# THE
# SAINT
## OF
# BRIGHT
# DOORS

# THE
# SAINT
## OF
# BRIGHT
# DOORS

VAJRA CHANDRASEKERA

TOR PUBLISHING GROUP
NEW YORK

THE SAINT OF BRIGHT DOORS

A Tordotcom Book
Published by Tom Doherty Associates/Tor Publishing Group
120 Broadway
New York, NY 10271

www.tor.com

Tor® is a registered trademark of Macmillan Publishing Group, LLC.

The Library of Congress Cataloging-in-Publication Data
is available upon request.

ISBN 978-1-250-84738-6 (hardcover)
ISBN 978-1-250-84739-3 (ebook)

Our books may be purchased in bulk for promotional, educational, or business use. Please contact your local bookseller or the Macmillan Corporate and Premium Sales Department at 1-800-221-7945, extension 5442, or by email at MacmillanSpecialMarkets@macmillan.com.

First Edition: 2023

Printed in the United States of America

0  9  8  7  6  5  4  3  2  1

FOR
**RUCHIRA**

# THE
# SAINT
## OF
# BRIGHT
# DOORS

# 1

The moment Fetter is born, Mother-of-Glory pins his shadow to the earth with a large brass nail and tears it from him. This is his first memory, the seed of many hours of therapy to come. It is raining. His shadow is cast upon reddish soil thick with clay that clings to Fetter as he rolls in it, unable to raise his head, saved from drowning in mud only by the fortunate angle of his landing. The arch of Mother-of-Glory's knee frames what he sees next. His shadow writhes slowly on its nail. Mother-of-Glory dips her hands in that mud to gather up the ropy shadow of his umbilical cord and throttles his severed shadow with a quick loop, pulled tight. The shadow goes to its end in silence—or if it cries out, if shadows can cry out, that sound is lost in the rain.

The next hours and years are lost to Fetter. Even this first memory is forgotten, until, as a boy already wearing thin his first decade of life, he explores the maze of his mother's house, looking for secrets, and stumbles across the lacquer box where Mother-of-Glory keeps a lock of his baby hair and the nail that tore his shadow from him. As he holds it in his hands that garrotting comes back to him, framed by the arch of his mother's knee, the shadow falling away, bloody rivulets in red mud.

Having relived the memory, Fetter looks at his feet with new understanding. He goes outside into bright sunlight, but no shadow appears beneath. He raises one foot, then the other, but it is as if the light passes through him. As if he's not really there. With both feet raised above the ground, he is suspended in the air, drifting slowly back to earth over a long minute, tugged aside by a light breeze. His bare feet drag a furrow in the soft dirt as he lands. This, too, is unusual. Mother-of-Glory stands firm on the earth, as does every other person he's ever met. His lightness of foot, he thinks for the first time, is not normal, and perhaps is linked to the absence of his shadow.

He doesn't bring up the nail with Mother-of-Glory that night, nor the next night, nor any night for a week. A week is about the limit of his patience, but he tries to make that week seem as normal as he can. He is neither more nor less inattentive than usual in the lessons with his tutors; when he goes out to play with the other kids, he is careful not to be more or less aggressive, or to spend more or less time at home, or to wander any further into town than he normally does, or to spend longer exploring the dry riverbed under the old bridge than usual. He is even careful not to experiment with his tendency to float. There will be time for that, he tells himself, when the lightness fills his chest in the mornings like he could breathe out and float away into the endless blue of the sky. He thinks he has achieved a sublime façade of ordinariness, hidden the turmoil in his mind.

He is nine years old, small, thin, and brown; his mother keeps his hair trimmed too short to curl. There is nothing between his mother and his mind but skin and skull.

Fetter plans how he will bring up the nail in conversation later and surprise his mother with his discovery as well as his self-control and skill in tradecraft.

But Mother-of-Glory confronts him first. She catches him after lessons one day at the end of that week and motions him to join her in the yard in front of the house, where she holds court and teaches her own lessons. Other, more mundane teachers will sit indoors with Fetter, or outside under a tree's canopy, or summon him to their brick houses in town. But Mother-of-Glory teaches under the blazing sun, as if to ensure that it, too, is learning.

"I see you found the nail," she says, seating herself on a tree-stump. Her tone seems serious, so Fetter remains standing in front of her. This is not playtime or bonding time: this is training.

"How did you know?" Fetter says, after a few seconds of furious wondering whether denial would serve any purpose, and then deciding that it would merely embarrass him. "I was so careful not to let on."

"You were quite good," Mother-of-Glory says. This is about as much of a compliment as Fetter gets. Mother-of-Glory is serious about the craft. "But you missed the telltale hair that broke when you opened the lacquer box. I've been checking it every day for years. What have you learned from this?"

"To always check for a telltale hair," Fetter says, though not sulkily. Mother-of-Glory disapproves of attitude, at least when aimed in her direction, but sometimes appreciates humour. She smiles at this, but waves her hand for him to continue.

"To plan better?" Fetter says, and this earns him a wince.

"Don't make an answer an ask," Mother-of-Glory says. "What you *should* have learned is to expect your enemy's intelligence. Look for countermeasures before you act."

"Yes, Mother," Fetter says. She seems not in the mood for questions, so he doesn't ask any. They are both silent for a while.

"Don't worry about not having a shadow," Mother-of-Glory says, finally. It seems to Fetter as if she was going to say something else but changed her mind. "The effect on your covert missions will be negligible. Nobody notices things like that. You'll have to learn how to stay grounded, though."

That's the only instruction that Mother-of-Glory ever gives

on the floating. Over the next couple of years, Fetter teaches himself how.

There are other oddities that he doesn't mention to his mother. He's not entirely sure whether they are real, or some kind of fallacy in his thinking or perception. It seems to him that he ages slowly. At ten he's smaller than his agemates; at twelve he looks like a child, and some of his peers have reached almost their adult height. Others haven't, so perhaps this is an ordinary oddity.

He discovers one day that fire doesn't burn him. Accidentally brushing his hand through a match-flame feels cool, as if the flame were a tiny waterspout. But several matches later he can't tell if this is a consequence of the flame being so small and ephemeral. Perhaps a bigger fire *would* burn him. There seems to be no safe way to test this without risk of serious injury, so he leaves it be.

He finds out, too, that he sees and hears things that others don't. He doesn't find it frightening at first. Some of the creatures he sees seem as much a part of the natural world as the squirrels slipping between bleeding-thorns, the kingfishers in the trees that weep over the river, the deer skittish in the wild grass. There are bulbous-bellied creatures that cling to the sides of people's houses, moving as if they were sucking in breath or slurping up something immaterial, perhaps feeding on something that Fetter can't quite discern. There are things that look like sea creatures, many-legged and tendrils waving, skittering across the main street as if it were a seabed. Others are more human in shape, and he understands them as being both natural and unnatural in the same way as people: dim and elongated, their gait a strange cousin to grace, or eerily multiple, toothy and long of tongue. Sometimes they speak in voices that sound raw and pained, and he pretends not to hear. He learns that most people don't see these creatures and manifestations; he learns that most people don't hear their whispering in the thick dusk. He learns to fear them from the reactions of others when he tries to ask. Acusdab is a small town, and the people feel outnumbered by the invisible laws and powers that they know crowd around them. The creatures are orders of being outside the house of humanity, he is told: they are antigods and devils. He learns that his skin should crawl, and so it learns to horripilate when one of them moves past his field of vision, even as he looks past to not betray that he can see them.

But, most of all, Fetter discovers that gravity finds him slippery, as if oiled. It is easy to fall upward, altogether too easy. All he has to do is breathe out and relax some clenched muscle in his lower belly, something that's always tight. He finds a terror in his yearning for the open sky, the call of falling up and up forever. Looking up makes him feel like he's standing on the edge of a precipice, and the urge to throw himself away is immense. He tries not to look at the sky.

He teaches himself that every step must be a conscious, willed act if it's to pass muster as ordinary human movement. Lift the foot, move it, press it back down to earth. He drills until it's second nature to test his footing, to subtly wriggle his ankle to make sure his heel is clamped firmly to the ground without making it obvious to the weighted what he's doing.

He's also learned to think of others that way—the weighted. The shadowed.

While Fetter is busy teaching himself these things, Mother-of-Glory gradually takes over his higher education. One by one other tutors fall away. Mother-of-Glory teaches him the core curriculum of a classical education: gramarye, dialectics, revanche, deferral, and murder. There are lessons in theory, and there are practice drills, what she calls his *exercises*.

Fetter learns the gramarye of summoning and binding. Mother-of-Glory tells him the invisible laws and powers used to come when called, to possess a human body and speak with a human voice, to prophesy, to teach, to leave when evicted. Everything is different now, she says. She does not explain why. He does his best to conceal that he can see them all the time, whether his mother is attempting to summon them or not. It is difficult for him to disguise startlement with his large eyes where the whites stand out like signal flares when they widen; he learns to keep his eyes low-lidded and still, as if always pained or fatigued, so as never to betray his shock at the doings of the invisible world. Headaches begin to curl in his temples.

In Acusdab, the invisible laws and powers—called devils by *some*, his mother sniffs, even though she too uses the word—are a high mystery. Even for her, they are the culmination of rare and difficult rites and not an ever-present horror, the blurred things that crouch in the corner of his eye while he pisses and brushes his teeth; the feeding things that cling to the walls of the house; the skittering things that circle warily around his mother's path, or away from her devil-doctors, the infamous, fearsome aduro of Acusdab.

Devils fear his mother far more than they fear the doctors. Devils will submit to a doctor's summoning and binding, as Fetter has seen many times in town, but Mother-of-Glory calls and calls and they don't come. She says she taught the doctors everything they know, but Fetter sees how the devils writhe and howl and jeer at her. She doesn't hear them, but Fetter watches, pretending he sees nothing but a failed ritual, wishing he could cover his ears and eyes.

When he summons, the devils obey, but he makes himself clumsy through the effort of pretending that he is not meeting their eyes, when they have eyes. He would make, his mother judges, a middling doctor, but this is sufficient. That is not the mission she envisions for him.

Murder comes even less easy to him. Mother-of-Glory all

but holds his hand for his first. She says she is multitasking, combining his training with the bloody end of an old family feud. It's past time, she says. The target is his grand-uncle, Mother-of-Glory's father's elder brother.

She drives him to this execution in much the same way she drives him to any other appointment, lecturing him the whole way while Fetter dangles a hand of out the window and tries to catch the wind and listens with half an ear. It's a long drive to the far edge of town, as if his grand-uncle settled as far away from his mother as he could.

Apart from fussing over Fetter's flawed underhand knife technique and reminding him to sing the song of sharpening under his breath to excite the molecules of the blade's edge, Mother-of-Glory takes this opportunity to reiterate her teaching of the lore of the Five Unforgivables. This is, in her pedagogy, the absolute heart of Fetter's education, red and meaty and pulsating. These are also the only occasions she talks about Fetter's sainted father, the Perfect and Kind, so Fetter sits up. These moments are his rare opportunities for hints of answers to a lifetime of questions about his father—manipulation so basic it barely counts, but Fetter resents it anyway.

"The Five Unforgivables are the major crimes as defined by your father's ideological apparatus," Mother-of-Glory says. She has given this speech so often Fetter knows it by heart, which is the point. "They are declared to be outside the jurisdiction of any regime of restorative or retributive justice. The Five Unforgivables are, in order of severity, matricide; heresy leading to factionalism; the sancticide of votaries who have reached the fourth level of awakening; patricide; and the assassination of the Perfect and Kind. By definition, they cannot be forgiven and cannot be redeemed. That means that if you commit any one of them, the cult will hunt you for the rest of your life, and make your name a curse for generations to come.

Your mission is to commit them all. Your father abandoned us. We were unchosen, cast out of his eschatology. We are going to destroy your father's cult and salt the earth where it falls. Now you say it."

Fetter repeats the catechism, obligingly. He could recite these words in his sleep.

They reach his grand-uncle's house. Mother-of-Glory parks outside out of sight, and they sneak in through a gap in the fence where a post is fallen and the barbed wire tangled low. Later, Fetter will understand that this opening would have been orchestrated by his mother—perhaps one of the devil-doctors came the night before to break whatever circuit of power might have protected this boundary. But at the time it seems fortuitous.

Fetter's knife technique turns out to be redundant, the song of sharpening useless. He ambushes Grand-Uncle puttering in his own little back garden, a lonely place full of sad vegetables, ideal for a first kill. Even with the advantages of youth and speed and surprise, he can't get his footing right before the old man disarms him, his wrinkled hand snaking out to twist Fetter's wrist until he lets go of the knife. Startled, Fetter forgets all his training, forgets to stay grounded—he leaves the ground altogether, his feet flailing and rising skyward, pivoting around the old man's grip on his wrist until he's upside down. Grand-Uncle shouts out in surprise and lets go, and Fetter instinctively grabs his mouth and throat to silence him.

After that, it's a hanging. Fetter, upside down, a rising noose. Grand-Uncle is lifted slightly off his feet, his desperate toes scrabbling at the earth and making patterns in the dust.

Even someone raised to the Unforgivables will have ingrained inhibitions against violence, which must be overcome in the heat and pressure of the moment. Mother-of-Glory has warned Fetter about this many times, but it's still difficult. A poisoned breath pools at the bottom of his lungs; it will never come all the way out again.

Grand-Uncle gets a foot planted on the ground and begins to struggle again, so Fetter frees up a hand and goes for the old man's face. He crushes his nose, jabs him in an eye hard enough to pop, claws at face and throat until there is red. It's high noon; when Fetter glances down at his feet, the sun is right there. He's standing on the sun. He tightens his grip on Grand-Uncle's throat, and remembers his first memory again. He is the garrotte. Grand-Uncle bubbles like he's trying to speak, but Fetter is rising again, and Grand-Uncle's feet leave the ground again, hung like meat.

The dead weight brings Fetter back to earth. The body settles and pools. Fetter comes down, twisting back the right way, until he settles on Grand-Uncle's chest like a carrion bird. He can't see his knife anywhere, but Mother-of-Glory is particular about follow-through, so Fetter gouges and claws until he's red to the elbow, until Grand-Uncle's face is a ruin that he can't even look at without his gorge rising. Fetter's heart is hammering in his temples. His entire body has turned into ice, so light, so clear. He doesn't notice he's drifting away in the breeze until Mother-of-Glory catches him by the ankle as he passes and drags him back.

Fetter wriggles his ankles and sets his feet firmly on the soil, clenches himself down. He does not look around, seeing from the corner of his eye that what seems to his mother a deserted vegetable patch is crowded by invisible powers. Many strange and terrible shapes have stopped to look at him. He looks at his bloody hands instead.

"That was the easiest it's ever going to be," Mother-of-Glory says on the drive back. Fetter is curled up sullenly in the passenger seat. His head hurts, and his throat too, as if he'd been screaming the entire time. He doesn't remember making a sound. He's cleaned up, but his hands are still sticky. He studies his fingertips carefully the whole way home, looking at the bruises and the cuts he doesn't remember getting, peering into the deep canyons of his whorls, looking for more of the flaking brown residue. He can feel it rasping when he rubs his fingers together.

"Next time," Mother-of-Glory says, "you'll have to clean the scene yourself. Remember, the First Unforgivable is matricide. After that, you won't have me around to hold your hand."

A couple of years vanish into higher education, including more exercises. Fetter learns to clean a crime scene. He calls these murders his *forgivable* crimes, as a way to subtly annoy Mother-of-Glory; she stops reciting the catechism so often but he already knows it by heart and, to his own annoyance, finds himself reciting it in the silences that it used to occupy. It helps him feel directed, that all this is aimed *at* something. The forgivable murders are covered by the constant violence of his extended family, Mother-of-Glory explains, timed and ordered to drift into the background noise of assassinations and funerals that structure the family calendar, feuds he doesn't keep track of. Most of Acusdab seems to be family and they don't need to know about the special mission she is training him for. There is no shortage of targets. Some distant cousins even attempt to assassinate Mother-of-Glory herself, which she turns into another lesson for Fetter.

This family didn't used to be like this, Mother-of-Glory says, sadly, as she prunes its tree.

Even with all this practice, Fetter cannot say if his skill in combat or the use of weapons improves. He eventually becomes accustomed to violence, which, he supposes, was the point in the first place. One day Mother-of-Glory pronounces him ready for the real thing. She packs him a lunch and gives him some money and a knife and a blessing, the words impatient and mumbled because she doesn't believe in blessings, not even her own. Such things are his father's territory.

"Remember, son," Mother-of-Glory says, compensating with pomposity for her deficits of piety or affection. "The only way to change the world is through intentional, directed violence."

And Fetter goes out into the world, armed and dangerous and thirteen.

# 2

Fetter's teenage years pass rough and jagged, full of cold nights and hunger and blisters on his feet. He learns to follow his luck, to listen to the roiling in his gut, and it keeps him alive. He learns mysteries and gains scars. His hair grows out long and curly. Eventually, his beard grows out too. He is no longer quite so small.

# 3

Looking back as an adult in the city—and having so painfully *become* an adult, he thinks, in an occulted process of total destruction and reconstruction, like the secret of what happens inside the chrysalis—he prefers not to talk about or consciously recall that time of his life.

When he makes conversation, on a third date like this one with Hejmen, for instance, he does his best to be open and vulnerable. It's easier to open up while they sit at an outdoor café in the darkening evening, lit by the smouldering canopy of the flame trees above. He'll talk about his childhood at length, but not about his teens.

Of course, he can't talk about the murders here in the city, but he can talk around them. He has learned how to describe them in emotional terms while leaving out the blood. Family feuds and estrangements are not so strange, though for most the knives are figurative.

He can admit now, from the safe perch of his twenties, that his childhood was spent in the thrall of a toxic, abusive parent. He has put away childish things. His mad, violent childhood; the indoctrination; his training as a child soldier in his mother's war against his father: these things, these people are in his past. He has grown up. He is making a new life for himself, all his own. His only purpose now is peace, he tells himself. To find some; to keep it; to age in grace; to never again raise his hand in violence.

He is, by his own best estimation, twenty-three years old, give or take a year or two. The dark brown territories of his skin, darkened further by the sun, are mapped by white traceries of scars, most of them faint. He doesn't remember how he got his scars—knife and jagged scale and thorn, broken glass and human nails—but he's sensitive about them. He wears his hair and beard thick and neatly trimmed, well-tamed with the city's conditioners, sleeves long and collars high. This is enough to hide most of his scars, except for the thin line that bisects his left cheek as if marking the path of a hot iron tear. When his face is in repose, the line looks unnaturally straight, so he's practiced a one-sided smile that hides it. The scars are only another thing that he doesn't talk about.

He doesn't mention, either, that his father is the Perfect and Kind, who is seen routinely on the TV talk show circuit and frequently quoted in the news, as a major regional religious figure and opinionator. Being related to him wouldn't be attractive, merely freakish. He does mention an absent father, so as not to seem overly obsessed with his mother. That, he has discovered, is not attractive either.

Hejmen is older than him and has a luxurious, chest-length beard, black shot through with grey. They met on a dating app and have been on three dates in two weeks, so things are going surprisingly well.

Hejmen noticed the absence of his shadow—that happened after the second date, when they went out for breakfast in the bright morning sun—but he took it in stride. Luriatis are like that. It's one of the reasons Fetter decided to live there. When he first came in sight of the city a few years ago, its towers of stone and glass golden in the sun, the white cranes in their arc across the skyline like a sheaf of arrows fired at once from a god's bow, he felt drawn to Luriat before he even knew the city's name. The air was wet, almost liquid, soft and healing on his skin. The city told him he was done wandering, done with his mother's quest. Now he is starting to feel like he belongs there. So many people come to the city from somewhere else that it's easy to feel at home. Fetter isn't even the only feral child of a messiah in his social network. There's a support group for unchosen ones, which was recommended to him by the therapist he's been seeing ever since he learned what a therapist was. He attends those support group meetings religiously, every Haruday at sundown. He hasn't told Hej about any of that yet, but he doesn't feel like he's hiding anything. It's early days, and he feels like he has time. He luxuriates in that feeling, stretching out in it like a cat in the sun. He supposes this is what happiness feels like. It's an effort to stay grounded in it.

∽

"What do you want to do with your days?" It's a question they ask every week at the support group for the unchosen, the almost-chosen, the chosen-proximate. Answers vary. Most people mumble or joke. It takes a long time, the veteran of the group remarks, for people in this group to start taking their own lives seriously. The only person newer to the group than Fetter retorts that maybe people need that time to recover.

"It's like floating," Fetter says. People nod and say yeah, though they can't understand what he means. He doesn't talk about the floating; he practices it sometimes, in the hope of turning it into a skill rather than a circumstance, but only when alone and unobserved. He doesn't talk much at group. There are maybe a dozen people who come and go, the unchosen detritus of as many religions. Today is a typical day, in that about half the group is present.

Of course the room is full of invisible powers. They fill him with an old fear that is almost comforting: Luriat is not as full of such beings and creatures as Acusdab was, but there are enough, and they crowd the meetings as if drawn to the support group's particular oddity. He is not sure how many of the others can see them. Perhaps none, judging by their failure to react. Or perhaps they have each decided, like him, that the only way to lessen the horror is to look away and never speak of it. He does not dare breach that silent agreement, if it exists; he has never stopped being sure, in his heart, that it would go badly for him if he ever allowed the invisible powers to know he can see them. So he unfocuses his eyes and allows his gaze to skim past their horrible shapes, their strange limbs, their implied multiplied eyes. They remain in the background. His head aches from the effort, but he has grown used to the pain of this unseeing. The room is dimly lit, which helps. It also obscures the absence of his shadow.

The group veteran is Koel, a woman in her late forties or early fifties. There are laugh lines around her eyes, but she rarely laughs. "The sooner you realize you've got lives of your own to live, the easier it'll be. All I'm saying," she says. She's told them before about her mother, who was supposedly the prophet of the Walking, a god that Fetter doesn't know. The mantle of prophet was passed on to her younger brother when her mother retired, and Koel found herself with all the training but no authority, no voice of god in her ear. Now, as far as Fetter knows, she is some sort of pamphleteer. She has an illegal press where she writes and prints her own seditious literature, which she then leaves in public places for people to read and distribute. She's supposedly also a playwright and independent filmmaker. He hasn't seen any of her films or plays, but he *has* seen her pamphlets being used to wrap loaves of bread, for children to make paper planes. She publishes regardless. She speaks of all this too freely. Any of them could betray her to the police. Devils, perhaps she is daring them to do it. No, perhaps she is only trusting them. Perhaps it is unconsidered faith, in the way of someone who grew up expecting her every wish would be as the word of god.

"I want to work on the bright doors," says the newcomer, and the whole group groans at this. Even Fetter groans, because he once tried to get a job working on the doors himself and knows how long the waiting list is. The newcomer is a young neutrois person named Ulpe with long, uneasy fingers. They've been at group for a few weeks but haven't yet shared much about their story of being unchosen except that it involves a man on fire, though whether literally or figuratively is unclear. Fetter and the others don't yet know if the Man in the Fire, which is the only way that Ulpe will refer to him, set himself on fire or survived a fire or merely lit a metaphorical flame of belief. They don't even know Ulpe's relationship to this man. But whatever that relationship was, it is so clearly of recent rupture that the groans are good-natured, even solicitous.

"You know it's never going to happen, don't you?" Koel is of course the one to say this, and her mock-severity is so full of mockery that it approaches true severity. "They'll especially not let one of *us* do it."

This is news to Fetter. "Why not us in particular?"

Koel shrugs. "Incompatibilities," she says, which Fetter doesn't understand at all. Some of the others are nodding—Ulpe looks blank, but they're new to the city and the group and so often look blank that it doesn't count—so Fetter doesn't pursue it for fear of once again playing the uneducated provincial.

༄

The bright doors of Luriat give the city its historic identity without intruding on its daily life. For his first year living in the city, there is too much to see and the brightly painted doors scattered around the city seem unremarkable. After a while, he notices how they are always closed, and how often there is somebody working on these doors—repainting them, always in bright, primary colours; testing, oiling, repairing the hinges, the locks, the knobs; filling in gouges or scars with putty, varnishing, polishing, wiping away stains, lighting incense, leading circles of prayer before them; shining ultraviolet flashlights, taking carefully flaked samples of the wood, the paint; leaving flowers, leaving small offerings of neatly sliced fruit and joss sticks with their thready smoke. The bright doors are distinct from ordinary doors, which don't receive such attentions and which are often, Fetter notices eventually, not doors at all. There are plenty of simple unobstructed openings in walls; arches and curtains of cloth or beads or translucent plastic sheeting; glass doors of varying degrees of translucency; half-doors or doors with inset windows; screens of netting, metal gates or grates, bars like cages. An ordinary Luriati door is always partly open or partly transparent, even if imperfectly. Only the bright doors are fully closed and opaque. From this Fetter gathers that it is the lack of transparency, the *closing* of doors, the unknowability of an other side, that differentiates the bright doors from mere entrances.

One day, unable to resist curiosity, he approaches a bright door on the street. He was walking the city, following nothing but his luck, when he happened across a rare unattended bright door. Nobody is fussing around it or keeping an eye on it. There are no police or witnesses. It's set in the wall of an unremarkable building which otherwise seems to house nothing but a luxury jeweller's shop. The entrance to the shop itself is an ordinary glass door set into the shop front, as far away from the bright door as possible. It's early in the morning and the shop is closed and the street deserted. He feels that familiar sensation in his gut: the sickening, queasy tugging that he has always thought of as his luck, his instinct, some deep sensitivity to the world that senses where he needs to go, what he needs to do, long before he can even articulate it. When it bubbles up in him, there is always something he needs to do, even if he doesn't know it yet.

He walks up to the door and tries the knob. It's locked. The wood is painted a cheerful orange, and up close he can see that the paint is thick and inexpert, with too many layers and stray brushstrokes and clumps. There are no signs or writing on or near it indicating danger or warning people away. He rattles the knob and becomes conscious of cold air seeping through the gaps where the door meets its frame. It's not the even chill of air-conditioning or refrigeration: it's the rustling whisper of a cold wind carrying an unfamiliar, bitter smell. The more conscious Fetter grows of the cold wind, the stronger and louder it seems, as if there is a gusting, howling wind behind the bright door, the kind of wind that might be funnelled through a mountain pass. At first he thinks it's the cold that unsettles him, when in point of fact Luriat is a city at low elevation, bordering the ocean, where the air is always warm and occasionally temperate and the wind comes from the sea. But then he thinks it's that smell he doesn't recognize, the way it's almost a taste on his tongue like ash. Or it's the way the chill in that air feels like the outdoors even though it's coming, by definition, from indoors, or at least from behind a door. If what's behind the door is the outside, then does that make all of Luriat—all of the world—the inside? The wind from the other side seems to intensify, as if there is a storm being held back by nothing more than this thin, over-painted orange door. The knob is freezing cold in his hand, though he can't tell if it was cold when he touched it. Perhaps it was, so cold that it numbed the skin of his palm. He lets the knob go, rubbing his palms together. When he takes a few steps away from the door, the gusts of cold wind recede, as does the sense of heavy weather on the other side. He has a headache squatting in the darkest corner of his temple, beating like an extra heart.

# 4

There is a crowdfunding campaign to bring the Perfect and Kind to Luriat for the next monsoon. Fetter discovers this by accident while clearing out his spam folder. His father's name catches his eye, and he digs out the message and clicks through to the campaign website. There he discovers a forum maintained by a small but enthusiastic local chapter of the Path Above fandom, and learns that they have run this crowdfunding campaign every year for almost a decade. The first few years they didn't make their target, or were shut down by opposition from the Path Behind, who are the established religion in Luriat. In recent years, they've successfully raised funds, but lost their bid to host—there are far too many southern cities that are bigger, wealthier, more wondrous, where the fandom is stronger and better organized—so the money they raised was rolled into the following year's campaign.

The crowdfunding page outlines their plans to hire out a major convention centre for the sixth-month monsoon season with included housing for the Perfect and Kind and his inner circle, the two saints and his amanuensis, as well as his other senior votaries, devotees, apologists, and other fans, as well as any donors to the crowdfunding campaign who contribute to the highest reward tiers.

Fetter imagines his distant, inaccessible father visiting his city, and considers donating a few fanons to make this fantastical outcome marginally more plausible. But no, he doesn't want to expose himself to his father's supporters; the Abovers and Behinders both surely think him obscure and forgettable, trapped under his mother's thumb in Acusdab, and they should go on thinking that. The Path Behind is dangerous—Mother-of-Glory wasn't wrong about that. He has seen enough of the world to confirm what he was taught. As a teenager in the hinterlands, he saw the aftermath of their more recent pogroms against the pathless; in Luriat, he sees their frothing, rabid demagogues on TV. He knows little about the Path Above, or what the differences are between these two halves of his father's religion, but it seems safe to imagine they are at least equally dangerous.

He considers reporting the crowdfunding campaign to the platform's moderators for hateful speech, to try to get it cancelled or at least inconveniently suspended. But the campaign's Abover language and positioning is carefully smooth, and offers grievance no easy purchase. Perhaps they are not as bad as the Behinders. Fetter leaves it be. There's over a month to the deadline. And anyway, even if he had wanted to donate, he doesn't have any money.

Luriat provides many free services to its residents, such as housing, food, and transport. As long as one's needs are modest, it is possible to live in Luriat and not need to work, at least for money. Most people do work, because money buys a better class of needs. Fetter has adapted in the opposite direction. He was assigned a small third-floor apartment on the east side of the city, near the coast but without a view of the sea, or indeed of anything. The apartment blocks in his area are crowded with newcomers. The district is called the Sands because it has a small beach, while most of the Luriati coastline is rocks piled up to prevent erosion. Many newcomers who arrive in the Sands will eventually request relocation to some preferred quarter of the city, or make enough money to rent privately. But Fetter has lived in the same building ever since he first came to Luriat, long enough to become an elder statesman of the Sands, given its rapid turnover. He finds himself advising others on how to navigate the city, and enjoying the sense of mission. He hadn't realized he was growing bored of floating.

People begin to refer others to him for advice. "Ask Fetter," they say, and so his name becomes known in this ephemeral society of strangers to the city. This is how he meets Caduv, who he will later induct into the support group of the almost-chosen. Late one night, Fetter responds to a knock at his door, bare-bodied and scarred. Apartment doors in these buildings are all metal grilles with a fine mesh against the mosquitoes, which most tenants compound with a curtain for privacy; the convention is to knock on the wooden doorframe. Leaning against the frame, Fetter takes in the unmemorable man standing outside and sees nothing to indicate that Caduv belongs in that unchosen community. He doesn't have the regal bearing of a trained prophet like Koel, or the aura of otherworldly damage that marks Ulpe, or, Fetter supposes, himself. It's only when Caduv opens his mouth to ask his question that Fetter understands. He hears it in his voice. Or even before voice, in the opening of the mouth alone, the browned and slightly uneven teeth, the furry, startling moss of his tongue, the way the ambient soundscape changes in preparation for Caduv's voice, as if they were suddenly not standing in the dull acoustics of a narrow doorway opening into a low-ceilinged corridor, but in a forest clearing under the open black sky, a natural amphitheatre with packed earth underfoot, rich dark soil made smooth by years of pounding feet, a stage for secret and sacred songs. Fetter shakes his head to clear away this image, so intense that it's almost a hallucination, though he doesn't lose track of where he is—the wooden doorframe under his upraised hand has a rough, splintering grain, which Fetter surreptitiously verifies by rubbing his finger along it—until the words trip out of Caduv's mouth.

"They said to ask you about applying for identity papers," Caduv says. The words are mundane, ordinary Luriati hellspeak dialect. The query is commonplace, the accent unfamiliar but unremarkable. But the voice doesn't sound like any voice on earth. It picks Fetter up and hurls him back to that nighttime clearing like a hard wind. He stumbles to one knee, catching himself against the earth before he falls flat on his face. He rubs his fingers against the soil, cautiously. Devils, but the earth is moist. It feels substantial. The sky is clear above him, a half-moon low and skulking behind the tree line to his left, a jagged line of mountains rising to his right. He waits for the vision to fade, because it surely must be a vision. But it doesn't. Until he hears the voice again.

"Sorry," Caduv says. "Are you okay? It'll clear up if you close your eyes and shake your head."

Fetter does this, and then does it again. He presses his thumb into the soft earth until the grain of old wood rises to meet it again, and when he opens his eyes he's where he was in the first place, standing in his own doorway with one raised hand on the jamb, looking out at a short man in a cramped corridor. There is no clearing, no forest, no open sky, no half-moon. He has not fallen or moved.

"Why a half-moon?" he asks. His mother trained him to track the lunar cycle because it's sacred to his father's cult, so he knows for a fact that tonight is the night after a full moon. The moon being off the beat is more unsettling than the vision. He's had visions before.

"I'm really very sorry about that," Caduv says. He introduces himself by name, reiterates his query as an explanation for being there, then remembers the unanswered question. "It's always the half-moon there. It'll be the half-moon when the Song of the Red is sung—"

"And you don't know which half-moon," Fetter says, guessing. "You don't know which year or month. But you do know it won't be you singing it."

"My fourth cousin won the tribulations," Caduv says, and stops because Fetter is waving off the explanation.

The story is back on familiar ground. Fetter knows how these things go. The cousin is the anointed Singer of the Red, custodian of what is presumably some sort of apocalyptic or salvific event to be prevented or triggered in some distant vale—it has to be pretty distant, because he's never even heard of this religion and the mountains in the background of the vision were unfamiliar. He doesn't need to know the details. Here in Luriat, foreign prophetic visions are detritus, not destiny.

"People here don't react to my voice," Caduv mutters. "I didn't think it would ever happen again. I came so far."

Fetter beckons him in and starts to rummage among his papers. "I have a cheat sheet somewhere," he says. He remembers that he is still bare-chested. Caduv saw his scars, but didn't react. They are insignificant to the other man, Fetter understands. Perhaps he should worry less about them. He pulls on a camisa anyway, and finds his notes on the Luriati citizenship application, with explanations, as he understands them, of all their tiny boxes to tick. As much as it seeks ways to identify the body, Luriat worries more about how to categorize it. Much of the application is concerned with assigning incoming citizens into their proper local hierarchies of race and caste, the grouping and typing theory inherited from the Alabi empire which ruled the entire supercontinent for a century and a half. "I'll translate the questions so you know how to answer, and I'll come with you to the Registrar's Office to help fill out the forms. But next Haruday, there's some people I think you should meet."

It's not unusual for people to come to Fetter like Caduv did, though they are usually less strange. It's not unusual for them to outgrow his help faster than he had expected, either. Sometimes they just need reassurance that there is help to be had, should they need it, and this knowledge is enough for them to make their own way. People volunteer their stories in turn: why they came to Luriat, what they're looking for, what they're running from. His gut instinct, the uneasy twinge that tells him to pay attention, is interested in these stories: he listens carefully. Some are escaping abusive homes or seeking fortunes, but most are fleeing plague or the frequent Behinder pogroms in the hinterlands, or sometimes from deeper south, from wars in the supercontinent that he hasn't even heard of.

Acusdab, with its doctors, has never been overly troubled by plagues—godly ills, the doctors called them, enforcing strict quarantines and harsh cullings—and saw no pogroms in his short life there, so Fetter is surprised by their prevalence in the greater world. Luriatis are well-inured to both. Their history, their calendar, is built around the succession of plague years and pogrom years. At first, Fetter does not understand how Luriat has survived so many disasters that would have wiped little Acusdab off the map. But he comes to understand that it is only cities like Luriat that *can* survive such things, and perhaps that it is only creating and then surviving them that creates the possibility of a Luriat. It is through the history of responding to these crises and disasters, he learns, that Luriat's free services came into being: small hard-won victories imme-

diately compromised by the frames of race and caste that control access to them.

There are no doctors in Luriat—at least, not in the way that
Fetter understands a *doctor*. There are hospitals full of medical
professionals, but not a single one red in the mouth. He doesn't
know how they style themselves: he has not fallen ill in years,
certainly not since he came here. His years in the city have so
far been blissfully free of both plagues and pogroms. When he
expresses this thought in group one day, Koel laughs at him. At
the time he isn't sure why.

It takes a while for Fetter to notice the patterns of the people
who come to him for help, and through them the changing
populations of refugees pouring into Luriat in their seasons.
There is always a trickle throughout the year, punctuated by
frequent, sudden floods—there are many undying wars loose
in the great supercontinent of Jambu, periodically lurching into
new territories and displacing the people who lived there, some
proportion of whom then find their way to all its innumerable
cities. Closer to home, the Luriati hinterlands are sick with violence; he learns slowly to read between the headlines, to understand that a *riot* is a pogrom, and that when a monk of the
Path Behind is on TV calling for *peace from both sides*, that it
means that the Path Behind is once again attempting to cull the
hinterlands of the pathless, and of the races and castes that they
consider low and other: his father's legacy conjoined with the
droppings of imperial Alab. Too, he learns there is plague abroad
in the distant southeastern subcontinent of Aggiopa, where all
those empire-builders came from, endlessly infecting and re-
infecting the world. Fetter isn't ready to grapple with a world so
enlarged, so bloated from pain.

The Sands, in its unofficial role of poor immigrants' district, is capable of handling the ordinary trickle of newcomers

to the city, but when it becomes a flood, or when it is known that the refugees might be fleeing plague, the Luriati military is called out and the newcomers shepherded into camps outside the city proper. The camps were occasional at first, Koel once remarked in group, and then seasonal, but now there are permanent camps, ever-growing, holding in quarantine those suspected of bearing plague or rebellion.

The Luriati military and police—Fetter has never been clear on the distinction; in appearance, armament, and practice they seem to blend into each other so smoothly that all police, soldiers, paramilitaries, drummers, first responders, tactical teams, home guards, torturers, and white-gloved traffic herders seem agents of a single enormous, ubiquitous, purposeful entity—range from involving themselves deeply or not at all in the lives of the newcomers in the Sands. He has no strong grasp of why they ignore several dozen new people and then descend in force to capture the next, and anybody that person might have known, and then anyone close to *those* persons, and so on, until sated. It is obvious that they fear infection, but infection by disease or ideas or identities? These intrusions too seem seasonal; he himself came to Luriat without trouble, in a balmy moment where no one worried about uprisings or outbreaks, not recognizing this grace.

About a year after he first moved to Luriat, after he had found some kind of footing but not yet begun to understand anything about the city, he witnessed his first mass abduction. His gut leads him to a building, not too far from his own, blockaded by armed soldiers, in dark blue uniforms, caps, gloves, and heavy black boots laced up to the shin. He notices the boots most strongly at that time, having spent most of his young life barefoot and only lately indoctrinated to the civilized practice of sandals. Closed shoes seem strange and painful in the heat, and in Fetter's eyes, the weight and solidity of those boots make it clear that they are not footwear but weapons. They are not for walking, but for kicking, for grinding down, for breaking doors, for bruising bodies and the earth. The soldiers—at the time, Fetter thinks they are soldiers, though he later learns they are the paramilitary tactical response unit of the police, a legal distinction whose consequences he never quite understands despite Hej's best efforts to teach him—keep him and everybody else at a distance while others of their number storm the building. There are drummers both on crowd control and surrounding the target. Their uniforms are the same as the others', except for the plume of the white feather on their caps and the short drums slung at their hips, on which they hammer out a grim tha-rikkita-thar of warding and anticipation.

There is a great deal of noise; the drums, the shouting, some shooting. A long line of people are brought out at gunpoint, hands raised and folded on the backs of their heads, packed into trucks and driven away. Some bodies are removed. Teams in protective gear swarm the building, either forensic examiners or plague specialists or both.

When the building is released from lockdown a couple of weeks later, Fetter goes to see and learns that almost a quarter of the building's residents were abducted. The remaining residents do not speak much of the experience; that is, at first they seem to speak of nothing else, in that they complain loudly and harshly, but after a while Fetter notices that the complaints are all about the inconveniences they themselves faced during lockdown, being questioned repeatedly by soldiers, having to ration food, and so on. They do not speak of the ones who were taken away. Fetter surmises that this is partly out of fear, as if there were a possibility, even now, of contagion, and partly because none of those left behind will confess to having known any of the abducted. Perhaps they are hiding that knowledge, too, or perhaps the soldiers rooted out and excised an entire social network of acquaintance and friendship and connection, leaving behind only those who could, at best, recognize the faces of the abducted, perhaps, without names, or knew a name but not to talk to, or had shared an occasional word, but never been invited to tea.

For months to come, Fetter asks around, very, very cautiously, but never learns what became of those people, which camp or prison they might have been taken to, or why they were taken. As far as he knows, none of them ever come back. The rumours are myriad, fantastical: some say they saw so-and-so in a different district a year later, buying tomatoes; some say they could have sworn that woman on TV last night was what's-her-name who was taken back then; many guess they are all quarantined for plague in one camp or another on the outskirts of Luriat; some suggest they are in a black prison in the hinterlands for terrorism; one tale-teller assures Fetter with complete sincerity that they heard from a friend's cousin's boyfriend's mother's physiotherapist's uncle who took a vacation in Remalu last month that some fellow they met there on a sight-seeing tour claimed to have been abducted in Luriat and exiled from the city for reasons that are undisclosed, or if disclosed, unclear.

The abandoned belongings of the abducted are quickly despoiled by their surviving neighbours, and the empty apartments reassigned to newer newcomers, who move in and go about their lives without trouble from soldiers with heavy boots. The season, Fetter understands, has changed again. Caduv, so recently come to the city, is as innocent of his own grace as Fetter had once been.

# 5

Caduv's first day at group goes exactly as well as Fetter had hoped. There are ten other people present, and all ten freeze, eyes open, muscles locked, the moment Caduv opens his mouth. Caduv has to coax each one out of the vision and apologize to them individually while Fetter chuckles quietly and eats the snacks. Group meetings are not usually so eventful.

Koel is the most cantankerous about the nonconsensual vision, perhaps irritated by being brought so close to somebody else's sacred mystery. She nudges Fetter, and he thinks she's about to say something to him about bringing Caduv in without warning—he has excuses and protestations of innocence ready—but instead she tells him to bring Caduv to see her sometime.

"After his paperwork is sorted out and he's had some time to settle in," she adds. "There are some things I'd like to talk to you both about."

Ulpe is more fascinated than annoyed by the vision, and pleased to no longer be the newest member. They quickly adopt Caduv, taking over from Fetter as his guide to the group and its culture. Caduv seems at first overwhelmed but, as the meeting goes on and settles into its ruts, also relieved.

See, Fetter thinks, though he wouldn't say this out loud. It's better to be unchosen together.

∽

On Tinday, Fetter takes Caduv to the Registrar's Office. Caduv speaks hellspeak well enough, accent notwithstanding, but can't read or write the Luriati script. In the long room set apart for this purpose, with rectangular tables crowded with people doing the same, Fetter fills in the paperwork while checking the answers with Caduv, who squints at the forms and says some of the glyphs seem very familiar, as if a distant cousin of the only script he knows.

"It's almost the same as Acusdabi—what we speak where I'm from," Fetter says. "They have a few more letters here, but it was easy for me."

"I've seen hellspeak written in fourteen different scripts so far," Caduv says. "This one has the curliest letters."

"You'll pick it up in time," Fetter says, but he doesn't truly believe that. Many newcomers to Luriat don't seem to. They make do with a newfound illiteracy. The city makes it easy to survive, as long as you can find someone literate to help you fill in the registration forms. Around them, everyone is getting help from someone. Many are forming impromptu little study groups of exegesis and interpretation; Fetter has already been consulted by some of them, as someone who seems to know what he's doing.

Caduv files the forms and hands over the biological samples, his fingerprints, his retinal scan, his cheek swab—somewhere, his DNA will be registered in the social categories to which he has been assigned, and feed into research that reinforces those categories—and they wait together in another long room full of supplicants until someone appears and starts handing out little yellow identity cards, laminated in plastic and bearing the relevant sigils of power and strings of haecceity that give access to Luriat's services. Caduv accepts his very formally, with almost a bow, to the bemusement of the civil servant.

"You're a citizen now," Fetter says, once they regain the street outside. The mud is fresh and the sun is hot; it's been raining while they were indoors, and now it's bright again. Fetter raises a hand to shield his eyes but, shadowless, achieves no relief. "Congrats. What will you do?"

"I thought I might retrain as a singer," Caduv says. "In one of the theatrical schools."

Fetter nods politely at this. Music and theatre mean nothing to him: the other man might as well have said that he intended to practice standing on his head. But he is glad, he supposes, on principle. Caduv seems to be adapting to the city, finding new meaning in his life. That should be how it's done. Soon he'll move out of the Sands to be closer to his vocation. Fetter tries not to envy. He has not yet found a vocation; perhaps he never will. His role as mentor and guide he welcomes and takes seriously, but more and more, he feels that it is something that happened *to* him because he was there and knew enough to answer questions. He didn't choose the role, it chose him. He is tired of that feeling.

His connection with Hej becomes more and more intense. Fetter isn't sure when things segue from dating to relationship, exactly. At first he tried to stick to dating, a concept he learned late in life from films and television—Mother-of-Glory scorned such things as disruptive technologies inimical to spiritual growth and a consistent training regimen—in what he understands to be its classical Southeastern Imperial style: dinners and incomprehensible theatrical performances and brunch and suchlike, followed by sex and postcoital tension. But after the first few weeks of attempted formalism, their interactions dissolve into a pool of complex organic reactions. The coursing of his heart becomes too wild to ignore, so much that Fetter begins to worry that it's audible from without, finds himself talking louder and faster to try and drown it out. Hej responds to his animation in turn, and the sense of excitement, of over-oxygenation, spirals. The air is too thick, the blood is too rich, too red. Hej takes to tracing Fetter's scars with his fingers and never asking about them, a conjoined intimacy and respect that finally breaks Fetter's commitment to high collars and long sleeves in public. They devour each other, again and again; they talk all the time; they entangle themselves in each other's lives and hearts and minds, so much so that in their moments of closest intimacy, stray thoughts spontaneously transmit themselves across the space separating their skulls and become audible, crackling and whispering, in the other mind's ear.

Fetter guards his secrets through all this because he is not at all tempted to speak of them. He does not allow them to rise to the surface of his mind, where they might become transmissible. It is heady to be found interesting in himself, not as the abandoned spawn of a messianic figure or as someone with a grand violent destiny. He has put away those childish things, he reminds himself, and so it is not a lie to omit them. Maybe some day.

"Maybe some day what?" Hej asks.

"*Maybe some day* is my favourite phrase," Fetter says, easily. "I like the idea that many things are possible."

‹✧›

Fetter takes Caduv to meet Koel.

"Why do we have to go meet Koel?" Caduv asks. "We see her at group every week."

"This is not a group thing," Fetter says, vaguely. Koel reminded him again recently, and this time it sounded more urgent, as if something had changed between the first request and this one, so Fetter has roused himself. Fetter has the impression Koel wants to keep the rest of the group out of whatever this is. Given her politics there is only one thing this could be about. He is obscurely offended that she didn't invite him into her world until Caduv appeared, but at the same time, now that he *is* invited, in whatever fashion, he feels a sense of excitement that he has not felt since he first came to Luriat. The mere possibility of a new mission—is it foolish? Is he still looking for someone to tell him what to do, who to kill, what to overthrow, even if he doesn't want to do those things anymore? But he cannot slow his heart. Lessons learned in childhood leave deep roots and are not easily plucked out by adult reasoning.

Koel lives in free housing too, but in an artists' district called the Pediment, slowly gentrifying at the south end and bordering the Sands on the west. Fetter and Caduv take the long way around to walk through those calcified southern streets first, to see the upmarket galleries selling objects of art made out of comprehensible materials and presented in more or less conventional forms: wood, clay, metal, water, smoke. Slowly, as they proceed north and east through it, the Pediment deliquesces and becomes poorer, the houses more dilapidated, the people less groomed, the commerce more casual, vendors populating pavements, spilling out into streets. The art, too, becomes stranger.

Perhaps it is the preponderance of art or humanity, but Fetter sees fewer invisible powers in the Pediment. The galleries host clusters of feeders clinging to their walls, slowly pulsating. As the street becomes poorer, Fetter sees the ones who are always there: the long-tongued, white-armed antigods that he has learned to associate with disease. For the most part, though, he sees only people, much larger crowds than Fetter is used to in the Sands. Many newcomers to the city, if not troubled or interned or driven away during their time in the Sands, move a little further inland to the Pediment. Fetter can see the appeal, and it makes sense that Koel would live there. In its own way, it is the perfect distillation of everything that is good about Luriat; the freedoms it gives, to those allowed to accept them; the space it creates for its citizens to make, to see, to hear, to be art, if they so desire and as long as that art does not cross the invisible lines of force that would bring down the boots and the drums.

In Koel's own neighbourhood of the Pediment, the current fashion appears to be a maze of religious and political rumours, as a form of participatory performance art. As they step through the narrow, crowded streets they pass from the territory of one rumour to the next, hearing and retelling them as they go, mixing and remixing, the stories leaving bitter flavours in the mouth. The rumours are usually simple and memorable. Some are incomprehensible without context, but most are clear.

"A general election will be called for the month of Second Vap."

"The daughter and sister of the Walking lives near here."

"There will be a coup after the election."

"The Perfect and Kind is coming."

"The first executions of the storm season will come in mid-Kinny."

"The coup will be before the election."

Fetter tries to negate the rumour about the Perfect and Kind as they pass through it, because it churns painfully in his gut, but there are enough rumour-repeaters that the message corrects itself. He supposes that some of these people must be contributing to his father's crowdfunding campaign.

"The Song of the Red will fail," Caduv says firmly to a small child sitting on a doorstep. His voice resonates, and several bystanders turn their heads to look at them. A hundred paces later, a passerby stops to murmur it back to them. Fetter glares at Caduv, who shrugs.

"Petty, I know," Caduv says.

Koel's house is difficult to find. The streets have grown darker and narrower, their shoulders always brushing others, the rumours quick intimate whispers in passing. When they finally get to her building, she is outside waiting for them, smoking a clumsily hand-rolled cigarette.

"Two strange ones are coming," she says to them, with a wry smirk. "I've been hearing about it for a while."

"We heard about you too," Fetter says, and Koel makes a face.

They go up to her apartment, which is in a building older and shoddier than Fetter's, but less crowded, and her space less cluttered. He expects paraphernalia, a hand printing press maybe, a mimeograph, a spirit duplicator, papers strewn about: something to indicate the life of a seditionist pamphleteer, filmmaker, and playwright. There is nothing like that. He asks about it guilelessly, and Koel laughs, which is rare enough that it makes Fetter and Caduv stare. That's a secret, she says, and Fetter remembers old tradecraft learned at his mother's knee. The details are vague, but it was once part of his training to hide, to make himself invisible, practice deferral. It didn't touch on pamphlets, but it did allow for conspiracies.

"This is about the voice," Fetter guesses, speaking to Koel but nodding at Caduv, who looks unsurprised.

"It's always about the voice," Caduv says. "I've listened to people reading from your pamphlets, and I don't disagree with your politics, but I can tell you up front that I can't change the vision or make the unchosen see it. Only the Singer of the Red has those powers. I just have . . . *this*. It's not useful."

Koel waves a hand and goes to make them tea. Her expression is thoughtful. Fetter expected her to be as outspoken as she normally is, to come right out with whatever it is she wants. But it turns out that she's capable of patience too. He supposes that this is part of the shared heritage of the almost-chosen.

Fetter tries to remember what he's read of Koel's politics in her pamphlets. Her thick columns of type detail complex histories of crimes and villains. He has gathered that she opposes the governing bodies, powers, principalities, and dynasties of Luriat, but it's difficult to follow the specifics of her grievances. His understanding of Luriati politics is muddy.

In Acusdab, politics was simple; there was that place with its devils and doctors; in it there was the family, hating and murdering each other; and like the bitter sun, there was Mother-of-Glory.

By comparison, Luriat has too many moving parts, too many heads, too many arms, a devilish profusion of writhing shadows and hidden blades. There are the two competing presidents and matching twin prime ministers; the governor-general representing the Absent Queen, and the steward of the Absent King (unrelated); the Parliament, in semi-permanent abeyance due to competing Dissolution Orders and Emergency Regulations, of elected representatives from the city and the haunted seats of various integrated and unintegrated hinterlands—Fetter was startled to learn that Luriat considers Acusdab a semi-domesticated Autonomous Territory. As such his homeland has no representation in the Luriati Parliament, but it *does* have a diplomatic legation in the city led by an Envoy Extraordinary and Minister Plenipotentiary, a woman he's never even heard of and whose claim to legitimacy seems dubious—what would Mother-of-Glory say? Too, there are the Presidential Task Forces, usually staffed by retired generals, that perform much of everyday governance unaddressed by the ongoing failure of Parliament; dozens of political parties, almost all of which appear to be formally or informally organized along lines dictated by the grouping and typing theory of Alabi race science; the city's Lord Mayor, who skips from embroilment to embroilment, one scandal to the next; the Council of the High Priests of the Path Behind, four old, withered, venomous men in blood robes; many warlords and drug barons, most of whom are also cabinet ministers; and the two great Courts of Summer and Storm, and their mirrored Constitutions with competing claims to supremacy.

Fetter has little understanding of how all these powers interact. Still, while the specificities of Koel's pamphlets have always remained opaque to him, the broad thrust is simple enough. Koel, like many other activists and agitators in Luriat, is opposed to the executions, violence, harassment, discriminations, disappearances, imprisonments, pogroms, and other tools of the death magic employed by the various limbs of the tentacular Luriati state against its people, and most particularly how they are *differently* employed against its various distinct peoples, as demarcated by the Almanac, the annual tally of ever-evolving races and castes. Fetter tried to read the most recent Almanac, but the task force of retired generals and high priests that compiled it wrote almost as abstrusely as Koel.

"You got people to read her pamphlets to you?" he asks Caduv, as Koel comes back with the tea.

"I went to some meetings," Caduv says. "They read from them and explained."

Fetter hadn't known Koel had any kind of readership, much less an organized one. A slow heat washes over him, a feeling of being left out, left behind. He wonders if their group, the almost-chosen, are more susceptible to this feeling. They were groomed to be insiders, given access to the mysteries, taught the secrets. And now they, or at least he, cannot stand to be the ignorant outsider.

*Why am I the way I am* is a question Fetter asks himself

a lot. He supposes that everyone does. His father's teachings begin from the same question.

"Are you willing to try?" Koel says to Caduv. Her bluntness is back. "I have some thoughts about your gifts, but only if you're interested in doing . . . more."

Caduv nods in a way that means *I'm here, aren't I?* and Fetter finds it also in himself to envy whatever inner capacity or facility allows Caduv to commit himself to an enterprise bigger and more obscure than can be seen in a single glance. He is interested in what Koel is building up to, but he is still sufficiently wary of her to think twice about a deeper commitment. Caduv, apparently, is not. He looks at the other man through the side of his eye and wonders what it would be like to be so sure of oneself—to have the song of your god in your mouth and still walk away, to choose music as your path in life as if there were no need to keep space for a destiny that might yet come crawling back, to pursue revolution in a place that hasn't even become home yet.

Koel looks at Fetter, as if sensing his inner roil, and says the words that cut through it. "I have something to ask of you, too," she says, and his gut clenches in alarm or excitement. "But first, I need to tell you both a story."

# 6

The story Koel tells is her own, though she hardly features in it at first: the tale of the Walking.

This sacred story (Koel says) is full of gaps. It has been told by mother to child for generations, and in each retelling, the mother kept some small part of it secret. This is called the prophet's portion: every prophet who has ever held the mantle has kept back a portion for themselves, such that every succeeding generation has less of the tale than the last, and therefore can access less of its power. Sometimes rumours are passed down by a prophet's aunts and uncles, but these could be born of envy and cannot be trusted. The most popular and enduring of these untrustworthy rumours is that there will one day come a point when the story is so garbled that the prophet loses all power and virtue, and at that point the Walking will walk again.

"Is it the prophets who are called the Walking, or the god?" Fetter asks.

It's both, Koel says, or neither. That distinction too is lost. Stop interrupting so I can tell you the story.

In a different country, in an older generation—we no longer know which country, Koel says, except that it was large and populous and somewhere on the supercontinent of Jambu, or how many generations it has been, except that it has been long enough for the tale to have lost this much—there was once a god, or the prophet of a god, who broke a law. The law may have been a law for gods or for people, or perhaps in those days there was not so much difference between the two. The law was a quarantine, a curfew, a forbidding. All the people or all the gods or everyone had been told to stay in their homes, to be alone, to not approach each other for fear of spreading an infection, a conspiracy, a rumour, or a truth.

All the gods or people obeyed this law except one: a woman who walked in a time and place and circumstance where it was forbidden, a woman who walked from home to home. She told the story, recruited for the cause, or spread the disease. Many learned the truth. Many joined the rebellion. Many died. The Walking walked until her soles wore away, until her feet were cracked and bleeding. She walked until her very flesh dissolved and then she walked on bones. It is possible she walks still, somewhere in the endless supercontinent.

Before she walked out of her own story, though, she lived many lives. She took many lovers, in the villages and towns and cities she walked to. Some of them accompanied her, for a time. She gave birth to many children, and formed such bonds with others who had their own children that they too called her mother. And wherever she went, she was beloved of street children, who called her mother and walked with her for as long as their small feet could bear. And to every child that ever called her mother, the Walking told her story.

None of her children followed in her footsteps—it was her rule that no two should go the same way. Most of them did not emulate her, either: after she walked out of their lives, as she always did, they decided that their mother's story was only a story. They may or may not have cared for the truth, joined the cause, or caught the disease regardless. The story does not tell of them.

Some of her children, though, *did* follow her teaching and

seek to keep it alive. They were forbidden from following in her footsteps, but the world was great and wide, so they each chose a direction and walked out into it.

*This* story, Koel adds, does not tell of most of them either. It is *one* story, about *one* lineage. But it acknowledges that there are other stories out there. Other lineages. Generation after generation, this pattern repeated. New lineages scattered into the world like seeds. Every generation's prophets kept their portions, and the story grew thinner and more fragmented.

Another enduring rumour among prophets and prophet-aspirants is that some day far in the future, on the other great supercontinent on the other side of the world, all the lineages will come together and join up their fragmented stories to retrieve the truth of the original teaching.

In my own (corrupt) lineage, Koel says, the practice is that only one of a cluster of siblings receives the formal title and the respect and standing that goes with it. The rest of us are spares, in case disaster strikes and the chosen prophet is lost. We have become a narrow, closed lineage, in direct contradiction to the spirit of the Walking herself. Nor does my lineage truly walk any more: the prophet does the rounds of our country, but it's merely a ritual progression carried out once a year to bless each little village and petty township. When I was unchosen, I walked away from it all. I walked out of my mother's house, out of her city, out of her country, out of the world I knew. I walked for many years before I came to *this* city, and here I stopped for a while.

"Why?" Fetter asks. He forgot not to interrupt, but he understands from Koel's face that the story is over.

"At first, to rest," Koel says. "I was tired, and my feet hurt all the time. Later, when I had healed up, I stayed because I'd met someone. Oh, don't look so surprised. This was years ago.

She was much older than me, and her lungs were weak. She died in a plague year long before either of you saw this city for the first time."

Fetter puts his hand to his heart and bows his head briefly. Caduv mumbles something, the words indistinct but somehow cooling, as if they were a soft wind.

"After that I stayed because of this fucking city," Koel says. "My days of walking the world may be done—if nothing else my poor feet couldn't take it now—but I can still tell the truth. I can still recruit."

"Or bring disease," Caduv says, with a smile that Koel answers briefly with her own.

"Recruit for *what*?" Fetter says. "I know you have your pamphlets and your . . . your *meetings*, but—"

"I wanted to talk to *you* about the door you tried to open," Koel says. She studies his face, perhaps seeing a flash of puzzlement. "The bright door. You told the story at group one day. It was before Caduv came. Oh, don't pretend like you don't remember. You've been interested in the bright doors for a while, haven't you? But nobody will tell you about them, or the ones that will talk don't seem to know anything."

Fetter opens his mouth to protest but then closes it again. It's true. He became—quietly, he'd thought, cautiously—obsessed with the bright doors after he tried to open one, but the headache it gave him was so bad that he has been wary of trying again. He brought it up in group to find out if others had shared his experience, but people had just mumbled sympathetically. He couldn't remember if Koel had said anything. Most likely she had just sat there looking at him.

There are too many secrets and lies about the bright doors of Luriat, Koel says. Here are some things that I have learned since I came here.

First are the things that everybody knows, if they live here long enough. The first of these is that the bright doors don't have an other side. Ah, I see it had not yet occurred to you to check. If you enter any building that hosts a bright door, or go to the other side of any wall that contains one, you won't find the back of the door. Go and see, you will find it is true. There is nothing there, just unbroken wall. Sometimes not even a wall, as the bright doors do not correspond to architecture in any predictable way.

Second is that any closed door in Luriat can *become* a bright door, if left closed long enough. Any doorway that can be shut and that can't be seen through when closed, if left shut and untouched for an undetermined length of time will vanish from one side and become unopenable from the other. There may be other conditions; they are heavily speculated upon but remain yet unknown. It is also unknown how far outside Luriat this effect can take place; there are records of it happening deep in the hinterlands. The door does not change in appearance, but it is tradition that such doors should then be brightly painted.

The bright doors, after an indeterminate time, become indestructible unless the entire section of wall surrounding them is destroyed first, in which case the door will go away as if it had never been. While the surrounding structure stands, however, the bright doors cannot be hacked open or blown apart. They repel force and steel. Knobs will turn and tumblers roll, but their locks, if they have locks, are unpickable. Or rather, it is simply that the locks are no longer the mechanism by which the doors remain closed, so picking the locks achieves nothing.

Not much more is truly *known* about the bright doors. If you ask around enough, you will find people who will tell you what they believe to be secrets: the secrets of their function, their purpose, their history. They may even believe these secrets. But their secrets are only contradictory theories and suppositions, with no credible witnesses or evidence in support. Some say the doors open into other worlds or other times; others say they might open into each other, if only they could be opened, providing instantaneous transport across the city; some say they are prisons holding gods or monsters; some say they are a complex and mysterious hoax or ritual carried out by a secret society.

The city has an entire bureaucracy dedicated to the study, worship, and containment of the bright doors—they get too many volunteers, and the waiting list is a barrier to weed out anyone without the proper connections of nepotism or bribery. Every single door is identified, named, and given its own committee, who must further approve the petitions of researchers and worshippers and suchlike. Depending on the waxing and waning interests and enthusiasms of their given committees, each door receives its own unique combination of attentions.

The only citizens who are banned from membership in these committees, unofficially, mind, are people like *us*. The foreign chosen, unchosen, almost-chosen. Anybody who bears a degree of potency, no matter how small, in a system of significance other than the Path Behind. If you knew how to read the strings of haecceity printed on your identity cards, you would find a particular string of symbols that marks you with this trait.

"How would they even know?" Fetter asks. "I didn't mention my background when I filled in the citizenship forms. Such questions are not even asked. I know those forms very well; I've gone over them hundreds of times."

"I don't know how," Koel says. "But they always know— they know a lot of things that you don't tell them. Their intelligence networks are extensive. Look, check your identity cards if you don't believe me. Here is mine, and *these* are the symbols I mean." She produces her card, small and yellow, and Fetter studies the symbols carefully. Comparing against his own and Caduv's, it is true that those particular symbols are shared by them all. But is that proof of Koel's claims, or merely proof that the city identifies *something* they share in common—he is already devising further tests, such as checking his card against those of other immigrants to the city. But Koel is still speaking, not waiting for him to decide where to lay his trust.

"If pressed, the committees cite *incompatibilities* as an explanation for why we are banned from this one thing," Koel says. "And there's a grain of truth in that. For most people, the doors are merely doors: mysterious, unresponsive, but otherwise unremarkable. For *us*, we very few, there are always strange manifestations, often physical pains or discomforts."

"I felt a great cold wind," Fetter recalls. "And it gave me a headache." This is about as much detail as he offered last time.

"I have tried several doors over the years," Koel admits. "Each time, I hear . . . something, something like a song or a chanted prayer. But it is very faint, in some language that nobody in Luriat seems to have heard before. It makes me ill, often for days."

"I have never approached one," Caduv says.

Koel turns to Fetter. "You had a very clear and distinctive reaction to that bright door, more so than most of us. I am curious. What if we could get you approved by one of those committees? What could we find out?"

"How? You said my identity card—"

"Let's say we can solve that problem," Koel says, and the phrase rolls off her tongue so easily that Fetter immediately understands that Koel has said such words many, many times in her life. "We would choose a door that is relatively neglected, a committee that is relatively disorganized, and we would have you masquerade, say, as a student of such phenomena from a moderately prestigious university, applying to the committee for a period of field study—"

"That sounds too specific to be a hypothetical," Caduv says.

Koel laughs. "The student's name is Peroe. He doesn't know me, but his mother is one of my friends—she comes to my meetings, you see. Peroe has only recently returned from a field visit to south Bbadu and is unofficially quarantined at home recovering from a mild case of the Aggiopan plague he caught there. He's not going anywhere for at least three months. She is willing to take the risk of lending his identity card for Fetter to use while he is confined; Peroe himself will never even know."

"This sounds so interesting," Caduv says. "I would love to—"

"I ask Fetter to do this," Koel interrupts, "for three reasons. One, Fetter is a match for Peroe; physiognomically, Alabi race science would group them together into a higher type than me or you, Caduv. Oh, I know neither of you understands what that means, but I assure you it is a factor when navigating anything in Luriat. Two, we know Fetter's reaction to the bright doors already, and it seems to have more potential than most of us, both more intense and less disabling. Three, I have something else to ask of you."

"What is it?" Caduv asks, at the same moment that Fetter grunts in disagreement. Caduv waves at him to go ahead.

"It's easy for you to say I suffer less," Fetter says. He doesn't want to get into his thoughts on race science now, in case Caduv decides to resent him. "The headache was very—"

"Oh, don't worry, I have something for that, too," Koel says. She switches her attention away again. "Caduv, you've mentioned that you're interested in the theatre?"

# 7

Hej forwards an email from the Perfect and Kind's crowdfunding campaign. Fetter stares at the message, his heart a plummeting stone. Perhaps the message is an invitation to mock it or to marvel at its quaintness. Hej forwards a lot, almost always without context, and will later either deride or endorse the content in person. Fetter hates having to guess his slant and ordinarily disregards the messages, but it is difficult to ignore his father's face on the screen. To his eye they do not look alike: his father's face is rounder, fleshier, a man in late middle age. Perhaps, he thinks, our eyes are similar, wide and dark, deep-set, and heavy-browed. Is this part of the physiognomy that Koel spoke of? Is my father also a *higher type*? But where Fetter's eyes have always been bruised and shadowed, his father's eyes are clear and blazing, as if alight. The eyes of someone who embraced their destiny instead of slowly throttling it.

The campaign is 94 percent funded, the message says, they just need a little more of a push—this year they've learned from experience and budgeted for the bribes that would get various concessions from city officials. This time, the campaign organizers are positive their bid will win the approval of the Perfect and Kind's site selection committee. There is a hopeful photograph of that committee itself, a large group of ordained votaries and lay devotees. The caption indicates that the chairperson of the committee is no one less than Salyut, the Saint-General, one of his father's two chief votaries and a member of his closest inner circle, the man who is perhaps most like the Perfect and Kind. Fetter studies the man's grainy face in the photograph. Perhaps if he had grown up with his father instead of his mother—if he had been indoctrinated differently, become almost perfect, almost kind, oh devils—he shakes his head. How can he explain any of this to Hej? He has gone too long without confessing the sordid truth of his origins. If Hej meant to mock his father, how should he even react? Fetter can no longer organize his thoughts on the cult of the Perfect and Kind. For so long he has understood the Paths Above and Behind as enemies, to be avoided and kept outside the boundaries of his life. Attempting to see all of it through Hej's eyes gives him a headache.

∽

Despite Koel's assurances, Fetter expects the meeting with the committee of her chosen bright door to be a gauntlet. But his meeting is in fact not even with a whole committee. There are only three members total, and he only has to meet one. He presses the button to ring the bell at the address Koel gave him, the committee chair's home, practicing his false name as he waits, rolling *Peroe* in his mouth so that he will remember to respond if called by it.

Unsurprisingly, the committee chair is wealthy. He lives in the Plantations, an elegant and bizarrely misnamed district far from Fetter's usual haunts. There are no plantations there; it looks like a suburb in the heart of the city. It's quiet and leafy, liquid silver running down the trunks of the weeping trees. The street is quaintly cobbled, and the greenery artfully pruned. Every house in the Plantations is a great mansion, or so it appears to Fetter. They are each several stories high, painted in rich, modest earth colours, outer walls free of bills and graffiti, elaborate gardens behind their tall gates. The committee chair's house is surrounded by a high wall painted in a blindingly clean pale blue. The door in the wall has a large glass window inset at face height, so that visitors may be observed before the door is opened, and, of course, to make sure the door can stay openable.

The door has a heavy brass knocker in addition to the discreet button for the bell. Fetter does not use the knocker because he suspects it is ornamental, perhaps a trap of etiquette. Through the glass window, he sees a young man approach unhurriedly and open the door to him. This is not the chair, of course; this is a servant. When asked, Fetter gives his false name and asks the man for his name in turn. He immediately understands this to be a great error of etiquette when the startled man blurts out his name—Siculu—then turns away quickly and gestures at him to follow. He was obviously not supposed to ask. He hopes that this came across as smarmy condescension or bohemian egalitarianism on Peroe's part, anything other than suspicious behaviour from Fetter.

This pretense is exciting. His heart is beating, but not painfully fast; his senses are alive. He hasn't felt like this since he was a child and still believed in his mother's plans, in his own destiny of glorious revenge.

Inside, the house has many small internal gardens and ponds, mazed by covered walkways that Siculu leads Fetter through. Again he attempts to make conversation with the man, who seems not much older than him, then catches himself being Fetter and not Peroe. Siculu does not respond this time, except to smile and nod politely. He is wearing ordinary clothes, as far as Fetter can tell: well-made, but not a uniform. So the committee chair is very wealthy, but probably not one of the city's true elite. Fetter has seen the convoys of the elite, with their long rows of vehicles, servants, bodyguards, drummers, elephants, spear-carriers, heralds, and motorcycles. Uniforms were a keystone of such displays.

Fetter is himself wearing new clothes for this mission. Koel helped him select them and paid for them, waving off the cost. Ordinarily, Fetter wears the cheapest clothing he can buy, baggy knee-length camisas and loose breeches, usually in bright colours and synthetics. He has been slowly drifting away from his habit of covering up. Koel insisted that Peroe would dress better, so Fetter is wearing form-fitting clothes in dull, respectable pastel blue, a sleeveless camisa and tight breeches that end just below the knee. The sandals on his feet are leather, not rubber. This, Koel says, is how a moderately well-to-do young student such as Peroe would dress in this season to attend such a meeting.

Fetter feels far more exposed in this costume than he is used to. He shaved his arms and legs as Koel instructed, and insisted she help him cover up the worst of his scars with makeup.

His scars were far less noticeable than he thought, Koel told him, though she helped him cover them up anyway, all the while pointing out that they were faint, pale little marks, practically invisible, and where visible, innocuous. "Many people have scars and marks from accidents and troubles throughout their lives," she said to him, in a scolding tone that he found faintly pleasurable. "You think people can somehow see how you got them. People can't see, don't care. I don't care. I've never asked, have I? At most, they will see the scar on your cheek and assume it was some small childhood accident. Just laugh it off if it ever comes up. I promise you, it never will."

They didn't talk about his greater deficiency, but he's lived in Luriat long enough that he no longer expects it to be noticed. He walked here in the sun, feeling the pleasant burn on his newly smooth arms, and casting no shadow. Nobody looked twice at him.

The committee chair's name is Tomarin, a tall thin man with an expansive smile and gestures. When they come upon him, he is lounging in a cane bucket chair, watching the birds in his gardens from the shade of a covered pavilion, eating something that Fetter doesn't recognize, large red wedges dusted with something that stains his fingertips. When he sees them, Tomarin bounds to his feet and welcomes Fetter effusively. They sit while Siculu fetches Fetter a drink. It is not tea, which is Luriat's traditional drink offered to guests, but something cool and a little disgusting.

"So, Peroe," Tomarin says, and Fetter rolls the name in his mouth again. *Peroe*, that's who he is.

Tomarin asks about his family, his studies, and his opinions on the bright doors—questions Fetter was prepared for. He answers smoothly, his nerves eased by realizing the older man is not truly paying attention to either questions or answers. As long as Peroe seems to be who he is supposed to be, the man nods along. His eyes never once go to any of Fetter's scars, and some small old knot in him uncoils.

Tomarin does not ask to see his borrowed identity card, warm in Fetter's pocket, but hands over a prepared letter of authority with official-looking stamps that gives Peroe, identification string such-and-such, the authority to study the door.

"Well, good luck with your studies, Peroe," Tomarin says. He is one of those men who constantly repeats your name. "You must come to dinner some time. And of course we must call a meeting of the committee—goodness, it's been a while! We're a bit lax, I'm afraid. Gerau has been away on pilgrimage, so only Coema and I are around. But perhaps the three of us can have dinner soon?" Fetter agrees, though he has by now eaten some of Tomarin's snacks as well and finds them also faintly disgusting. The red stain they leave on his fingertips is oily, and he wants very badly to wash his hands clean. He remains silent because he is unsure if this would be considered rude: Tomarin has made no move to clean his fingers.

Koel's briefing identified Tomarin as a minor player in the spice trade, Coema as a government official in the Ministry of Health, and Gerau as a wealthy retiree who is frequently, and currently, away on pilgrimage. Koel was confident of being able to prepare him for Coema, so dinner is not too intimidating a suggestion.

"Have you been to see Nine Yellow Oxen yet?" Tomarin asks, and Fetter is lost for a few moments before he remembers that this is the name of the committee's assigned bright door. The actual catalogue entry, Koel told him, is just a long string of numbers, but the practice is to translate the formal numeric designation into a nickname involving animals and colours, through a schema that Fetter does not understand at all. The colours in the names do not necessarily match the colour the door is painted—Nine Yellow Oxen is painted red, he was told—which in any case might change at the committee's whim. Perhaps it was yellow before. The oxen he cannot fathom.

"Not yet," Fetter says. He had not wanted to risk being questioned near the bright door without a formal letter of authority on his person. "But I look forward to spending time there."

⸎

Koel is harder to get hold of these days. She's apparently working with Caduv on a new play.

"I haven't written a play since . . . well, I co-authored two," Koel says, and by the long-soured old grief in her voice Fetter guesses that her lost love must have been her collaborator. "They were very well-received," she adds, after a moment. "By which I mean they were both banned—one can be spoken of but never performed again, and the other may never even be spoken of. Since then, I've done short films and street theatre and various performance art projects, but I've never returned to the stage. I thought perhaps with Caduv it might be time."

"Can he act, though?" Fetter says, and is surprised into laughing by his own whiny tone. Koel laughs, too.

"Well, he has presence," she says, eyebrows raised, smiling. "The script will be a little stylized to compensate for a lack of experience."

Fetter feels like she emphasized that *he* just a little, as if to suggest that Fetter, with his floaty, light-footed ways, lacks such presence. Not that she knows quite how light-footed he really is. Devils, but that stings, and he's unable to come up with a retort that wouldn't make him feel worse. He falls back on his own training and experience; he nods and keeps his silence.

The bright door called Nine Yellow Oxen is located in an extremely public space on the edge of the Plantations, where the faux-suburban aesthetic blends back into the urban density of the surrounding districts. The door is set in the high outer wall of a building that is being demolished; in its stead, judging by the rain-stained billboards that bracket the construction site, will rise yet another condominium tower.

The wall that contains Nine Yellow Oxen only exists for a few steps in either direction from the bright door. A fragment of wall preserved while the rest of the demolishing and reconstructing goes on unabated. As Fetter learned from Tomarin, a bright door may not be intentionally destroyed without permission from its dedicated committee. The committee has withheld this permission thus far, as seemed obvious to Fetter, because they are slow at committee work and for the most part not very interested in the door. To hear Tomarin say it, they had *preserved the door for research* so that Peroe could complete his study of it before they allow the new owners of the property to, at last, demolish this last unsightly fragment. This demolition will also have the happy consequence of dissolving the committee and freeing them of this tiresome civic obligation, at least until they are reassigned to another such committee for a different door.

Koel explained to him that the truest explanation for the delay was probably ongoing haggling over the bribe. The closer the new building gets to completion, the more anxious the new owners will be to demolish the fragment containing the bright door, and the higher the price that Tomarin can set—Fetter still isn't sure if this is more likely than the committee's laziness, but the ways of city money are strange to him. In Acusdab, money meant old copper discs stamped with the insignia of kings and queens long dead, though Mother-of-Glory's household rarely paid for anything in cash. In Luriat, money is both a lot more and a lot less. The city's cash is traded in paper of various denominations: fanons and rupiyal for most people, and the rare varaagam, the pig note, for people like those on his committee. But in truth the city runs on credit, not cash, and he dimly senses great rivers of wealth flowing far over his head.

In the meantime, the new building will set its own wall slightly back from this stray bright fragment, and it will erect its own entrance a hundred steps away, a construction worker tells Fetter. At the moment, the work is focused on the careful demolition of the old building, and all of Fetter's work at the bright door is accompanied by the sound of swinging hammers.

Throughout his first day at Nine Yellow Oxen, three different policemen ask to see his identity card and his letter of authority. They are polite afterward, which is more disturbing. He spends that entire first day squatting in front of the door

and writing down observations without touching it, not wanting to trigger anything just yet. For the moment, he just wants
everyone to get used to his presence, including any invisible
laws and powers that may haunt this area. He has seen several
out of the corners of his eye, but they have not paused to look
at him, and he desperately wants to keep it that way. His gut
has been queasy and grumbling ever since he approached Nine
Yellow Oxen. There is some ill luck or danger here, but he
can't spot it. He feels skittish, half inclined to run back home,
to the safety of being Fetter.

Perhaps ill luck for Fetter can be transmuted into good luck
for Peroe. They are very different people. Peroe, for instance,
has brought a thick notebook and a pencil. He meant to pretend to make notes, and instead finds himself making notes in
truth. He doesn't even know the formal name of Peroe's field of
study—Koel said he studied *phenomena*, suggesting that bright
doors were not the only object of such studies—much less its
thinkers, theories, practices, or terms of art, but he finds himself making what he considers to be commonsensical notes on
the door's positioning, environment, approximate proportions,
colour, state, and aspect. This is partly because he doesn't want
to have an empty notebook if a policeman happens to glance
through it, but also because he is serious about this opportunity. Perhaps Peroe would have formal training, but Fetter's experience with the bright doors, as Koel keeps reminding him,
is unique. No training could replicate it; therefore, whatever
method he invents is canonical. If only his gut would settle.

On the second day, he makes contact with the door. Sitting
cross-legged on the concrete slab before it, knees sticking out
over a ditch and the sound of hammers in his ears, he leans
forward until his face is a handspan from the wood. The wind
is difficult to discern at first, because he is expecting it, feeling
for it, and his skin is alive with sensitivity. Every touch of air

feels like the touch he's waiting for. There is something erotic about being so open to the world. He feels naked, vulnerable. His penis stirs and he shifts his legs uncomfortably, resisting the urge to casually brush a nail across his nipple through the thin cloth of his camisa. One of his oldest scars bisects his left nipple; it doesn't feel as much as the other, but because of this he has always been partial to it. He hasn't seen Hej in days, what with one thing and another. The list of things that he hasn't told Hej is growing with every step he takes into Koel's world.

Ah, there—the wind is still nothing more than the faintest of breezes, but the bitter scent is unmistakable.

Fetter notes that down, in case anybody is watching him. *Day 2. 5th hour, dawn watch: wind and bitterness.* There are too many people around: he feels conspicuous, shadowless in the bright sun, observed by many eyes—when he looks, of course, nobody is paying attention. No invisible powers either. The demolition crew are hard at work, and, behind him, the morning traffic has grown. He can tell without looking that the deep rumbles are buses, the jingle-jangle rattles are bullock carts, the throaty whines are tuktuks, the shuffle and slap are the rubber soles of foot traffic.

He reaches forward cautiously and, remembering the dangerous cold of the doorknob on the bright door he'd touched before—in blessed silence and unobserved, what luck that had been, when his gut was pushing him at the bright doors rather than away from them—places the tips of his fingers gently on the wood.

Nine Yellow Oxen is different from that other bright door in several ways. Where that one had been orange, this one is a pale red. Once it might have been brick-red, but the coat of paint is thin and faded. The wood is of superior quality: it looks thick and heavy, and has no splinters. Instead of a globular knob, it has a curved, ornamental brass handle. It has not been maintained so well, but it was once a proud door, so well-fitted to its frame that the cold otherworldly wind barely seeps through.

He has the beginnings of a headache—he fumbles for the little cloth bag of painkillers that Koel gave him and extricates one. The black ball is so small he can barely hold it between two fingertips; it is just a little oily, enough that his fingers will retain a faint metallic scent. He swallows it whole. He does not yet have the sensation he had felt that other time, of a great howling wind on the far side of the door. Only that light breeze. He feels it faintly on his feet, then raising the soft hairs on his shins. It makes him feel unbalanced, as if he could tip over. He does not reach for the door handle. Not today.

# 8

When the ringing starts, Fetter mistakes it for birdsong: the trilling of some distant, insistent creature. He is at home, taking a break from researching Nine Yellow Oxen by burying himself in a book, as he often does in the afternoons when it's too warm to go outside and squat on hot concrete in direct sunlight. The book is called *Exorcism Rituals in the Luriati Hinterlands*, which Fetter was alarmed to discover is a region that includes his hometown. Acusdab used to be so far away when he first came to Luriat, but one of the new highways has reached out across the plains and dragged it closer. The city claims cultural dominion over all the territories it has begun to so entangle. He remembers some of the rituals in the book from childhood, being performed on himself or on others. Possession was commonplace there, and exorcism likewise. The book says the devils of Acusdab are fading away, perhaps repelled by the highway and the modernity it brings, and without possession, nine-tenths of the lore are already lost. The book is an attempt to document the remaining tenth. It includes interviews with many hinterlander exorcists, though Fetter doesn't recognize any of their names. The aduro of Acusdab don't seem to be included. He checks the publication date on the book, and it's relatively new; the author must have travelled the hinterlands not long after Fetter left home.

The trilling in the background is persistent. It's a telephone. Not his mobile phone, which lies quiet on the table next to him, but a landline. Does his apartment have a landline? He vaguely remembers seeing a receiver when he first moved in. He hunts for it. The apartment is full of books and dust. He can afford books but not bookshelves, and because he lacks windows, the apartment traps becalmed sea winds that take a wrong turn, depositing the dust of a thousand shores in a fine layer over Fetter's books. After the first few months, he grew resigned to the dust. The books make it harder to clean and take up too much space, but he can't stop himself from collecting them. It's the only thing he really needs money for, living in Luriat, and to support this he works every now and then—often as a guide for Aggiopan tourists, because his Alabi is pretty good after all this reading—just to get paid so he can buy more books.

The freedom to learn about whatever he wants makes him giddy, and he has far more books than he has been able to read, stacked into unsteady towers, often collapsing into piles that he hasn't restacked yet. Many of the newer piles concern the bright doors, though as Koel warned him, most of them are full of nothing but speculation. Some of the oldest piles are novels, a form he was briefly fascinated by when he first came here. The trilling sound is coming from beneath such a pile. Fetter brushes aside dusty paperbacks with lurid covers, partially nude human figures clutching weapons and each other against the sun or the sea, or against monstrous beings. At the bottom is a telephone with a rotary dial, plastic once shiny and blue, now dull and discoloured. It is ringing, but when Fetter picks it up and speaks into it, there is nothing to be heard on the other side, only the pure silence of disconnection. The landline is not plugged in. When he replaces the receiver it starts to trill again. Filled with foreboding, he finds the connecting cable, plugs it in, and tries again. This time there is static, which resolves into his mother's voice. It's been years since he heard her, but her rasp rolls those years back like the tide.

"I'm dying," Mother-of-Glory says.

Perhaps the phone has made her sound thin and scratchy, or perhaps she's always sounded like that and he's only now hearing it with adult ears. It makes his throat itch.

"How did you get this number?" Fetter asks.

"I divined it in the entrails," Mother-of-Glory says. Fetter wants to ask *whose* entrails but she is already saying something more. It was lost in a burst of static, but it was probably her answer to that very question. He doesn't want to ask her to repeat herself, in case the answer is vile.

"How are you dying," he says, instead. "What does that mean?"

"The doctors," Mother-of-Glory says, and Fetter has a vivid memory of Acusdabi doctors, their mouths red from betel, black instruments in their hands. "The doctors will tell you it was cancer."

"But it isn't?"

"The doctors will tell you it was cancer," she repeats, as if she's practiced this line to herself in a mirror and is determined to get it out before she hangs up. "But it's disappointment in you."

After the weekly meetings, Fetter gets into the habit of staying behind, ostensibly to help clear up but mostly to brief Koel. He does not tell her that his mother got in touch. He has not mentioned it in group either; something about the way that Koel remembered and instrumentalized the story of his first encounter with a bright door has soured him on sharing in group. Now he speaks less and listens more.

But despite how it began, he is excited by his research. It feels good to have a task again, a purpose, especially one that touches so closely upon the numinous. He feels more connected, though to what he could not yet say.

Koel is not as interested in what he's learning as he is. "My interest is not in Nine Yellow Oxen," she admits. "I will not pretend otherwise. I know *you* have a great interest in the doors, which is why I created this opportunity for you—now I ask you to do something for me."

"You want me to spy on the committee," Fetter guesses. Devils, but old lessons stir like sour mother's milk.

"Well, for a start, I just want you to accept their dinner invitation, when they formally make it," Koel says. "You should understand, you will only be invited to eat with them because Tomarin has Peroe pegged as racially acceptable and, much more importantly in this case, an acceptable caste. Peroe's family is lesser cultivator-caste, so Tomarin will invite you to a friendly dinner but won't act as your patron or get involved with your fortunes. Still, it's something—Tomarin wouldn't have spat on *Fetter* if you were on fire."

Fetter grunts. The Luriati caste system is overly complicated. It seems like every district, every tributary township, and every village in the integrated hinterlands has its own system and hierarchy, and their multifarious points of contact are ever contested. Acusdab had its own caste and clan politics, but Mother-of-Glory had long since warped such things to revolve around herself, and by association, him: he never had to think about it as a child. He's ill-equipped to navigate a hostile foreign caste system, unclear on its signifiers and kinetics. He has to rely on Koel to understand what he doesn't.

"I want Peroe to be friendly to Coema," Koel says. "He's also cultivator-caste, though a much more prestigious variant than Peroe's—I need to check against a copy of the Almanac, but I'm pretty sure. He should be eager to sponsor Peroe. You will find that Coema shares your interest in the doors but is far too busy to study them, much less pay real attention to the committee. So he will *want* to talk to you."

"Isn't that dangerous?" Fetter asks. "If he's an expert—"

"He isn't," Koel says. Her hand moves to the side as if swatting Coema away, a pest. "He's a dilettante. You've already read more on the subject of the doors than he has. His is an idle interest in cataloguing the folklore of the doors; he plans to write a book when he retires, or so he has often announced. Myself, I think this is unlikely, but the important thing is that he thinks that he thinks that he wants this. Just make sure you have some small new thing to say about bright doors every time you meet him."

"How often do you want me to meet him?" Fetter finds the committee the least interesting part of his life as Peroe so far.

"Let's start with *once* and see how it goes," Koel says, laughing.

Mother-of-Glory calls back, irregular, unpredictable. She is the only person who ever calls Fetter on the landline. Disconnecting the receiver has no effect: it rings anyway, no matter how he tries to disable it, even after he's removed some of its component parts and shattered others. He stops only when he realizes the obscene possibility that he might reduce it to dust and nothingness, and still be pestered by its ringing. It's easier to just answer, while there's still a receiver he can pick up to make the ringing stop.

At first the calls are full of grim mutterings, threats, and accusations. After she grows used to him answering, she seems to relax a little, so he tries to make conversation. She seems eager for this. She encourages questions and answers most of them, but not others. When he asks her about the Envoy Extraordinary, Acusdab's alleged ambassador to Luriat, Mother-of-Glory relapses into a sulky silence, forcing him to change the subject.

She asks after him, finally; how is he doing, *what* is he doing? She asks about the city, about the famous bright doors of Luriat. Fetter pointedly refuses to hide Hej from Mother-of-Glory. She tuts at him.

"You have to be careful in the city," she says. "They have laws against sodomy."

"If they do, they don't enforce them," Fetter says. "I see lots of people together—"

"That's not how laws *work*, son," she says. "A visible law is a ploy, a little play. A mummery in waiting, waiting for you to become interesting. Never give them a reason to care who you are."

"I don't—" Fetter begins, and then falls silent, thinking about the growing complexity of his second life as Peroe. Or is it his third life, if the first was the small sharp one his mother shaped and armed? Is he risking becoming interesting to the visible laws and powers of this city? In the silence, Mother-of-Glory hangs up again. Their conversations are getting longer, but they're also growing less unpleasant. Sometimes it's nice to hear the phone ring, when Hej is busy and he's feeling lonely.

Tomarin texts him after a few weeks to invite him to dinner, as promised. Coema will be there also, Tomarin says. But when Fetter arrives at the house and is ushered to a small dining space in one of the inner gardens by a servant—not Siculu this time, but a tall young woman, pushing Fetter's clumsy estimate of Tomarin's wealth further up—he finds three people around the table, not two. Tomarin himself is at the head of the table, dressed more formally than before in an austere pale-yellow camisa. Fetter feels underdressed, wearing the same type of Peroe costume as before. Koel only bought him a few changes of clothes and said it was all right for a student, even from a moderately well-to-do family like Peroe's, to be a little shabby. He hopes she's right. He keeps his arms and legs shaved all the time now, and his beard and hair neatly trimmed a little shorter than he prefers, so that he can fit into upper-class company at short notice. He's stopped wearing makeup to hide his scars, though. Koel was right about that, and the worst of them are on his back and chest, anyway.

The man to Tomarin's right must be Coema, who looks exactly as Koel described him: a little older than Tomarin, large-bellied, and hairy, with a government moustache and a thick mat of curly hair on his forearms, even on his fingers below the knuckles. He's wearing a light Southeastern Imperial-style shirt with a wide, open collar that shows more of his hairy chest. Is all this body hair daring or crass? Either way, Fetter decides, it is a kind of power.

To Tomarin's left is a silver-haired woman who could be no other than Gerau, the pilgrim. She is even taller than Tomarin and, to Fetter's eye, dressed more formally in the Luriati style, in a drape of rich, deep-red fabric over a fitted bodice. Fetter wonders if Peroe would apologize for being underdressed, and then decides no, Peroe would be oblivious. He smiles, greets them, and sits across from Tomarin.

The table is square and not too large. Tomarin's garden is peaceful, elegantly lit by candles in clay lamps rather than crude electricity, and by the silver light of the three-quarter moon, dark enough that Fetter's shadowlessness is moot. The food is served by Siculu, who nods almost subliminally to Fetter, and the tall young woman whose name he doesn't know. They look a little alike: perhaps they are kin. Perhaps the two

of them are Tomarin's only servants? Fetter speculatively re-
vises his estimate of Tomarin's wealth again, assuming that the
truly wealthy would keep small armies in servitude.

The food is better and less alien than Fetter expected. For a
while, the conversation is light and mostly over his head, as the
other three discuss things that he does not understand at all;
the doings of their mutual acquaintances, business partners,
colleagues, families, and so on. Coema asks Fetter about Nine
Yellow Oxen in exactly the way that Koel had prepared him
for: with a burst of enthusiasm and interest that quickly turns
out to be shallow. The other two indulge these turns of conversation that touch upon the numinous otherness of the bright
doors, but are more interested in discussing their own affairs,
so the conversation keeps drifting away.

Everyone is drinking—Gerau a pale Aggiopan wine, Tomarin and Coema arrack—so when Siculu murmurs the question
at him, Fetter asks for arrack too, in case this is a gendered etiquette trap. Alcohol is not free in Luriat, so Fetter has not had
much opportunity to drink it. The arrack burns his throat a
little and he tries not to cough.

Fetter slowly figures out that Coema and Tomarin are distant
cousins by marriage—presumably this is why the aristocratic
Tomarin tolerates the cultivator-caste Coema—and that they
share some old family feud against some other relatives; that
Tomarin seems to know everyone in the city who has any money
at all; that Gerau is religious. Dismay grows in him: she is, like
many in Luriat, a believer in the Perfect and Kind. More than
that, a *true* believer, the kind of bright-eyed zealot his mother
spent his childhood warning him about. This appears to come
as no surprise to the others, who don't blink as Gerau talks
about Fetter's father at the dinner table. So her pilgrimage—her
pilgrimage—

"Did you see *him*?" Fetter blurts out. The words are out

before he can bite them back, and he can't disguise the naked interest that drives them. All three look at him curiously, and Gerau nods slowly, as if re-evaluating her assessment of him as a person.

"I did and I didn't," she says, after a moment. When she looks directly at him, the spikes and curls of her silver hair look both expensive and militant, like precious instruments of violence. "The Perfect and Kind monsoons at Kalaki, and the crowds of pilgrims are simply enormous, an absolute ocean of humanity as far as the eye can see in every direction. His sermons are held in a large stadium, and I could certainly not afford the premium tickets to stand at the front. Most of us pilgrims heard his voice on the speakers and saw his face projected on the giant screen behind him, but of his mortal person I saw only a distant blur, and of his unmediated voice I heard nothing."

Fetter blinks at the suggestion that this obviously wealthy woman is an impoverished pilgrim in some other context. He has been trying to understand Alabi race science and studying the Almanac that Koel let him borrow, but it's only now that he understands that Gerau should be considered racially distinct from the three men at the table. Is that part of this show of poverty or humility? No—Gerau is a little fairer of skin, a little narrower of features; she probably has Aggiopan ancestors, perhaps even Alabi, and therefore is both higher-status than the others for being more Southeastern Imperial in her very meat and cells, but also lower, for not being purebred. Alabi race science, as Fetter understands it from his reading, places great value on inbreeding populations to allow racial traits to pool and thicken. Wealth works this way as well, pooling and agglutinating and breeding with itself. He is beginning, he thinks, to understand this world better.

Perhaps Gerau is hinting at deeply inbred superstrata of wealth so much higher than her own that she is recontextualized in their presence as poor. Perhaps Kalaki is so much greater a city than Luriat that the latter's gentry are the equivalent of the former's peasantry. How is *he* supposed to get near the Perfect and Kind if—no, he reminds himself, he doesn't need to do that, it was just a nightmare of his childhood. He is no longer bound to kill his father. He doesn't even have to see him.

"Did you know there's a crowdfunding campaign to bring him up here?" Fetter asks, and the others all chuckle. Gerau laughs out loud, startling him. He'd only meant to make conversation. He's a little drunk, he realizes.

"She knows that quite well," Coema rumbles. "She's only its organizer, it would be odd if she hadn't heard of it."

Gerau waves this away. "I'm not *the* organizer. I'm on the committee, that's all. But I'm glad you've heard of it, young man. I've been complaining that our social media outreach isn't strong enough."

"My boyfriend forwarded it to me," Fetter says, and filled with horror, bites his tongue so hard he thinks there might be tears in his eyes. It just slipped out, too—where *is* his luck tonight? He'd *never* called Hej his boyfriend before, what did it even *mean* that he's out here saying it to strangers? And what if these rich city people were bigots like his mother warned? They could have him arrested, on the spot. But no, they're already chuckling again. This is something they do a lot, Fetter has already noticed, these infectious waves of amusement, not the open-mouthed laughter of the genuinely mirthful but a sort of rumbling, shaking, controlled titter, a hahaha, a hohoho. Their laughter means they are far beyond the possibility of offense from the likes of Peroe. It means they are in control: of this conversation, of their lives, of his life, of the world. Or so they think: if they knew who he was, what he's done, what he was *for*, they would scream in horror. He reminds himself that he gave that life up, threw it away.

"If 'cool' young people are forwarding the campaign to each other, I think you don't have to worry about the social media," Coema says, clumsily. The man is a caricature, Fetter thinks, but then he sees the beads of sweat on his moustache. There is some tension between Coema and Gerau that he had not previously recognized. Fetter quickly rifles through his memories of the evening—yes, Coema is a little too amused and tolerant of everything Gerau says; he takes the pose of the knowing, rational, modern man, who is civilized and tolerant of the irrational but has no time for it. Gerau meets this with naked faith. She dares him to mock her with the blaze in her eyes, and with her poise and presence.

"Well, I approve of your friend," Gerau says to Fetter, smiling with such brightness that his spirits feel lifted even though he is in no way seeking her approval. "If he wants to volunteer for the campaign, please put him in touch with me, we can always use more young people. And you're welcome to join him!"

"Always recruiting," Coema says, and another wave of titters crosses the table, hahaha, hohoho.

Fetter rolls the name *Peroe* in his mouth again, conscious of his own intoxication. He needs to switch to water. Oh, this mustn't get more complicated. "I'm afraid he's away on field research," he says, as smoothly as he can. "I don't think he'll make it back in time."

"Ah," Gerau says, unblinking. "He must want you to go in his stead. Well, I understand that completely. I always try to share the teaching of the Perfect and Kind with the people important to me, to see if it helps them like it has helped me. I tell you what—if the campaign funds successfully, I'll put your name down as one of my guests, and you will be able to attend a sermon at the premium tier."

"You've never offered *us* premium tickets, Gerau," Tomarin says. He's not chuckling yet, but Fetter can feel the titter bubbling in the man's throat, ready to pop in response to whatever Gerau says.

"Oh, you two are useless," Gerau says, with a smile. An hour ago, Fetter might have called the tone of voice fond; he is getting better at understanding them. The titter circles the table again. He tries to smile broadly in sync with it.

"Thank you so much," Fetter says, once the laughter dies down. This isn't about me, he reminds himself; this is about Peroe, a student of the mystical and the otherworldly. Peroe would leap at the opportunity. "That is extremely kind of you. I'd love to." He can just not go. Claim a minor illness or an unfortunate conflict on the day. He just needs to say *yes* now, because Peroe would.

Gerau beams at him. "We're very hopeful about bringing the Perfect and Kind to Luriat for the first time. The crowds will be much smaller than in the south, even for the free sessions. The premium experience will be quite intimate, much less commercial compared to the big southern tours. It will be wonderful."

"Speaking of commerce," Tomarin says. His voice contains precisely the same minute trace of boredom whenever he changes the subject away from the Perfect and Kind, if Gerau is talking, or from Nine Yellow Oxen, if Coema is talking. He starts talking about an abstruse Luriati corruption scandal that the three of them seem very well-versed in; they've been discussing various aspects of it on and off all evening. Fetter wasn't even aware of it before tonight. It seems part of a shipment of medical ventilators donated—no, sold at cut rates—by some Aggiopan-owned foundation from East Kantak had vanished, and the city's opinionators were divided on whether to blame the donor foundation, Kantaki shipping, corrupt port officials, the Ministry of Health, or organized crime. Somehow this too devolves into low sniping between Gerau and Coema.

Fetter listens to them talk, eating to prevent himself from blurting out anything more. At some point he broke out in a sweat but it's cooling on his body. He feels light-headed and exhausted, as if he'd been running for his life.

Later in the evening, as if it had nothing to do with anything that had happened before, Coema turns to Fetter and says, "I have the privilege of mentoring a small group of researchers doing some interesting work on the bright doors. You would get on with them—they're young and enthusiastic, like you!" Coema glances at Gerau, who is seemingly talking to Tomarin and not paying them any attention, and wets his lips. "They're working on a big project that I think you'd be interested in. Give me your number, I'll ask Pipra to text you."

# 9

When Fetter tells Koel about the dinner, she whistles in appreciation and says that's more work than she expected him to get done in one evening. He's not sure what she means, but it seems that she's happy he's on good terms with Coema. He wondered if he should wriggle out of this meeting with this Pipra, whoever she is—as Coema promised, she texted him an address—but after the conversation with Koel, he decides he should give it a shot.

Getting closer to any kind of real research on the bright doors is compelling; still, he worries that the more people Peroe is exposed to, the less well he will hold up. These are scientists, not rich dabblers like Coema. He'll have to play up the ignorant student who is happy to learn from them. That should be easy enough; it's true.

He follows the address to a partially abandoned shopping mall in a suburban district called Cooksferry so far away from his corner of Luriat that it takes three hours in a bus to get there. The traffic is intense. Cooksferry reminds him a little of the Plantations, with its spaciousness and greenery, but here nature feels natural, messy. The trees are untrimmed and wild from neglect, not fine-tuned into an aesthetic by generations of wealth. The abandoned shopping mall is nestled into an empty bylane off Cooksferry's main road, where it abuts a large, overgrown plot of land not merely wild but gone feral. Great crawling thorn trees and whipping brambles burst out of that nest of misplaced wilderness to invade the mall itself, sharp enough to shatter plaster and leave whip scars on brick; scaled vines climb the mall and penetrate its windows, displace the insulated metal sheets on the roof.

Fetter finds the entrance on the far side of the mall, which is still tame enough that a thin handful of shops are still operating: a mini-supermarket, a pirate software store, a few dusty shops selling clothes nobody is buying.

Pipra appears when he texts her and guides him away from this desolation. She leads him deep into the bowels of the dying mall.

The deeper they go, the wilder the mall becomes. Squirming vines tangle in the fluorescent lights, only a fraction of which work; the stuttering light and permanent gloom are helpful, because otherwise a building full of scientists would have surely noticed his shadowlessness. Tiles have been shattered by roots, and there are shards of pottery all over the floor. The walls are stained with mud and dirt, as if someone has been trying to encourage this invasion of nature. A pattern of brown handprints on the walls follows them deeper into the complex.

"That *is* mud, I hope," he says, gesturing.

"Hmm? Oh, yes," Pipra laughs. "Clay from the riverbank. There's a bit of a marsh out back where that empty lot borders the old canal. The team's not yet at the point of smearing shit on the walls. Or blood, I suppose blood could make that colour. Isn't it curious how primeval artforms recur like that?"

Pipra is young and enthusiastic, as promised. She is perhaps a few years older than him, in her mid or late twenties. She reminds him of Gerau in some way, rather than Coema. At first Fetter thinks it's the short hair, but no, it's the eyes, blazing with a certainty very much like faith.

They see more of Pipra's team as they cross the building. She introduces them in passing; Fetter doesn't retain any of their names and simply waves at them. They are arranged in small teams of two to four people, sitting in front of doors. *Closed* doors which are obviously not yet bright. He hadn't understood how easy it would be for him to tell the difference. The bright doors radiate significance in a way that ordinary closed doors do not. He's never seen so many of the latter since he came to Luriat.

The teams of watchers seem to have been camped out for some time. There are sleeping bags, portable stoves, unkempt beards, frazzled hair in caps. The air-conditioning is spotty; some spaces are too cold, others are sweltering. Researchers sit on the ground or on portable chairs, watching the door in front of them at all times. All observed doors are closed; there is a network of open doorways so that people can move around, as Pipra and Fetter are doing.

"Every non-transparent shop door," Fetter says, at last. "Every janitor's closet. Every office door."

Pipra beams at him. "Very good!"

"You're testing how long it takes for an ordinary closed door to . . . become a bright door?"

"To *translate*, yes," Pipra says. "Sorry for the jargon, we're making it up as we go. This building was part of a famous corruption scandal from a few years ago. Both the owners and the construction crew were from outside Luriat, and they bribed the Public Health Inspectors that would have kept them from installing so many vulnerable doors. Then they started getting bright doors—there's First Blue Heron on the second floor, and over there, what used to be a door to the basement. It hasn't got a designation yet. Anyway, they lost all their money and the building was impounded by the Ministry of Health. And that's when the boss gave us license to run some experiments in it."

"Coema?" Fetter asks.

"Ooo, *Coema*, is it," Pipra says. "We call him *boss* behind his back, and *sir* to his face. He's *only* the Second Senior Assistant Secretary to the Ministry. How do you know him again? Are you his illegitimate son or something? Should I watch my mouth? Oh shit, too late—"

They both laugh, and Fetter waves it away. "He's on the committee for Nine Yellow Oxen, which I'm trying to write a paper on." Even with practice, he's surprised how easily that rolls off his tongue. "He said I should meet you all. Sorry, I'm very bad at understanding how the Ministry works—I didn't even realize he was such a big wheel."

Pipra taps the side of her nose in a gesture that Fetter doesn't quite follow. It feels halfway between acknowledgement and warning.

"We want to observe a translation event in real time," she says. "Did you know there isn't a single authenticated case? Not *ever*? Recording equipment doesn't work; the recording always cuts out the good minute or two, and equipment gets damaged, making for very expensive failures. There is anecdotal evidence of observed translations, including from people who we've interviewed, but they vary wildly on the details and are considered unreliable. So we're putting teams of trained observers on both sides of every closed door and waiting it out."

"How long has it been?"

"Three weeks," Pipra says. "We've already missed two translations while everybody was somehow distracted or blinking or napping or snacking or taking a bathroom break at the same time *despite clear instructions*—" This last bit is a shout, clearly aimed at one of the teams in earshot. Several of them raise their arms, as if in surrender.

They arrive at the other side of the mall. A large brute tree branch has intruded through the outer wall; large cinderblocks lie scattered on the ground in a way that suggests that the tree punched a hole in the wall one day and pushed an arm through. The cinderblocks are covered in fallen leaves, curved like twisted smiles. Warm sun filters through the foliage, mixing strangely with the faint fluorescent light from a single half-blackened bulb.

A solitary watcher is staring at what Pipra identifies as the last closed door on this level. It's an unremarkable plywood door, painted blue. It is closed only by a small bolt, without any locks or knobs. Pipra relieves the watcher, sending them back down the way they'd come, presumably to rejoin their original team.

"Sit," she says, suddenly, taking Fetter's arm and plonking him down in the portable cloth chair. It sags a little under his weight and, alarmed, he straightens.

"You're low on bodies," Fetter says.

"How insightful," Pipra says. "Was it me having to watch this last door all on my ownsome that gave it away? Eyes front please. No blinking."

"Are you serious?"

Pipra turns her huge eyes on him for a moment and he feels a little unsteady in the chair. "*At least* try to blink as little as you can. Alternate eyes for relief."

"What are we looking for, exactly?" Fetter says, eyes front, trying not to blink, wanting very badly to blink. He's not sure if she's hazing him. She sits cross-legged to his side, also staring forward.

"When this door translates," Pipra says, pointing at it. "This side will be either the front or the back of the bright door. If it's the back, the door will vanish—we want to know what that looks like. Does it pop out of existence? Does it make a noise? Is there a puff of air? A farting sound? Does it fade slowly? Do all its parts fade at the same rate, or will the bolt fade before the wood? Do invisible monsters from an elder world come and dismantle it? How exactly is the missing door replaced by *wall*, when those bricks were never laid by human labour? Is the new wall from a parallel universe identical to ours in all respects except for the existence of this one door? What does that imply about the layout of shopping malls in parallel universes? What happens that makes cameras stop working, regardless of the technology they are based on?"

Fetter digests this. "And if this is the front of the bright door? Won't that look exactly the same?"

"It will look exactly the same," Pipra says. "But Janno on the other side of the door will ping us so we know something's happened. And if there is something to be seen in the moment of translation, we will see that too."

They spend an enjoyable afternoon together, chatting and watching a closed door that remains stubbornly mundane. Pipra has snacks, which she shares: fried manioc chips, bitter and familiar. Pipra is full of interesting facts about the bright doors, but he's already encountered many of them in his reading. Apparently so little is known that the line between dedicated amateur and professional expert is quite narrow.

"Well, thanks for stopping by, Peroe," Pipra says, at last, when the light leaking in from outside turns golden. He feels an odd pang at the false name in her mouth. "I hope you enjoyed your tour of duty, but you don't work for the Ministry and we're not paying you to do this, so you should probably go home and do something more productive, like stare at a blank wall all evening."

"I bet we could make this door translate right now," Fetter says. He feels reckless, tempted to brag about his own strange encounters with a bright door. Oh, if only that wouldn't bring so many questions he didn't want to answer. "If we coordinated with Janno to look away for a few seconds."

"This has been suggested," Pipra says. He's still looking at the door but he can hear the scowl in her voice. "I don't think the door would deign to cooperate. And anyway, if it did, it would only be to spoil our project."

"If it's waiting to be disregarded before it translates, then you'd have to adapt the project anyway," Fetter says. "If it's been waiting for weeks and weeks and someone's eyeing it all the time, getting impatient—"

"They're not sentient, you know," Pipra says. "Supramundane, yes, but they're still doors. They don't have feelings."

"I mean," Fetter says. "How do you *know*?" He turns to look at her, which feels dangerous and electric. She meets his eyes, and very slowly, smiles in the half-dark. Her smile is blinding, like her eyes.

Pipra raises her walkie-talkie to her mouth and mutters into it. "Team Fourteen? Janno, we're trying a disregard window again. Start protocol in two minutes, observation check once every minute."

"You've tried this before," Fetter says, a little disappointed. He'd hoped for praise, he realizes.

"We have," Pipra says. "It would be very convenient if we could control the timing of translation, even if it puts dampers on our data-gathering. So we tested intentional disregard early on. It didn't work."

"Oh," Fetter says, feeling small. "Then why now?"

"We tried that at the *beginning*," Pipra says. "When we first set up in here and closed all the doors. None of them had been closed for more than a few days at that point. But if you're right and—"

"If the doors are getting frustrated?"

"*If* the length of time they're closed could cause some sort of buildup—oh, the metaphors are so tricky in this work, so messy." Pipra sighs. She's rummaging in a pack under the chair, one eye on the door. "I've been assuming an equal probability of translation at any moment, but if the gambler's fallacy doesn't hold in this case, if a longer wait *does* increase the likelihood of translation, then it's worth trying again. Ready?"

She stands and walks behind him. He tries to stand as well, but she pushes him back into the chair. "I only have one pair of earplugs," she says. "So plug your ears with your fingers, please."

"Are we not facing away?"

"Disregard protocol says we have to be able to resume observation as quickly as possible," Pipra says. He tries to turn to look at her so she's not a disembodied voice, but she taps him on the head. "Sit still. Plug your ears and close your eyes. Don't resume observation until I let you go."

He plugs his ears with his fingers and asks a question but the words he hears through his bones are a different dialect and he isn't sure what he asked. Pipra's hands slide around to cover his eyes, which he still hasn't closed. He shuts them quickly as her hands clamp themselves to his face, cool small palms over his eyes, and he understands she's not going to risk the untrained observer peeking. He opens his eyes again behind her hands and wonders if she can feel his eyelashes moving on her palms. Her littlest fingers cross on the bridge of his nose.

With two senses shut away—nothing to see but darkness, nothing to hear but the echoing silence of his own head—his other senses are uncomfortably alert. He's very conscious of Pipra's proximity, of the contact between her hands and his face. She smells like clean sweat, but there is a trace of something sweet in there, a sickly-sharp scent underneath. Perhaps the last traces of a perfume. Her skin is cooler than he expected, and his face flushes with heat in response. The heat spreads across his face and neck, across his entire body. He is mildly aroused, he realizes, embarrassed. His nipples are painfully tight, his penis stirring. He takes deep breaths to force his body back to quiescence, and smells the faintest bitterness on the air. A familiar bitterness, which wasn't there before.

The walkie-talkie chirps, which he doesn't hear, and it vibrates, which they both respond to immediately. Her hands are gone from his face. When he removes his fingers from his ears, he hears her talking excitedly to Janno. He hears Janno indistinctly through the door as well. Or, through the wall, rather, from the other side. Because the door *has* indeed translated. He can tell, instantly, by looking at it. It looks the same in every way, an unremarkable, anonymous, blue plywood door. The tiny bolt is still closed. He feels a dreadful temptation to stand up and go unbolt it.

"I didn't think that would actually work!" Pipra is saying. He's not sure if she's talking to him or Janno on the walkie-talkie. Perhaps both.

"You're *welcome*," Fetter says, grinning, and she allows this with a grin of her own. "Now what?"

"Now we both write down every sensory detail we can remember," she says. She hands him her notebook and pen. "You go first. Don't leave anything out!"

Of course he leaves things out. The heat in his body, the tightness, the stir—He's pretty sure those things had everything to do with Pipra touching his face and nothing to do with the bright door. He doesn't write that he could smell Pipra, which seems like it would be insulting. But embarrassed at having nothing to write, he mentions the bitter smell that accompanied the translation. He writes as if it were the first time he'd smelled it, and is vague enough that it could just as easily be explained by the decaying vegetation that lies thick on the ground nearby, the mulch of fallen leaves and strips of bark covering the tiles below the branch piercing the outer wall.

Pipra reads his notes, nods, and doesn't ask about the smell.

He wonders if that means it's a known datum or whether she's dismissed it, but he's afraid to ask in case he gives himself away.

Janno comes around the long way and joins them to add his notes and lack-of-observations. He's a tall lanky man about Fetter's age, but while Pipra is relaxed and casual, Janno is restrained and informally deferential in a way that reminds Fetter that Pipra and Janno must belong to different racial or caste designations—he can recognize a subtle accent in Janno's voice now, the hellspeak that is almost the same but not quite. He is not yet Luriati enough to know *what* the difference is, or what precisely it means. On top of that, and perhaps because of it, they are both government employees in a formal hierarchical relationship. They all are, aren't they? The whole team works for the Ministry of Health, like Coema, who outranks them all in every hierarchy. He wants to ask about their relationship to their boss, but he doesn't want to interrupt their excitement. Fetter isn't all that excited himself, but Peroe is over the moon. It's a strange feeling, being more than one person.

It's late when he finally leaves them, with promises to return and provide further brilliant insights that they totally could not have come up with on their own—even Janno cracked a smile for that one. Pipra, Janno, and the others are planning a series of induced translations with carefully graded increases of sensory observation and timing: cotton wool instead of ear plugs, filter goggles instead of closed eyes or blindfolds; doors reopened and reclosed to reset the timing at staggered intervals to test what Pipra is calling *frustration theory*, in honour of Peroe's contribution.

He *does* want to come back. It's not just Peroe who is excited. Fetter wants to feel the easy fellowship of this group again, so different from the support group and its solidarity of shared loss. He wants to see Pipra again.

# 10

The drums wake him up, and at first he thinks he's a child again. He's in that maze of a house, Mother-of-Glory somewhere within, an impossible gravitic presence like a planet on two legs, and outside the devil-doctors are setting up for another summoning ritual. When he gets up and goes outside, he'll see them massing in Mother-of-Glory's estate—unfenced, because isn't all Acusdab Mother-of-Glory's estate? Her gravitational field does not have a crisp boundary but only weakens with distance; in theory, it has no end. The devil-doctors will be making the seeming-pots for a blessing grid, erecting barrier fences and elaborate decorative constructions, all out of carefully cut twists and arcs of young pale-green coconut palm leaf; when he goes outside, they'll put his small clever hands to work making more. Some doctors will be practicing their whirling dances, spinning like tops, faster and faster. Some will be practicing the drums, high and low.

But these drums are not quite the same. Those praise and gather, these tug and insist. The realization creeps in under his eyelids and pulls them open even as his gut snarls and churns in warning. He sits up, hands clutched to his stomach. His arms and legs are not thin, short, child-sized. There is hair on his chest, on his arms, on his face. The dream—was it a dream, or only a stray memory on the threshold of waking?—has left him with a doubling of vision and sensation. When he stands up with his grown man's body, his legs feel weak, as if his adult weight is being borne by those little child legs after all. He stands still for a moment so that he doesn't stumble. Though, Fetter supposes, he can stumble if he wants to. Nobody would know. Nobody is here to see.

He waits, anyway, until he feels steadier. Unhurriedly, he washes his face, cleans his teeth, puts the kettle on. He does these things semiconsciously, but off the beat. Only then does he open his front door and walk out into the passageway to look for the source of the drumming. His third-floor neighbours have already gathered at the outer balcony.

"What is it?" they're asking each other. Of course they don't know. They're all very new to the city. Even as he joins them, he can see they are turning to him for answers.

"Nothing good," he says, at last. He remembers the drumming that accompanied the raid, when soldiers arrested all those people a few years ago. Have they come for his building? Who are they looking for this time? Automatically, some part of his mind is preparing a screen of lies.

But this drumming isn't like that drumming either. A different rhythm. He looks out over the balcony: it is a procession. A line of prisoners is being led through the street. Today there are more drummers than soldiers, fewer heavy boots to stamp the time. The drummers wear the same uniforms as that day, but the drumming then was a warning beat, an ominous, low, never-finished growl, keeping people away, keeping them still. Today, it is louder, more triumphantly incantatory, a summons.

*Come and see*, the drums are saying. *All you, come look, and remember.*

The plumes on the drummer's caps wave in the breeze. He thinks of white anemones undulating in soft currents.

The prisoners walking in line are not manacled, but they are dressed in the rough grey government-issue sleeveless camisas and knee-length shorts that he knows from the news to be standard prisoner costume. Their heads are shaven, as punishment or as practicality. It helps curb the spread of lice in Luriat's overcrowded prisons and overflowing internment camps. They each wear a garland of bright red flowers. Their faces are lowered, but he can see that they are of all ages, of all genders. They are not, he thinks, of all races and castes. There is no way to tell this by merely looking at them, but part of being Luriati, perhaps the major part of citizenship in this city, is being able to look at such a procession and *know* this.

Devils, but he is truly Luriati now.

Absent-mindedly, he scratches his bare thigh—he's come out in his nightshirt and boxers—and sees the others are looking at him with a kind of quiet horror. He knows his face is still, his demeanour calm. He understands: they think he is unmoved.

What do the flower garlands mean? The flowers have five large bright red petals. They lie on every grim grey chest like a ring of fire. It is a common flower that he's seen before, often used in worship. They grew in Acusdab, too. Is this worship? Some kind of Behinder ceremony? No, he remembers: Luriatis call these hurtflowers, and he's never understood why, until now.

He leans out over the balcony to see where the procession is going, turns to see where it's been. The line is long but not endless; he can see both the head and tail of the procession. It seems to have entered the Sands from the Pediment. That makes sense, too. These marked prisoners are obviously being paraded as a warning, and who needs that warning more than the artists and the immigrants? All that remains to be seen is if the procession itself, the shaming, *is* the punishment, or whether it is only the prelude to something worse.

He does not explain his thoughts to the others. They've all

heard the drumming, watched the prisoners, seen the hurtflowers with their soft petals like bloody tongues. The summoning drums have been answered everywhere he looks. The pavement on both sides of the procession is crowded with watchers, and every balcony is packed. In the hollow silences between drumbeats, there is the roiling susurrus of the crowd questioning each other, asking what this is, what is happening, where are they taking them, what are they going to do?

There are only so many possibilities. He returns without a word to his apartment for long enough to gulp down a lukewarm tea, to dress hurriedly. Then he too joins the crowd below.

Outside, the atmosphere is even more charged. It's different watching from street level, part of the crowd that slowly follows the procession along the pavement. It makes him part of the procession's frame of reference, rather than a distanced, still observer. Many seem to be doing what he's doing. The compellence of the drums is powerful, but no more than the dread urge to find out.

The crowd moves more slowly than the procession, trailing it like a slow wake. Fetter is impatient; he starts to overtake, to angle himself between shoulders and hips, to mutter apologies like imprecations as he slips through the crowd like a breath. He peers at the faces of the prisoners, looking for a face he recognizes—someone from the Sands, maybe even one of those people he saw taken once, though he is ashamed to not remember any of their faces with clarity. None of these people seem familiar. Most faces are lowered, chins tucked against the red flowers, as if breathing in their scent to the last.

He catches up with the head of the procession. The crowd extends forward into the distance, those keeping pace with the procession, like him, mingling with new observers being summoned by the drums. At the very front of the line of prisoners is a head drummer with two plumes in her cap. She's short, muscular, grim; her hands are callused, perhaps from a lifetime of drummery. Her part in the rhythm is minimal—she is the director and navigator. He tries to guess whether she is leading them on a predetermined route, or searching out a clear path to their destination. If we rushed out and formed a human barricade across the street, if we prevented them from getting any closer to where they're going, she is the one who would bark orders to the others. Perhaps she wouldn't even speak with her mouth, but only with her drum. They must have done this many times. He imagines that they must have drum-codes that can be transmitted through replication all the way to the back of the procession in seconds. Do they have a code for *citizen uprising*?

But such a movement of protest and prevention would not be spontaneous. Unlike the prisoners' faces, Fetter recognizes many faces around him in the crowd—they are people who live around here, who he sees all the time. Some he's spoken to, helped with some small thing or the other, bought from or sold to, fucked or been fucked by, passed the time of day with, passed by with a nod. A much larger proportion of faces he doesn't recognize at all. This audience has not been organized to any degree. He's been to a few of Koel's political meetings now, and grown familiar with the faces there; he sees none of them here. The terms and conditions of free government housing prohibits even tenants' associations. This crowd is atomized, aerosolized, no matter how dense it is; individual particles, not a massed wave.

His stride grows impatient again; he outpaces the procession altogether. A few people are walking ahead of him, too. They seem like they're heading for a destination.

It can only be a site of execution, he thinks. He must harden himself to not cry out at the sight of it. Why does the thought dredge so much fear out of him? Has he not killed? Is he not himself a monster?

Ahead is the Coast Road and the actual sands of the Sands, one of the few small, dingy stretches of beach on the Luriati coast not piled with great rocks against erosion. The track of the heavy rail out of Luriat parallels the coast like a dotted line on a map, a border separating the city from the sea. The sea looks onto the backs of buildings, as if the entire city is turned away in a sulk. Fetter never thinks how close he lives to the water. The rumble and grumble of the crowd around him segues seamlessly into that of the sea.

Fetter reaches Coast Road and turns south. Others around him seem more hesitant to commit to a north or south turn until the procession catches up and makes their decision for them, but Fetter has followed the logic of the procession and the queasy tugging in his gut. He expects what he finds a few hundred yards down the way, the wooden platform constructed on the widest spot of the beach.

In his first year living in the Sands, he came here more often. The sea was new to him, then, and it had called to something deep in him, some atavistic urge to drown, to hold his breath and hurl himself into the calm dark of the low waters—he has never so much as dipped his head below the surface, much less explored deeper water outside the safety of TV documentaries, so he doesn't know where the call of the abyss comes from. He never indulged it; he has never even learned to swim. He contented himself with getting his feet wet and feeling the pull on his ankles, wondering at himself, the obscured movement of strange desires in the deep. After a while, other things had taken his attention and he stopped coming, forgotten even that there *was* a beach here, so close to home.

The beach is not a busy one, in his memory. He has never seen any constructions on it before. It is already crowding with people, others who have figured out the procession's destination, or who have seen this before and know what to expect. They are gathering in front of the long gallows platform built across the entire southern end of the beach, just before where the anti-erosion rock wall begins again.

The far end of the platform, which is still being assembled, stretches into the water. The team fitting the preassembled modular parts together is thigh-deep in ocean. Luriat must have these by the score, portable, reusable. The wooden planks and supporting beams are slotted together and the horizontal crossbeams raised aloft and reinforced with thick wooden plugs. Perhaps the damp air has warped one of them; one of the crew pounds away with a mallet until it yields, and then the final crossbeam is up. The assembly crew cleans up and withdraws from the sea side of the platform, wading back to the sand and vanishing into the crowd just as the line of drummers and prisoners arrives. Each of the wide crossbeams support multiple nooses. It seems at first like an arithmetic problem set by a macabre tutor: how long will it take for all of the prisoners to be executed, given $X$ nooses and an average time of execution $Y$? But Fetter can't bring himself to count nooses any more than he could count the prisoners. The drumming has not stopped. If anything it is louder, more insistent, more final. *Come now*, it says. *Come and see before there is nothing left to see.*

A few drummers climb the platform and space themselves out along it; most position themselves in front of it, or in and around the crowd. The beach is full of people now. Bodies brush up against him on all sides. Even if he rises up on his toes to peer, he can't see an end to the crowd. There are unearthly presences hovering in the distance that he pulls his eyes away from. How long has he been here? It feels like an age. He is freezing in the wind, his face cold as ice. Most faces in the crowd are either flushed with blood or drained of it. He is not sure what his own face looks like. The crowd mutters and rumbles and roils. As the first wave of prisoners drops, he is distracted by a tug at his sleeve.

"You look different," Pipra says. The face he least expected is pale and strained. He looks around for Janno and the others but doesn't see them. This beach is a long way from Cooksferry.

"How so?" he says, automatically, but a fresh surge of alarm overtakes his already-overwhelmed heart. He is not dressed as Peroe—he just threw on whatever clean clothes were nearest at hand when he left home, and those are Fetter's old clothes, cheap and baggy and colourful. His camisa is bright red and patterned in gold, loose at the shoulder and hanging down to his knees, sleeves down to his knuckles; his breeches are a lurid purple, wide at the hip, narrowing and laddering into soft folds at the ankle.

He is barefoot. The soles of his feet hurt, abraded by the walk. He glances around the crowd again. In truth, it's Pipra who looks out of place here in her pastel colours and sleeveless camisa. She looks bed-rumpled, her hair every which way. But many of the people around them have such small signs of disorder: uncombed hair or beards, missing shoes, camisas unbuttoned at the neck, mismatched clothes. Perhaps the compellence of the drums is stronger than he thought.

He tries to bring Peroe to the front of his mind, his face, but he fails. He even asked Pipra the wrong question, the one that would focus *more* of her attention on him, though perhaps she was already doing that as a welcome relief from what is happening in front of them. Fetter tries to correct himself. "I mean, how are you here? I thought you were full-time in

Cooksferry." He realizes midway through speaking that she can barely hear him over the noise of the crowd and the drums, so he leans down and speaks into her ear.

"I visited a friend in the Pediment last night," Pipra says. She too tucks her face into his ear to speak. "Stayed over and woke up to this." Her face is very warm next to his cheek.

One of the drummers on the platform ceases drumming long enough to announce a list of charges, but their voice is reedy and carried away by the wind from the sea. Fetter thinks he catches words like *sedition* and *conspiracy* and *terrorism*, but he isn't sure if those words were spoken or whether he simply expects to hear them. He dreams, waking, that the platforms are altars of wood, of stone; he sees garrottes, great bloody two-handed swords with no point. It seems to him then that he is in another world, perhaps in the past, or another present with a different history. But then he blinks again and shakes his head, and there are not heads being rolled into piles, no swords being blunted on stone and sharpened between every third cut, no thick-armed garrotters in hoods. There are only the scaffolds and the thick boiled ropes, stiff and unyielding. He shakes his head again, but the world holds still.

In this world, the bodies are not dropped to break the neck, he realizes, once he manages to not avert his eyes at the death. They are gently lowered into the open trapdoor by the technicians, who only let go once the rope is at full extension. The prisoner, their hands bound behind their back, or in some cases bound to their lifted-up ankles, thrashes and wriggles for a few minutes until they are finally still. In this world, faces are not hooded. The hurtflower garlands hang off necks, in parody of the nooses they predicted. The prisoners rise and fall, wave after wave, to break upon the sands. The crowd around them moans and roars and howls, whether in approval or protest Fetter can't tell. Perhaps both, in proportions that slowly shift and swell like tides. The noise seems to be beyond language, set to the rhythm of the unending drums. In his arms, Pipra is making a noise like keening. He listens to it with his chest for a long time before he understands that he, too, is making a sound.

# 11

Hej is a clerk for the Summer Court, which worships the Seventeenth Schedule and will soon close for the wet season. Fetter meets him for lunch at a streetside kadé across from the Court, a grand old building fronted by a forest of enormous, elaborately carved wooden pillars. Fetter has learned enough of Luriati architecture to recognize it as colonial-era, but Hej sees him staring at the pillars and identifies them as Late Second Occupation, Abjesili style.

"You should see this up close," Hej says. He waves down a waiter to claim a table by the window and orders food and tea for both of them without sitting down. Like most Luriatis, Hej is a great believer in tea. "They'll take a minute anyway, so come on, I'll show you while they cook."

Hej looks different in the middle of his workday. He's oiled and braided his beard and wears an Alabi-style button-up shirt with long sleeves, his hands neat and brown against the sky-blue cuffs. He leads Fetter outside, across the square, and toward the home of the Summer Court.

They don't enter it; Hej leads Fetter along the side of the building instead, past the first row of wooden pillars and into the wide, stone-floored colonnade that encircles the complex. The pillars are all around them, irregular and unnerving. Long and fluted columns are interrupted and enwrapped by intricately embellished decorations: leaves, vines, explosions of fruit and flower. It is as if the pillars anticipate their eventual ruin and abandonment, the jungle that will some day claim them.

"They're beautiful," Fetter says.

"Beautiful imitations," Hej says, smiling. He leads Fetter around a corner, and the colonnade opens up on a small cobbled square, tucked away from the main street. "*This* used to be the entrance, when the place was built in the Middle Second Occupation. The old front entrance is lost. They say it became a bright door in the Early Third and the Alabi governor-general had half the complex demolished to get rid of it. So nearly all the columns are Alabi or Luriati reconstructions of the Abjesili style, some quite old in their own right, except for *this* one. This one is original."

The column that Hej is pointing at is much like the others, except that the decorations are sparser—there is a single lonely wooden vine that breaks the regularity of the fluted column, and only two open flowers. The wood also looks different, perhaps not at first glance but at a second or third. Does it look older because Hej just said it was older, Fetter wonders, or would he have thought that anyway? It's not the colour or the grime or the texture that's different, exactly, but something about how the pillar occupies space. It seems . . . heavier, somehow. It reminds Fetter of the bright doors.

"Be careful if you touch it," Hej says. "This is genuine Abjesili hauntwood, apart from where it's been repaired. Sometimes people are sensitive, I've seen people faint. I'm not, you know, but I still don't like touching it."

Fetter can't see any trace of repairs or any markings to indicate the boundary between old and new. He's heard of hauntwood, though. "The haunted forest that surrounded imperial Abjesil, yes? I think I've read about it."

Hej touches a finger to the pillar, grimaces, then withdraws it, shaking his head as if the contact had filled his skull with flies. "Hauntwood is how Abjesil built the world's first global slaver empire. For centuries, they'd lived in fear of the haunted forest around their city, until they learned how to cut down those trees and carve their spears, their arrows, the stocks of their long guns, the wheels and struts of their chariots, their slave collars. They conquered Aggiopa first, and eventually most of Jambu. They thought their tamed devil-forest was eternal. For a hundred and fifty years, they used up their hauntwood . . . by the end, even on useless decorative shit like this. But the forest was dying the whole time. What's left of it is walled off—biodiversity protected areas, you know? Most of the surviving hauntwood artefacts in Jambu are in museums. The Summer Court is too traditionalist to give this thing up, though. They won't even put up a plaque here because they don't want tourists coming to poke it. Sure you don't want to?"

Fetter declines, laughing. "I'm too scared," he says, easily. "What if it gives me nightmares?" In truth, he's worried that hauntwood might trigger a reaction like the bright doors, some kind of unholy incompatibility that he couldn't explain to Hej without unravelling too much of his life. And there's a deep unease in his belly, a feeling like a light fever, when he draws too near to the hauntwood. But it's also just fun to have Hej tease him about his fears, and flirt about being protected from old ghosts.

They go back to the kadé and their claimed table. Neither the tea nor the food has arrived.

"Our legal system is a huge tangled mix, you know, of Abjesili and Alabi holdovers from the Second and Third Occupations," Hej says, sitting down. Fetter mirrors his movements and posture. "You'll notice both the Summer and Storm Court buildings are in the Abjesili style. It seems everybody who came after, for over two hundred years, literally everyone, the Alabi Empire, the postcolonial government, the Courts themselves, everyone just agreed that, you know, the Second Occupation style looks better. All those odd little fruits and flowers are just so much more elegant and charming than grim old Alabi memento mori, or worse, boring Path symbolism." Hej laughs, and Fetter laughs with him, less for the joke—all of Luriat's buildings in their various styles look equally strange to him, the endless skulls and bones, the suns and moons, the war-beasts, the sea-beasts, the kneeling slave-youths, the ubiquity of his father's stylized face and hands upheld in the seal of teaching—but more for the pleasure of laughing with Fetter's chest, not Peroe's.

Fetter has been feeling cramped in Peroe's life. With Hej's eyes on him, he feels more like himself; better yet, he feels like the him that Hej knows, the best version of himself he has made so far. He wonders if he should find a way to mention Pipra, to be absolved of his reaction to her—but no, Pipra is Peroe's problem, not Fetter's. He tries not to think about the beach. It has been over a week but the drums are still echoing in his head.

He watches as if bespelled while Hej unbuttons his cuff and rolls up the sleeve of his right hand, revealing his wiry forearm and some of the tattoos he covers up for work. He wants to bend down like a thirsty animal and rub his face along those arms, to nose for the pits, to find that thick smell of the burrow, of home. Then the tea arrives, the ceramic chipped and the liquid a dark brown that makes Fetter think of medicine.

"Another Alabi thing, I know," Hej says, laughing. "Is it still strange to you? You have that big-eyed look again."

"What, tea?" Fetter says. He can't stop swallowing. "No, no. I'm quite used to it. It's just been a weird week." *I saw wave after wave of people murdered as if by a machine. My mother called again, she thinks I should dump you. I want you so much*

*right now but I might also want someone else.* "I've been thinking about being a kid, I suppose. We didn't drink tea in my
village." *Village* is how Luriatis like Hej talk about places like
Acusdab. He's learned to translate.

"You've said. It's odd, I always thought tea was quite popular in hinterlander villages," Hej says. "If they can make time
for tea, you know, between riots."

"My village was hinter than most," Fetter says, just to hear
Hej's laugh again, though the bit about *riots* puts a sudden bitterness in his mouth. They're not riots, he wants to say, but he
is afraid to hear out of Hej's mouth what he knows he would
hear: the measured, calm, reasonable voice of a liberal monk
of the Path Behind, calling for peace from *both sides.*

Then the food arrives, flatbreads, sambar, and chutney
North Jambu style, which Fetter remarks on is almost the
same as ordinary Luriati style. Arguably, Hej says, the former
includes the latter. This little Luriat-dominated tongue of land
protruding up into the great and endless ocean, these twenty
thousand square miles of peninsula north of the Hanu range,
has always held itself a little apart from the rest of North
Jambu. Fetter never even thought of it as a *peninsula* before; it
was everything he had ever known, it was just the world. His
world gets bigger by the day, but at the cost of getting smaller
and smaller at the same time. Even the wars are small—but
isn't it the same wars all the way south? The fruit of the Occupations, as much as those carved in hauntwood.

They eat and discuss the supercategories of cuisine. Jambu
is far too large and varied to be said to have simple regional
cuisines, Hej says; there are too many exceptions and nuances.
He seems about to launch into another of his rolling, languor-
ous rants, which ordinarily Fetter likes listening to, but today
the urge to interrupt is overwhelming.

"I saw your forward," Fetter says. He's been planning this sentence for days, so his heart picks up speed. "The one about—"

"Oh yes," Hej says. "The Perfect and Kind. I know you're probably not into it . . . Is it silly? He's never come this far north before and I'm not, you know, *practicing*, but I did grow up in the Path and it feels like a big deal. I just thought I'd check it out. Last big show of the summer. So do you want to come with?"

"You know it's not a . . . a *concert*, right?" Fetter says, and he's laughing too much from the sheer relief of discovering that Hej is not secretly a true believer like Gerau. He tries to rein in his laughter before it turns into sobs, but Hej seems to be laughing along.

"I know, I know!" Hej says. "I promise to take you to a concert, also. I just feel like this is kind of historic, you know? Living messiah on tour, finally coming to our hometown? It's worth the price of a ticket, at least."

Hot and cold blooms flare at once in Fetter's chest, the warm glow of *take you* and the hot burst of *our hometown* against the icy spikes that he associates with his father and *living messiah*. And there's the added complication of Gerau and her invitation—that's for Peroe, not Fetter, and they can't be allowed to touch. But surely it will be crowded, and Gerau will never find him and Hej in the cheap seats. And perhaps, perhaps it will be good to see his father in the flesh, at a safe distance.

"I'm game if you are," Fetter says, and this time he hits the perfect note of indulgent affection and casual excitement, as if cold spikes are not piercing his warm heart.

# 12

There's a story I need to tell you, Mother-of-Glory says, her voice throaty and echoing on the line. Fetter pictures her alone in a vast auditorium, but there are no such places in Acusdab; he imagines her instead squatting, bony and sharp-chinned, on the rocks by the lake, pulling the sky down over her head like a shawl, her voice echoing over the water.

It's the story of why my name is Mother-of-Glory, she says, and why your name is Fetter.

But I already know this story, Fetter tries to say, but she's already interrupting him.

You *think* you already know this story, Mother-of-Glory says. You've heard versions and fragments from your tutors, your cousins, from people in Acusdab. But you've never heard it from me, so let me tell you what's true.

A long, long time ago, Mother-of-Glory says, before the sun and the moon, before the fall of devilry, all of this land north of the Hanu mountains was once a great island. It had no name, except that we called it our great island, our strange and wonderful island, just as we had no names, except that we called each other friend, kin, best beloved. Mortals and devils lived free and together, sharing our worlds. Our greatest city was called the great city of our strange and wonderful island, but it was not the city of our ruler, for we had no rulers. In our language, the word for woman was the same as the word for queen.

The day your father came to our strange and wonderful island, I was the first to meet him. That was where everything went wrong.

I was a daughter of sea folk, an apprentice diver. Do you know what that is? Perhaps not; the gulf of pearls is gone and the art does not survive in this part of the world. We would dive into the cold water, naked but for a knife and a basket, holding our breath and clutching a heavy rock with a line tied to it. Down in the dark, not breathing, wary of sharks, we would cut free the oysters and fill up our baskets. We were wealthy, respected folk: our pearls were prized across our strange and wonderful island and beyond. In the great cities of the plains they wore our pearls, and in the mountain fastnesses, and in the mighty western trading cities at the muddy lagoon of the singing fish, and at the port with the deepest harbour. At the sacred northern temple overlooking the unbounded ocean that crowns this half of the world, they used our pearls in ceremonies to honour that great unbroken water; in the southern peninsula, the learned of the great universities would gift them to visiting scholars from the mainland.

I was sixteen and already a master diver. I had been diving since before I became a woman. I was wealthy. I had my own house by the sea, a little further south from the others because I liked the quiet. I had a lover, another diver like myself. My parents had warned me not to love another diver, saying the art would drive us apart in the end, but she was fierce and beautiful and together we held our breath so long that our hearts burned with holy fire. I've often wondered if my parents were correct in their dire projections, whether the shared art would truly have embittered us some day, or if we would have drifted apart and taken other lovers. I think my parents simply did not like my best beloved; she was loud, and rude to her elders. She was also brilliant: at the age of fourteen, she invented a new style of nose clip for divers, and a year later, we were all using them.

What was her name? I told you, we didn't have names. I called her my love, my best beloved, my heart, the fire in my belly that warms me when the sun goes down. She called me things like that, too, only some of them were ruder. Even after all these many years I can't bring myself to repeat them to you, my son. I have absorbed the stilted mores of the mainland now, the clothes and manners and shames. The sea folk were a free and prosperous folk; we went about naked in the sun, except sometimes for our pearls, the ones we'd decided to keep because we loved their flaws or their perfections. My love and I took turns wearing pearls, playing the lover and the loved. That day we were alone on a long golden beach overlooking the gulf. I was the beloved, adorned in nothing but pearls, and she was fully given over to my adoration.

Your father came upon us and surprised us then. In the distance behind him, we could see where his boat had come to rest, and the long line of footsteps that we had not heard, buried as we were in each other. Further behind him, over the sea to the east, we could see ships coming into view.

He spoke to us in his mainlander language, which we spoke only roughly. From what we said and what we'd been doing, perhaps from the richness of the treasure I wore, he took me for her queen and her for my servant. And that was true, in that moment; it didn't occur to either of us that it meant something different to him. I'm not sure the misunderstanding even mattered. He only began as he would continue.

Our great and wonderful island, until that time, had already had much intercourse with some parts of the mainland, through trade and travel and the exchange of scholars. But the continent to our south was vast. It narrowed to an arrowhead below our island, so that the further south you went, the east and west coasts of the continent grew ever further away from each other, hosting entirely different peoples and civilizations. We traded mostly with their northernmost peoples, the trading cities of the arrowhead's tip on the opposite shore of the gulf of pearls—too far to see but close enough that any of us master divers could swim there if we wanted to. Our universities dealt mostly with their famed fellow institutions on the east coast of the mainland. At that time, there had been little direct traffic with the west coast of the mainland, which was a different country altogether, especially the deep south-west where your father was from.

He and his people were a pirate fleet, he admitted, scorned and hated all the way up the mainland's west coast, forced further and further north as every city repulsed him. He was a prince, he said, a deposed prince from some kingdom far in the south-west, thrown out of his country for being an uncontrollable monster of violence and debauchery. His followers came with him, already in their hundreds, a ragged fleet of ships and boats and barges. His name, and he was the first person I knew who had a *name* in that sense, was Victory. He said, carelessly but with a certain relish, that all along the west coast they called him Cruel Victory.

"But I'm beyond all that now, O northern queen," he said to me, never taking his eyes off me. I wasn't sure if it was my body or my pearls that he desired more. "We have come in peace; we are done with our time of troublemaking. We are tired of the sea. We wish to settle here, and start again."

My love had stalked off in a huff by this point; I was dimly aware that I was in for a loud argument when I got home. But I was fascinated by him; even then, even before his rise to true power, he was imbued with charisma, positively glowing with it. The kind of person who can lead hundreds of people across half the world.

My love saw right through it all the moment she laid eyes on him. She loathed him. What? No, nothing happened to her. Later, she accused me of cheating on her, even before I cheated on her. We fought and fought. Eventually she left me. I don't want to talk about it.

I wish you could have known her, though.

Oh, she died long ago, like most people in this story. If we together had been your mothers, your story would be so different. So would mine. She had no patience with men like your father, and saw through them easily. I . . . well, when I was young, I saw through no one. I only learned such things later, too late.

My infatuation with Cruel Victory was short-lived. He was a handsome, charismatic man, but not a good lover or mate. He was confused, I think, by our wealth, or perhaps our understanding of wealth. He wooed me as a queen, and I'm still not sure if he was attracted to me or whether he thought he was making the alliance that would allow his pirate crew to settle on our strange and wonderful island. It did help his cause; I introduced him to my parents, my uncles and aunts. My eldest uncle, who at that time was my favourite, was particularly taken in by him, enthralled by his charisma, the palpable force of his heart.

Between the blandishments and persuasions of my uncle and me, my parents were induced into friendship to Cruel Victory, even warmth. My family introduced his people to the rest of the sea folk and suggested lands where they might settle. Eventually, when I took him as a lover, my parents liked him better than she who I'd loved before—he spoke well to them and was respectful, polite, and persuasive. And my father laid great store on his elder brother's word, so my uncle's endorsement made things so much smoother. On such small things do worlds break.

You met him briefly—your grand-uncle—when you were a

boy. Do you remember? I owed him something for his part in all this, I felt. Interest accumulated over the ages.

It didn't take long for your father's people to spread across the island, to visit and settle in the other cities, to inveigle themselves into power structures wherever they went. They did not conquer us by violence; they *were* violent at times, but the island had known war before. In truth, they conquered us before we knew they were invading, perhaps without even *them* understanding it was an invasion. They were a cult, the first cult we had ever known, and we had no defenses against them. They infected us with strange ideas from the south-west. They brought doctrines of shame and disgust for the body and the glorification of the perfected mind. They asked us to look at our bodies not as the clean and perfect instruments of living that we had known, but as bags of flesh containing the thirty-one parts of impurity: the hairs of the head and the body; the nails and the teeth; the skin, flesh, and tendons; the bones and marrow; the heart, liver, and kidneys; the lungs, pleurae, and spleen; the intestines large and small—the shit and undigested food; the bile, phlegm, and pus; the blood, sweat, and tears; the fat, sebum, and spit; the mucus, the synovial fluid, the piss. They asked us to reflect on this and be repulsed: is the body not disgusting?

Like this, they brought endless categorizations and subcategorizations and enumerations of being and experience. They brought, almost incidentally, the politics they knew, of centralization, of the consolidation of power, a politics of thrones.

As their control over the island strengthened, Cruel Victory grew more and more powerful and more and more restless. He took on new names, new habits, new practices. First, he took the name Blessed Victory, for, he said, he had put cruelty behind him. Later he found even victory too warlike a name for a prophet of peace, for that was what he was becoming: he

truly believed that peace could come from the ideological sub-
jugation of all peoples of the world into an organized system
of life, one that he would devise to be perfect and complete.

He spent years building and refining his system, but at that
time it was simply a matrix of moral instruction: do this, don't
do that. Nothing that everyone didn't already know. His doc-
trine lacked the numinous, the otherworldly power that he
knew he needed to complete his cult and legitimize its mundane
role.

He never quite lied to me. He never quite does. It was true
that he wanted me, for a time. It was true that he came to our
strange and wonderful island looking for a new start. It was
true that he was tired of piracy and that kind of old-fashioned
trouble. It was true that he was tired of the sea.

He grew tired of me, too. He missed the soft pale women of
the land of his birth. I was too dark, my skin too rough and
tough from salt and sun and sea, my hair was wrong, too short
and thick and curly instead of shiny and straight and long, my
mouth too big.

Once in a fight he called me ugly. Some of his closest confi-
dants, you know, his innermost circle, his boys, they made that
my name—my first *name*. They probably still call me the Ugly.

I almost broke up their band, you see, by taking him away
from them, by distracting him. They've always hated me for
that, but I only distracted him for a little while.

He left me while I was pregnant with you, not long before
you were born. He had the grand realization that he had to
leave to grow. He was still living in my fine house by the sea,
as my mate and partner, but it had long begun to chafe on
him. When he looked at my house he saw a hut. We had been
together for some years and he had learned much from me and
my island, but most of all he had learned contempt.

He had been studying our arts, the powers of our devilry.

This was the unspoken reason he had come to us, you see. He had heard rumours, increasing in detail and accuracy as he came up the west coast of the mainland, of our strange and wonderful island, where devils lived among mortals in plain sight and where the very air glowed with power. More than anything else, he came to us to learn that power, our art and technology.

And he did learn. While he lived with me, he first learned what was ordinary, everyday power in that time and place. The songs of sharpening, the songs of freshness, the songs of light in the dark that you can hum in your chest and belly. The songs of love and binding, the songs of beauty and joy. All these I taught him my own self.

Oh yes, I taught you one of those too, remember? Though it now has only a small fraction of its efficacy, after the cataclysm. I hope you practice it, the song of sharpening. I once sang it to my knife every day before I dived into the cold water of the gulf of pearls.

Your father and his people ranged across the island to learn such things. He and his closest band of associates learned more and more from other peoples of our strange and wonderful island. In the mountains he learned the dances of the hunt and the honey, the dances of the fire and the bear. In the universities he spoke with theoreticians and designed his own models of power. On the island's far shore he learned the songs of other sea folk, different from ours. From this parallax too he learned more about the fundamentals of power, its components, configurations, and flows. Oh, he was a fine scholar in his own right, I grant. He probably did a great deal of original work. Who knows? He made it so we can't know. It wasn't an accident that the cataclysm destroyed all records of his research.

He spoke with the devils among us, too, who were not immune to his voice and his ideas. They had never encountered such a hunger for new technologies, this desperate yearning for knowledge that was of use not in the day or the night but in some other realm of thought, separate from the body and the life it led. They answered questions that none of us had ever thought to ask.

Only two of his fellows could keep up with him at all—you know them today as his chief votaries, Salyut and Magellan, who became the Saint-General and the Saint-Errant. The final member of his inner circle was his cousin Vido, Blessed Victory's amanuensis and occasional lover. Vido was a weasely little shit then and he is one now. He never understood anything about anything, but he was born with eidetic memory, and Blessed Victory recruited him for use as a recording device, invaluable in his research and fieldwork.

In the meantime, while he accumulated more and more power and knowledge, his legend as a peacemaker also grew. He put himself forward as an expert mediator, resolving some very public disputes in the east and in the south of the island. We in the gulf of pearls heard of these famous victories and shook our heads. Or at least, I did. My parents never stopped loving him. I was perhaps the first ever to *stop* loving him, even before he left me, before the cataclysm.

I didn't want to be the pregnant wife at home while he travelled our strange and wonderful island and learned far too many of its mysteries. But I wouldn't join him, either, because I didn't *want* to know those mysteries. I didn't even want to be near when they were revealed. Do you understand? These are the mores of an elder civilization. We went naked, felt no shame for our bodies, but we had a deep sense of propriety around mystery. We would never attempt to learn the sacred mysteries of all disciplines, for the purposes of cross-indexing them and cataloguing them. We chose *one* discipline and mastered it—perhaps we would change that discipline once or twice in a life. We would not question the devils that lived among us for the mysteries of their being and their world; we gave them the dignity of being themselves, not objects of study. They were part of our strange and wonderful island, like we were: sometimes they were familiar and worked or played or loved or fought us; sometimes they were strange and ignored us; sometimes they were violent and dangerous and preyed on us, and had to be driven away. But we never saw them as a resource to be exploited. That, too, was one of his innovations.

Because of these long-dead proprieties, though, I am afraid I cannot tell you much about your father's power. How it works, how to subvert it, I do not know.

I do know that when he left me, he was already something more than mortal. He had long since stopped being Blessed Victory, but he was not quite yet the Perfect and Kind—almost, but not quite. By then, he was calling himself He Who Shall Cause the Truth to Be Revealed. His followers called him the Revelator, and his flag was the sun and the moon. Through persuasion, election, viral marketing, coup, and conquest his followers had already raised that standard across the island. All our disparate civilizations were becoming unified in their obsession with him.

I had not seen him in a season; I was heavy with you, tired and sleeping much. I am told he visited our home while I was sleeping; I am told he looked in on us one last time. I am told that he turned away and left without saying goodbye. That is what he himself said of the matter, later, down south, in what we once called the mainland.

We are told that he said these things in a sermon, remembered and faithfully repeated by Vido on numerous occasions. Many versions of it, often garbled, were written down by various scribes, reporters, scholars, and informants. Copies of those reports found their way to me, in the months and years to come, as I sought news of your father.

This is what he said, as best as I can reconstruct it:

"O monks, know that I had to leave him, my son, my only, my glorious son; I had to leave her who gave him to me, the mother of glory, the woman I had loved and married—

"O monks, know that I could have named my son Glorious Victory, in truth, because he was born with the signs of a great destiny, like I was: he was born to be a prophet or conqueror, one who masters the wheel of the world.

"But I did not name him thus, O monks, and why did I not name him thus? Because when I looked through the flesh of my wife's distended belly and upon the face of my sleeping son within, I understood that I loved him so dearly that if I allowed it, this love for my only son would bind me tight like a chain and prevent me from reaching my own great destiny, prevent me from bringing peace to the world. So I named him Fetter, for he was the final chain upon me that I had to break before I could ascend to perfection."

This is how he speaks of us. This is all he ever says in public about you or me, since he broke the chain and walked away.

That night he walked to the beach, where his inner circle had already gathered. I imagine, for this part is not recorded or spoken of anywhere, that one of them asked about getting him a boat. Probably Vido, the sycophant.

The Revelator's goal was to return to the mainland and convert it—he was not satisfied with our strange and wonderful island, which he had already mastered. For him, perfection meant the world, and the world meant the world-island, the supercontinent of great Jambu. His inner circle would have known this; that blood-robed cult he left behind probably did not, though they would have supported him in this as in all things. He didn't take the Behinders with him, though. He was starting again for the last time: he only took his general, his knight, and his memory.

If Vido asked him about a boat, I imagine that he laughed.

He waited for an hour when the sun and moon were both in the sky, such that the sky itself raised his standard for him, and then he took the miles and years in his hand and, making a fist, he smashed the island into the mainland so hard that it raised the Hanu mountains where the gulf of pearls used to be.

But he didn't want to kill everybody in this cataclysmic collision, or cause earthquakes that would shatter cities across the world. Perhaps he thought of me, sleeping so nearby. More likely, he thought of you. He had broken the chain of love, but he had also moved beyond cruelty, so he said; he moved the collision of island and mainland into the distant, forgotten past, long before there were any people to see it.

He made it so that it had always been this way.

He made it so that I had always lived at the foot of the mountains; he made it so that I had never been a pearl diver, because there was no beach, no sea to dive in, and no oysters to catch. He removed the gulf of pearls from mortal memory.

He made it so that my sea folk were hunter-gatherers far from the water; it was as if we had always been that way. But on that first morning we all still remembered the old world and not the new one, and we knew our songs were wrong.

He made it so that we had never been a strange and wonderful island, but merely the northernmost tip of the great world-island, the supercontinent of Jambu, whose arrowhead was blunted and distorted by this addition.

The Hanu mountains did not only take the place of the gulf of pearls; they took the place of our great southern peninsula and all its universities. All our learning and theory carefully stored in their great libraries was wiped out, including, and

I believe this was intentional, all the formal records of your father's research.

Instead of an island, sea-girt and unique, we became one more province, one more hinterland in this endless continent. With the loss of our records and theoreticians—they had not been killed, do you understand? They had either never been born, or been born and led other lives, clutching fading memories like a mad dream of another world. Without them and that learning, we could not explain any of it.

He folded time, too, in ways that to this day no one understands. As he changed our past, he folded a long future into it. Thousands of years of history that hadn't happened— and yet now, overnight, had always been. Now we remember the ancient rise and fall of kingdoms that should have come long after our deaths; now we are told of, and some even say they remember, the First, Second, and Third Occupations: the intrusions of empires that had never existed before you were conceived. Time is rolled up like a wet cloth having the water wrung out of it. You were conceived thousands of years ago, but you were *born* into a new world. Do you understand? I am in late middle age, as I would reckon it, but I remember things so ancient they are lost to history; I am also twenty-five centuries old. I forget this sometimes, lose hold of the reality before your birth. It is a strange feeling, my son. For what feels like my entire adult life, I have felt cored like a fruit. I am not *well*. I have not been, since that day.

With the island becoming—having always been—part of the mainland, our strangeness thinned and we lost all devilry. Whatever natural, seasonal flows of power had led to its slow, millennial build-up and concentration on the island had been rerouted to spread thin across the world. The world of devils faded from ours; we stopped being able to see them, to speak with them, to play with them or love them. Only fear is left.

Oh, and it's only after we lost them that we began to call them *devils*. That, like so many other things, is the work of your father's remnant cult, which ebbed and flowed but regained its power after learning and incorporating the lessons of the Occupations—the arrogance of adventurist Bbadu, the haunted lawmaking of Abjesili slavers, the monstrous race science of dead Alab.

That cult, which was once your father's invasion of our great and wonderful island, today call themselves the Path Behind, a name they claim is because they worship *the transcendental path behind the illusion of the mundane world*, the original teachings of the Perfect and Kind. But we who were there and remember, we know that it was only because in the morning of that new world we looked at them in contempt and called them left-behinds.

The Behinders reclaimed that mockery, perhaps without even knowing what they did, as memories of the other world were lost. For most people, those memories faded quickly; for some, more slowly, or only in part. Mine, and perhaps mine alone, have stayed sharp and total, not that it helps much. I *remember* how we spoke of the Behinders and the devils, before, but it's like coins and clothing and the other trappings of the modern. It is now meaningless to mock the Path Behind when they are risen to such heights of ideological and political power. And now that they have faded from our sight and metaphysics, it's almost impossible to refer to the laws and powers of this world as anything except devils.

With his great exercise of power completed, the Revelator walked through the Hanu mountain pass—he had pressed his thumb down as he formed the range, so that there would be a pass for him—into greater Jambu, followed only by his three closest companions. All the power that had once accumulated and circulated on the island leaked out behind him. He had learned from us everything he could about power, and then taken learning and power away from us.

When he came out of the other end of the mountain pass and stood on the soil of his home continent again, he said it was done; he had accomplished what he had set out to do, and had found the unbreakable peace beyond peace. He would dedicate the rest of his life to teaching. He was now Perfect, and Kind.

# 13

Fetter is silent for a long time after Mother-of-Glory finishes speaking. She is also quiet. The line crackles between them, and behind that static he can hear Acusdab's birdsong. Suddenly he misses it.

"When did you come to Acusdab?" Fetter asks, eventually. "I thought you had always been there. I thought I was born there."

"You were born in the shadow of the Hanu," Mother-of-Glory rasps. Her voice is hoarse, and he feels guilty for making her talk so much when it's obviously difficult. He tries to protest, suggest postponing the rest of this conversation for another day, but she keeps talking. "No, don't stop me. Today I answer questions. Tomorrow I may not feel like it.

"Everybody I knew was losing their memories of the elder world. My parents forgot everything quickly. Some retained fragments. I was the only one who truly remembered, and it sickened me to be with those people—it was as if they had been replaced by strangers. So I took you and left that place. I walked inland because I never wanted to smell the sea or see a mountain again. Acusdab was a small village in a shallow valley where there still remained some small trace of power; I could feel it in the air, the way it made my skin crawl. I knew there were devils there, even if I couldn't see them. I found it comforting."

Fetter opens his mouth but says nothing.

"What words did you just swallow?" Mother-of-Glory asks, tiredly. "Never mind. Keep some secrets, they're good for you. I also discovered a local scholar who retained some memories. In time, I had others brought there. I lied earlier"—she says this casually, without a smile in her voice—"when I said I *never* accompanied your father or learned any of the mysteries myself. I understood it was wrong, but I did learn a little. I had grasped enough of the fundamentals to develop my own practice.

"I taught doctoring to lost fishers and lone scholars. It . . . changed them. Oh, I know you probably still have nightmares about the devil-doctors. They are not a good thing in the world, I admit. But I needed to build a power base before his left-behind cultists came for me and mine. And the devils, too, had changed. Possession became commonplace, as they sought to regain the visible world. So the doctoring was necessary on two fronts. I don't regret it.

"Acusdab was just a little village when I found it. I made it a fortress. Later, I called my family here, all my sea folk, my folk-who-lost-the-sea. They were struggling to survive as hunters; I taught them to be farmers where I could protect them, here, in my country.

"I will never again be caught sleeping while someone else changes the world in the night.

"But I recognize—" Mother-of-Glory stops for a bout of coughing. "All right, I think I'm almost done talking. Let me just say this. I recognize that Acusdab is only a refuge. It is a defensive posture. It isn't enough. That's why I trained you, my son. You are our only weapon that can reach *him*."

"I'm not anybody's weapon," Fetter snaps. It's almost automatic. He's spent so long unlearning that childhood fanaticism that even with all the affection he feels for his mother now, it grates against his heart when she speaks like this.

"Yes!" Mother-of-Glory seems cheered by this. "Good! You

are free and young and capable. You've found a city to live in and a man to love! You can do anything! But your father will come to your city, as he will eventually come to every city. They will love him and his talk of peace and compassion. Everybody does. Then when he leaves, he'll leave behind a fresh seeding of his Path Above that will leach into everything you love. He's been doing this all across Jambu.

"Oh, he's had a harder time conquering the mainland than he thought, and much of it is his own fault. As his new history unfolded, he found a world that had become crowded with anointed ones, cults upon cults to compete with. The Path is not the biggest or most powerful cult in the world today, nor the second, nor the third. Most of the world remains pathless and free. But it is perhaps the fifth or sixth, and that is still too much of a victory for my liking.

"Look at what the Path Behind alone has done to Luriat. Study the rest of the island—the peninsular hinterlands beyond the city. Understand what is happening there, the pogroms and prisons. Those are the old embers left behind by your father's last trip to these territories, in the years before you were born. When he comes back, he will bring the Path Above to your strange city, too, if only to spite the two of us. He'll unify the Path, and then he'll come for you, if you don't get to him first."

"I'm sure he doesn't even remember I exist," Fetter says, and he tries very hard not to feel bereft. "Maybe you. But he never knew me at all, so why would he?"

"Of course he does," Mother-of-Glory says. "You were his heir, before he unchose you. And if he's forgotten, Vido will remind him. That's what the little shit is *for*. Make sure you kill him too, there's a good boy."

"I already told you I'm not killing anybody," Fetter says. Conversations with Mother-of-Glory often take this turn. If he's not careful they can get into a loop of yes-you-will-no-I-won't.

He asks a question to break the cycle before it starts. "Why did you call Luriat a strange city? What was it like, before?"

He's not sure he entirely believes Mother-of-Glory's account of events, given her political slant and her deeply antagonistic account of his father, but the story of the cataclysm makes sense in some way more fundamental than fact; it explains, if nothing else, the emotional geography of his childhood, even if it's only a mad fantasy of his mother's. Whether it's real or not, this is how *she* sees the world, and understanding that makes his life, so heavily shaped by her, seem clearer.

"It wasn't," Mother-of-Glory says. "That's why it's strange."

"What do you mean, it wasn't? What was it—"

"Before the cataclysm, it wasn't *there*."

Then there comes a week when Fetter shows up to group and the group isn't there. Or rather, the group has been reduced to its core, a subset that now includes him. This is no longer a group dedicated to mutual support. This is Koel's group. The space seems emptier than usual, though they've had meetings with fewer attendees in the past. It's less about the space they take up and more about their absences. This is not that group of people who came here to feel like themselves, who filled up this space with their attention and presence. No one in *this* group is entirely present, not even Fetter. Everyone is neck-deep in plot, entangled in things that are too complicated to even talk about. He has not talked in group about getting back in touch with Mother-of-Glory, and he's gladder of that, now, after having heard her story, her old mad secrets. He's not ready to talk about those things with anyone. Even in this room full of the almost-chosen, he is no longer, he thinks, just one of them.

Koel is there, naturally, and Caduv. Fetter is surprised that Ulpe is also there and the first to speak, though the other two seem to take it in stride.

"The Perfect and Kind," Ulpe says, meeting Fetter's eyes before looking away. He is startled, as if accused, but Ulpe continues. "The Walking. The Singer of the Red. The . . . Man in the Fire."

"We are not any of them," Koel says, as if agreeing. Fetter wants to argue, immediately, that this is not what Ulpe has said, that in fact Ulpe has not said anything, merely named what sets them apart, what they are set apart from, perhaps what they are set against.

"I know something about the others," Fetter says, instead, looking at Ulpe. If this meeting is going to be a rude one, if he was supposed to be surprised, taken off guard, he can be as rude as the next. "But I don't know anything about the Man on Fire. Please tell us about him."

Ulpe looks discomfited, and it's Caduv who corrects him. "It's the Man in the Fire. Not *on* fire."

"That's an interesting distinction," Fetter says, unblinking, at the same time that Koel overrides him with—"What's important is that *we* are on the same side."

"A truism," Caduv says. "I think what Fetter is trying to say—"

"I can try to say it all by myself," Fetter says. He just laughed, he thinks, a little like Gerau and Tomarin and Coema laughed around their table. "If we are on the same side, then why don't we all know what we're doing?"

"That's why we're here," Koel says, in an appallingly reasonable tone that makes Fetter's complaint feel like a whine. "I've asked each of you for a favour—"

"Only one?" Caduv says. His face is neutral; it's hard to tell if he's making a joke. "You've asked me to speak to a number of people, and I was counting *each* of them as a separate favour."

"If you like," Koel says. She gives him a smile that instantly irritates Fetter. He recognizes that she is playing favourites in order to spur him and Caduv to compete. Would he have seen that so clearly if he hadn't recently re-established contact with his original controller, if Mother-of-Glory hadn't been quite so matter-of-fact about her own manipulations?

"So the group was only ever a recruiting tool for you," Fetter says, and Koel dismisses him with a shake of her head.

"Any group is a recruiting tool for me," she says. "I am the godsdamned Walking."

Fetter and the other two respond to this with raised eyebrows and little skeptical smirks. Koel raises her arms to strike a pose, then laughs at herself.

"You know what I mean," she says. "It's my heritage, my training. I didn't start the group, and I didn't join it for this purpose. At first I was just looking for . . . connection, I suppose. But you have to understand, while we are all unchosen together, I'm not like the rest of you."

Devils, Fetter thinks, the familiar curse a little flat after hearing his mother's story. But it is uncomfortable to hear a profound truth about his own condition repeated by someone else in a way that makes the insight sound like a shallow and self-serving brag.

"Oh, don't look at me like that," Koel says. She's smiling again. Fetter has never seen her so relaxed, so upbeat. For all the time he's known her at group she has been a bitter, biting, cynical presence. Now she's laughing, expansive. Even her posture has changed. She is no longer sitting ramrod straight and stiff-backed and glaring. She is leaning back in her chair, her long legs stretched out in front of her in leggings and battered boots. Her shoes look dusty; her soles are worn. She has been out walking the city.

"Did you send the others away?" Ulpe asks, and Fetter is glad to hear someone else ask it. So it's not a conspiracy of the rest of them against him alone; his heart catches and expands in his tightening chest. It's a conspiracy of Koel against the rest of them—is that even a conspiracy? He can't think of the word.

"Not exactly," Koel says, opening her palms as if to say: patience, these are all my cards. "They are spontaneously self-quarantining. We won't see them again this year. They know to do this because they've lived here longer than the three of you, and they know that they're marked. In a plague year, the likes of us are always suspect. It is *sensible* to hunch over and make yourself small. We are the ones who are not sensible."

All three of them speak at once, and she interrupts them with an upraised hand. "You three are the newest. I didn't recruit you: you've recruited yourselves. You're the only ones in this group who didn't even know a plague year was coming, and you're the only ones whose anger hasn't been sucked dry yet."

"I'm not angry," Caduv says, and Fetter smiles a little. At least he's not *that* unself-aware. He meets Ulpe's eyes; they, too, are smiling. Koel is outright laughing.

"My dear Caduv," Koel says. "You are a deep well brimming with rage. There's no reason to be ashamed of it. Everyone in this room is the same."

"You think you're the Walking," Caduv says. "You're the only one in this room who doesn't seem to understand that you got kicked out of your world."

"I'm the only one in this room who has a tradition to fall back on," Koel counters. "Fetter over there is supposed to either become his father or kill him, or both. Not a lot of wiggle room. Ulpe . . . well, I respect your privacy, so let me just say that Ulpe needs to *prevent* the Man in the Fire from ever coming out, which puts them at odds with their people. To put it mildly. And you, Caduv: you want the Song of the Red to fail, or your cousin to fuck up, but you don't really want to *be* the Singer any more. You don't want to go back, you don't want to create a new sacred song, you're done with that life. You want to be what, a musician? The three of you have all set yourselves against the worlds that made you, in one way or another. I'm not blaming you: the worlds that made you are shit, and it's right that you should struggle against them."

"So is yours," Fetter says. "So do you."

"So I do," Koel says. "Except what I want is to *fix* mine. I want the shit flushed out, the corrupt lineages broken, but I believe in the work. In my art. I see myself as the true custodian of a tradition that could still matter, in the hands of someone who's willing to make it mean something. I don't think any of you would say the same about your own traditions." She pauses. "I've told you all the story before, I think. A long time ago, I lost someone I loved very much to one of Luriat's plague years. I've lived through several cycles of plague and pogrom since, and lost loved ones to both. Most people who've lived here for decades could say the same. These cycles are partly an emergent property of a long and complex history dating back to the death magic of the Occupations, and partly engineered and refreshed in the present, through the myriad great and small actions of hundreds, perhaps thousands of people in various positions of power. A scholar could live their whole life writing books about it, and many do. What *I* want to do, ultimately, is to break the cycle in which plague and pogrom for the segregated, disaggregated many lead to power and profit for the few. At least for a little while. I want to *show* people that the death and the loss we've learned to accept are neither a curse to be borne nor a price to be paid, but are the efficient functioning of Luriat, working as designed."

Fetter's head swirls with fog and light. He is familiar with some of this rhetoric from his brief expeditions into Koel's pamphlets, but there is so much he doesn't understand, even though brief bursts of illumination seem to suggest entire vistas that he had not previously considered. He has spent most of his young life feeling old and world-weary; suddenly he feels young and stupid. He is not quite certain of his age any more, but he knows he's in his early to mid-twenties at most. Caduv is perhaps a little older, Ulpe perhaps a little younger. Koel is so much older than the three of them. He'd always known that, but somehow it had never truly felt like a difference before. Now it feels like a vast gulf. We are still children, he thinks, obsessed with ourselves and our own lives. She is an adult, with an adult's fears and an adult's mad plans. Like a feral beast. She is too dangerous—he should flee. She will get him killed doing something he doesn't even understand.

He doesn't move. Neither do the other two. He can see some of the same new self-knowledge in their eyes. The same light, the same pain and fear.

Perhaps Koel sees it too. She's more sombre when she speaks again. "I know this is too much. We still have a little time. I will teach you what I know, and I will tell you how to learn more on your own. I brought you all together here and now because—after a very long time—there finally seems to be an opportunity for intervention. There are many groups in the city who sense it in the air, and I, too, feel the possibility of action more direct than our little play. A plague year is coming and the war in the hinterlands is about to heat up again: this is why we are cultivating contacts in the Ministries of Health and War, because if both cycles hit Luriat at once it will be a White

Year, a year of death like we have not had since I lost my love. For the powerful of Luriat, that is both a moment of absolute consummation and absolute weakness. If there is going to be a change, that will be *the* moment."

"I don't want to kill anyone," Fetter blurts out. The other two look at him strangely—he hasn't talked about his childhood murders in group, has he? Only that his mother groomed him to kill his father? He can't remember what he has or hasn't said in group, or who was there to hear it, only that he has almost certainly said too much and paid too little attention—but Koel nods as if she had guessed as much.

"I will never ask that of you," Koel says.

"'The only way to change the world,'" Fetter says, knowing that none of them will know that he's quoting his mother, "'is through intentional, directed violence.' How could this even work without?"

"I didn't say there would be no violence," Koel says. Her face has stilled but Fetter is not sure if it's to hide her feelings or to not betray her secrets. "As you say, it is impossible to change the world without it; the power of rulers is always based on death magic, and you can't topple that without violence. But I won't ask it of *you*. There are others."

Caduv immediately asks how many others and what others and where are these others, and Koel simply smiles.

"This is a baby revolution," Koel says, after the pause stretches out long enough to make it clear that she is not going to answer the question. "A small, weak, vulnerable thing, long gestating, barely born. We are all its parents together, and we must feed it and protect it. Of course we are not the only ones; it will take a big clan to raise this child. But be aware—they grow up so fast."

# 14

Fetter, as Peroe, has been visiting the bright door called Nine Yellow Oxen every day for a couple of weeks when it happens. He is in his customary posture, sitting cross-legged on the concrete slab in front of the door, doing his best to ignore the crowded street and the construction work, to briefly forget the complexities of his lives as Peroe, as Fetter, as all the Fetters he is simultaneously trying to be. He has his notebook out and is documenting the fine details of his senses, beginning with the most ordinary and gradually working his way to the subtle traces of the otherworldly. He has made contact with every part of the door by this point, in a careful, controlled fashion, an imitative scientism he associates with Pipra: he has traced its great unblinking rectangular territory, both with and against the grain; tested its strength, its give, the points of sensitivity where he estimates the hinges to be positioned, and around the lock. He has taken the handle in his hand twice, braced for . . . if nothing else, for a headache, of which he has had several so far. The painkillers that Koel found for him are helping, and he can avoid the headaches if he limits contact, especially with the cold metal of the handle. Is it some kind of conductivity? Or is it that the handle represents intentionality? Perhaps the door can sense his will to open it, or rather not the door but the phenomenon that presents itself as a door, or more precisely still at the *site* of a door—he writes all this down. Perhaps the casual habit of thinking of the doors as doors is the problem. He leans forward, as he has done frequently, his face a handspan from the wood, his eyes half-lidded and his nose flaring, sniffing for the scent of another world.

Because his eyes are half-closed and unfocused, at first he doesn't understand what he's seeing; it looks like a faint pattern on the surface of the door, at more or less eye-height as he sits on the ground. A circle of dots larger than his head, very indistinct but gradually becoming clearer. The dots are white, he thinks, and then amends that to off-white, a dirty white. The pattern is quite distinctly visible now, and he attempts to sketch it quickly, excited. It takes perhaps two or three minutes to become fully visible, even at close range. Do the doors manifest patterns that nobody is noticing? Has he discovered something new? Nothing he's ever read or heard about the bright doors mentioned such a thing.

He places the tip of his pencil directly on one of the white dots. Is there a bump? Yes, the dots are dots no longer; they are little bumps, like blisters. Their colour has not changed. They do not seem to be wood. He counts them, then counts them again, realizing new dots have appeared, roughly still in the same circle. The original dots now protrude slightly from the wood of the door, enough so that he can tap their little points with the pencil. He is careful not to touch them with his fingers: they look sharp enough to cut.

A deep unease wells up in his belly, climbing rapidly into nausea. He takes deep breaths to control it and glances to his left and right; there are people everywhere, but nobody has stopped to stare. Could this be a common occurrence that he somehow missed learning about? He has been feeling especially ignorant since that last conversation with Koel. Perhaps this is—he is distracted from his own thoughts by the realization that the sharp little points have extended further from the door, and that they have an angular shape that reminds him of nothing so much as . . . is he just being paranoid? He scuttles backward, startled, then scrambles to his feet.

He's not paranoid. They are teeth. He knows this because he's seen them before. They're a *devil's* teeth.

He walks backward, slowly, onto the pavement, and then a little to the side. The queasiness in his belly is intense and he thinks he might puke; he imagines bending over the ditch and letting out a scream of vomit. But he does not; the clenching and spasming eases once he's gained a little distance, as if his gut wanted to drag him out of the devil's way.

Nobody else is reacting: Fetter has long since established through careful questioning that nobody in Luriat sees devils. Not even the other almost-chosen, unless they too are concealing that ability from him. Perhaps they see other things that he can't, he thinks, a little wildly. His heart is pounding.

He has seen *that* creature before, or one of its kind—some devils seem to be kinds, others seem to be unique—long ago when he was growing up in Acusdab. He hasn't been so close to one of the invisible laws and powers since he was a child. His head was almost in its mouth. Would it have moved through him as intangibly as it is moving through the door? No, he touched it, his pencil made contact with its teeth, its frighteningly solid teeth. He *tapped* on its *teeth*. Whatever principle makes the closed door permeable to it, the devil is not intangible, at least not to him. Perhaps devils were always tangible. He's never dared to touch one.

The mouth is entirely protruding out of the door. It is a cone of twisted flesh, filled with a circular row—no, multiple, concentric circular rows—of triangular, pointed teeth, distended outward like a saw. It has been moving slowly, so glacially slowly, but as more of the head emerges it speeds up; the head bursts through with what feels like impatience, and then shakes itself as if to tear free lingering cobwebs. Its feet are next, rotating in great arcs around its twisted body. Its body is long enough that its hindquarters are still behind the door when its head reaches the pavement.

Pedestrians unthinkingly move around the devil. They show no sign of seeing or sensing it, except that they move to avoid it. It, similarly, ignores them, the great head swinging this way and that.

It looks exactly like the creature he remembered from Acusdab. It was a familiar devil; he knew it to haunt the jungle paths near the mangrove swamp. It looked like a parody of the crocodiles that it shared its environment with; it looked like the nightmare that a crocodile might have. If a giant crocodile were taken and twisted like rope in the hands of a malevolent god, made into a long reptilian braid of flesh and scales tipped by a circular saw of a mouth, teeth jutting out like a cluster of arrowheads, it might look like this. This could be the very same devil, or some distant cousin.

The devil moves as if it's trying to untwist itself. It rotates around its axis, undulating to keep its balance, legs wrapping and unwrapping around its body to swing over its back and land on the ground. It looks permanently unsteady, ruined. It has black eyes tucked into ridges all along the length of its body, able to see in every direction except, Fetter hopes, directly ahead. He got out of the way before any eyes came through, but what if it can *see* through the wood of the door as easily as it could cross it?

Fetter slowly moves further away, as inconspicuously as he can. He crosses into the construction site for a moment to take a look at the back of the wall fragment that holds Nine Yellow Oxen. As always, there is no door on this side. More importantly, there are no hindquarters of a great crocodilian devil. There is no long, massive tail so twisted upon itself that the tip looks like a drill bit, the bony ridges digging into the scales.

He knows what it should look like: he once spent an hour in a wheezing tree as a child, listening to it breathe and surreptitiously watching a tail just like that pass below. It should still be visible from this side if the devil were crossing through the wall, as devils do sometimes, and it came upon Nine Yellow Oxen by accident.

But his initial impression is correct: the creature is coming through the bright door from somewhere else, even though the door itself has remained closed the whole time. He walks back out to the pavement, buffeted by crowds. He has lost sight of the creature already—no, there it is. It has crossed the road, somehow, and is moving away.

Fetter returns to the door, maintaining a healthy distance in case the creature is followed by others.

The devil is significantly wider than the door at its broadest. That doesn't seem to have stopped it. The wall around the door is not damaged. The bright door is not just the wooden door itself, then—and on the heels of that realization comes the other.

The bright doors are not locked. They are not even closed. The bright doors of Luriat are *wide open*.

# 15

Fetter doesn't leave his apartment for several days. He stops answering his phones: Hej and Koel both call him on his mobile, and he doesn't answer; Mother-of-Glory calls on the landline, and he doesn't answer that either. Finally, Hej comes to see him—a native Luriati, so alien in the Sands. His knock at the door is familiar and insistent, so Fetter hauls his body off the bed and opens it. Hej tries to hug him, but Fetter won't allow it. He does let him in, though.

"Have you eaten anything today?" Hej is asking, and Fetter isn't sure how to answer. His head aches and his body feels hollowed out, so perhaps not. He tries to shake his head but that makes the pain worse, so he waves a hand instead.

Hej has brought a little bag of fruit, dried green slices of something that Fetter has never even heard of. It's a little spongy in his mouth but not too sweet, speckled with tiny, crunchy black seeds. He eats a few slices while Hej makes tea—in the last while Hej has been stashing a better grade of leaves in Fetter's tiny kitchen for his own benefit. Fetter remembers that he has painkillers in the house and finds the little bag that Koel gave him. Hej watches him take one.

"That's the good stuff, isn't it?" Hej says. "My aunt has a prescription for her megrims. I didn't know you had them too—they're supposed to be very expensive."

"I didn't know they were expensive," Fetter says, at last. He has the feeling there was a long delay before he answered. "A friend gave me these."

They drink the tea.

"What happened?" Hej says.

Fetter opens his mouth to say *The world is full of holes and monsters come out of them except my mother says they may not all be monsters, and for some reason I thought I was safer from them in Luriat because it was so far away from Acusdab, but I've learned that Luriat is practically on top of Acusdab because the world is much bigger than I thought it was and my life so much smaller, and it turns out all the old monsters from the marshes back there are just as at home in the city as I am, so what does that mean for my escape from myself? Am I just another lurking devil from the swamps? Is there no safe place in the world?* What comes out is "My mother got in touch with me. She's dying. Cancer."

He's obscurely proud of this almost-forgotten tradecraft, his trained defense mechanisms working even as his body and mind are deep in rebellion. Hej hugs him—this time he couldn't escape, but the spontaneous contact feels painful, as if his surfaces are scraped raw. He thinks about lies, and how they sit smooth and bulbous in his belly. They hardly discomfort him now. It's just that he is full of them; he can't add any more.

"I may have . . . had a moment with this woman I met," he says. "Her name's Pipra, she's a researcher at the Ministry of Health. I thought I should tell you."

"What's a *moment*?" Hej says. Incredibly, he is smiling.

"She covered my eyes—it was for an experiment for her research, oh I don't know how to explain it." Fetter is tired already and regrets opening the subject. "Anyway, she just happened to touch my face and I found that, I mean, I felt . . . something." He doesn't mention the *other* moment, the one at the beach, at the executions. He tries not to remember it.

"You're allowed to find other people attractive, you know," Hej says, with a calm that is both reassuring and worrying. "You're touch-starved, so you are. Someone touches your face and you think you're sleeping around."

"I just wanted to be honest," Fetter says. *For once.* He rubs his fingers in a gentle circular motion at his temples until Hej brushes his hands aside and takes over.

"You're the most honest person I know," Hej says, easily, and this is so painfully jarring and wrong that Fetter lets it slip away immediately without engaging with it. Hej's fingers are broader and warmer than his own. "We haven't talked about this, but it's okay if you want to be with other people sometimes. I'm not a jealous person, as long as I'm the one who gets to come and take care of you when you're sick."

"Are *you* with other people sometimes?" Fetter feels the hot flush in the question and understands himself to be what Hej has just defined as *a jealous person.*

"No," Hej says, laughing, and Fetter relaxes; Hej would have felt the muscles of his face spasm and settle under his fingers. "I would have talked to you about it first. Besides, I'm way too busy this year."

Fetter is quiet for a little while, sinking into the sensation of hands on his head, massaging his temples and scalp. Hej is gentle with his tangled curls. He feels content, even though he hasn't solved anything or told any of the truths that matter.

"Why are you so busy this year?" he mumbles, after what feels like an hour. Hej is still massaging his scalp, so it has probably only been a few minutes. He's lying down, his head in Hej's lap. His reasoning mind is returning. Food, tea, medicine, the company of a loved one: sometimes pain can be waylaid.

"Well, you didn't hear this from me, but the Summer Court is drafting a sequence of lockdown orders," Hej says. His tone is light. "We thought it wouldn't happen before we closed for the season, but . . . well, it'll be official soon enough. We have a plague year coming."

Hej has lived all his life in Luriat, Fetter thinks: he's older than me, so he's been here longer than Koel. This is how familiar a born citizen is with how the city works. Hej's family have lived in Luriat for generations; he's told Fetter the family legend about his great-great-great-give-or-take-another-great grandparents who first came to the city. *Eight generations in Luriat,* except according to Mother-of-Glory, Luriat didn't exist until a few months before Fetter was born. Yet still not a new city, but a new old city that came into this world with a long dragging tail of history, full of new ancestors and new old money.

"Will it be a White Year? What's a White Year?" Fetter asks. He remembers how Koel used the phrase, but he's curious how a Luriati native would speak of it. Hej's hands freeze in place, their warmth leaching away until he rubs them against each other to warm them up again.

"White is the Luriati colour of death," Hej says, eventually. He is smiling fondly again—did he stop smiling briefly when the question was asked? Fetter isn't sure: his eyes are nearly closed. Hej begins massaging Fetter's scalp again, but slower, as if his fingers are beginning to tire. "We wear white for funerals, for mourning. White flags mean death. A White Year is what people call a particularly bad year for the city. Usually plague, but also violence, looting, riots. We haven't had one in years. I don't think it'll get that bad this time. Especially if we can get the quarantine in place, which we're well on track to do. Don't worry about it, you have enough on your mind."

For a long moment of freefall Fetter has no idea what Hej is referring to. The bright doors? Koel's secret war with the city archons? Then he remembers—oh, my dying mother.

"I should warn you, though," Hej says. "Your mother's in

the hinterlands, right? You shouldn't try to visit her now, if you were planning to. It's not a good time for you to travel out of the city. You'd get quarantined when you come back in, and you don't want that."

Fetter makes a muffled noise of acknowledgement.

"The camps," Hej says, and there's a hadal note of rue in his voice that Fetter doesn't recognize, something so far underneath the surface that no light penetrates. "The camps are not a good place for someone like you."

Mother-of-Glory has been calling every day, and he hasn't been answering. When he finally picks up the phone again, she is angry and cruel, as if their relationship had been reset back to that very first call when she first told him about her cancer.

"I want you to know that you're killing me," she says. "I'm dying, and it's at your hand. Do you understand?"

"Yes, Mother," Fetter says. He's tired, and there's no talking to her when she gets like this. "Everything is always my fault. I understand."

"You *don't* understand," Mother-of-Glory says, viciously, and suddenly Fetter is furious, enraged like he hasn't felt since he was a teenager. He is surprised by the depth of rage and violence that rises in him—where is all this coming from? Where does it pool and ferment when it's not spilling from his eyes and his ears and his nose and his mouth? But no, it's not spilling from his mouth; he clamps it shut, the muscles of his jaw tight as a trap, vibrating with effort. He can't breathe or see or hear over the red roar but he swallows the words back down as they come.

He doesn't say: Oh I *do* understand, Mother, I understand more than you ever did. I kept secrets from you, after all—you never knew that I can *see* the fell things that you only remember. As a child I watched your devil-summonings falter and fail while you shouted and sweated, dancing for them. I never told you that the devils were there the whole time, watching you, mocking you, some of them imitating you, howling.

Oh, it was awful! So much more awful than you knew. Things with rows and rows of teeth grinding them in mockery of the furious working of your jaw; things with elongated arms and too many joints raising them to the sky as you lifted yours, unfolding and unfolding endlessly; things with voices that sounded nothing like voices, things that were never meant to speak, imitating your chants in wordless grinding moans with orifices that were not mouths, bleeding themselves to do it. They knew your stance of supplication was fake, you see. They knew you were impatient with the rites you yourself had concocted. When I was younger, I thought that they howled because they feared you, but I slowly understood it was *you* that was weak, that the devils were stronger than you. Even as a child, even through my fear of those awful beings, trying not to huddle in the firelight while you and the devil-doctors danced and howled and the devils themselves swirled and encircled in their masses outside the circle of light, howling back at you, so loud to me that I had to clench my fists not to clap them over my ears in fright, even then I knew not to tell you. Not only because it was my secret to keep, but because I knew that you could not bear it—you could never bear to be the one who didn't know, you could never bear to be weak. I want to tell you so badly now, and I think I would have, just to hurt you, if it didn't mean baring a secret I've kept for so long.

But as he doesn't say these things, he hears Mother-of-Glory's tone of raging and ranting decline into one of scolding and finally fall silent; he has no idea what she has been saying for the past few minutes, any more than she knows what he hasn't been saying.

"You've gone soft in the city," Mother-of-Glory sneers, at last. "You were a knife once, and now you're limp as a string. Where is the son I made? You think I'm blaming you. I'm *congratulating* you."

"What?" Suddenly his mind is whirling, like dead leaves in a strong wind. He can't nail down a single thought. Bits of his childhood flutter to the front of his mind and are instantly washed away by flashes of his adulthood, and even dark shards of his intentionally forgotten adolescence. "What's—what are you saying?"

"You've killed me after all," Mother-of-Glory says. "Through heartbreak, frustration, and disappointment rather than the blade I was expecting, but oh, it hurts like a knife all the same. My congratulations to you, son: soon you will have committed the First Unforgivable. It's not too late—you haven't failed yet. One down, four to go. Do you remember what comes after matricide? Now you say it."

"Heresy leading to factionalism, sancticide of votaries who have reached the fourth level of awakening, patricide, and the assassination of the Perfect and Kind," Fetter recites, the words scooped out with a jagged trowel from the deep earth of his belly despite himself.

"Good boy," Mother-of-Glory rasps, and Fetter wants to cry from his loathing of the warm feeling that fills his chest, rising like bubbling black water, submerging the tumult inside of him as if none of it mattered. "That's my boy."

# 16

By Eerieday evening, Fetter's healed from his megrims and about ready to go back to work. He's thinking about what he's going to say to Koel and Caduv and Ulpe at the next meeting—he's never talked about the invisible laws and powers, he doesn't want to start now, but he might need to tell them *something*. And oh devils, doesn't he need to warn Pipra, keep her safe even if it means laying bare his secret worlds? What if something terrible comes through one of those doors they're making? What if they get too close, unknowing, in their academic enthusiasm? Would it hurt them? Would it move through them without a trace? Fetter is drinking a cup of Hej's tea and worrying about all this when Caduv knocks at his doorjamb.

The moment he brushes aside the curtain, Fetter flashes back to their first meeting, just like this. He is even in the same posture, his hand on the same wooden doorjamb. But this doesn't feel the same. They were strangers then, brought together by the otherworldly; now they are . . . friends? At least allies, bound by an extremely worldly conspiracy. As if to reflect that worldliness, Caduv has a bloodied lip.

"Someone object to the voice?" Fetter asks, standing aside for Caduv to enter.

"Not the first time," Caduv says. He heads for Fetter's kitchen, and from the sound of the freezer opening, Fetter assumes he's looking for ice. "Koel doesn't know I'm here, by the way."

Fetter thinks about that. Koel has been careful to keep the

members of her conspiracy apart as much as possible; each has their own mission, unknown to the others. Operational security, Koel says, with a little laugh to puncture the pomposity of the phrase. But if Caduv is here, that means he's decided to breach this protocol. That, and the bloody lip, suggests a single likely reason.

"Need some help?" Fetter says.

Caduv finally reappears. He's holding a chunk of ice in his bare hand, pressed to his mouth. "Koel figured out that people tend to do as I ask."

"Unless they decide to punch you instead," Fetter says.

"Unless that," Caduv says. He attempts a smirk but his mouth is still too tender for that; he winces instead. "My current mission is to steal some records from a Ministry of Health sub-office. It should have been easy. My plan was to casually bump into a security officer on his day off and ask him nicely to leave some doors unlocked."

"I thought the vision only appeared to people like us," Fetter says. "The holy leftovers. Is that not true?"

"It's not about the vision," Caduv says. The chunk of ice in his fist is slowly melting, lines of ice water slaloming down between the fine hairs of his forearm and dripping off his elbow to the floor. "The vision is a reaction to the incompatibilities between sacred paradigms, for people like you and Koel. But she figured out that everybody else experiences only a . . . side effect, a kind of persuasion."

Fetter keeps his expression politely interested, but he is suddenly wary. If Caduv will admit to that much so easily, how extensive *is* his power? Is he capable of manipulating Koel and Fetter and the others? Has he been doing that all along? He struggles to remember whether he's ever gone along with things just because Caduv said so. But he might have done that anyway. He already intends to help him with whatever he needs tonight—it's because he finds this exciting, isn't it? Not because Caduv is controlling him?

He's been quiet too long. Caduv sighs. "It's not like that," he says. "Whatever you're imagining, it's not like that. It's not mind control or mesmerism or anything so absolute. And it really doesn't work on you all, or anybody who sees the vision when they first hear me speak—that reaction means you're incompatible, beyond reach. I've tested it."

"You've tested it," Fetter says, and despite himself, it comes out in the boyish, unsteady voice of that young murderer, the other, long-forgotten Fetter. It's a voice he hasn't heard out of his own mouth in years. Caduv recoils.

"*Not* like that," Caduv says, again. "Never on you. Koel volunteered—no, she made me do it, she devised experiments with herself as the subject. And like I said, it's not that kind of . . . it's a *tendency*, more than a power. Do you see what I mean?"

"No," Fetter says. He is startled to realize he enjoyed the other man's flash of fear. Caduv has always felt like Koel's favourite, and yet here he is, having failed at something while Fetter's own projects are going . . . well. The memory of teeth arises and he buries it immediately. He makes an effort to relax. He has always understood, if vaguely, that there was something special about Caduv's voice. Of course Koel would have articulated and defined it. "Tell me, then."

"People who don't see the vision, they have a different reaction to my voice. They're vulnerable to suggestion," Caduv says. The ice is gone. The last of the water slips through his fingers as he clenches his fist and then lowers it, dripping. The drops are pink from blood. "I suppose I've always known that, but I never explored it in a methodical way on my own. When I was young, I thought people were just nice to me, you know? At home, I thought it was about my status. Even those of us who lose the tribulations are considered special. Later, after I left home, I thought people were being kind to me because I looked like my whole world had fallen apart. Which was true, I *was* lost. And here in the city, people were helpful. I thought they were being—"

"Kind," Fetter says. The word drops like a stone from his mouth.

Caduv pauses, perhaps aware that he's on dangerous ground, and then continues. "It fails often enough, for no reason that I can see. Sometimes people just don't want to cooperate, or I hit a limit to what I can ask them for. They might do something small or innocuous, but nothing big or complex. I could never have asked the security officer to copy the records for me, for instance. I couldn't even ask him to leave the doors unlocked all night. I thought I could ask him to be a little lazier than usual, though. He usually locks up around seven and then goes out for a meal at a nearby kadé. So I suggested that it would be fine to forget to lock up the building tonight while he went out. But he was completely immune to my voice. That's rare, but it happens sometimes."

"You should have just bribed him," Fetter says, drily.

"I don't think that would have worked either," Caduv says. "The man was surprisingly honest. He punched me in the mouth and said if he sees me around again, he'll break my legs before he calls the police."

"So what do you want me to do?" Fetter asks, feeling more amused than aggrieved now. "Do you want me to punch him for you?"

"No, no," Caduv says. The blood on his lips has dried and Fetter resists the urge to reach over and scrape it off with a nail. "That doesn't matter. I want to complete the *mission*. I need to get those records out tonight, because I'm pretty sure that man will report the incident to his manager tomorrow morning when the office opens for the week, and his manager will re-port it to the Second Senior Assistant Secretary, who will either increase security, or move the records, or worst of all, destroy the records."

"So you fucked it up pretty badly, is what you're saying," Fetter remarks. His voice is quite level, he thinks, though his thoughts are racing. The Second Senior Assistant Secretary to the Ministry of Health—that's *Coema*, isn't it? He heads for the kitchen. "Do you want more ice? It's starting to swell up."

"Yeah, thanks," Caduv says. "And yes. Please. Help me do this."

Fetter hands him ice wrapped in a hand towel, which Caduv seems faintly puzzled by. Fetter guides the other man's hand to his face and presses it to his split lip.

"I'm perfectly willing to help," Fetter says. "I just don't know what you're expecting me to do that you can't. *You* have this power. I'm just me."

Caduv waves at him with his free hand. "Of course you have power. You have no *shadow*. You're like a ghost. Or . . . or a cat. You don't make noise when you walk. People don't notice you. You could break into anything. You could go anywhere. Koel always says you could be the greatest burglar in Luriat if you wanted to."

Fetter bites back an exclamation of surprise, then another one of ill-articulated outrage. So they've all noticed the absence of his shadow over the years. He'd assumed as much, but it's gone on so long without an acknowledgement that he feels vaguely offended to have it pointed out. "Koel has never asked me to—" he says, then remembers his undercover missions. "Well, not like that. Not breaking and entering."

"No," Caduv says. "She just meant you had talents that you weren't even using. I think she'll ask you for something like that one day, but she's just waiting until she needs it. Wouldn't you do it, if she asked?"

Fetter digests this. He has no real objections to burglary. Luriati concepts of property crime are quaint to him; in Acusdab there was no such thing as *property*. The invisible laws and powers of the world go absolutely anywhere they want. They aren't bound by worlds, never mind the pretension of ownership. In some ways, he's still more like them.

"Yes," Fetter allows. "Probably. All right. I'll at least take a look, and if I decide I can't do it, I can't do it, no complaining. All right?"

Caduv closes his eyes. "All right. Thank you."

"This office. Tell me everything."

✎

At Fetter's insistence, Caduv stays behind in Fetter's apartment. Fetter pointed out the danger of Caduv being seen and recognized by the security guard, but in truth it's just that Fetter wants to do this alone. He tells himself he doesn't want distractions, but it might be a witness he's avoiding—to his secrets, to his possible failure. His shoulders are stiff and his jaw tight, but there is a thrill rudding deep in his belly. Setting out into the night with the blatant intention of breaking the laws of Luriat feels good, if unsettling. It reminds him of being free and wild, wandering the world. He's allowed this city to civilize him, so gradually he didn't even feel the loss of that wildness. It would be good to have a little of it back.

It's too easy for him to slip out of thinking like a citizen; he becomes more like a feral creature, like a jackal moving through nighttime streets, black and yellow under the lights. The city as a wilderness environment. Terrain and ecologies. Obstacles.

It's easy to find what he's looking for, given the street address. It's a three-storey building on a quiet street that would have been twenty minutes from the Sands on the light rail. Instead, he took a tuktuk part of the way and walked the rest, avoiding ticket records and train station cameras. From a distance, the target building is obviously some sort of office, square and narrow, the walls a dark institutional maroon studded with rows of windows on each higher level, dark at this hour except for the light in the lobby. Caduv called it a sub-office, but there's no sign, no government sigil over the door, no particular indication that it belongs to the Ministry of Health. Perhaps there's some sort of sign in the lobby, but Fetter has no intention of approaching it or the man puttering about inside, who wears no uniform but could only be the incorruptible security guard, a tall, wiry man with a greying moustache and a limp.

Caduv said the records he needs are on the second floor. The building does not seem especially secure. There's a padlock on the gate, and the wall around the building is about ten feet tall and topped with broken glass, typical for Luriat. Fetter can see through the wide bars of the gate when he walks past: there is a small parking space and then the glass door to the lobby, where the security guard is just settling down at his little desk with a cup of tea. None of the visible windows are barred. There are no security cameras.

To the left of the building is a closed-up shopfront with a locked metal grille. To the right is a tall waking fig, its aerial roots seeping all the way to the pavement slabs, framing a small temple of the Path Behind. Both of those things are as ubiquitous in Luriat as they are in the hinterlands, except the waking figs in the city do not grow so large as what Fetter remembers. Or perhaps he was just smaller then.

He enters the temple grounds as if he were a worshipper. It is not crowded, except for some common devils—unseen feeders on the walls of the monks' huts in the back, their tendrils waving lazily as if in underwater currents. They rarely move, and never quickly. He ignores them. He wanders to the sandy area set apart behind the tree and sits there for a while as if meditating. When there is nobody in sight, he gets up and walks the few paces to the boundary wall of the Ministry of Health building. This is the first barrier.

He wonders what Caduv thinks he's doing, exactly. Probably not this.

Fetter places a hand lightly on the wall—rough concrete, grainy—and breathes out, and when that breath is gone, he breathes *out,* just a little more.

Slowly, his feet leave the ground. He has not done this often since he left Acusdab, but he hasn't *not* done it either. It is a useful ability, and Fetter has practiced to make it more so. He keeps his face resolutely forward, never looking up; he still fears the possibility of falling forever into the sky, of drowning in the thin air of the upper atmosphere, becoming a perfectly preserved corpse storming the heavens unto eternity. The wall is his focus against that nightmare, the contact between his palm and the concrete, the scrape as he rises.

As he reaches the top of the wall, he draws his feet up, as if he were leaping very slowly instead of floating. It's easier, he has found, if he thinks of it as a leap. It feels more controlled. He rises above the wall; his fingertips leave concrete and touch jagged glass, too lightly to be cut, crouching in the air. His sandalled feet reach forward a step—resting on the edge of the wall for just the moment he needs to push off as powerfully as he can, at an angle that is nearly horizontal. He arcs through the air across the gap from the top of the wall to the nearest second-floor window of the Ministry of Health building, perhaps a few yards. He looks neither up nor down nor around. There would already be shouts of surprise if someone had seen him, but there is almost nobody about on the street and he should be invisible in the almost-dark. The waking fig's long rootfall shields him from the streetlights: he is speckled in their shadows. The only sound is the tree rustling.

He clings to the side of the building like a gecko, testing the window. It is locked; he moves sideways, weightless, keeping a firm grip on handholds and testing the next window, then the next. He is prepared to break glass and risk the security guard hearing the noise if he has to—he is calm at the prospect, because he does not fear that man. Should he fear his lack of fear? Does it suggest a comfort with violence that he thought he'd grown out of? Distracted, he almost misses the improperly latched window under his hand and curses under his breath. A firm tap or two on the slightly warped wooden frame releases the latch on the inside, and a few minutes of patient struggle with his fingernails opens the window. And then he is floating inside, from the open dark to a crowded dark. He lands with utmost caution in the centre of the room, not knocking anything over. And he breathes in, and clenches that muscle deep in his belly, the grip that he has held for years without ever letting it slip. His feet skid on the floor, trying to leave it again, but he wiggles his ankles to remind them to stay grounded. And it is done—he stands up, there are no alarums, and he is inside, his eyes adjusting to the dark. He leaves the window very slightly ajar.

There is something odd about the inside of the building. It feels like the faintest touch of fever, a sickening.

This office is obviously in frequent use. He is in a room that looks like it's shared between a dozen workers; there are many tables arranged throughout the room, squashed up against each other with barely enough room to move between. Every table is covered in the detritus of white-collar drudgery. Most of it is paperwork of a particular kind: off-white file folders stuffed full with paper, tied with pink ribbon. Stacks and stacks on every table.

There is writing on the file covers, but it's too dark to read: he can only make out the spidery traces of letters. He has a small torch in his pocket, but he doesn't dare use it yet. The light might be visible through the windows, and who might take note of such a thing?

Instead, he waits for his eyes to adjust a little more to the darkness, then moves through the room in complete silence. He's never truly paid attention to his stealth; it isn't something he does consciously. His footfalls can be noisier, if he wills the soles of his sandals to slap against the ground, but usually they are too light to be heard. He hadn't thought it remarkable at all. Of course Koel would consider it a talent to be used. Everything is grist to her mill.

None of the internal doorways have a door that could close. This is typical in Luriati public and shared spaces. There are little plaques next to each doorway briefly identifying the purpose of the room, sometimes simply with an acronym or a numeric code that presumably makes sense to the people who work here. He moves through the building unhurriedly, tracing the writing on the plaques with his fingertips to read them.

The sixth room he checks is the one that Caduv told him to look out for: the plaque says, in an abbreviated shorthand that he would not have understood if Caduv hadn't already explained it, that the room contains equipment inventories for a subgroup of quarantine camps. Fetter struggles to remember the details of the conversation between Coema, Tomarin, and Gerau that he'd recounted to Koel. This seems related: he's looking for records relating to a donation of medical ventilators. The scandal that had been discussed at dinner, he recalled vaguely, was that some of the equipment had gone missing, presumably stolen and sold for a profit. Why would Koel be interested in that? Perhaps she wants to bring Čoema down for corruption.

This room is small and contains only a wall of cubbyholes, each holding a tall stack of files. They look much the same as the others he's seen in this building, except the files are a darker colour—he can't tell what colour in the gloom. It has no windows and it's nowhere near the stairs, so he judges it safe to use his torch.

The light seems harsh and loud in his hand. He almost switches it off again, breathing hard, but the silence remains. His night vision is gone, though. Nothing exists except for the little pool of light on the file in his hand—it's a pale green. This is the wrong file. He puts it back, checks the next. Caduv had him memorize the code of the file he's looking for, a string of numbers and letters. The room is well-organized; it's easy to find the correct row and column. The file is thinner than the others, but not empty, tied with the same pink ribbon as all the other files. He peers around the ribbon and sees there are at least a few dozen sheets of paper in there, all typewritten, most of them looking like official letters. He double-checks the code on the file cover. Well, secrets don't advertise themselves. Most likely whatever information is in the file would mean nothing to him but everything to Koel. Still, he resolves to read it himself before handing it over.

The mission is complete and he should leave. But something about the building is still nagging at him, that sense of fever or sickness that struck him when he entered, the uneasy tugging under his skin, in his gut. When he switches the torch off and closes his eyes, he can feel it pulling him to his left. He exits the room and, hesitantly, moves left. It's the direction of his exit anyway, so why is he hesitating? He finds the room with the window, but the sensation lures him a little further down the corridor—his eyes have readjusted and he's moving as if it were well-lit—until he thinks *here* without knowing what he's say-ing *here* to. Another small room of crowded desks and paper-work. Why is there *so* much paperwork in this building? He's seen a few computers, but old ones, big clunky beige beasts. The room is unremarkable to his dark-adjusted eyes, but his uneasy gut calls him to a particular desk. Then to a particular drawer, which is locked.

He squats in front of the lock, irresolute. He doesn't know how to pick a lock, but it seems absurd to be defeated by so small a thing. The feeling of sickness is stronger than ever; his skin feels itchy, his throat fogged, his belly roiling. He knows this feeling: it is the feeling he thinks of as his luck, the nausea and fever of significance. It has never been so strong. Some-thing in there is important, more important than the file he already has in his hand. Or at least, more important to *him*. He considers the consequences. This is already a theft, he rea-sons; they will eventually realize this file is missing, and they will know it was stolen on this night. The security guard will even say he was approached by a suspicious character, a short and nondescript man. There is no need to be overly subtle. He just needs to not be caught.

Fetter braces himself against the table with one hand and breaks the drawer open with a determined wrench from the other. It makes a great cracking noise like a thunderbolt. He lets the broken drawer hang, and grabs the entire fistful of paper within, clutching it and the stolen green file to his chest. He can hear hurrying footsteps from the stairs as he ducks into the corridor, and the wavering light of the security guard's approaching torch.

When the man bursts into the corridor, he isn't armed, not even with a baton. He looks slightly crazed and more than a little terrified—his moustache is quivering furiously as if his mouth is making silent words beneath it, perhaps curses, perhaps prayers.

Fetter is expecting him to shout, but he seems unable to. The man runs down the length of the corridor to the room where the noise came from. He does not look up as he passes Fetter pressed still and horizontal against the ceiling. When the guard enters the room, there is finally a loud imprecation, as if perhaps the man had been expecting the noise to have an innocent explanation until the moment he saw the broken drawer. Fetter has already landed, soundless, and found his way to the window he left ajar and out into the night.

# 17

The sickness is not fading. He feels drunk, his feet unsteady. He finds his way home without incident, but it takes real effort not to trip on the stairs of his own building. In his apartment, Caduv almost has to catch him as he falls forward. He recovers enough to set the paperwork down and go to the kitchen. He drinks water, feels a little better, and then puts the kettle on.

"You got the file, great," Caduv says. Fetter looks out of the kitchen, wanting to warn him to keep his distance from the other papers, but Caduv is holding them unconcernedly while he unties the pink ribbon and starts to leaf through the contents of the green file. He waves his handful of tainted paperwork at Fetter. "What's all this?"

Fetter doesn't answer until he's made tea and brought out the cups. Caduv has put the stack of loose papers to one side, preoccupied with reading the file; Fetter carefully sits on the other side of the table and examines himself. The clawing, clogging feeling in his throat and gut is still there, the hot squirm just under his skin, growing more intense again. He drinks the tea quickly for the burn. He thought it was only the intestinal, lurking uneasiness of his gut instinct, that feeling he has so often relied on, but it should have faded after he made his choice to take the papers, whatever subliminal currents trigger it appeased by his acquiescence to its urgency. But this time, it persists, becoming more intense with proximity to the papers. It doesn't seem to have any effect on Caduv.

He asks Caduv about what he's reading, and *how*. "I thought you couldn't read."

"I'm not illiterate," Caduv says. "I just couldn't read the Luriati script when I first came here. I've learned."

Fetter nods in light apology. "What does it say?" he asks, again. His head is starting to feel soft, so he gets up and walks back to the kitchen for more tea.

He doesn't get an answer until he comes back with his cup: "We're on the wrong track, it seems," Caduv says, and Fetter understands why that admission was like getting blood from a stone.

"You can afford to explain it to me," Fetter says. "After the trouble I just put myself through." The break in the kitchen has him feeling better, so he approaches the tainted paperwork directly this time, spreading the papers across the table with his hand, which stings lightly at the touch as if dipped in something red and spicy. He drinks his tea while he reads, in the hope that the heat will keep his throat clear.

Caduv sighs. He hasn't raised his head from the green file in a while. "This file contains copies of medical equipment requests and inventories from the quarantine camps for the last financial year. I am trying to figure out which camps suffered the most from the shortage when half that shipment went missing."

"Why?"

"What do you mean, *why*?" Caduv seems affronted. "Because it fucking matters, that's why. They will deprive some camps to supply others, and that means they're condemning some to die—the people they care the least about."

"I understand that," Fetter says, absently. He's feeling cold, both from the fever and, he thinks, the draining excitement of his mission. He can't muster outrage at the thought of atrocity; in him there is only that old lake of cold, simmering fury, and it is impossible to tell if it has swollen or not from these fresh tributaries. His eyes, and half his attention, are still on his own stack of paperwork; he is feeling sicker by the minute. "But why are *you* trying to figure this out? Your baby revolution—the demands of parenting? Your goal can't be to expose Coema for corruption. The file is stolen, and there can't be anything in it that he couldn't dismiss as falsified. So it's useless as evidence. Which means you're looking for information, not evidence, and you're looking for it *urgently*, which is why the file had to be stolen one way or the other. So either . . ." Fetter falters, distracted by belatedly understanding what he's just read. He wants to turn that paper over to see what it says on the other side, but he doesn't want to touch it again.

"Either what?" Caduv says. He's scowling, perhaps at Fetter's question, perhaps at the contents of the green file. "What *are* you looking at? Why did you take those papers as well?"

Fetter looks at him, helplessly. "They're about my father," he says. "I found them. I had to know." This seems to be the truth. He just hadn't known that before this very minute.

Caduv shakes his head. It's as if there was nothing else that Fetter could have said that would make him lose interest faster. Caduv has no time for other people's mysteries. "Finish your thought," he says. "Information and not evidence, yes. Urgency, yes. You don't need me to explain, it seems."

"You're trying to figure out how to help them," Fetter hazards. His attention has shifted; he just wants Caduv to leave so he can think in peace. "Do you have a secret supply of ventilators that you can use to save them? Did Koel buy the black market ventilators with her secret stash of crispy pigs she's been keeping under her mattress this whole time—"

"No, no," Caduv says. He's smiling. "All wrong. Not even close. The problem is . . . we know where all the camps are located, even the unofficial ones. Security is tight everywhere. We have the resources to liberate *one*. Maybe. After that they'll increase security and be aware that we exist. But we don't know who is in which camp. They keep that information where we can't get at it. We can't waste our efforts on the wrong one. The people we're looking for, they'd be the lowest priority for the Ministry of Health, so we thought we could at least get an idea of where to look based on the equipment allocations. But there was no significant shortfall anywhere, according to this." Caduv's smile fades. "Either they already addressed the ventilator shortage somehow, or more likely, these records are falsified. We'll have to figure something else out."

Fetter's head is spinning, but he's not sure if it's from the fever or from the incongruous image of Caduv and Koel staging a raid on a quarantine camp. In his mind's eye they are holding hands, like children about to wander into a wild wood. Maybe this will be where Koel's *others* come in, whoever they are. Her killers, who are sparing him of that duty of the revolution. He is on the fringes of whatever is happening in these subterranean movements. Perhaps even Koel is not at their centre.

"You've got something on your mind," Caduv says. He's closed the green file; he's even retied the pink ribbon. "Is it about your father? Why would the Ministry of Health have files about him? I thought he'd never been within a thousand miles of Luriat."

Fetter doesn't feel obliged to keep his mother's secrets, but he doesn't feel inclined to share them with Caduv, either. It's too much to talk about. "He hasn't," he says, instead. It's not even a lie, is it? "And somebody at the Ministry—well, Coema, it's obviously Coema, doesn't want him to come here."

"Oh?" Caduv cocks his head at this. "Quarantine?"

"No," Fetter says, then scans the spread of paper again. "I don't think so. That must be handled by a different faction. This is a confidential in-house research paper on apotropaic shielding, specific to my . . . the Perfect and Kind. My father.

The Ministry of Health has acquired some holy object which the author of this paper believes will result in a resonant feedback loop. I'm not sure why. The paper refers to it as Relic *a*. It doesn't say what it is, but its dimensions are quite small. You could hold it in your palm. The paper says the Perfect and Kind will be unable to come within range without being physically affected. The effects become more severe the closer it gets to him, and the longer he spends within range—indigestion, mild fever, severe fever, seizures, status epilepticus, and possibly death." Perhaps some ghost of this effect is why Fetter feels ill.

Caduv studies Fetter's face. "This is an assassination plot, then?"

"I don't think so," Fetter says, before he thinks about whether he thinks so or not. Does he not think so? Does he merely hope not? Does it feel like something is being taken from him? "He'll figure it out when he starts to get sick, presumably, and retreat out of range. He's not all-knowing, but knowing enough . . . This is a warning. A warding. Coema wants to spoil Gerau's event."

"So the relic will probably be planted somewhere near his base of operations in the city," Caduv says. "A convention centre, yes?"

"A big one," Fetter agrees. "Gerau's campaign website said it'll be that place up on Boiling Point. In the Plantations? I can't remember the name. They keep changing it every time a different president gains control of the Plantations. But it's huge and it has the private park adjoining, so the fans can camp there while the Perfect and Kind and his official staff stay in suites above the convention centre itself. There will be a million places to hide this relic in or around it."

"It seems like a lot of trouble just to spoil the show," Caduv says.

"Seems like the exact right amount of trouble," Fetter says.

"Coema didn't even have to do any of the work. Other people would have researched the artefact, hunted it down, analyzed it, and written this paper for him. It's an in-house paper, so it's already a Ministry employee. So Coema can just give them the job of hiding it somewhere at the convention centre, whatever it's called this year—"

"The Godsfaction Dedicatory Convention Centre," Caduv says. "I went to a concert in one of their halls a month ago. I got fucking confused finding it because it's been the Kingsfaction Dedicatory Convention Centre ever since I got to Luriat and I didn't know they were in the habit of changing the name. Everyone I asked for directions would just say they had no idea what I was talking about, because apparently the Planters are in on the joke."

"Oh *yes*," Fetter says, remembering. He's seen the cowdung-khaki uniforms and the feathered hats of the Colonial Police out there when he's visited Tomarin's house. The military and the paramilitary wings of the police traditionally belong to the Kingsfaction, but the Colonial Police belong to the Godsfaction. Technically they belong to the Absent Queen, but the Godsfaction have been allied with her since the Late Third Occupation. Fetter is annoyed to know some of these distinctions and histories, having picked them up from Koel and her pamphlets and the tainted osmosis of life in Luriat. He misses the blessed ignorance of his early years in this city, when every jackboot was the same to him. "Yes, the Godsfaction president runs the Plantations now, so it should be the GDCC again. It doesn't make much difference which president is up there, but they just can't seem to resist the symbolic name changes—I've seen it happen at least three times."

They share the snide laugh of the knowing outsider. *Fucking Luriatis, am I right.*

"How's the play going?" Fetter asks, after a minute. He's

avoided learning more about it, out of some sense of increasingly obligatory jealousy, but he's gathered that the play is finished, or at least ready to be performed—Koel seems to never quite stop working on anything, so maybe she will keep changing the words even as they are spoken.

"It's going," Caduv says, shortly. Then: "We got the amendments back from the censors and Koel's applied for the police permit. We might even be able to stage a show or two before the lockdown kicks in."

Fetter makes a noise of affirmation and heads toward the kitchen again. How many cups of tea has he drunk? But no, he needs a break, before his head starts spinning again or the fever rises too much. He's not sure if it's the paper itself that is affecting him like this, but the implications are ominous. Perhaps this is why he feels sicker than ever; maybe this is not his own body's sensitivity to significance any more, but rather because the paper discusses Relic *a* so intimately that it is imbued with an echo of its properties through the law of contagion. Or perhaps the physical material of the paper came into contact with Relic *a* itself, as the author worked on it.

"Oh, can you check the author of that paper for me?" he calls, from the safety of the kitchen. "There should be a signature at the end, I forgot to look." He doesn't feel up to getting close to the accursed thing again. Out of Caduv's line of sight, he wipes the sweat from his face. He opens the freezer door and puts his head in the cold. His bones feel weak, as if they are slowly beginning to melt under the flesh. If this is what he, the *son* of the Perfect and Kind, feels after close proximity to nothing more than a paper *describing* the relic, then surely Relic *a* itself is immensely dangerous to both his father and himself. He wonders how close he needs to be to feel the relic. It must have been in the city for weeks, and he's felt fine. He hasn't been near Boiling Point in that time, though. He must avoid the whole street. No, he should approach it to find his limit, to find the relic's effective range, in case he has to. In case—

In the living room, Caduv starts reading a name, a little laboriously. He's not yet mastered the way Luriatis style their names: every person has a string of preliminary names, the name of their house or clan if they're of an approved caste, any heritable titles or epithets, any honours or glorifications, and then, only at the end, their personal names, the short names that they use in everyday life. They'll use the full name to sign off on anything sufficiently formal, and apparently this extends to official government reports. Fetter is about to yell back across the house to skip to the end when Caduv finally reaches it himself, a name that in hindsight is perfectly obvious. Why *else* would she have been given a whole team to run her offbeat experiments with? She must have taken that academic freedom in trade for doing Coema's dirty work. Of course it's Pipra.

# 18

It feels like an omen: the email is repeated threefold. First, forwarded by Hej, as usual without adding a comment: the official update that the campaign to bring the Perfect and Kind to Luriat has successfully funded. Second, the same email, forwarded by Gerau to the email address he'd made for Peroe. Gerau added a note: *I haven't forgotten! One guest seat at a premium sermon is reserved for you. Look forward to seeing you there.*

Third, the same update, sent to his *own* email address. He must have clicked the "keep me updated on this campaign" button at some point, though he has no memory of doing this. Or perhaps Hej signed him up? At least his email address doesn't give away his name; he's still using the government email, assigned along with the apartment and its internet connection. Though if his father's people have access to the citizen registry—but no, only the Path Behind holds that kind of power in Luriat, and the campaign is run by the Path Above, and they seem to loathe each other. *Did* he really sign up for email updates on the campaign? Was he that incautious? But perhaps it seemed less so when he first saw the campaign, before he became Peroe, became entangled.

There is more to the update, beyond the headline and squee at the top. There is a picture of Salyut again, the Saint-General; he has issued congratulations and promised a visit by representatives of the site selection committee. There are further hurdles for the campaign to overcome; it is only one of many campaigns across all of Jambu that have successfully funded and are pitching their cities to the Saint-General and his committee. But then why is Gerau already talking about his reserved premium seat, as if the selection were a done deal? What could she know? Has she brokered a deal with the Saint-General? Is the site selection process a mere formal veneer over a straightforward bribe?

Either way, the email in triplicate teaches that he must deal with it three times over. Peroe must accept Gerau's invitation, so he can regretfully decline on the day. The Fetter that Hej knows would probably go. They could sit at the back, make out during the sermon, go drinking after. He'd keep both himself and Hej lost in the crowd, far away from Gerau and her premium seats. And finally, there is the Fetter that has kept secrets from Hej. Is that last one the same Fetter who goes to the meetings, the one who knows Koel and Caduv? Perhaps. But if so there is one more of me, he thinks, because I've kept secrets from them, too. The last Fetter, the one who may have already committed the First Unforgivable.

He wants to let out a scream of frustration, but he's afraid if he cuts loose he might not be able to stop, and it would only frighten his neighbours. He is on a devil's back, unable to dismount, in danger of being thrown or devoured, forced to ride it through. This devil will tire and kneel before he loses his grip. He opens his mouth to a precisely controlled degree, and instead of a scream, he says "Ah." It sounds loud to him in the silence, like a temple bell calling the hours for the faithless.

Fetter goes back to Cooksferry a few days later. The research team is familiar now. He passes Janno in an abandoned cor-

ridor, his hands dripping red with clay and making prints on
the wall tiles. Janno grunts in recognition, but does not speak.

In the distance, at the end of a long corridor, Fetter sees a
white-armed antigod stalk past. He shudders and turns the
other way.

Pipra is not at her usual door. He doubles back, finds her
walking and talking to two people at once, issuing instructions
and receiving updates. He accompanies them silently until she
finishes talking to the others. One of them peels away; the other
stays as Pipra turns to Fetter, apparently considering themself
included. "This is Avli," Pipra says. "They're newly seconded
to our team. Avli, this is Peroe: sir thought we could be helpful
in his research, and he was very helpful in turn with the FTTs.
Per, come see the rig! Avli's going to take their first turn at it."
She keeps talking, a steady stream of superficial patter, much
of it couched in technical details that are incomprehensible
to Fetter and probably would be to Peroe too. Fetter slowly
catches on that she's just preventing him from talking in front
of Avli. She doesn't want him blabbing—what? About their
last encounter, at the beach? He wouldn't have brought that
up even if they had been alone, and he thinks she would not
have either.

Her stiff tone is absurd to his ear because he knows how
Pipra ordinarily talks. Doesn't she call Coema *boss* behind his
back? Then we are not behind his back now, Fetter thinks: Avli
is his eyes.

Avli doesn't look like what he'd imagine a Ministry spy to
look like: small and ferrety, cunning and slinky. Instead, they're
the youngest-seeming person he's seen at the Cooksferry site,
broad-shouldered, smooth-faced, and cheerful. But then Avli
speaks, and Fetter realizes that they aren't a spy but something
worse: a replacement. "I'm afraid I've been thrown in the
deep end," they say, apologetically—it's aimed at Fetter, but

he suspects it's a sidelong apology to Pipra, one that's already been given several times and not accepted, going by her impatient eyes. "I've been assigned to take over from tomorrow, but *only* till Ms. Pipra finishes the other thing and comes back."

"What other thing?" Fetter asks.

"It's classified, Avli," Pipra snaps. "Please try to remember little details like that."

The "rig" is an ordinary plastic office swivel chair with a blue cushion and a high back, into which Avli is deposited. There are two other team members present but they are keeping their eyes on the door, so Pipra recruits Fetter to help her strap Avli into the seat with heavy cuffs that look like they might be dog collars, at the wrists, the neck, and the forehead. The rotating part of the chair's axle has been modified to control the degree of its motion; it is firmly affixed to a long metal rod that sticks out behind the chair, connected to a waist-high wooden cabinet which, as Fetter discovers on trying to shift it at Pipra's direction, is very heavy. The connection of the rod to the cabinet is governed by a large metal protractor; Pipra loosens the screws and directs Fetter to roll and rotate the chair into a position of her liking, and then gradually re-tightens them at a precise angle. Avli doesn't speak at all during this process. At first they laugh a little nervously as Fetter moves the chair, but then they fall silent.

"We worked through every minute of arc to find the perfect side-eye," Pipra says. "It's impossible to be too precise, given that the human head is this great big awkward bulgy *thing*— can you tighten that forehead strap by one more hole? Avli, for the love of science stiffen your neck. Peroe, you're with me; we flank the door, three steps in front of it, our eyes on Avli. Everybody else clear line of sight; come back and resume observation in five minutes. Avli, eyes forward and count off five minutes without blinking."

Avli tries to say something, but Pipra snaps them to silence. Fetter keeps his mouth shut, though the hairs on the back of his neck are standing up from the proximity to the door—to what might soon become a bright door. He had meant to warn Pipra of the dangers, but he still can't think of a way. He's not even sure the dangers are real to her.

Pipra being temporarily reassigned, so soon after Gerau's crowdfunding campaign completed? Pipra, Coema's chief researcher into Relic *a*? This could be it. She must have been asked to emplace it. If he can accompany her, volunteer to help—no, she said it was classified. Maybe he can follow her without her knowing. He might be able to find out where Relic *a* is, or where it will be. Surely if he can get close enough, he will be able to sense it. Does Pipra know what she's part of? He doubts it; Pipra doesn't seem like the type of person that Coema would trust with the details of his plots and machinations. Her interest would be in Relic *a* itself, and her reward for working with it would be to work with it. Much like Koel does for him with the bright doors, Fetter thinks, ruefully.

Avli is counting seconds softly under their breath. "Thirty-five . . . forty . . . forty-five . . . I really *really* want to blink, Ms. Pipra. Um . . . sixty-five—"

"I'll tape your eyelids open if you do," Pipra says. "I have the tape *right here*. And stop trying to look at me. Eyes forward!"

"Sorry!"

Smell blooms like low heat at the back of his neck. It's faint, even fainter than before, but the bitterness is unmistakable.

"There," Pipra says, with satisfaction. "Did you get that, Peroe? The indicative scent."

"Yes," Fetter says. "Do you also smell it?"

"I smell *something*," Pipra says. "About one in ten people we've tested seem to be able to smell something at the liminal peak. The smell seems to differ by person. You reported an astringent scent; to me it smells sickly sweet. A few seem able to pick up traces of it even *after* the translation, especially with practice, but I can't. Yet. It fades for me as we pass the liminal peak. Have you ever smelled the indicative scent at a bright door before?"

"No," Fetter says. Lying seems safer. He doesn't want Pipra to be jealous, or worse, suspicious. But he's also taken aback at the suggestion that there is some small effect, even for ordinary people—that is, people who are neither chosen nor unchosen—no, that doesn't make sense, does it? They are all unchosen too; it's just that the degree of their unchoosing is greater because they were never *almost*-chosen. Perhaps that distinction is finer than he'd thought. It means there's no such thing as ordinary people. Perhaps that means the dangers are also real to them. His gut is churning, as if the bitter scent had disturbed it. There are devils right here in the Cooksferry mall, moving about its corridors. The urge to say this, to call out the invisible laws and powers, is almost overpowering, as if he were carrying a stone in his mouth, large and hard and smooth from the years.

"What we've accomplished with the rig is *unique*," Pipra says. "It's so delicate a balance that if Avli over there so much as twitches an eyeball in this direction it will collapse. But until then, for *as long as Avli doesn't blink*, it is a bright door and not a bright door; it is neither a bright door nor not a bright door—don't you *dare* blink! Are you crying? It is perfectly poised on the horns of the tetralemma. The liminal peak can be held to the limit of human will and fine motor control over the eyelids, and the incomplete translation then reversed. All right, Avli, you can close your eyes."

Avli slams their eyelids shut. It seems almost audible to Fetter, like a loud clack. Pipra turns around to look directly at the door. Fetter doesn't move. Thick tears have indeed etched

Avli's cheeks. "Sorry, Ms. Pipra," they say. "I'm not crying, it's an involuntary tearing response. It happens—"

"I wrote the report you're about to quote back at me," Pipra says. "I know why it happens."

The other two team members return and begin unstrapping Avli from the rig. The bitter scent is gone. When he turns around, the door is just a door again. Closed, not bright, not liminal.

"The process doesn't work on doors at a frustration load of less than six weeks," Pipra says, to Fetter. "The more the better. This one's at eight."

She mustn't ever see me near Relic *a*, Fetter thinks. She will know—she *will* know, and he can't be sure of what she'd do.

# 19

Fetter goes to the play's opening night—its title is *The Leopard's Bane*—because Koel insists he come. At first he thinks she's just worried there won't be anybody there, but then she tells him which theatre it is: one of the grand playhouses in the Plantations, not the shabbier establishments in the Pediment.

It seems Koel is better known as a playwright than he'd thought. Her comeback is *news*.

In the build-up to opening night, he reads her name in the ordinary newspapers—in the back, in the arts section, but still—instead of in the byline of her own pamphlets. The arts sections fill up with remembered praise for her old play, the one that can be mentioned but not performed. He is surprised, and Koel's explanation is unhelpful: she speaks only about the political details, such as who owns which newspapers and the balance of Godsfaction or Kingsfaction stalwarts in various editorial teams. Fame, she says, is how a ruling class conditions artists to docility and incorporates their work to lesser ends. Sedition, unrest, and even revolution are useful to political actors currently out of power.

Caduv offers a different explanation, while chatting backstage on opening night.

"It is intended as temptation, I think," Caduv says. He is in full stage regalia, sleeves slashed and puffy and vividly orange, dark green leggings tight. His half-mask—a snarling big cat, the titular leopard—is pushed up over his hair. His ankle bracelets tinkle distractingly whenever he shifts his weight. "Keep the boundaries of allowed speech vague, and you can claim that your enemies have crossed them whenever you need to suppress them. The Ministry of Information and Mass Media is nothing more than a blacklist-in-waiting."

Fetter nods tiredly. It's the same attitude Mother-of-Glory has to the law. Fetter himself thinks of the law less as strategic or rule-based and more as a muddled, dangerous beast. A rabid leopard, like Caduv's character in the play. None of the others understand that the law might do anything, at any time, to anyone, and justify itself any way it likes—it is feral, like the invisible laws and powers of the world of which it is a pale imitation. It's because none of them can see the devils, he thinks. That's why they're all so optimistic about worldly law.

"Will you be dancing? In public? Showing off your calves like this?" he asks. Caduv glares.

"He just has a few steps," Koel says, appearing suddenly. "You'll be fine, you've practiced it to death." She's dressed formally, and entirely incongruously to Fetter's eye: a flowing drape over her left shoulder and across her body, over a tight, low-cut strapless bodice, exposing a thick panel of startlingly white tattoos on her dark brown skin, crisp-edged and broad like a banner across her shoulders and chest, nestled underneath her clavicles. He hadn't thought Koel wore so much ink, but these would be covered by the camisas she ordinarily wears. The tattoos seem abstract at first, geometric shapes, curves, sharp points. Then, as she turns to glide away from them, Fetter thinks they look like stylized teeth, as if Koel had made an upper jawbone out of the top of her torso. He wonders if she has a lower jaw tattooed on her belly to match, but if so, it's covered by both the bodice and the drape. It is unsettling, but this is exactly how Koel would wish to present herself: aggressive, dangerous, the iconoclast artist.

Still, despite the exposed tattoo, she's being a different Koel tonight, less aggressive than he's used to. She swans between knots of performers, speaking softly to them. Earlier, Fetter saw her bantering with her well-dressed audience as they came into the lobby. She even did the laugh that he associates with Tomarin's dinner table. It's a false front, but not one that worries about that falseness; she is wearing a shield whose weight has long since grown familiar. A little show for this night of performance, for all these people who will go home and congratulate themselves on facing the danger in the art, when the real danger is in the Walking getting her boots dirty.

Koel takes her seat in the front row. Fetter skulks backstage for as long as possible, then when Caduv and the others take the stage for a final huddle, he leaves by the side door and comes around to the lobby, meaning to sneak into the audience from the back.

The lobby has emptied of people, but his heart judders when he turns the corner and is confronted by a devil. He almost trips over his feet and has to catch himself against the wall. The devil is not just a feeder—there are some outside but he hardly registered them—or even a wandering antigod. He has never seen its like. It turns to look at him immediately and he sees the intelligence in its eyes, the glow of *recognition*. It knows he saw it, from his startlement. It is lying flat on the ground, the size of a large dog. It pulls itself forward on human arms, licking the floor beneath it with a long tongue protruding from something almost like a human head that goes down to the upper jawbone. The teeth are human; the tongue is more like a cow's. It has no lower jawbone. He can glimpse some exposed inner flesh or cartilage, as if a jawbone had recently been ripped away. It is bleeding copiously and crawling through its own blood. Its hindquarters are a bulbous, long, voluminous skirt of flesh, with folds and pleats, dragging like a train through the blood, spreading a fan of gore behind it, showing the path where it's been—in from the street, at a glance, on a direct path toward the main entrance. He can't tell if it's clothed in something that looks like flesh, or whether that is its actual flesh, and if so whether it has more limbs somewhere in there.

He freezes in place, trying not to meet its eyes, then bends over and simulates a coughing fit, covering his mouth, to provide a reason for his stop and stumble. It's a poor ruse, but it's all he can muster. The top of his head prickles, as if still under the creature's glare, but when he eventually straightens up again, it's gone. The spreading lake of gore shows that it entered the auditorium, moving through the closed doors. He approaches the door and peers through its small inset window of frosted glass, but the auditorium lights are off and he can't see anything. He opens the door and enters cautiously—looking down at his feet as he steps in the gore, shuddering to see his own footprints in the red train, darkening to almost black—but he can't see the devil, and someone hisses at him to close the door and stop letting the light in. The play is about to begin.

He shuts the door behind him and waits in the dark, breathing as evenly as he can as his eyes adjust. It's standing room only back here; he has to mumble apologies as he pushes his way through people to find a space and stake a claim to it, brushing shoulders on both sides. There is no sign of the devil, and it's too dark and too crowded to see if there is invisible blood on the floor. His legs feel cold. He raises his eyes resolutely to the stage, where the curtains are still closed.

There is drumming.

He's avoided finding out too much about *The Leopard's Bane* in the past few months, out of a sense of well-earned pettiness. This hasn't been difficult. Koel and Caduv rarely discussed it in front of him, and he is only mildly acquainted with the other people in Koel's theatrical troupe. He's occasionally shown up at Koel's house when they were rehearsing, got by with smiles and nods. He knows a few by name, most only by face. Koel, characteristically, has not mentioned if any of the troupe are part of her conspiracies. Caduv has mentioned that many of them are semiprofessional or well-regarded amateur stage actors, usually part-timers; Caduv took to this new social world with great facility. When the curtain parts and the lights fall on the actors in their stylized opening poses, Caduv—the mask now covering his eyes and forehead—looks just as much an actor as any of the rest.

Caduv inhabits the leopard well. Or perhaps it is the leopard that inhabits the man. The lighting briefly casts a swirl of spots over him, evoking the markings of the pelt that his costume doesn't have. Without preamble, Caduv opens his mouth— Fetter only has a moment to gasp, because he feels it like a punch in his gut even before it comes—and *sings*.

There is black earth in Fetter's mouth, in his eyes, weighing down his limbs like water. He is drowning—no, he won't drown, but he can't move, his muscles strain—and then they break through, and he digs himself out, blinking and spitting. He hauls himself out of the earth, kneeling in the mess of his own grave. Clods fall out of his hair. He rubs a hand over his face. His heart is pounding, his hand shaking. He dares to look up. The sky is clear, the half-moon low to his left. The vision, he thinks, it's the vision that Caduv's voice brings out. This isn't happening. Why is this happening again?

Just below the waterline of consciousness but exposed in shallow waves, Fetter is aware that he remains upright and unmoving, breathing shallowly, his shoulders touching others', only his fingers spasming. But then the vision swamps that awareness, and he's digging in the earth again, trying to prove its irreality to himself. It is rough and grainy on his palms, as real as anything he's ever felt.

He looks at the half-moon, a brilliant silver cup in the great hollow night. There's a half-moon outside in the real night; the theatre's orientation and the timing of the performance are such that the true half-moon mirrors the position of the vision, from the perspective of the audience. Or it would, if they were also experiencing the vision. But they couldn't be, at least not like this—*this* is just for him, and perhaps for Koel in the front row. He imagines her patiently kneeling in black earth in her finery, waiting for the vision to fade so that she doesn't make any sudden movements to startle the gentry she's sitting with. The thought is amusing: his mind fills in the clods of earth in her hair, her disgusted face as she spits it out of her mouth, and he feels his heart calming. All right, he thinks, standing up to mirror his real-world posture. This is a brief dream. It will fade away in a few moments. Perhaps the alignment of the true and false moons makes it possible for him to see the vision again. Perhaps this staging was deliberately engineered to strengthen the properties of Caduv's voice. Or perhaps this is the consequence of practice and intention, with all the work Caduv must have put into preparing his performance. Fetter has no illusions that tonight is about pure art for Koel. This is an attempt to use Caduv's voice to influence this audience, to whatever unknown proximate ends serve her greater goals.

He tries not to wonder if that bleeding devil sees the vision, too. Is it still here in the dark, slithering among the audience, slowly covering the floor in a mat of blood? Is it, too, crawling in black earth? He tests his footing carefully, but there is no sense of stickiness.

The vision fades as his train of thought grows more cynical, more knowing. For a while the vision is superimposed over his sensorium, so that he feels at once both the chill breeze of that silent amphitheatre and the chillier air-conditioning of the theatre; so that above him is the ceiling of the hall but also a deep dark sky with stars in strange constellations. He looks for Caduv and finds him brighter, as if he is present in both worlds. He's still singing, but now the chorus joins in. Fetter can't figure out what they're saying, can't quite pick out the words—it's rapid Luriati hellspeak in a more formal register than he's used to. He regrets that he knows so little about theatre that he can't even tell if the play is traditionalist or modernist.

Slowly, the vision fades and the story of *The Leopard's Bane* comes together. The words become easier to follow, or he adapts to the idiom. Caduv is the narrator, supported by the chorus; he is also a monstrous and tragic beast, as suggested by his costume, a leopard-spirit but fleshly and worldly. The chorus are dressed as the fallen spirits of his victims. He is danger and violence, sex and death. He becomes a wild young queen's de-mon lover, then a devil of a father to a prince and princess, then a monster king to a country. Fearing his wildness, his violence, the queen, the prince, and the princess plot his overthrow.

It's at this point that Fetter recognizes the bones of the story. This is an adaptation of the origin story of the Perfect and Kind, from the unexpected perspective of Fetter's father's fa-ther. He's heard versions of the story before—it's popular Be-hinder lore, woven into Luriati folk culture—but never from the point of view of his monstrous grandfather. He's never thought about his paternal grandparents before, and he's not sure if the leopard mythos is part of the original story or an innovation in Koel's script. He thinks of the story Mother-of-Glory told him about Cruel Victory. This leopard sired that prince, young Victory, before he became so cruel. Perhaps this is the story of how he becomes so.

To overthrow the king, the queen makes the first move. Her

task is to distract him with nostalgia. They have become estranged as they aged, but she comes to his bedchamber one night like he used to come to hers, when he was her demon lover. She summons up their carefree younger days.

In the morning, the princess comes to the king in his throne room, first as a petitioner and then as a daughter. She makes her claim to the throne as the elder child. She asks her father to do right by her, by their country, and abdicate.

The king, caught between these claims on his past and his future, paces the hallways of his palace not even noticing that they are empty—the queen and the princess have ordered all their staff and servants and ministers and guards away on one pretext or another. The prince comes up upon him then, and the king asks him ruefully what demand *he* has come to place upon his father. The prince smiles and says his only claim is to his father's heart. Then he stabs the old beast in it with a long knife, even as his father attempts to embrace him.

Dead, the monster becomes an invisible devil, who continues to narrate the story. His leopard nature comes to the fore; Caduv exchanges his mask for one heavier and redder in the tooth, his camisa for one with longer sleeves. The slashes are bloodstained now and the sleeves are too long. They flop past his hands and dangle like dead paws.

The chorus, too, change their costumes. They are no longer the ghosts of the mortal dead but a host of invisible devils. Life goes on, and death comes by. The devil lover weeps unheard at the queen's funeral pyre while the chorus sets up a bone-rattling wail. The devil king loiters palely in the background, unknown, as his children contend for the throne. The princess's claim to her mother's throne is the more legitimate. She exposes her brother as the assassin, declaims to her court with great sadness that despite his human-seeming form, he is a monster just like their father. The court is shocked. The prince is vilified and cast out. The princess takes the throne. Check and mate.

The play ends on the lone prince, swearing vengeance and ruin on the world, huddled in baffled despair under a spotlight. The invisible leopard comes up behind him and lays its trailing sleeves, its dead paws, over his shoulders. It is at once a father's embrace, an inversion of the patricide, and his pelt as a monstrous trophy hung around the prince's neck. The spotlight swirls with leopard-spots one last time as the prince ties the sleeves together at his throat. The curtains close to a deep roar from the audience, a guttural noise that Fetter is surprised is coming from his own chest, matched by a furious clapping from his own hands, as much as from everybody else.

Backstage, Fetter shoves through the crush until he finds Caduv in the middle of the playgroup, and laughing, embraces the other man.

"That was incredible," Fetter says to him. He has to shout it directly into Caduv's ear because the room is riotous with giddy actors and their admirers. Caduv seems startled by the hug, but returns it. He is sweating, his makeup smeared, but beaming happily.

This is what fulfilment looks like, Fetter thinks. Caduv chose his path and made it work. He'll envy this later, he just knows he will, in the wee lonely hours of being Fetter, floating out of his bed if he's not careful, waking up on the ceiling from dreams of loss, or in the daytime frustrations of being Peroe, when nothing works right and he can't fulfill his urge to know, much less the more complex goals that Koel puts on him. But in the moment, his friend is happy and so is he.

Koel comes to find them a few minutes later. "Magnificent,"

she says to Caduv, kissing him on both cheeks and the fore-head. In her heels she towers over him. "As wonderful as I always expected of you." She glances at Fetter, suddenly, nods him closer. "Did you . . . ? When he first sang?"

"Oh yes," Fetter says, laughing again. It seems funny now. "I definitely did. Thought of you sitting in the front row trying not to spit."

"Too real," Koel says, smiling. "I was sure I was going to have a coughing fit and throw off the whole show."

"I'm so happy with . . ." Caduv says, gesturing incoherently. "I'm so happy. Thank you." He seems to address this to Koel, which makes sense, but also to Fetter, which does not. Koel pulls the three of them together into a hug.

But when their heads are closest together, Koel whispers, "I think it *worked*. I could feel it take." She lets them go, touches Caduv's cheek as if in blessing, and congratulates him again before she moves away to speak to her other performers.

Fetter wants to ask what worked—what subliminal instruc-tion did Caduv feed this audience of the wealthy and influential, exactly—but he can't ask in the middle of the crowd. Half the audience seems to be backstage at this point. He begins to turn to head back to the hall, but Caduv grabs his hand and the back of his neck to pull him close again, the sudden nearness hollow-ing out Fetter's belly.

"Coema just walked in," Caduv whispers. That voice so close to his ear sends an echo through his entire body, as if opening an endless night above him. He feels like he might float away into it; he clutches Caduv's forearm to stay grounded. "He hasn't seen us, but he'll probably come find me soon."

"Back door," Fetter says, in acknowledgement. Untangling himself from Caduv, he walks directly out. He doesn't turn around to look. He doesn't hurry.

One of the reasons he stayed inconspicuous in the back of

the hall was because Koel invited all the members of the Nine Yellow Oxen committee, along with numerous other members of the Luriati gentry. In fact, she invited far more of them than would fit into the hall, which both Fetter and Caduv demurred at until Koel explained that society theatre events in the Plantations did this as a matter of course. As predicted, most of those people didn't attend.

All evening, Fetter kept an eye out for the people who knew him as Peroe, but didn't spot Coema. Technically, there's no problem with Peroe being seen at the play—he now dresses Peroe-style all the time—but he prefers to simplify and minimize his out-of-context contact with those people. Koel wagered that Tomarin simply wouldn't show his face at the theatre due to lack of interest, not even for social clout, and Gerau would have heard about the play's themes and found it offensive to her politico-religious sensibilities, so Coema was the only one of the three who was at all likely to show.

Fetter wonders if Coema will bring the play up at his next dinner with Gerau, even recommend it, while she simmers or openly denounces it. It's hard to say: he has only the barest inkling of their dynamic. And how much of what he saw was a social performance for his benefit? In the absence of young Peroe, a playing piece casually tossed into contention, are they cordial to each other, accepting of their differences? Or was it only the presence of an outsider that kept their tempers cool that night? Maybe other such dinners devolve into shouting matches ineffectually refereed by Tomarin. Fetter can imagine both scenarios, but neither seems more or less plausible.

Perhaps they are all more like Peroe than he knows. When Peroe goes home, he ceases to exist and there's only Fetter left, someone they've never met and whose history or truth of circumstances they could never guess no matter how brilliant they are as judges of character. Perhaps there is no Gerau and no Coema beyond the roles that they play across the dinner table, beyond the relationship that might have so much consequence if Coema's plan for Relic *a* goes through.

It seems excessive for a prank, considering its author; it seems petty, exaggeratedly vindictive, outright dangerous. He *ought* to be siding with Coema, the skeptic and unbeliever, but this scheme only makes him sympathize with Gerau instead.

# 20

Fetter goes back to Cooksferry, ostensibly to help. Avli greets him cheerfully but seems worried; they must associate Peroe with Pipra and assume he has more access or connections than he has in truth.

"I knew you'd be short-handed with Pipra away," Fetter says. He tries to borrow from Caduv, to put as much warmth and intimacy into his voice as he can. He found Avli on a solo vigil on a door deep in the complex. Things seem lax today: he passed several other doors that only had one person watching them. "Is there anything I can help with? I can turn the bolts on the rig or whatever you need."

"We're not doing any rig tests while the boss is away," Avli says, smiling in response. They seem relieved. "Strict observation duty only. We're to rack up frustration load on doors, nothing more."

When Avli says *the boss*, Fetter realizes, they mean Pipra, not Coema.

"I haven't seen Janno today," he says. "The team seems a bit thin. Did they all go with Pipra?"

"Oh no," Avli says. "It's just her on the thing. They're all here, they're just not all at their stations right now."

He reads Avli's flush and guesses. "It takes a toll on people," he says, sympathetically. "Janno was deep into the wall art phase last time I saw him."

Avli sighs, nods. There is a slight but noticeable relief in their posture: they hadn't been sure if Peroe knows, or is allowed to know. "Nobody's immune. Even the boss has had down days," they say, with a small, confidential smile. "She told me to expect it myself."

"So soon?" Fetter says. "I thought she'd be back long before you got to that point."

Avli flushes even redder. "The boss says it can happen fast. Have you—I don't know how much time you've—"

Fetter shakes his head. "No, I come and go," he says. "Haven't spent enough time here at a stretch to feel the effects. You all are the ones at risk." He's out on a limb here; he does not in fact know the nature of the condition, beyond what little he's observed on his visits to Cooksferry. But this conversation is about making a connection, and he's in a hurry. He *needs* Avli to trust him, though he's not sure they'll ever give away where Pipra has gone. He's feeling his way through this conversation as if through a swamp; he has to smile and pretend that he's not chest-deep in the mire.

"I don't know about *risk*," Avli says, with a little laugh. "The effect doesn't seem lasting. Last time Janno was up, he told me he'd been through it three times already. He'll be back to work before the boss comes back."

"Where *is* Janno, anyway?" Fetter says. He's following his instincts without being sure where they lead. "I had something I wanted to talk to him about."

"Oh," Avli says. Their voice sounds even smaller. "He's with the second-floor congregation, near First Blue Heron. You should go say hi, maybe it'll help snap him out of it."

"Does that even work," Fetter says, with a sad smile. His gut is already tugging him away. "I'm willing to try, though."

"Haha," Avli says. They don't laugh, they actually say *haha*. Fetter wonders, uneasy, if he overstepped by making Peroe seem too confident or intimate with the team, playing on Avli's own insecurity as a newcomer. It's too late now. He leaves Avli staring at their door and goes to look for this congregation.

He still doesn't know what the affliction is, except that it seems to be brought on by too much time spent on the Cooksferry project. Too much exposure to bright doors, or ordinary doors at high frustration load. Maybe the observers only hold the doors back from that transition by pouring in the light of their eyes, the quiet of their hearts. Perhaps the doors drain those resources from their door-keepers, who develop deficiencies. Could the rate of their deterioration have been worsened by Pipra's experiments with the liminal peak? He feels a sediment of guilt over his own contribution to that.

Pipra would have tried it anyway, he thinks, then derides himself for wanting credit but not blame.

He's taken a close look at First Blue Heron before, the oldest of the Cooksferry mall's bright doors, just to press its image into his mind. He's made sure to visit each bright door in the building at least once, to actualize their massed looming threat, which he feels every time he enters the building as the heat of a pending storm on the back of his neck.

That day, First Blue Heron's environs were deserted: there were no watchers on doors that had already translated. First Blue Heron had translated long before Pipra's project began; it had been the first sign of the failure of the mall project. Before it changed it was the main entrance to the small luxury film theatre on the second floor, blatant and impossible to miss. The theatre itself is still accessible, but only through the emergency exits on both sides, now propped permanently open. From the inside, there is nothing but a blank expanse of wall where the entrance ought to have been. When Fetter visited the theatre, he had an irrational impulse to close both exits after himself, to wait for them to translate and cocoon him in a room that was inaccessible from the outside world. He remembers that thought and shudders. At the time it felt terrifying and yet somehow delicious. Now it feels only obscene.

Today, First Blue Heron is crowded. Fetter wonders if Avli said *congregation* because they were reminded of a place of worship. He feels like he's approaching a grand ceremonial altar in a busy temple. First Blue Heron is enormous and showy at the top of a short series of steps. The door would be wide enough for ten people to enter abreast, were it open; when the door's two halves were pushed inward and open, grand and welcoming, it must have made patrons feel like they were entering an occupation-era palace. The colonial majestic, a familiar aesthetic. Closed, the door looks heavy and expensive, the painted wooden surface ornately carved in what Fetter now recognizes as an Abjesili style—a starburst when the door is closed, that would draw the eye and the punter inward if the door were open—elaborated by floral and fruiting designs curling around that geometry as if it were a trellis. He doesn't recognize any of the fruits or flowers, but then he never does in this style of sculpture. Perhaps they are meant only as nonspecific abstractions. Perhaps these were the haunted fruits and flowers of old Abjesil, or exotics from the far expanse of their slaver empire.

Janno is sitting underneath one such bell-shaped flower, leaning on the door with his face pointed up. His exposed throat works, as if he were trying to swallow falling spores.

Pipra's team crowds the hallway leading to the theatre: in the space in front of the ticket office, among the burgundy velvet ropes and brass stanchions that once organized the queue and are now fallen and piled into disarray like so much seaweed and driftwood; up the steps to First Blue Heron itself; even a few people leaning against the bright door, like Janno. The more alert acknowledge Fetter as he passes, with a nod or a muttered hello, before they go back to watching the less

responsive daub the walls with river clay. They've brought clay
in by the bucket, as well as by every type of container they've
been able to find in this building: metal pails, wastepaper baskets with mud oozing out of the little airholes, plastic trash
bins, cardboard file boxes slowly disintegrating as the mud
soaks through, even jugs and cups. The daubers are intent on
their work: Fetter cannot elicit more than a distracted mumble from any of them. The daubings seem meaningless to him.
There are marks that could be symbols or writing, curves and
slashes and odd shapes, but he doesn't recognize them. It's not
any variety of hellspeak he's ever seen, nor is it Alabi or Abjesili
script. Perhaps they are making art, not language. Nearer to
the bright door, he sees more of the familiar handprints, as if
even this cursory attempt at symbolism or communication is
being pared down to its essence as they push deeper into the
door's range of influence, reducing to ever more minimal asser-
tions of presence, of existence. *I am here, I am, I.*

He approaches Janno cautiously. First Blue Heron's presence
is intense up close; he has been smelling its bitter scent for some
time. He climbs the steps until he can see Janno's upturned
face. His eyes are open and staring. His entire body is twitching
slightly, as if in a seizure. *Is* he having a seizure? Fetter touches
him gently, and when Janno doesn't respond, Fetter takes him
by the armpits and pulls him away. Moving him seems less
risky than leaving him in contact with the bright door.

Janno's posture doesn't change, but he's not entirely dead
weight; when Fetter hauls him up, he allows himself to be lifted
and walks down the steps partly under his own steam. But then
he gives way again, as if exhausted, and Fetter lays him down
carefully on the ground, curled up and lying on his side.

The almost-chosen, Fetter and Koel and others, have a different order of reaction to the bright doors, but here is more
proof almost anybody has reactions to the bright doors, even

to not-yet-bright doors, at high levels of exposure. So the difference is one of degree, not of kind. Janno has had more exposure than most. Perhaps too much.

Fetter goes back for the others leaning on the door and brings them down the steps one by one, laying them on their sides like Janno. He may not understand what's happening to them, but he *does* know that contact with the bright doors is best avoided.

Keeping a wary eye on First Blue Heron, Fetter squats, then sits cross-legged next to Janno's head. The other man's face is still rigidly upturned, his mouth and throat working. He doesn't seem to be choking, at least; he is breathing hard but evenly. Fetter sits and breathes along with him.

Very gradually, he thinks he sees a relaxation in Janno. It's so slow it seems illusory at first, as if Fetter is simply imagining the relief he wants the man to feel. But the tight cords of Janno's neck have softened, and his mouth and eyes have slowly lidded shut; Fetter adjusts Janno's head so that he faces forward, checks on his breathing again. He seems to be sleeping.

The others that he moved, too, have reverted to sleep. He doesn't know them, but their reactions were much like Janno's, if less severe.

Further away from the door, the daubers and daub-watchers mull around. Some are still talking to each other in mumbles that Fetter can't understand.

He walks up to First Blue Heron again. He is always tense near bright doors since he realized they were open, ready to spring away at the first sign of something coming through. The cold bitter wind is strong on his cheeks now that he's not distracted by the need to rescue someone. Cold wind through an open door. Perhaps the things that come through have been preying on these people all this time, leaving psychic wounds in their wake.

Would Mother-of-Glory know how to read the clay-daubed symbols on the wall? She claims to remember the lost knowledge of an elder age. Perhaps he should ask her when he goes to see her.

This is how the thought comes at him; sidelong, clinging to the back of another thought like a tick, or a child.

He speaks the thought in the open agora of his mind, experimentally: *I'm going home to see her.* It echoes strangely. She's dying. He should do this—no, he *wants* to do this. Does he?

A stir of movement in the corner of his eye: the sleepers are waking. Fetter backs away from First Blue Heron, never quite turning his back on it.

Janno has made it to a sitting posture. He looks up as Fetter approaches—the glance is so normal that Fetter says hello automatically, and is startled when Janno grunts an acknowledgement.

The other sleepers have staggered to their feet; they're wandering away from the door, back toward the outer edges of the congregation. Perhaps they will go back to a safer preoccupation.

Fetter kneels next to Janno and tries to check his pulse, which Janno swats away.

"Are you all right? Can you speak?" Fetter asks.

"Of course I can speak," Janno says. His voice sounds rough, as if he hasn't used it in a long time, or perhaps as if he has been weeping. "I just fell asleep for a bit. Should get back to work."

"Are you . . . recovered?" Fetter doesn't even know how to ask this question. "You were in some kind of fugue state. Do you remember?"

"Hmm?" Janno looks at him. The man is far from recovered: his eyes are clouded, confused. "Peroe, help me? Where's Pipra?"

It seems he just wants help to stand up. Fetter lifts him,

but Janno stumbles as soon as he lets go, so he pulls the other man's arm over his own shoulder and starts guiding him away from the door. Janno follows peaceably.

"I was going to ask *you* where Pipra was," Fetter grunts. Janno is heavy, and Fetter has to work extra hard to keep himself grounded—to lift up the other man without kicking off the ground in front of everyone. It's quite possible that nobody would notice if he did, or they might chalk it up to a hallucination. Perhaps the congregation would build the myth of a floating man into their symbology.

Devils take it, he's not going to have a better chance. "Isn't she away on the relic project?"

"She's away," Janno echoes. "Relic."

"Yes," Fetter says, both relieved to have reached the subject and tense to be on the threshold of what he's looking for. "She talked about the plan to put Relic *a* in place."

"The emplacement test," Janno agrees.

Fetter leads Janno away from the congregation, out of the bright door's line of sight and, he hopes, its immediate zone of influence. Janno shuffles along as he is led. More distance is better, Fetter thinks. For Janno to recover, and for privacy.

"She tried to explain the test protocol the other day, but I didn't really get it," Fetter hazards. Janno has overheard dozens of such conversations between Pipra and Peroe on various parts of the Cooksferry project; hopefully in his befuddled state he will remember only that Peroe seems to be in Pipra's confidence and not that the different projects have different security ratings.

"Emplace and range test," Janno says. He's not slurring—if anything he's enunciating slowly and clearly, but this only makes him seem less lucid. If Fetter didn't already know what the bright doors can do, he would have thought Janno and the others were getting high eating strange mold off the walls of these wilding hallways.

"To test the effective apotropaic range," Fetter says, citing from Pipra's paper. When Janno doesn't respond, he tries another gambit. "It's very fascinating . . . is she off at Boiling Point today? The GDCC?"

Janno looks puzzled. "No," he says. "Probably at the office having more meetings. Or the emplacement site. Let me sit down for a minute." They've reached an abandoned observation point on the second floor. There are a couple of low-slung canvas chairs, a backpack of provisions, a sleeping bag, and a door propped open with a brick.

Fetter helps Janno into one of the chairs and hands him a bottle of water from the backpack. Then he sits in the other chair and says "Meetings?" like it's not the *other* thread he wants to pull on. He needs to distract from his wrong guess at the emplacement site.

Janno is chuckling at the thought of meetings. "She's still negotiating with that Saint-General. Coordinating the test. What's-his-name. He insists on videoconferencing so she has to be dressed up all the time."

The fine hairs stand up on Fetter's neck and his belly runs cold—if Janno is telling the truth, and he doesn't seem to be capable of complex deceits right now, then the situation is not quite as Fetter had imagined it. If Pipra is working with the Saint-General himself, whose signature he last saw in the email forward from the crowdfunding campaign, then perhaps Coema and Gerau are not at odds like he thought? If the Saint-General is coordinating a test of Relic *a* with the Ministry of Health, then surely . . . His mind is racing ahead, and with an effort he drags it back.

"Salyut, right?" he says, trying to suggest with his intonation that this is a vaguely remembered name dredged out of his memory, and not burned into the very folds of his brain. "I thought his site selection committee reps were due here soon."

"Oh, didn't you hear," Janno says, chuckling. He's been drinking the bottle of water steadily and is now pouring the last of it over his head. "Latest is that the old stick is coming himself, just to be sure. He's going to sit there with Pipra at the emplacement site tomorrow morning and personally accept the handover after the test. Like he thinks we might not put it back in the box quickly enough and fry his boss like an egg."

Fetter joins him, falsely, in laughter, still dealing with the overturning of his assumptions. His mind snags on details—*the old stick*—yes, Salyut is famously conservative and difficult, and Janno mentioned that Pipra had to dress up just to videoconference with him. Formal officewear, to dress like the civil servant she's supposed to be, which she would never do of her own accord. And *tomorrow*: that's dangerously close. If he hadn't come looking for Janno today, he might have missed it.

So Relic *a* isn't being hidden away as a dangerous prank to spoil his father's event, like he'd been imagining. It's a formal handover, a grand collaboration. Salyut would be an honoured guest in Path-obsessed Luriat, so this will be a ceremonial occasion, with a high chair with a white cloth on it for Salyut, a bowl of water for someone, probably Pipra, to wash his feet, an official Ministry banner on the wall, maybe some light speechmaking. Would they use a Ministry office for this? No, they'd want a ceremonial open-air pavilion for someone of the Saint-General's rank. A purpose-built field site. Should he ask? Not yet, he thinks, let me pull a different thread first so I don't seem too intent.

"I didn't know they were planning to hand the relic over," Fetter says. "Is the test going to be in person? I wouldn't think the Perfect and Kind would want to be in a room with it, even for science."

"No, no. Oh, that was one of the very first batch of conditions," Janno says, smiling. His head and shoulders are drenched from the water but his eyes seem less fogged, though his pupils are still very wide and there's something off about his smile. "The range of the unshielded relic, according to lore, is eighty miles. The Perfect and Kind has graciously agreed to confirm its ill effects at the outermost edge of its range, a closed test of apotropaic effectiveness in the spirit of scientific inquiry, and so on and so on. But given that the test involves highly sensitive material and his own personal wellbeing, he insists on secrecy and demanded that his representative take custody of said material immediately afterward. He promises the Abovers will share the results of their own findings afterwards . . ." Janno is laughing again. "Of course they won't, that'll be the last we see of it. But getting them to agree to the range test is a big deal."

Fetter finds himself laughing too, this time with some hysteria: *eighty miles* means that if the relic had ever been taken out of its shielding while Pipra was studying it, it would have affected the whole city and a significant quarter of the Luriati peninsula—all the way south to Acusdab, even. If the relic affects him as it is supposed to affect his father, and his reaction to Pipra's paper seemed to suggest this, Fetter might have sickened and died without knowing what was happening. The mere fact that he's alive means that the relic hasn't been taken out of its shielding. If he hadn't come looking for Janno today, he might have died tomorrow without—he should leave the city immediately. His thighs tremble with the effort of not leaping to his feet and breaking into a run. No, no: he still has time. How much time? He can take the train out of the city tonight. But first he needs to figure out how this range test is organized.

If the Perfect and Kind is willingly taking part in a test of Relic *a*—and how this overturns his idea of the war between Coema and Gerau! Are they working together, then? He can't fathom it. Fetter shakes his head to focus. His father can't just take a flight from Kalaki to Luriat. He'd have to approach the city by land to control his speed, and to be able to hastily backtrack at the first sign of symptoms. He and his entourage would probably fly from his monsoon camp at Kalaki to the northernmost city with an airport that's safely far out of the relic's range. Probably Pearlprince or even Burrflower, south of the Hanu. Then he'd hire vehicles, and a convoy of the Path Above would drive north from there. He would have to recross the pass in the Hanu mountains, just like he'd done two thousand years ago: the mountains are about twice as far away as the relic's purported effective range. The convoy would proceed north ever more slowly and carefully until just outside the presumed range of Relic *a*, say a hundred miles south of Luriat. Not far from Acusdab.

In Luriat, the relic would be ceremonially unshielded by Pipra with Salyut glowering on. In the south, the convoy of vehicles would slow to a crawl, or perhaps the Perfect and Kind and his entourage would simply get out and walk. Yes, they would probably walk; his father and a thousand monks of the Path Above undertaking yearly barefoot peregrination between southern cities is a famous seasonal event, often accompanied by TV crews. Though if this experiment is kept secret at his own insistence, maybe he and his people would walk without cameras just this once.

If Salyut the Saint-General is going to be sitting with Pipra the whole time, he would be coordinating by phone with someone in the Perfect and Kind's entourage, timing the unshielding and getting status updates. Probably with Vido the amanuensis, who seems to get all such practical odd jobs. Fetter can't imagine his father on the phone. It seems disturbingly bathetic.

It would take this procession of monks a day, perhaps, slowly walking north on bare feet, checking the Perfect and Kind's health every few minutes, to determine the outer limit of the relic's effective range. Maybe half a day? Surely not more or less, if they are being both cautious and urgent on their way to reclaim the relic.

If Pipra is correct in her calculations, the procession would stop about eighty miles south of Luriat when symptoms became unmistakable. Salyut would then seal the relic back into containment and take possession of it. The relic would be unshielded for half a day or more, during which time Fetter cannot stay in Luriat. But he has until tomorrow. His heart calms a little, though it is still racing.

Is it a coincidence—it could not possibly be a coincidence—that the range test would have the Perfect and Kind stopping near Acusdab? Fetter feels an overpowering urge to go look at a map. He's still not good at positioning Acusdab in relation to the rest of the world, but he studied Luriati maps after Mother-of-Glory told him her story and he knows Acusdab is about halfway between Luriat and the Hanu mountains. So with Relic *a* in Luriat, the relic's effective range must end somewhere in Acusdabi territory.

Could his father be planning to attack his mother under cover of this experiment? Or maybe it's not an attack, Fetter chides himself. Leaping to assumptions of violence and conflict, is that not part of the childhood indoctrination he's trying to put away? Just like he had thought Coema and Gerau mutually hostile when they were apparently collaborators, perhaps his father is only attempting a late rapprochement. He would, after all, be walking barefoot into his mother's territory; he might even be sick and weak when he arrives, knowingly and willingly defanged and made vulnerable. Surely this is intentional, a deliberate baring of his throat. A peace offering. The thought makes Fetter feel faintly sick, a low tide of bile rising up his throat.

"Where are they setting up the emplacement site?" Fetter

asks, at last. His tone is casual, and he tries to project as much of Peroe's earnestness as he can. "I should go help out. Pipra will be glad to have someone to talk to while they're covering everything in coconut leaves and white cloths to keep the old stick happy."

And it's easy as that. Janno, his pupils still dilated wide and black, laughs in acknowledgement and tells him.

∽

The pavilion has been assembled in a children's playground, attached to a school at the north end of the city. *North*, not south like he would have guessed: further away from the direction of the Perfect and Kind's approach. Fetter supposes this is out of an excess of caution. He wonders if it was Pipra's idea.

He too approaches with care, like he'd imagined his father doing: he takes a tuktuk, which he can control better than the light rail; he tells the driver to drive slowly, and constantly interrogates his body for signs of discomfort, of which he finds none except the varieties that come from the interrogation itself. Is his throat closing up, or is it just a prickle from exhaust and pollution? Is his body temperature rising, or is it just hot and sunny? Is his belly clenching? Are his balls tightening up? And so on.

In the end, despite having told himself he wouldn't do it and that he's still as safe today as he was yesterday, he gets off the tuktuk early and walks the last few miles. He's hypersensitive, hypochondriac, and paranoid, but the walk is uneventful. He doesn't even see a single devil. In his own body, apart from a slight and not unpleasant tiredness in his feet and shins from the walk, and mild dehydration from being out in the sun, he feels no ill effects. Or perhaps those *are* the attenuated effects

of the relic, he thinks uneasily, whatever fraction of its effect
might act on Fetter as his father's son. But it's not the feeling
of unmistakable illness from when he found the papers about
Relic *a* and brought them to his apartment. That sensation is
entirely absent. This is worrying and confusing, but at least it
doesn't prevent him from going ahead. He keeps moving.

He finds the school: it's been closed to students and its
premises commandeered by Ministry of Health staff. There is
a military escort, but it's small. A couple of armed soldiers at
the gate, barely paying attention except to check his identity
card. Fetter shows his borrowed card with a smile and walks
past as Peroe without being troubled further. There are people
all over the playground itself, setting up equipment behind and
between the swings and slide. He still doesn't feel any symptoms at all—he feels fine, he tells himself, dismissing the bubbling sense of panic. He feels a little stupid for approaching so
cautiously, and a lot more stupid for approaching at all. But
this is too good an opportunity. He'll never get this chance
again after the Path Above takes possession of the relic.

The pavilion is already complete. It's a large eight-sided hut,
built on the only open patch of ground, whose frame is a metal
and plastic scaffold that is clearly prefabricated and must have
taken only a few minutes to assemble. Long white cloth covers
seven of the eight sides and stretches overhead as canopy, with
wide gaps left open for cooling breezes. It's an industrial-grade
rapid-deployment model of the wooden Behinder preach-huts
that he's seen many times in Luriat and the hinterlands. Ordinarily, a group of Behinder monks would sit in an open circle
inside the hut, chanting in harmony, while the faithful knelt on
mats on the ground outside. Here there are no faithful, only
Pipra's technicians and Ministry bureaucrats. There seem to
be more of them than is strictly required; perhaps this is why
Fetter is not challenged. Some are setting up equipment, pre-

sumably to measure the relic's output tomorrow. Others are just standing around in little knots talking.

None of them—not soldiers, not scientists, not bureaucrats—notice or react to his oddity. He found it charming at first, how unremarkable his shadowlessness is in this city, but he's come to see it as part of a deep Luriati unwillingness to acknowledge anything that would require overturning their world, whether in physics or politics. A crowd like this wouldn't acknowledge the fact of a hinterland pogrom or a prison camp either. To them, such things are the invisible laws and powers of the world, to be left unseen or at least not looked in the eye. They hide behind *unfortunate incident* or *tense situation* or *welfare camp for internally displaced persons* or *a trick of the light.*

Pipra is easy to find. She's inside the pavilion, alone, looking stuffy and sweaty in conservative officewear. The tight sleeves of her bodice are modest and elbow-length. The drape is impatiently gathered and wrapped around her waist to keep it out of her way, a treatment the stiff, formal fabric resists.

The pavilion's interior is austere. There are a couple of ceremonial coconut-leaf pots on the ground—bare earth, grass plucked and soil stamped down—and a small pile of clean, pale green coconut leaves beside them, as if someone had been interrupted in making more pots. Pipra is squatting in front of a rugged field laptop balanced on one of a disarrayed cluster of large opaque plastic boxes. Her headphones are on. The screen is facing away from him, but Fetter has a moment to wonder if she's videoconferencing with the Saint-General before she looks up and sees him.

She looks startled, at first, and then something undefinable comes to her face. Her eyes narrowing—but that could just be from the glare of the sun behind him—and her lips tightening, as if to swallow the first, and maybe also the second and third, words that came into her mouth.

She mumbles something into her headset that Fetter doesn't catch, then removes the headphones and closes the lid of the laptop.

"So," she says. "Avli?"

"Janno," Fetter says, smiling. "He thought I should come help out." Then, catching the grim set of her mouth, he adds: "Don't be angry at him. I know he wasn't supposed to tell me, but he's having a rough day."

"Insistent, was he?" Pipra says, face stiff.

"Well, no," Fetter admits. His face stilled in automatic response to Pipra's expression. He tries smiling again. "I thought you'd be glad of a friendly face and a helping hand. I can make the rest of those things, for instance." He points at the coconut-leaf pots. "Also, I wanted to see you."

Pipra smiles a little at that, then rises to her feet. She has a little box in her hand—she must have been clutching it in her lap. It looks oddly familiar. "Did you really," she says. "Or did you want to see this?" She opens the box before Fetter can say anything, and he understands how foolish he's been when she takes something small out of the box and throws it to him.

He catches it out of sheer instinct, his fist clenched tight around something small and hard. His heart is pounding, suddenly. His gut flares in foolishly belated alarm.

This would be a very stupid way to die.

But he doesn't die. There's a long moment where he's not sure if he *has* died and is only waiting for his body to fall, but it slowly dawns on him that his heart is already calming, that he's broken out in a sweat and his knees feel weak but that he's still upright. He doesn't feel sick, apart from the shock. Nothing has happened.

"You look like I just threw you a grenade," Pipra says, and now she *is* laughing, though it still sounds a little acidic. "Relax, it's just a relic. That little thing is what this whole production is about. I don't know how much Janno told you."

Relief floods through him—she doesn't know that he knows, she doesn't know who he is. He badly wants to sit down, so he does, lowering himself shakily to the ground beside the pile of coconut leaves, so that it at least seems like he's preparing to go to work.

He opens his palm, at last.

"It's called Relic *a*," Pipra says. "It's a mandibular third molar. A wisdom tooth."

The tooth is faintly yellowed. It has two roots like legs beneath its squat crown. It seems unremarkable. It is not radiating any otherworldly energies into the skin of his palm or striking him dead from the sheer overexposure. How? Fetter clears his throat, digging for Peroe within himself, then says, carefully, "Ew."

Pipra beams at him. Now she looks delighted. "It's *clean*. Lore and rumour also say it's ancient, though nobody can seem to agree on a timeframe. Some tests suggest it's a couple of thousand years old and others that it's only a couple of decades old, so maybe it's some kind of hoax. Either way, it's a Behinder artefact. Or I suppose I should say an Abover artefact? I'm not sure. Your Path is all the same to me."

"Not much difference, really," Fetter says. He hadn't realized Pipra was pathless, but Peroe, or at least, the Peroe he's made for himself, is hardly a devout Behinder and wouldn't remark on it. He keeps his voice casual, unable to look away from the tooth. But no, he doesn't need to pretend to not be fascinated by the relic. Peroe would be, too, for scientific reasons if not religious ones. "What does it do?"

"Apparently, it's dangerous," Pipra says. "Not to just anybody. Only to the person whose mouth it allegedly came out of."

"The Path . . . so one of the Saints? Or . . . not the Perfect and Kind?"

Pipra nods, as if he were a slow but diligent student. "The Perfect and Kind himself. I am definitely not supposed to tell you that, but since you're here and have gifted me with that look of absolute terror, you can in fact make the bloody pots. The old stick will be here tomorrow morning for the test, and the boss's friend is very particular about how we're supposed to receive him."

"That's not the lady who runs the crowdfunding campaign, is it?" Fetter asks. Having survived this close encounter with sudden death—he still doesn't know why he didn't collapse the moment Pipra opened the box, let alone when the tooth made contact with his hand—he is starting to recover from the shock, to rethread the nest of deferral in his heart, hiding what Fetter knows behind what Peroe knows, but this part is easy. It's Peroe who's met Gerau and Coema, and it's Peroe who knows Pipra, and it's Peroe who's here. "I've met her—she's on the committee for my door."

"Oh right," Pipra says. "Gerau, yes. She's . . . interesting. She'll be here tomorrow, too. And no, you *can't* come, even if you do know her and the boss. Please don't suddenly show up. They'd probably indulge you, but you'll get me in a world of trouble later with the Ministry."

"Sorry," Fetter says. "Should I get out of here? I don't think anybody particularly noticed me."

"No, today is fine," Pipra admits. "There will be a security sweep tonight to prepare for the VIPs, but as long as you're gone by then, nobody will care. In the meantime, get to work! And give that back here."

He hands the tooth to her, carefully. It's strange to think that he just held his father's tooth in his hand. "Never occurred to me that the Perfect and Kind would have to get a wisdom tooth extracted," he says. He watches her hands as she puts it back inside the little box. The inside of the box is lined, a pale pink, soft and velvety. When she closes it, he sees that the lid is ornately decorated in a style that seems very old-fashioned and familiar to him. He wishes Hej were here, to explain whether it's Abjesili. It seems to be metal and not wood, so probably not.

Pipra goes back to the laptop, so Fetter shifts his attention to the coconut leaves. There is a small knife next to the pile. He picks that up, selects some likely pieces of leaf, and starts to work, cutting, folding, bending. He can sense, without quite looking, Pipra glancing in his direction every now and then. It's good that he actually knows how to do this.

His hands are clumsy at first, but the skill recalls itself at the touch of the soft leaves on his fingertips. He learned this in his mother's house, a traditional craft across the hinterlands. The young coconut leaf, fresh and pale, is a perfect medium for sculpture. It's flexible enough to be curved and twisted around itself, but stiff enough to assert its own pressure, to contribute to the shape. Mother-of-Glory once told him that the art was old when she was young, long before the coming of the Path.

"Once upon a time," Fetter says, as if speaking to the construction taking shape in his hands. "A long time ago, nearly all of this . . . land, everything north of the Hanu, was jungle." He'd almost said *island*. Mother-of-Glory's stories have squirmed deeper under his skin than he'd thought. Isn't he retelling another one right now?

Out of the corner of his eye, he sees Pipra lean back a little from the laptop, and knows she's listening. "It was wild, like the people were wild then, but it was known-jungle. It wasn't the stranger forest that once covered all Jambu before the Ten Thousand Years of Ash, when the people were still exploring outward from the Land of the Wintering Crane, in the oldest days.

"In the known-jungle, the people knew every tree, every path, every beast by face and family. They knew where to find food, where to find shelter, where to cut and make their green cities, when to sacrifice the cities back to jungle.

"For seven times ten times a thousand years they did this, until the entire jungle was built upon reclaimed cities from one age or the other. This is what it meant for jungle to be *known*.

"For three times a thousand generations, when they sang their songs, they named the bards that first sang those songs in the great green halls that were now rich black soil under the oldest roots of the most ancient trees. They knew the pools and currents of ancestral soil by name.

"And when they made their halls and houses, when they made their art and monuments, when they made their amplifiers and containment fields for their devils—" Fetter hesitates, the word *devil* awkward in his mouth. In his mind's hollow, he says *laws and powers*. He looks through the corner of his eye, but no, still no devils.

Then he goes on: "When they made these things, they made them like this, out of leaf and bark and wood. They built their cities to rot. They loved the smell of decaying plant matter; it was part of the song to them, the promise that the jungle would accept the sacrifice. To make things that would *last*: they would have considered that obscene."

"You're fascinating," Pipra says, after he's silent for long enough that it's clear he won't continue. "Where's that from?"

"*Exorcism Rituals in the Luriati Hinterlands*. Roughly paraphrased," Fetter says, smiling. "As told to the perhaps overly credulous author by some old coot just past Acusdab, and as generously interpreted by him. It's my favourite part."

"Acusdab," Pipra says, like a sigh. "Of course. I've read reviews of that book. You make it sound more interesting than they did."

He's not sure if she means Acusdab or the book. He shouldn't have mentioned Acusdab at all. Peroe has no connection to that place, except having read about it in a book. He can't remember how much of the story he just told was from the book—some of it was, for sure, but his words, the intonation, the rhythm of it, that was pure Mother-of-Glory.

Something in him likes to cross the boundaries of his selves, to bring Peroe ever closer to the brink of Fetter. For all his early training and his recent practice in lies, there is nothing so tempting as confession. Or perhaps it's just the desperate feeling in his heart, the sense of things ending.

The first pot takes shape under his hands. It took longer than he thought, but he had to recall the way of it. The second one comes a little faster; the third flows into shape like oil.

He's humming under his breath, an old song whose words he's forgotten. At first he vaguely thinks it's some Luriati pop song that he must have heard when he first came to the city, even though he has no love for that kind of music. It's the small knife in his hands that reminds him what it is: the song of sharpening that Mother-of-Glory taught him so long ago.

The knife doesn't seem to get any sharper, but then, it was never dull.

What he's making is a seeming-pot. The art of the coconut leaf is about semblance, a magic of sympathy and evocation. Everything made from them is a seeming, a mimicry of a real object that evokes its symbolic function in a fleeting, biodegradable form. A seeming-canopy evokes shelter without providing it; a seeming-spear evokes protection without the capability for violence; seeming-fences represent boundaries without enforcing them.

The seeming-pots, then, represent fullness and containment. They are placed in a grid, reinforcing each other, around a site to declare it temporarily sacred. Ground zero of a marriage, for example, or a funeral. Mother-of-Glory assigned him a similar task at his grand-uncle's funeral, the very one he had murdered while she watched—to take a little knife and a pile of coconut leaves to make seeming-fences around the closed coffin. He remembers admiring her gall, but at the time he had thought the exercise to be about himself, to train him against displays of guilt. It's only in hindsight that he understands that it was more for her: that it was less gall and more spite, just tremendous, petty vindictiveness, her triumphant excision of a very old grudge, a triumph so secret that she didn't even mention it to *him*, her knife, until years and lifetimes later. He can't help smiling.

"You look happy," Pipra says. "Those are good. Where'd you learn to do that? I got the first two done earlier by this kid from Look-There-Lies-Land."

"I don't even know where that is," Fetter says, laughing. "A coastal town, I assume."

"Yes, up north," Pipra says. "Hinterlanders, don't you know. They have a big tradition of devil dances up there. I would have got him to do the whole set, but he's my best software guy so I need him doing equipment calibrations, not the fucking décor that we need to have to not piss off the feudal throwback monk from hell. I thought I'd have to beg the kid to work an evening shift."

Fetter nods. "I did a semester in the field studying hinterlander funeral practices—south of Luriat, but it looks like it's much the same style." Sometimes he doesn't even know how he lies so smoothly. Where did that even come from? "I'll make sure they don't look mismatched. How many do we need for the whole set?"

"Seven inside," Pipra says. "Eleven outside the pavilion, and twenty-three around the site boundary. Thank you so much!" And she's back at the laptop.

Fetter rolls his eyes, or rather, Peroe does. That's just for her benefit. In truth, this is the best possible job he could have. He has time to plan and an excuse to move freely around the site, ostensibly placing the seeming-pots.

With the very occasional quick glance, he keeps an eye on the little relic box. Pipra's grip on it has become less white-knuckled.

After a while, she puts it down on one of the plastic boxes next to her. He wonders if that's the first time she's put it down all day. Maybe his arrival *has* been helpful to her. Maybe she likes having him around. A sense of mourning rises in him.

This is the end, he thinks. If I do what I'm thinking of doing, this is the end of Peroe. I'll be throwing away all the work I've put in with Coema and Tomarin and Gerau, giving up my access to Nine Yellow Oxen, to the Cooksferry experiments, throwing away my seeming-Peroe. And yes, along with the mourning there is guilt, though he doesn't want to look at it.

I never *did* anything with Pipra, he tells himself. This time there's no *yet* in it, but that doesn't help. The guilt is about the lies now, because the lies are so close to being over.

Stealing the relic is easier than he'd dared to hope for. For a long time, he works on the seeming-pots with great concentration. There are three concentric circles: one inside and one outside the pavilion's walls, and a greater circle encompassing the entire team and all the equipment. He borrows a notebook and pencil from Pipra to calculate precise positioning to avoid disharmonics, and walks around to reposition pots frequently, perfecting the enclosure, growing ever more invisible to the people around him.

He makes small talk with Pipra on and off whenever she's in the pavilion. She gets busier as the afternoon wears on into evening, called away more frequently by one or more groups of people. She leaves the relic box in the pavilion, along with her laptop.

"Don't worry, I'll wrap these up and be gone before the security team gets here for the sweep," he says, as she comes back into the pavilion after a dozen such interruptions. "Thanks for letting me hang out and help."

"Thank you, you're great," Pipra says, automatically, distracted. "I'll see you at Cooksferry sometime soon?"

"Sure," he lies, and this is the first lie that's felt false in his mouth. It sticks to his palate.

There's one last step before the *last* step. He tears a page from the borrowed notebook and writes a brief note. He worries over its phrasing briefly, but it's short enough. It's the signature he spends the longest time over. He folds and refolds the note as if it were a coconut-leaf sculpture, though the paper lacks vitality and he can only make a basic flower shape. A tiny white lotus, smaller than his littlest finger.

When he's ready, he picks a moment—a very brief moment, as it turns out, but long enough—when he's alone in the pavilion with the last seeming-pot. His thumbs ache from the work, but his belly is unclenched, his feet light and fleet, aching to move. When the moment comes, he moves without thinking, smooth as if oiled over rails. He puts the knife down where he found it, with the last leftover bits of unused leaf, picks up the last seeming-pot in one hand, so far so normal, then he takes three quick sideways steps out of his life, his lips a little open and his breath shallow, his feet light and quick. He opens the relic box with his free hand, palms the relic while slipping in the folded paper white lotus to replace it, closes the relic box, and walks out of the pavilion, all in the space of a few breaths, just as Pipra walks back in.

Fetter mouths *bye* at her and she waves, barely seeing him. Oh good, he thinks. I finally hate myself. He feels it land in his gut like a rock, winding him a little. He can't seem to get a deep breath going again.

He still doesn't rush. This is what training is for, deferral and revanche: to wait in silence and act without hesitation.

Fetter takes a few minutes to make sure the last seeming-pot is properly placed. Then he walks casually out of the school premises, smiling at the soldiers at the gate, and flags down a tuktuk with the hand that's not holding his father's wisdom tooth tucked between thumb and palm.

It's harmless. It can't hurt him. He hadn't prepared for that, but it changed his ordering of priorities and consequences: it changes the possibilities arrayed before him.

The tuktuk takes him back into the city proper. He doesn't go home, but to the nearest light rail station. If Pipra's discovered his theft already, the Peroe identity will not stand up to scrutiny—it was a flimsy cover meant for light subterfuge, relying on everybody taking him at face value. The Ministry's investigators will find fingerprints or DNA evidence and identify him as Fetter from the citizen database. It's possible, if not yet likely, that the Ministry has already sent troops to his apartment building. It's too risky to ever go home again, though he is reasonably sure this has not happened, that in fact Pipra hasn't yet realized the relic is gone, and most probably will not until morning when she opens the box to show to Salyut. That's if he's lucky, and he has so often been lucky.

*Please let me be lucky one more time*, he thinks, though he doesn't think of this as a prayer and he's not sure who he's addressing it to. Not destiny or fate, which he still dares abjure. Perhaps just the world that surrounds him, the other to his self, the not-Fetter that has always enwrapped him, held him close when nobody else did. Hasn't he led a charmed life, when all is said and done? One more night is all he asks for.

He takes the light rail across the city to the coastline, head down and nodding and anonymous with one hand loosely slung onto a strap, the other hand in his pocket, fingers curling around the tooth. He imagines it red-hot, crisping his fingers where he rolls it between them. He tries not to wince. At the station, he buys a ticket for the heavy rail, the fast overnight train south to Acusdab.

# 21

Morning light out of the window reveals the long-abandoned fields of outer Acusdab gliding by. The train is already slowing. Outside is the familiar detritus of slash-and-burn agriculture gone to an uncanny half-rot, punctuated in the middle distance by long-limbed devils like radio towers or scarecrows. Indistinct and further away, vast creatures move slowly like great cranes. The water in what had once been fields is reduced to a thin black gruel, the air still and dry, so dry. He breathes it in and the old forgotten thirst comes back to him. Already Luriat's humidity seems like an interruption in his life, a brief submergence—he clamps his jaws and resists this impression.

He's not walking back into his old life. He's visiting his mother, who is dying, with his father's tooth in his hand.

All night he felt alone, cut off from the world. He feels distant, disregarded, as if the world's attention was elsewhere. He supposes this is good. This is where he ought to be, alone and unseen.

Deferral, revanche, and murder. The old curriculum.

With a drowning feeling, he faces the thought he's been pushing away since he took those irrevocable sideways steps and threw away two of his lives: both the identity of Peroe, all the friends and relationships he made wearing the name of that stranger he's never met, his . . . connection, perhaps, with Pipra, which is over before it even started; and much bigger than that, the identity of Fetter, the Luriati Fetter, the new self he wore in the city, the one familiar to Koel and Caduv and all the people he's met and known and helped and loved in the Sands and in the city, the life he'd truly thought of as his own.

He thinks of Hej and he aches. He thinks of Hej's face, his smile, his hands, the low burr of his voice, the scratching of his beard. He aches, but there is also a low shameful breathing out, release, relief. All those lies of omission, all the secrets he's kept; he can let go of that guilt from never opening up, never sharing his truth, never loving more than he feared.

*I can never go back to Luriat.* He holds that blazing-red thought carefully, at arm's-length as if with tongs, his face half turned away from its heat. That life is over. All those lives are over; Fetter in disguise, Fetter the rebel, the lover, the friend, the advisor, the false scholar, the true student, the liar, the cheater, the thief.

He imagines that the Ministry of Health will have sounded the alarm over the theft by now. Pipra will report to Coema, who will be outraged by the betrayal. He will loop in Gerau, who will bring her believer's fanaticism to her rage. Health will call Defense, who will sweep aside the flimsy protection of his false identity as Peroe with contemptuous ease. Perhaps they will go after the real Peroe first, the student whose life he stole, the student he's never met. But that misdirection will not last long; soon enough Defense will know Fetter's face and name. They will summon a swarm of paramilitary police to his apartment building, surround it with drums, kick in his door, arrest everybody that he had ever known or associated with. The guilt starts to coalesce in his belly like a stone.

Oddly, Fetter discovers he's not so worried about Koel and the others in the group. He is confident in their ability to weather this storm, either to brazen it out with Koel's connections and Caduv's power, or to go into hiding, to vanish into some underworld. His guilt centres on the people in the Sands and those who'd passed through it: his casual friends and acquaintances, all the people he's helped, answered questions from, accompanied to one office or the other to fill out forms for them. And the real Peroe, and his family. The police would come for them all. The heavy boots and the drums, oh devils, the drums. There are so many people who know his name, who've knocked on his door, who've come to him for help. He had signed so many government forms as a witness or reference; they have his haecceity strings, and the database will throw up every single one of those people as a suspect in a terror network. Innocent people, his ever-changing neighbours in the building, people across the Sands telling each other to *ask Fetter*, people who've moved all over the city by now, all those people who were never chosen by anyone except the people who loved them, never tangled in any destinies except their own, the innocently shadowed, the guiltlessly weighted. By what right had he done this to them all? When Peroe's mother lent her son's identity to Koel, it was supposed to be for discreet access to some councils of the moderately high, not grand theft and scandal. He should have been able to return Peroe's identity after concluding his "research," with no one ever knowing that there had briefly been two of them. Now the real Peroe and his mother will both be arrested for collusion, at best, unless Koel steps in to protect them.

Why is it Koel's role to be the protector and not mine, Fetter asks himself, though he already knows and dislikes the answer. He had not even thought of those his actions would hurt. No, that's another lie. He had thought of them, but his need had been more urgent. He had considered and refused the role and responsibility of a protector, even when the mantle attempted to settle on his shoulders. Hadn't he long been bored of being the answerer of questions and the guide of lost newcomers? He tries to summon up some of that devilish, uncaring urgency again, that wilful agency, that memory of fire, but it dissipates in the quiet and enforced inaction of the train.

The stone in his belly starts to climb his chest. Its weight has a finality to it, as if his innards are petrifying, holding him down. He wonders if he could float now or ever again, even if he relaxed his stance and allowed himself to unclench; perhaps guilt will be his ballast from now on.

He does not test this, because he doesn't know that it's true. No, isn't it nonsense? He berates himself. He tries to think logically. What has he set in motion? What has he accomplished?

The Saint-General must have been informed by now. Or if not now, then very soon, when he arrives at the pavilion and finds it in disarray. Salyut will rage and reach for his phone. So his father must know, too.

But it would be too late for a warning, wouldn't it? That was what Fetter counted on when he took those sideways steps and threw away so much and so many.

His father would have already passed the Hanu mountains. Right now he is either being driven north in a vehicle, walking on foot, or camped for the night. There is no way he can outpace the train.

Fetter can't resist a smile. He can see it reflected in the glass of the half-open window of the carriage. An ugly smile. He's ashamed of it, but he can't seem to wipe it off his face.

The overnight train south is quick as the stab of a knife. It's as if he suddenly stepped close to his father, reaching him all at once from a great distance. He thinks of his long-unpracticed technique, the long-unsung song of sharpening. A simple arithmetic of murder: he moved south fast on the train while his father was moving slowly north on foot or in convoy. A surprise killing blow, impossible to dodge.

If his understanding of Pipra's paper was correct, if Relic

*a* has the effects on his father that she predicted, then the old man would have seized and died at some point during the night, as the fast train swept south with the relic bright and hot in Fetter's hand, his eyes red and unsleeping.

Did the Perfect and Kind die in his sleep, in a tent, twisting and spasming and falling from his camp bed, only to be discovered in the morning?

Had he died with his eyes suddenly rolling back, a death rattle in his throat, in the back seat of a hired SUV while Vido shouted helplessly from the driver's seat and almost overturned the vehicle trying uselessly to stop, to turn, to drive back faster than the old man could die?

Had he died walking, falling like a felled tree between one step and the next, the sainted light in his eyes cutting out like a lighthouse going dark forever?

# 22

There are devils gathered for miles around Mother-of-Glory's house.

At first, Fetter doesn't recognize that their attention has a focus. It seems only that as it approaches Acusdab the slowing train draws into a sea of devils, more than he's ever seen at one time. The train halts. He steps off onto the platform, eyes fixed straight ahead, pretending not to see the invisible world restless and swarming around him.

Devils don't swarm, in Fetter's expert opinion. They don't crowd each other. They're not like people, or animals; they don't have a language of touch, display no social behaviour that he's ever seen. There is a reason the older term for devils is *invisible laws and powers*, Fetter reminds himself. Mother-of-Glory taught him this, and he's seen it in his reading, deep in the heart of abstruse footnotes. The devils are not a people or a species. They don't groom or fuck or fight or die. They may not be alive, or even truly be a *them*, as he understands the theory, not beings with a consciousness or sense of self that a mortal would recognize. They are principles of the world's operation. They are gears and wheels; they are interlocking, grinding teeth. Or so it is supposed, at the most sophisticated level of mortal thought that he has ever encountered. There is no telling if this is any more or less true than the childhood terror of monsters that they still evoke in him.

There are people moving about the station and the street

outside, too—Acusdab is not a big town, and Fetter has already recognized some faces, though not so much that he could put a name to them—and the devils seem to avoid them, much as they always do. The devils sidle alongside and around, never occupying the same space as each other or any living thing, plant or animal, but passing intangibly through all manner of inorganic material at will, including the earth itself, sinking in and rising again, never quite underfoot. Even in haunted Acusdab, the devils have never filled up so *much* of the negative space before, devils like water in the air, an unfamiliar humidity. His skin horripilates despite his best efforts at self-control. He keeps his eyes down and walks as if deep in thought, allowing his feet to lead him home.

It's a walk of a few hours to his mother's house from the train station, uphill with a gentle slope. He had thought it was closer. Of course, he hadn't taken the train out of Acusdab. Back then there had been no train, no station, no nearby highway, no faint traces of oil or city smoke in the air. He breathes it in, discarding those minor notes, and tries to remember: heavy, bright air, mostly clean of pollution. Woodsmoke, easily distinguished from exhaust. Cowdung. The bitterness of fields gone fallow. Dust on his tongue, his skin giving up the stored water in its cells. He blinks to keep his eyes from drying out. He should have brought a water bottle, like a tourist. Left the empty plastic on some devil-doctor shrine amidst the red hurtflowers.

The doctors' shrines are everywhere in Acusdab, in much the same way and for the same functions as Behinder temples in Luriat.

Acusdab feels smaller than he remembers. It's become a province, both in the world and in his head. When he was a boy it *was* the world, but more than that, it was a sovereign territory, an ancient nation. As a boy he ran these dry low hills, sloshed thigh-deep in the swamps, never coming to a border until the day he left—until he was *sent out*. It's still formally an Autonomous Territory, with that Envoy in Luriat representing it, but now that he's come back, he can't help but see Acusdab through the eyes of the people he knows from Luriat. Would Hej find it dull and bucolic, empty of culture? Would Pipra find it interesting enough to study? Would Koel deign to walk from door to door in this exhausted, enervated place? Would Caduv want to come and perform here, where there is no theatre except the dry, exhausted grass at the foot of a hill, where there is no music aside from bawdy drinking songs and red-mouthed ritual chants that climb the hearer's spine like a thorny creeper?

Well, perhaps he would. Caduv understands that kind of power.

As Fetter nears the house, he hears drumming, rhythmic shouting, the stamp of heavy feet. He knows that sound. The doctors are dancing. He raises his eyes from his own feet; he's prepared, braced so that he won't freeze or stumble at the sight of devils or doctors, though he still almost does. For hours, ever since he arrived—no, ever since he left Luriat—the hollow of his chest has felt like a dark well, deep and obscure. Now cold water wells up in it, flooding in from the base of his spine, filling him up, shocking his lungs and his heart.

Further up the path is his mother's house. The sun above is bright and merciless. The earth all around the house has been cleared for what seems like a mile. Before him are doctors and devils, dancing. The soil under their feet is dark, as if watered with sweat, or perhaps it's blood—some of the doctors are bleeding from their bare feet, from the hooks in their bodies that lead to their wrapping chains of bondage, from their ears and rolled-back eyes. At first sight, it seems that there is no pattern to the dance, the dancers seen and unseen responding to different calls. The devils move as their inhuman bodies allow, spidery limbs trembling, crawlers writhing, elongated bodies swaying like trees in a storm; the doctors spin at wild angles, flinging their arms out and bringing them back in, their feet a blur, howling through their fishhooked mouths, the drummers among them lifting and stamping their feet in rolling, folded rhythms as if the earth itself were another instrument. Then the movements resolve themselves in Fetter's wild eyes, and he sees them as great wheels within wheels of dancers, encircling and slowly rotating around Mother-of-Glory's house, the devils moving sunwise and the doctors opposed. He blinks, and he sees them all together, not a sea of dancers but a whirlpool with his mother's house in its maw. As he walks into it the clarity and organization of the dance vanishes, and there is only swirling chaos around him.

The only blessing is that doctors and devils alike ignore him. The devils slip out of his way and back into place as he passes, avoiding contact smoothly and without apparent effort, just as they dance amidst the doctors without, as far as he can tell, touching a one. The doctors do not move out of his way, though Fetter thinks this is no more a rudeness than the devils' avoidance is a politeness; they are simply caught up in their ritual and do not register his presence. There are few of them, relative to the devils; Fetter walks around them instead. He wonders if they are far gone enough to see the invisible laws and powers that surround them.

The sun beats down on him so fiercely that he can feel his scalp desiccate, the individual hairs wilting. The heat in Acusdab is like a weight. He'd forgotten that.

The house seems lonely when he reaches it. The doctors and devils do not approach closer than a few yards from the door. The boundary is guarded by a lone tree-stump that has not been plucked out of the bare earth. His mother used to sit here when she taught him. The house feels mean and poor to him now. It is large but low and ramshackle, one expansive storey sprawling horizontally, not like the rising towers and stacked mansions of Luriat. He used to think of it as a vast and singular space: now it seems segmented into parts that fit and interlock imperfectly. Most sections are wattle and daub, thatched in dry coconut leaf; some are brick and mortar, unplastered; others are metal with paint peeling off in weeping diamonds, perhaps repurposed containers. The brick sections are roofed in cracked clay tiles—he remembers his childhood bedroom like this—and sometimes in asbestos sheets turned black under the sun. Sometimes there is no ceiling. Inside the house, deeper in the maze, he remembers tunnels and rooms of cold grey stone. He's not sure which sections of this house are the oldest. It should logically have been the stone, he always thought, but it always felt foreign, as if it didn't belong at the top of this low dry hill. The wattle and daub felt oldest to him, then and now.

The garage out back is probably still just three wooden poles holding up a rusted tin roof and sheltering the same puttering old car she used to drive him to his practice murders in. He can't remember its colour. A pale green? Perhaps it had been bright, once. He wants to walk all the way around the house sunwise and scout the territory before entering, perhaps confirm his fading memory of the car. He recognizes this desire as procrastination.

The door to the house is closed. It seems strange to him now, a simple closed wooden door with no inset glass or other transparencies, but there are no bright doors in Acusdab. He opens the door and enters the house. After these hours of travelling, he feels urgency; the cold water in him rising to his throat, brackish, making him thirsty.

Inside, the temperature drops from the unbearable directness of sunlight to a more muted, intimate heat. He half expects to see her as soon as he crosses the threshold, coming to greet him or berate him, but she's not there. There is a smell, though, a pervasive stink of kerosene. Before his eyes adjust to the half-dark, he stumbles on something. He looks down at his feet and sees a bundle of oil-soaked wood—there are many all around him. This house is a funeral pyre.

He moves through the house as if in a dream, stepping between the stacks of oil-drenched firewood waiting for a spark. There are no devils inside, no doctors. The house is empty, except for firewood and the smell of oils. As he moves further in, he smells something other than kerosene. A familiar funeral scent, oil of sweet basil. He follows the scent, doubling back whenever it gets weaker. Eventually, he turns a corner and sees an open doorway where there should not be one, glowing with blinding light. He's too deep in the house to have reached the outside, and yet there is a door. He walks through it. His eyes are lidded low against the sun, but it still blinds him for a moment. He steps backward to the threshold and leans on the jamb to steady himself.

He is not outside. It is a large inner courtyard, enclosed by walls on all sides, some intact, some broken. He doesn't remember any courtyard in the middle of the house, but as his eyes adjust, he sees the wreckage that fills it—the ruins of walls of wattle and daub, old dry coconut leaf thatch and firewood stacked upon it, the scattered trash of the house's former contents, pots and cloth and broken-bladed knives and staves of wood and spilling jars in stains of dark fluid and broken chests and shattered metal lockboxes and piled twists of ola parchment and shards of crockery, all rising into a rough mountain at its centre—and he understands. The courtyard is new. The doctors must have broken down this entire section to turn the house into a pyre. This new funereal courtyard is absolutely soaked in oil of sweet basil; the smell even overpowers the kerosene. He walks into the open space, the scent wrapping around him like a cloak.

The courtyard is larger than he'd thought at first, like an inedible seed gutted from the flesh of the house—the house that looked intact from outside, but is in truth a rind of itself. He remembers a particular one of his mother's many storage rooms, where he once found a lacquer box with a lock of his baby hair and the nail that ripped his shadow from him. That was about where he's standing now. He wonders if that box too is broken open and buried in the rubble. The box and the hair would burn, he supposes. Maybe the nail will be all that's left in the ashes, other than the strange bones of the house in stone or brick or metal, whatever will refuse to burn or melt. Now he understands why the doctors cleared so much land around the house: they're wary of starting a forest fire.

Fetter walks carefully over the rubble, feet slipping on stray bricks. He follows the rising of the slope with his eyes, and then with his feet, climbing carefully, and then on all fours as he reaches its apex.

And there she is, lying at its top. If she'd been raised any higher, he would have seen her rising above the house as he approached. As it is, the pyre is only a little higher than the roof—what's left of it, an encircling barrier. The house is itself at the top of a gentle hill, so they've raised her up as if for a sky burial. She's the highest point for miles around. She's dressed in white, her dark and shiny skin a net of fine wrinkles. White for death: that's a Luriati fashion. Even Acusdab has not been immune.

Her feet, the first thing he sees, are bare and clean. He climbs to the top and sits by her, carefully finding a mostly intact wooden beam to rest his weight on.

Mother-of-Glory opens her eyes. "Oh, you're here," she says. Her voice is a dry rasp and her tone is without inflection, so he can't tell if she's surprised by him or disappointed in him. Probably both, as usual.

"I'm here," he says. His voice is warm and rough. It shocks him when it comes out of his mouth.

# 23

"Well," Mother-of-Glory says.

Fetter waits to hear more, but she is silent. Her eyes are open, though, and looking at his face. He opens his palm and shows her the tooth. It's been clenched in his fist for hours.

"I've committed the Fifth Unforgivable," he says. The assassination of the Perfect and Kind. Then he remembers. "And the Fourth, too." Patricide. If the Perfect and Kind had known his own son would be his assassin, he could have designated one fewer Unforgivable and optimized his schema.

"No," Mother-of-Glory says, though she's smiling. She lets out a hacking cough. When she speaks again, her voice has a worrying, liquid burr to it. "Where did you get that?"

"Luriat. I stole it from someone," Fetter says. "No, I have killed him. I timed it right. He came too far north to have survived." He explains his reasoning and his actions, in brief. He doesn't explain how wretched he feels at his betrayal of Pipra, his abandonment of Hej, the people he condemned to prison or worse. She would only grunt at such distractions. He spends more time on the theft. He feels a need to emphasize his cleverness, so he describes it in detail.

"You stole it back," Mother-of-Glory says, and makes a noise that he thinks is a kind of laugh. "That thing was stolen from me a few years ago by a visiting researcher. Thank you for returning it."

Fetter is not sure if Mother-of-Glory has ever thanked him

before, but this is almost lost in the swirl in his mind. "What did you mean, *no*? Is it a lie, about the power it has over him? They were sure it would kill him if it got too close. He's coming north by convoy—he should be very close to here. He must be in range."

"Oh, it would have killed him, if he were near," Mother-of-Glory says. "That was how I made it. But you underestimate your father, son."

"You *made* this?"

"I slapped it out of his mouth myself," Mother-of-Glory says. "The night he left us."

"You said you were sleeping!"

"I never said any such thing." Mother-of-Glory frowns. The wrinkles in her face change, like a net slowly bowing in deep water. "That was what *he* said of us. I told you his story, the one which named both of us."

"You were awake?"

"I woke before he left," Mother-of-Glory says. "We fought. He didn't originally mean to leave the island behind, you see. He was building an ideological empire. He wanted me to be his subservient plenipotentiary in the north, you the heir to his new throne. I slapped his tooth out of his mouth. I summoned every bit of power I had, called in every favour owed from the invisible laws, mustered every dreg of puissance I had ever learned, and I picked up his bloody tooth and put into it my curse. I banned him from my island for as long as I lived. I told him to get the fuck off my land. He spat blood and walked away quickly, even as the curse began to settle and the tooth slowly began to exert its influence on him. The rest is as I told you. His breaking of the island was revenge for what I had done. He took away what made us special, took away our lives and memories. But he could never cross the Hanu again as long as I held this boundary with the tooth in my possession, and so his cult fractured. The Path Behind formed from all those left behind in his absence, from the strange, fractured heresies they came up with without him."

"Heresy leading to factionalism," Fetter says. "The Second Unforgivable. You already committed it."

Mother-of-Glory nods. "It was not enough. He can still reclaim them."

"He can't if he died when I came south," Fetter says.

"It was a good effort. A very good effort," Mother-of-Glory says. She sounds consoling, and this scores a jagged scratch across his heart. "But you must understand what you are up against. Here in my place I am a power in my own right, but a small one as such things are measured—you are a strong little weapon, perhaps, if not a power—but *he* is a true power, a chosen one. He has raised mountains and broken time over his knee. He cannot be defeated by an overnight train and good timing. Without his own tooth in my house, even my curse could not have kept him away."

"I don't understand how he could have escaped," Fetter says.

"By deciding never to have been there," Mother-of-Glory says. She is speaking very slowly now, the hoarseness of her voice deeper and rougher. "He comes because he knows I am dying. When I go, the curse will break and the tooth will just be a tooth. He may have been walking slowly, triumphantly, to see my pyre. But when he felt your attack, he would simply choose that the world be otherwise."

"He can do that?"

"He did it with the mountains," Mother-of-Glory reminds him. "He did not come into danger: it will have been so. There *is* a world where he was walking north while you came south on the train, but this is no longer that world. Now that you have attacked him, now you have struck and missed, he knows you.

In this world where he knows you, he never came north over land at all, never came within range of the curse. He merely waited until I died, then took a plane to Luriat."

Fetter starts to say that's not possible, and then looks south. The Hanu mountains are hazily visible on the horizon.

"Go south and see, if you don't believe me," Mother-of-Glory says. "Walk the swamp path south from Acusdab. It will lead you to the main cart track, which now connects to the southern highway. Walk on it for a few hours—a day, two days—as long and as far as you need. You could walk all the way to the mountains. You will not meet your father on the road."

Fetter says nothing. He already believes her, but he resolves to confirm it for himself. He tries to organize his thoughts, which whirl as if caught in a firestorm. So much that had seemed settled and ended is now undone. So much is up in the air again.

"And the tooth?" he says, at last. He's still holding his palm out, the tooth sitting on it. His mother shrugs, and he turns his hand over, letting the tooth fall and vanish into the small gaps in the makeshift funeral pyre.

"The tooth was an old weapon," Mother-of-Glory says. "It served. It is blunted. You are the new weapon."

"I failed, though," Fetter says. He shakes his head. He refused this quest once. Why has he taken it up again? Because he had seen the world the Path Behind has made? Because his mother asked? Because of the pogroms and the Almanac and the camps, or because she was dying and he wanted her to die happy?

"Don't forget how the world may be changed," Mother-of-Glory says, and closes her eyes.

Intentional, directed violence—his attempt was certainly directed, as precisely aimed a strike as he could have made, knowing only what he knew then. Why had she never told him his father's capabilities? But then she did, when she told him the story of the Hanu mountains. That had been a lesson but he had only thought of it as a kind of origin myth, a slightly fanciful history of himself. He had failed to account for it as a tactical reality.

Perhaps it is the intention that is lacking. He acted without truly understanding why he's acting: he has not been intentional so much as instinctive, floating on the opportune confluence of opportunity and method. And here he is, the fire at his back, still not understanding—

The funeral fire is lit, he understands too late. It has been lit for a while. His eyes were hazy, looking at his mother's still face and then looking at the mountains in the far distance. Slowly he understands the haze is partly smoke, from the burning shell of the house around him. Now that he's noticed it, the fire picks up speed. It is red and roaring, already climbing the pyre, though he feels no heat. He looks at his mother, but she doesn't move again.

Fetter stands, careful of his footing. The pyre is already starting to shift and give way underneath him. He descends the way he came, and makes it nearly all the way down before he loses his footing and falls forward. He catches himself on his hands, bruising one hard and unbalancing when the other breaks through a termite-softened plank. For a crazed moment, he thinks he will pull his hand out to find himself holding some talisman from his childhood, like the nail that once ripped his shadow from him. He pulls, and his hand comes out bloody but empty. He staggers to his feet. His clothes are blackening and curling. The fire is all around him, a great wavering orange-red storm, underfoot and overhead, burning the very clothes off his body. But he feels nothing. The fire is cool on his skin, like a soft wind. He remembers, dimly, childhood experiments quickly abandoned. It seems he guessed right as a boy. Fire doesn't burn him. Fire wishes him no harm. He could stand here and wait for the pyre to burn down and walk out clean but for ashes.

He doesn't blame the doctors for lighting the pyre with him still inside. Those childhood nightmares are poor creatures after all. They probably didn't even know he was here.

He walks out of the fire without hurry, finding his way by touch. Outside, the dance is still going, even faster and more frenzied than before. He turns and looks at the fire once he is outside of its embrace, and it is a pillar rising into the sky like a beacon. He wonders if his father sees it from wherever he is.

The clothes have burned off his body, but he feels no shame because there are only doctors and devils to see. The fire has touched no part of him: his skin is not even warm and his hair is untouched, even his eyebrows and lashes and fine body hairs. He thinks not of his mother, nor the tooth he brought south in his fist, but again of the nail he didn't find and hasn't seen since he was a boy.

Then he walks away, down the hill on the south side, looking for the swamp path, the cart track, the highway, with his mother's black mushroom cloud rising behind him.

# 24

Three days later Fetter is on the early morning train back to Luriat in stolen clothes, holding a ticket he bought with stolen money. The clothes are ill-fitting, the oversized camisa's short sleeves falling to his elbows. His skin itches. He avoided other trains because they seemed too full of refugees. There is no war in Acusdab—well, there *has not yet* been war in Acusdab, though who now knows what will befall it—but the train station was full of people fleeing Behinder pogroms deeper in the hinterlands, carrying their belongings on their back, clutching each other's hands. He avoided them and waited for a moment of relative emptiness, not wanting to be counted in their number. His train has only a few refugees. It makes many brief stops as it nears the city and grows crowded in turn, but the people around him are mostly commuters from the shallower hinterlands.

The train is well outside city limits when he notices that people around him are talking about his father. Mostly they talk about war and pogroms and the flood of southerners running north to Luriat, yes—and is that not still about his father? They talk about hinterlander monks of the Path Behind leading those pogroms against the pathless, firebrands and firestarters like Ripening Wisdom, their speeches quoted, sometimes with the approval of light and chuckling condemnation. You know: our boys will be boys; someone had to say it; that one's not much of a monk but by the gods he has the right of it—*those* conversations he has heard a thousand times in Luriat. But this time they are also talking about his father himself, not only as a causal principle, but in the flesh.

At first Fetter doesn't notice this distinction, lost as he is in frustrated reverie. He searched the road south for his father almost as far as the mountain pass before giving up, and it seems natural to his weary unconscious that his father should occupy everybody's mind as much as his own. But slowly it occurs to him that the quiet conversations he is eavesdropping on are part of the outside world, not an accompaniment to his own thoughts.

From fragments and mutterings, he gathers that the Perfect and Kind arrived in Luriat a day or two earlier and is already holding sessions for vast crowds. The speakers are more concerned with the effect on traffic than of the historical import of this visit.

Fetter is still mulling this over when the train stops at a station just outside city limits. Soldiers enter the train, checking every person's identification. Fetter barely has time to remember that his identification is lost—Peroe's borrowed identity card would have burned up in the fire along with his clothes, and he hadn't spared a thought for it until just now—before he finds himself trying to explain his lack to an impatient soldier, who keeps his weapon pointed casually at Fetter's chest the whole time.

He is bundled off the train along with a dozen others. Some, like Fetter, have no identification at all; some do, but have been designated suspicious for other reasons. They are all searched, any belongings examined, then taken to a small room just off the station platform. There is no door to shut, this close to Luriat, so the detained group can see commuters coming and going outside while they sit on a long bench. Fetter sees devils, too: white-armed antigods, long and thin, moving in eerie rhythms, effortlessly not touching the people around them except when they reach out and pat someone on the back to plague them. The devils do not turn to look at him, and he is careful not to attract their attention. He wonders if they can smell the smoke of his mother's pyre on him. He wonders if they were there, dancing for her.

The detainees are processed three at a time by uniformed officers sitting at desks in front of them. A pair of armed policemen flank the entrance.

The queue proceeds in order of seating, which was random— Fetter sat near the leftmost edge of the bench and discovers that he is therefore at the bottom of the queue. The policemen's desks are only a few feet from the bench, so the interviews are audible to those waiting in the queue. Both questions and answers sound inane to Fetter. Dry questionnaires and recitations of addresses and claims. The policemen seem as weary as the detained; they hardly seem to listen to the answers, coming alive only when they speak to each other, in an unending and incomprehensible stream of banter and gossip.

Waiting for his turn, Fetter tries not to grind his teeth or to think of his father in the city.

As each of the detainees completes their interviews, they are returned to the bench to sit and wait. By the time it's Fetter's turn, the entire queue has reformed itself with him at its head, as if he has been regurgitated. He feels like a spat-out bone. A policeman nods tiredly to him, and he moves at last from the bench to the interview station. His calves and thighs are cramping a little—perhaps the bench was just a little too low, forcing an awkward posture, or perhaps he is just tired from all the walking he's done in the last couple of days.

The small chair at the interview station is also a little short. He wonders if the discomfort is intentional, but no, he thinks, it is simple indifference. The boredom on his interviewer's face makes him feel forgotten and disposable, but it would have been easier to fight that feeling if he had sensed intentional manipulation. Even manipulation would speak of a kind of care that's absent in this room. They don't care, because the outcome of this room is already decided. He tries to pay more attention to his immediate situation. This is dangerous, and he is being careless. If only he didn't feel so tired, so sick of everything, his father, this unsane country. If only he weren't worn out from strange grieving, aching from effort that he had been *warned* would be fruitless but that he couldn't stop himself from doing anyway—

The policeman asks his name, race, caste, residence, origin, and any proof or documentation he might have of any of those things.

He almost blurts out Peroe's name. But no, there is nothing on him to tie him to Peroe. Instead, he names himself Fetter, gives his assigned race and caste from memory, the address of his apartment in the Sands, and . . . what is his origin? Acusdab, he supposes. He says that, which earns him the slightest raised eyebrow. The policeman has been writing down his answers on a piece of paper—not a form, just a stray piece of paper with a jagged edge as if it had been torn from a notebook. But he pauses on this last answer.

"How do you spell that?" the policeman asks, and Fetter spells it in Luriati hellspeak. The policeman writes it down, frowns, scratches it out and rewrites it differently. "Like this?"

Fetter peers at the upside-down writing, which spells out something like Cusdaba, or perhaps Cusadaba. He tries to correct this, which irritates the policeman.

"You don't even know where you're from," the policeman says.

"Luriati dialect has a few extra letters that Acusdabi doesn't have," Fetter says, starting to explain, but the policeman waves this away.

"When you come to a new place, you should learn the language," the policeman says. "And get a shadow, while you're at it. Don't they have those where you come from?"

"This one doesn't even speak the language?" asks the policeman at the next table, still scribbling away at his notes on his last interviewee. He doesn't raise his head to look at either his colleague or at Fetter, who tries to figure out the difference in meaning, if any, between the detailed notes the other policeman is making and the few scrawled and misspelled lines documenting his own interview. Is it just that one policeman is more conscientious about documentation? Is it the other detainee or himself in greater trouble?

The policeman in front of Fetter doesn't answer, but instead leans back, ignoring Fetter and speaking to the other policeman. At first, Fetter doesn't understand at all what they're saying. It's almost as if the policeman's accusation has somehow come true, as if he no longer speaks the language—and that's not possible because spoken Luriati is virtually indistinguishable from spoken Acusdabi, notwithstanding the incomprehensible difference in pronunciation the policeman identified. But then the words start to sound familiar again, and Fetter understands the policemen are just speaking in unfamiliar slang, some kind of cop cant peppered with references to their institution and its various politics, their fellows and superiors, their workloads and favour-tradings.

In fact, the policeman is thanking his colleague for covering for him on airport VIP security detail the other day. It becomes clear slowly, like a fogged mirror, that the conversation he is following in fragments confirms Mother-of-Glory's prediction. The Perfect and Kind arrived by air three days ago, the plane landing only a few hours after the funeral pyre would have burned out. At that time, Fetter was still stumbling south, naked but for the ash in his beard and hair, searching by the side of a highway, or perhaps still stubbing his toes on rocks on the cart track. He stopped dead, he remembers, to let a large green rat snake cross his path. He thought he heard something; he looked up. He does not remember seeing a plane in that pitiless sky, but he had not been seeing clearly, right then. He almost stepped on the snake—he froze because he thought it might have been a devil, something serpentine in shape but otherworldly in origin, but as far as he could tell, it was just a snake.

The policeman is looking Fetter in the eye, suddenly, as if aware of his thoughts, or his attempt to follow the conversation, though this was hardly eavesdropping since they were after all talking right in front of him—Fetter looks away, uncertain, and in that moment the policeman stands and hits him in the face.

The blow isn't particularly painful; more a slap than a punch. Fetter is startled into a kind of wakefulness, a wariness, that feels more like himself. It was the first use of overt violence in the room, and he feels the other detainees become alert behind him. He's not sure if he was singled out, or if it's just that he was the last in the queue. The slap seems to signal a phase shift: the policemen all stand and usher the group out of the door. The armed policemen outside guide them out of the train station. They are shepherded into the back of a dingy brown van, which is slightly too small to hold all of them. There are no seats; they sit on the floor, crowded against each other, rocking when the van starts moving. One policeman is in the back with them, so the prisoners do not speak.

✎

Fetter's first prison is a comfortable hotel turned quarantine centre. The prisoners are led in a line through an empty parking lot and into a deserted lobby. They catch glimpses of uniforms that are not police or military, and Fetter guesses they are hotel staff, seconded or pressed into service as de facto prison staff. He didn't get a good look at the hotel's environs when finally released from the back of the van, but it seems to be somewhere green and peaceful, with no other buildings nearby. He hears birdsong and sees extensive grounds that look less well-maintained than they ought to have been, undead trees that seem artificial. He sees no birds. Perhaps the sounds are recordings.

The lobby is a large, modernist space with abstract sculptures and artfully exposed brick, a high ceiling with antique wooden rafters. The style is entirely Alabi, except that some of the sculptures are upmarket interpretations of Behinder iconography.

There is an intake desk in the lobby where every prisoner is photographed, fingerprinted, cheek-swabbed, throat-swabbed, nasopharyngeal-swabbed, blood-sampled, temperature-tested, and strip-searched. The staff at the desk are in full-body protective suits complete with masks and gloves, even though the accompanying policemen and soldiers are unmasked, ungloved, and in their ordinary uniforms. The prisoners are allowed to put their clothes back on afterward. Apparently they were supposed to be issued a standardized uniform, but there has been a mix-up and a delivery has not been made in time. There is some griping and cynical laughter from the people that work there. The prisoners do not participate.

The line of prisoners is led up several flights of stairs, where they meet nobody, and down a plush carpeted corridor, where they are fed into rooms one by one through doors of thick frosted glass.

The van had driven for what felt like hours, but from the glass doors Fetter knows they are still in or near Luriat. The policeman locks the door behind him; turning, Fetter can see him on the other side of the glass before he moves away, blurred but recognizable in his uniform. Pipra once told him that there were standardized measures of how frosted glass could be before it ran the risk of triggering the phenomenon of the bright doors. High-end hotels and stores made heavy use of frosted glass at the approved limit of opacity.

The room is small, air-conditioned, and comfortably, if blandly, furnished. There are heavy curtains on the windows and blocking the view behind another internal frosted glass door—an en suite bathroom, Fetter assumes. He looks back at the door to the corridor and finds the curtain rod above it on the inside. No curtain, though. This space was built for guests but has learned to hold prisoners. He tests the door to be sure it's locked. He searches the room and the small bathroom methodically. There are no obvious cameras or recording equipment, though there are plenty of places they could still be hidden which he wouldn't find without tearing up the room. The windows are sealed shut, but they are unbarred and the glass is clear and thin, ordinary window glass. Seeing this, Fetter relaxes a little.

He'd wondered as he was led out of the van, when he was briefly out in the open, whether he should try to escape into the sky, to leap and rise like a flame—breaking a lifetime's habit of secrecy and providing, no doubt, a nine days' wonder to police and prisoners alike. But it was too dangerous under an open sky. He would have no way to break his upward fall, and he has never been able to descend unassisted. The thought raised ancient childhood terrors of falling forever into the sky, of passing alone through the clouds, the eerie storms of the troposphere, choking as the air grows thin, a frozen body perhaps forever staring in the dark. He'd choked a little on his own spit, and one of the policemen gave him a pitying look, as if to call him a coward for choking on fear even in such luxurious accommodations, even with no sign of ill-treatment. After that he kept his eyes fixed firmly on the earth until he was under the hotel's roof again.

He isn't sure if the floating is still part of him. He has felt weighted ever since he walked out of his mother's pyre. Perhaps it burned out of him then. Perhaps if he had tried to float, he would merely have flopped pathetically under the eyes and the no doubt mocking laughter of the police. He resists the temptation to test it now, in his seeming-privacy. He cannot be sure he is not being recorded. He doesn't want to become their science experiment.

Still, it's a relief to see the window's thin glass. It makes him feel less trapped. It soothes the claustrophobic twisting in his belly. He could break the glass of the window. There is a small wooden chair in the room, which looks heavy and expensive. If he threw that chair, the window would definitely shatter. He is on, he believes, the fifth or sixth floor. He could float out of the window and move quickly along the building's surface, moving himself along window ledges and awnings. But he would probably still be seen. The problem is not getting out of the room, but escaping the area without being recaptured. In an urban area, or in a jungle, he would have had access to a third dimension of movement, but in wide flat open spaces like the extensive hotel grounds he saw outside, he could only run like anybody else. And, he reminds himself, he can't trust the floating without testing it, so even if he broke the window he might have to climb down five or six floors with his hands and feet. He is not at all confident he can do that as a weighted person. He certainly could not move quickly enough to get away. That would be the end of this low-security incarceration. If he is going to try to escape, he must wait for a better opportunity.

He doesn't truly believe the floating is gone. All his life has been defined by his tendency to float, and the necessity of keeping himself grounded, staying tight and clenched with his feet firmly placed on the ground. It could not possibly change so easily, so quickly. And yet—

Fetter sits on the edge of the bed and, gripping the wood of the bedframe, tries to allow himself to rise just a little. Not enough to be recorded by a camera or even noticed by an observer, just enough to lift the soles of his feet—he's barefoot, and the soles of his feet are filthy; how long has he been barefoot?—off the carpet by the breadth of a few hairs, to lift his ass just off the bed, just high enough that a helpful assistant could slip a sheet of paper underneath him as a kind of magic trick. But there is no helpful assistant, and he can't tell if it's working. He feels still the contacts in his seat and soles. It is impossible to test the ability under the threat of surveillance. He just can't be sure.

He sighs and allows his weight to drop back into himself, falling back to lie on the bed, unconsciously dirtying the clean hotel sheets with the ash and grime he doesn't even see he's still covered in.

# 25

After he's been removed from it, he estimates he only spent a few days in this first prison. Perhaps a week. It seems like much longer. At first, he opens the curtains every day to measure the passage of time, but grows irritated by light and leaves them closed, letting himself drift into the no-time of this no-place. The discrete tick tock of timepass becomes a liquid gurgle, as if he is submerged in the unending flow of a river in which the boundaries between objects dissolve into a slurry that passes into silt through his hands. No, there is no grit between his fingers, no hands, no eyes with which to not see them. There are moments of coming back to himself, marked by the slow understanding that he has not been himself. There: those are his hands. The veins bulge, climb the parallel bones like vines.

He discovers his own filth and cleans himself. The hotel-prison does not do laundry, but he cleans his own ill-fitting stolen clothes and sheets as best as he can in the bathroom.

When he grew tired of searching for his absent father and thought of coming back to the city, he followed the queasy sensation in his gut as he had long since learned to do, the discomfiting engine of his unconsidered decisions. It turned him down a small driveway off the highway where he found a small cluster of houses. It was a bright day, nobody about under a blazing sun. He walked through the first open gate and found an unlocked house, from which he took some clothes and money. He would have begged for help, or run away perhaps, if he had found anybody there, but the house was open and empty, with a cooking-pot simmering on the stove as if the residents had merely stepped out for a moment, or were lingering elsewhere in the house. An elderly dog lying under a couch raised its head to look at him, yawned, and went back to sleep. He didn't endanger this luck by attempting to choose his clothes or loot valuables. He simply took a handful of cash he found on a table—enough for a train ticket, which was all that mattered—and the topmost items from a pile of laundry, to cover his nudity so he could board a train: a camisa that must have belonged to someone with much broader shoulders, and soft long breeches tight at the calves, both much-worn and faded. Both are so stained from the ash of his body that they don't quite get clean, no matter how much he scrubs. He sits naked on the floor until his clothes dry.

There is nothing to do or read or look at, except the unchanging view of greenery out of the window or the TV in the room. He keeps an eye out for intrusions from the invisible world, but there are none to be seen, unless some of the specks in the sky are aviform devils.

He leaves the TV running with the volume low. There are six available channels, five of which are popular Luriati news and entertainment channels. He tries to follow the news, but it's as if his ears are packed with mud. He recognizes names, but the sentences bury themselves uncomprehended in the sludge. He tries to let the news rain on him. Perhaps some of it will sink in.

His father is prominently featured. The Perfect and Kind's first interview in Luriat is rerun so often that Fetter begins to recognize the footage as a ritual, the sacralized movements of his father's face, the ironic smiles and the iconic raising of a brow at what, Fetter reverse-engineers, must have been some small impertinence from the interviewer, a young woman wearing glasses with severe black frames and a dark purple lip.

Fetter can't quite understand the questions or the answers, and he wonders again if the policeman's accusation has dislodged language from his brain, but he can still follow expression and tone, and the interviewer seems to him more aggressive than he would have expected for the first interview of the Perfect and Kind on Luriati television. He would have expected Gerau and her coterie to have fed the programme softball questions. Perhaps it's all the same to the Perfect and Kind, one of the world's top ten living messiahs, a media personality for twenty-five centuries. His father seems unruffled. After seeing the interview another dozen times, Fetter thinks his father might even be . . . not amused, exactly, but perhaps entertained. Appreciative. Perhaps the Perfect and Kind is bored of sycophancy.

Fetter channel-surfs, lying in bed. His father is far from the only monk of the Path to feature in interviews. Celebrity monks of the Path Behind appear frequently on TV; he is familiar with their faces from the last few years of living in Luriat. They all have names like Ripening Wisdom or Shining Jewel of Truth or Huxley-from-Riverside, and they each cultivate slightly different areas of interest and modes of rhetoric that echo and reinforce each other but do not quite overlap. Ripening, for instance, is focused on street-level violence: promoting it for himself, organizing it among his supporters, denouncing his victims for provoking it. Shining is always haggard from staging a fast-unto-death to pressure some aspect of the Luriati power structure to promote temperance, vegetarianism, or abstinence among the people, or conversely, to bar or constrain Almanac-disapproved castes from involvement in the food and beverage industry, retail, or hospitality; from memorializing their dead; or from engaging in competitive worship during particular phases of the moon—especially in cases where a once-approved caste has fallen from grace in succeeding editions of the Almanac but the mundane world has not adapted quickly enough for his liking. Huxley's pet subject, meanwhile, is what he claims are the differential birth rates of races in Luriat, and the resultant dilutions and extinctions that he fears.

And there are other monks, endless others, from both the Path Behind and now also the Path Above, who have staked out territory in Luriat's culture wars. One endorses a faith healer from the hinterlands whose lucrative cult is compatible with Behinder lore, despite its increasing tally of preventable deaths; another promotes a racially exclusive social network for entrepreneurs, the app not having launched yet but due any day now; one monk reiterates that it is necessary for the racially pure to overcome the demands of the market and buy racially pure goods even if they are of lesser quality or more expensive or both; yet another calls for military intervention to protect a new ancient Behinder site of worship that he has just discovered, which is to say designated, in the far hinterlands, surrounded by races that he declares enemies of the faith. Even the occasional pathless talking head is featured, as long as they are sufficiently self-abnegating. Names and causes blur together as Fetter flips through the first five channels.

The sixth channel shows an empty room with a small wooden chair standing in the middle.

The picture is black and white, a little grainy. There is no audio, not even a hiss of white noise. It's difficult to tell the chair's scale with nothing in the image to compare it to. After flipping past the channel a dozen times, Fetter thinks the chair might be child-sized. At first, it is only an oddity. It might be a still image, perhaps some kind of test broadcast or a placeholder image for some channel currently not broadcasting. Perhaps it references some Luriati slang or idiom—asking the viewer to sit down and wait?—that he is unfamiliar with, a possibility he is more willing to consider than ever. Despite having lived in the city for years, despite having earned Luriati citizenship, he has neither been part of nor understood it.

He tries to remember his strings of haecceity, shifting his identity card back and forth in his mind's eye, the plastic laminate reflecting the light. He can only visualize fragments, never more than three or four sequential letters, numbers, or symbols out of the several dozen that form each string. Even those fragments might very well be from Peroe's borrowed identity card, which he studied more recently than his own. He had been in the habit of carrying both cards (Fetter in the left pocket, Peroe in the right) when he felt that he might need to switch quickly. Had he done that this time, and lost both in the fire? Or did he leave his own card behind in the apartment, as he sometimes did if there was a chance of being searched? If he *had* left it behind, then the police would find it when they searched his apartment. That would confirm his identity as a citizen but also entangle him in the investigation of the theft of the relic. He groans out loud and channel-surfs again.

The channel with the chair grows more painful to look at each time. He understands it is bothering him only after he is already discomfited, a lump in his throat, a slight difficulty in breathing. When he surfs past it, he sometimes catches brief glimpses of movement, as if someone left the frame just as he tuned in, a blur of departure so quick that at first he's not sure he saw anything at all. He flips past the channel again and again for an hour, perhaps two, before it finally happens again. After that he notices the blur irregularly but often, and begins to dread the channel. He has a theory of what the broadcast shows, and is not eager to see it; he doesn't want to see that blur resolve itself into victim or torturer, a threat or preview of what's to come. He avoids the channel, using the number buttons to select channels instead of cycling through them all. But that feels like giving the empty chair too much power. After half a day he finds himself almost desperate to see it again, to know that nothing has changed. He almost screams when he finally switches back and sees the empty chair.

Something has changed. On the grainy black-and-white screen, the stains on the chair are hard to see until he's looking for them. He thinks some might be blood.

They move the prisoners out of the luxurious hotel. Fetter listens and gathers that the hotel is meant for the moderately wealthy to while away mandatory quarantine in a plague year. It was never meant to hold prisoners, a policeman remarks in their hearing. This is the first formal confirmation that they are prisoners and not temporary detainees awaiting processing. Perhaps some of them were the latter: their numbers have almost halved. He asks if the missing have been released, but the policemen do not indicate that they have heard. Nobody speaks to any of the prisoners as individuals, in fact, only issuing broad directives such as: follow me, through here, down there, stand, sit, wait, strip, bend over, squat, stand, cough, raise your arms, put this on, go over there. The prisoners are strip-searched again, and finally assigned standardized, shapeless clothing: white sleeveless camisas and white knee-length shorts. So girt, they are guided outside, where there is a large, once-yellow bus with metal grills over the glass windows. The side of the bus has large stenciled letters that read DEPT OF PRISONS, with slightly smaller letters beneath that read CUSTODY, CARE, CORRECTIONS.

One of the prisoners is manacled and chained to the metal bar of the seat in front of her, but not Fetter or the others, who simply sit. A single armed policeman is in the back seat.

The bus driver is not in uniform. The bus moves out, unhurried. The hotel grounds are large and lush. Once they pass its gates, there is a long drive on a lonely road flanked by coconut plantations before they reach an unfamiliar highway with traffic on it. Fetter tries to orient himself, but can only guess. It doesn't look like the southern highway—this one is elevated high above the ground, with massive concrete barriers on both sides. There is no sign of the coast in any direction, only sporadic construction, green and fallow land, and the coconut plantations that have an air of neglect or abandonment. He dimly recalls, from another life, hearing Tomarin, Gerau, and Coema discussing with relish a scandalous white elephant of a new circular highway around Luriat and the story of who profited from it, a lesser scandal whose details have long since faded from memory. From the position of the sun they may be inland and southwest of the city, heading north. Not toward the city, but not away either, merely circumnavigating it. He tries to remember the locations of Luriat's prisons and internment camps. He should know that quite well, having followed Koel and Caduv's plans, but those maps seem to have been burned out of his memory. He feels adrift in landscape, as if he could be anywhere.

A pod of devils paces them for a while, vast and fleshy and swimming through the air, their protuberances almost scraping the side of the bus. They seem interested in the bus—perhaps in Fetter? He avoids looking directly out of the window until they finally bat away, heading north over the plantations, brushing the uppermost tips of the swaying coconut palms with their tendrils.

Is he getting closer to, or further away from, a room with a small chair in it?

He should be familiar with this tight-clenched feeling inside of him, with the effort he has made all his life to stay grounded; it is frustrating to know that he is not immune to terror and manipulation. Recognizing the gramarye of dehumanization does nothing to prevent it from working its way upon his body and his mind.

The first time the bus turns off the highway, his heartrate quickens. They drive down small bumpy byroads and stop outside the high gates of a large anonymous building. What can be seen above its wall looks more like an abandoned factory than a prison. There are armed soldiers or police in uniforms he doesn't know obscurely and intermittently visible through the bars of the gate. Flashes of white stutter, too, and Fetter thinks of a great heron, until he recognizes a white-armed antigod stalking just behind that gate. His skin ripples in revulsion; he doesn't want to be led through that gate, to pass near that thing.

The prisoner who was manacled to a seat is carefully unlocked and accompanied by two officers, chained at the wrists and ankles as if she might attempt an escape. She does not. The gate slides partway open for her and a few more prisoners to be taken inside, like a half-open mouth. For perhaps twenty minutes nothing happens. The gate remains open; the bus continues to idle; the policemen mumble to each other indistinctly. Fetter and the other remaining prisoners stare through the smeared glass windows. Fetter's pulse has slowed again. It's not his turn yet. This is some type of prison, but it's not for him. His clouded thoughts part and reform, obscuring what is bright and hot in him.

He is startled back to attention as three new prisoners are escorted out of the gate. They each shuffle as if they too were manacled at the ankles, though they are not. As each one steps through the gate, a long white arm passes over their head as if in blessing. The prisoners' hair is ruffled as if by wind. They are guided onto the bus, which reverses and makes its way back to the highway.

The second and final stop comes after a longer drive. It could have been an hour or three or five: Fetter's sense of time has disintegrated, leaving him drifting in his mind and memories. He didn't notice when the bus turned off the highway again. It is evening. They are parked outside another high gate, this time set in a tall wire fence. Through it can be seen, indistinct in the gloaming, a vast landscape of makeshift shacks and plastic sheeting; many people, a few in prisoner's uniforms like himself but most in ordinary clothing; and inevitably, the bright flash of white-armed antigods in the distance. The landscape of habitation stretches as far as the eye can see—the horizon is speckled with buildings, too. The far boundary of the camp is not visible. The wire fence marches off straight into the distance in both directions, with no sign of curvature to suggest that it encloses a space. It seems more as if the fence cuts across the entire peninsula: Fetter has a vision of it running into the sea on both sides, hundreds of miles apart.

There are police at the gate, and gun emplacements on both sides of it.

Fetter and the others are led off the bus and through the gate. There is a small intake station where they are again fingerprinted, cheek-swabbed, and nasopharyngeal-swabbed by policemen wearing masks and gloves. Each of them is assigned a district by the officer who collects their fingerprints.

"District three-five-seven-nine," the policeman says to Fetter, a number that he clutches at and immediately loses. The policeman is muttering numbers at a rapid clip to each person in full earshot of everyone, so Fetter's head is jumbled with numbers. Plus, he has no idea what the number's significance is and is not sure if he's meant to remember it—he guesses it's where he's supposed to reside in the camp, but his mind latches onto the fact that there are four digits to the number, implying a potential ten thousand districts to the camp. There shouldn't be that many, unless these so-called districts are very small. By the time he's completed this thought, he and the others have been guided through a long narrow corridor and out of the intake station, and sent into the camp.

"Go find your assigned district," a policeman says, dismissing them. The other prisoners all walk into the camp as if they know where they're going, no two going the same way. Fetter hesitates, waiting for his gut to lead him, but there is no queasy tugging, no prickling feeling of unease to push him one way or another. In the end, he chooses a direction at random and starts walking.

# 26

The prison camp is at least as enormous as Fetter assumed it could not possibly be. He has no idea how deep it goes. He seems to have entered an entire town with its own neighbourhoods and a grid of roads that grows more haphazard the further he walks. The roads are dotted with signboards and billboards. Fetter thinks they might explain the layout of the camp, but in the gathering dark, they are hard to read. He approaches a small signboard on a pole, hoping for a street name or district, but it is painted with a single word in large letters in Southeastern Imperial script. He doesn't recognize it as an Alabi word: it seems to be all consonants mushed together. Perhaps it's Abjesili or one of the myriad other unfamiliar Aggiopan languages that use the same script.

Later he finds out these are not words at all but acronyms or brand names. The signs are here to represent whichever state entity, foreign government, non-governmental organization, or corporate social responsibility programme sponsored each section of housing.

He goes deeper until the asphalt roads give way to packed-down earth, most so narrow they are only fit for foot traffic, and there is plenty of it. There are people everywhere. A little ways in and he is the only prisoner in prisoner's uniform. It marks him as an outsider, a newcomer; he can see the sidelong glances and the avoidance.

The styles of construction of the habitations that flank the roads seem to come and go in waves, as Fetter wanders from district to district. In one, every building is a metal box, thin sheets enclosing a single room that holds one or more families. In the next, lines of tents in what must once have been bright United Nations blue but is now faded to patchy paleness by the sun. He is cursed and shooed away as he trips over guy-ropes. There are clearings like little town squares, where people queue at tube wells for water. Some areas have electric lighting, with cables strung between intermittent poles and harsh bulbs hung in tents. Others are only lit by cook-fires and kerosene lamps.

Fetter tries to ask for directions—he gets responses in half a dozen dialects of hellspeak, most of which are near-unintelligible to him—but he doesn't remember the number of his assigned district, so there's not much anybody can do.

In a district without electricity, he follows his gut to a man in a turban tending a cook-fire. He is offered mushy rice and flavourless dhal. Here he briefly becomes part of a group of unaffiliated individuals, and he sinks into their membership gratefully. He spends a few days with them, learning the ways of the prison. The cook, a devout follower of some religion Fetter doesn't recognize that places great store by charity, gives him old clothes to wear so he's no longer marked by his prisoner's uniform. It's a relief to be able to blend into the background again, to not draw eyes. Parts of prison culture become clearer. The cook explains that dry rations, supplies, fuel for cooking, donated clothing, and so on are intermittently provided to each district, which must organize itself to request and collect such aid from its patrons, if any such patrons exist. This, apparently, is district four-four-one. The cook asks Fetter what district he was assigned to.

"I don't remember," Fetter admits. "It was three thousand and something. Is that much further in?"

The cook shrugs. When he came to four-four-one, he says,

there were only four hundred and forty-one districts. There used to be a fence right where you're sitting, he says.

Unlike his first prison of isolation, this one mandates social interaction. No matter where Fetter goes in the camp, there are people there. Every district has its own politics. Some are large and populous, others small and furtive. He is far from the only person in the wrong district. There is a sizable itinerant population, most of whom are running from their assigned districts due to some trouble or the other. A few, like him, are still searching for theirs, in the hope of finding a space demarcated for them.

"You have to find your district," another searcher tells Fetter. "That's where they'd mail your summons for court. If you don't show up for court, there will be penalties."

Instead of the floating, unstructured void of isolation, Fetter is faced with the choice of endless variations on structure, endless interaction. He keeps moving. Most districts are indifferent to his passage, as long as he doesn't attempt to poach their scarce resources. Some are actively paranoid, chasing him away and forcing him to circle around them. There are enough districts where an itinerant can get fed out of a sense of charity, or in exchange for labour of some sort, that he doesn't go hungry. He digs ditches for drainage. He helps install a fence, at first confused about whether this is the edge of the camp, but no, it's merely a district boundary enforced by a faction with more goods to protect. He repairs huts that have come apart, or tents that have been uprooted by wind. Once he spends the night in an enclave of northern Behinders and is forced to join them for half an hour of chanting before he can get fed in the morning. Soldiers descend on some districts more frequently than others, targeting by Almanac. He gets caught up in these sweeps several times, but they're always looking for someone else, and he suffers no more than the occasional shove.

There are devils everywhere in the camp, as in the outside world. Most huts and tents have feeders clinging to their walls or fabric, sometimes making the surface of the tent puddle in a way that he is continually surprised no one else notices. Gangling antigods stalk the camp, bringing plague. Deaths are common in camp. The bodies are taken away by soldiers in full personal protective gear, to be cremated without ceremony.

✑

Fetter's plan is simple and confused: if he keeps walking, he will find the outer fence again. The camp is surely too large for every stretch of fence to be guarded by armed soldiers at all times, so he should be able to find a disregarded stretch where he can float over the fence by night and escape. Or he will find his assigned district and finally fit into the scheme of things. At least then he'll be in his proper place in the system: he feels a great hunger to be filed correctly. He wants both of these things, sometimes at the same time.

Nobody asks him why he's in prison. He doesn't ask them, either. He's not sure what answer he would give. Is he in prison for not being able to convincingly identify himself as Fetter? Is it because he has been caught impersonating Peroe? Stealing Relic *a*? Attempting to assassinate the Perfect and Kind? Carnal intercourse against the order of nature? Speaking with an accent? Having no shadow? He's asked about this last in prison a lot more than he was in the world. He shrugs and says it was a childhood accident.

Every few streets—or as he goes further in, every few districts—there are sentry boxes holding armed soldiers, relieved regularly by vehicles that drive up and disgorge more. The loud-speakers on the boxes' roofs broadcast numbers sometimes, interrupted by squealing feedback. This is confusing to Fetter until someone explains that the loudspeakers are summoning specific prisoners by their assigned numbers. Fetter doesn't even remember being assigned a prisoner number, much less forgetting it.

"I thought summonings were issued in the mail," Fetter says.

His answerer scoffs. "There's no mail out here." At first, Fetter thinks they mean in the prison, but he has seen soldiers with sacks of mail in other districts, and he has been assured by multiple people that this is a good reason to stay in one's proper district, to receive mail. He hasn't seen those sacks in a while, so perhaps they mean that the outer districts have amenities that the inner districts do not.

Districts are not numbered in a regular way, at least not as far as he can tell in his meanderings. District six-one-one is bordered by district two-nine-three-seven on one side, which gave him hope of finding still higher numbers in that direction. When district five-eight-nine appeared on the other side, he was lost again.

How long has he walked without finding either his assigned district or a border fence? Some part of him still tracks the phase of the moon, but he caught the plague a couple of times. Each time he spent a few days—perhaps a week, perhaps more—in semiconscious, delirious haze, burning up with fever. The first time he was taken by soldiers in protective gear to a hospice tent, but there was little medicine and no equipment. The second time he merely huddled at the back of a metal-sheeted hut, broiling slowly with fever and the heat of day. Both times he felt he was near death, but both times he recovered. He feels healthy now, if weakened, but due to that lost time he is no longer sure if he has been in this prison for eight weeks or ten or more.

Mobile phones are common in the camp. Sometimes soldiers confiscate them, but more often they let it go, especially in the inner districts. Some sentry boxes don't even have loudspeakers, so the soldiers in those areas maintain lists of local prisoners' illegal mobile phone numbers. Phones ring often in such areas; the ringing is authorized and relatively safe. He borrows a phone a couple of times, intending to call someone—but who? These calls would all be tracked. Even if he had a number for Koel or Caduv, which he doesn't, he couldn't risk it. The only number he knows by heart belongs to Hej, who he can't bring himself to call. Phones are useless to him. But Fetter still almost weeps the first time he hears ringtones ring out free like birdsong.

After weeks of trading physical labour or simply begging across the camp, Fetter follows his gut to a district, one-one-nine-oh, which is a kind of provincial centre. It contains an actual brick building that hosts police, military, and a privileged bureaucracy drawn from among the prisoners themselves. It is one of several regional headquarters for prison administration, a provincial secretariat that oversees this cluster of districts. The military and police offices coordinate security, the Ministry of Health sub-office coordinates food and medical supplies, and the civilian secretariat is the point of contact between the outer world of state actors, charitable donors, and other involved parties with the inner world of organized district committees. The secretariat wrangles negotiations for supplies and services, acts as a conduit for complaints and petitions, and attempts to resolve minor disputes without calling down jackboots.

With a little effort, Fetter wrangles his way into the secretariat, trading on his literacy and extensive familiarity with Luriati citizenship paperwork and race science. He may not have any formal qualifications, but he can quickly fill forms in several different dialects of hellspeak and, given a recent Almanac, figure out who gets priority for rations and medical care, not just at the top of the hierarchies of race and caste, but step by painful step, all the way to the bottom.

He is brought in as a hanger-on and dogsbody, but when he proves capable of abstruse paperwork, he rapidly ascends to the formal position of assistant to the secretary of the province. He's fingerprinted, cheek-swabbed, nasopharyngeal-swabbed, and registered in the system as taking on this role. All the formality is a farce. It is not a difficult hierarchy to climb. The few other staff are either semiliterate or unwilling to fill in forms, so he has no competition. Even the secretary of the province is only a prisoner like himself, and has no real status. So at long last, Fetter gets a regular job. He reports in at the fourth hour of the dawn watch and clocks out at the sixth hour of the noon watch, like a salaryman, though his salary is paid in meals provided and a temporarily assigned tent in district one-one-nine-oh.

He attempts to use his access to the computer at the provincial secretariat to find out what his correct district *is*, and how to get there, but is frustrated to learn that he is not in the provincial database at all.

"You're in, hmm, entirely the wrong province," the secretary tells him, looking over his shoulder. "I don't even know how you got here."

"Which province should I be in, then?" Fetter demands. "Is there a map, or a list of which districts belong to which provinces?"

The secretary shrugs. He only knows the one province for

which he is responsible. The secretaryship is an elected position, but it is subject to recall at any quarterly meeting of district coordinators, so the role is as fragile as the province's mood. Fetter imagines that its holders would tend to the nervous, and this one is no exception—perhaps more so than others, because the secretary is also pathless. His sole act of religious defiance is a small clay lamp that he lights every morning in his office, in front of the absence of a shrine.

As far as the secretary knows, nobody in the province has ever been heard in court, or indeed even been formally charged. Nobody knows precisely why they're here, though everyone can guess at one or more possibilities. It doesn't exactly help Fetter to know his situation is the norm.

"Technically, all this is in, hmm, a space of legal uncertainty and nobody *can* be charged until that's resolved," the secretary explains. He has an annoying habit of hmming and making loud smacking noises with his lips as he talks.

Fetter recalls, not without pain, conversations with Hej. "Doesn't the Seventeenth Schedule have provisions for prisoners' rights to representation?" he hazards.

"Unfortunately, we do not fall under the jurisdiction of the Summer Court," the secretary says. "This prison was established under an order from the Storm Court, so the Twentieth Schedule is ascendant."

"And that makes it legal?"

"The Storm Court has so far, hmm, refused to hear petitions on the matter," the secretary says. "We fall under older counterterror instruments with broad, ill-defined powers. The extent to which prisoners, hmm, nominally have rights under Luriati law depe—"

"Can't we go to the Summer Court instead?"

The provincial secretary blinks at this fatuity and shakes his head. That, he explains in a way that leaves Fetter even more confused than before, is not how Luriati law works at *all*. The distinction between Summer and Storm as competing supreme courts dates back to an ancient unresolved power struggle between Godsfaction and Kingsfaction administrations during a coup of one by the other—who was couped by whom is lost to history—which sundered all civic authority from helm to crotch into halves that achieved a complicated détente over the generations, forming a vast nested array of entangled loops of power. "The Summer Court has no jurisdiction here," the secretary says. "They would just throw petitions out of court."

"But if neither court will hear petitions—"

"Yes." The secretary nods, pleased. "Now you see the problem."

# 27

Fetter's third incarceration sneaks up on him. Its earliest har-
binger is a phone call. He learns later that this call is not the
first: there was a wave of calls to mobile phones across districts where he's been sighted, a voice asking *where's Fetter*,
met with confusion or irritation. When the phone call finally
sneaks up on him, it has grown wise to the ways of the prison.
It comes to the provincial secretary's landline in their small
office in the secretariat, and it picks the secretary's day off, so
Fetter is the one to answer it.

He puts the receiver to his ear and makes a questioning
noise that isn't quite a word.

"Fetter?" the voice says, as it has said many times before.
Even through the crackle and hiss of the overtapped prison
phone, Fetter has a sudden brief vision of a clearing open to
the night sky—a half-moon rising to his left, mountains like
teeth to his right—and he bites down hard to stop himself from
blurting out the name. He needs to identify himself in a way
that Caduv will recognize.

"Always the half-moon," he says, and hears the answering
exhale. "How did you even . . . no, I suppose we shouldn't
speak about that. Not much we *can* speak about on this line,"
he adds, quickly, though Caduv probably doesn't need to be
warned that the line isn't secure. "I'm surprised."

"Surprised I found you?" Caduv says. The voice is tinny but

he can feel the power in it, as if it were giving off a heat that makes his ear sweat. "Or surprised that I would look?"

Fetter notes the *I* instead of the *we*. Has Caduv broken away from Koel? Or is he just being conscious that the line is tapped and not revealing more than he needs to?

"I thought you'd be busy," Fetter says. "Trying to balance a career with . . . the demands of parenting."

Caduv laughs. "I strive for synergy, as always."

"I thought you had priorities," Fetter says. "I distinctly remember listening to you talk through your priorities."

"Well, I didn't need to say it then," Caduv says. "But of course you're a priority."

Someone shouts Fetter's name from elsewhere in the building. He recognizes the voice: a plague doctor in the Ministry of Health sub-office next door. The Ministry of Health forbids personal calls on their land lines, so employees frequently barge into the secretary's office to use the phone for free calls.

"Lots of claims on your time?" Caduv asks.

"Claims to the phone, I think," Fetter says.

"My only claim is to your heart," Caduv says, and Fetter is so startled that he goes silent. Caduv doesn't wait for a response. "I'll see you," he says, and leaves Fetter listening to a dial tone.

It takes an hour for Fetter to remember that it's a line from the play. He feels obscurely hurt by this, as if wounded in someplace unreachable from the surface of his thoughts. He's never thought of Caduv that way, has he? So why should the trick make him feel . . . like this? Caduv is obviously using the line so that the listeners of recordings or readers of transcripts will think it an endearment between lovers. An illegal one, under the Storm Court's ban on homosexuality, or rather, their re-fusal to nullify the Third Occupation's ban on homosexuality, preserving the Absent Queen's ancient revulsion for carnality against the order of nature.

He's wondered sometimes, in his endless hours of specula-tion, if this is the real reason why he's been arrested. Maybe Hej snitched on him; maybe Fetter is to be charged with the unnatural corruption of a court official. Maybe his mother was right to warn him of these laws that lie in wait like predators. Perhaps that is what Caduv is trying to hint at. Or perhaps he meant only to distract eavesdroppers, while being certain that Fetter would understand the reference to the play.

It's not a good code, Fetter thinks. In the days before he fled the play was increasingly popular and it seems entirely likely that somebody in the prison administration or the surveillance apparatus has seen it, and even more likely that the play has been flagged by the censor board and all the actors watchlisted. But they have no prearranged code for this situation, so Caduv would be improvising, which suggests urgency. Are they plan-ning to break him out?

The thought sends him spinning. Incarceration has dam-aged his ability to focus; he finds himself drifting too easily. He grinds his heels into the ground. *My only claim is to your heart* is what the prince—Victory, becoming cruel before he becomes perfect, or kind—tells his monstrous father before killing him.

Is Caduv referencing Fetter's failed assassination? That can't be right: the world has changed, leaving no evidence of the attempt. Perhaps it's a reference to how the queen and the prin-cess prepared the ground for the prince's attack by distracting the king. Fetter is exhausted just thinking it through. Caduv said *I'll see you* at the end. Is that another hint or only a col-loquialism? How did Caduv know to find him here, inside this huge place? It has to be his registration as an employee of the

provincial secretariat. He was entered into a database somewhere, with his name, his fingerprints, his DNA. That information is accessible to anyone who can get into the right databases
or ask the right people. The more he considers this, the more
confident he is that between Caduv and Koel they could gain
that access. So the purpose of the call would have been to make
sure that he knew that they know, to warn him that he should
be ready for whatever they might have in mind.

It's strange to think that Caduv and the others might be
planning to break him out, that those plans he'd once been pe-
ripherally aware of might now revolve around him, or that the
consequences would be upon him so quickly.

What about the prison break they were originally planning—
the people they were searching for, who would have been de-
nied medical help? Fetter now has a better idea who such people
might be, having done so much data entry recently. He tried
to ask about *priorities* but is not entirely sure how to parse
Caduv's response. Had they already carried out that original
plan? Are they redirecting the effort toward him? What about
their original targets? Are they being abandoned for his sake?
Fetter is tired of guilt. He wants to call Caduv back and say,
*No, leave me here, rescue your political prisoners instead. I
got myself into this through my own carelessness, I'll get myself out—if I even deserve to get out.*

He feels this thought push him deeper into the mire of himself. Does he think he deserves imprisonment? Why? Is he pun-
ishing himself? For what? His mother's death? His failure to
kill his father? He tries to sift through the heavy sediment of
guilt in his heart, the one that Caduv almost seemed to lay
claim to. He thinks its cause is neither parent but his own act
of cruelty in throwing himself away without thinking through
whether he acted out of righteous political rage or twisted

filial love and hate. He threw away both his names, abandoned the people who loved him under either, put everyone who ever touched his lives at risk, and he failed—he sacrificed all of this for nothing. He deserved to stand in the wreckage of all his lives. It is the merest and most unearned grace that his father's meddling with time undid that damage, to whatever extent it has done so. It seems unlikely by now that his imprisonment has anything to do with his theft of Relic *a*. If that had been the case, surely they would have connected Peroe and Fetter by now. He should have suffered the consequences, but he hasn't. He seems to have been forgotten in here.

But he *did* those things, even if the world changed to undo them. He remembers his old world, like Mother-of-Glory remembered hers. His guilt outlives the world in which it was born.

And maybe nothing has changed. Maybe in this history he still stole the tooth and went south, as he remembers doing. Maybe the police just haven't made the connections yet, or there is a jurisdiction issue . . . He tries to still his mind. There is a way out that he can still bear.

He writes a letter of resignation before he leaves the provincial secretariat that night. The secretary will see it in the morning and update the database, signaling Fetter's departure to Caduv and stalling whatever plans were underway. By that time, Fetter will be in another province, in a direction chosen at random. He leaves immediately, not stopping to return to his assigned tent for the night but walking in the direction of the nearest provincial boundary. His luck seems to have abandoned him: his gut makes no suggestions. That usually means all options are equally bad.

Caduv won't be able to find him again in this endless prison if Fetter is careful not to register in another database. Caduv won't be able to risk himself or abandon anyone else for Fetter's freedom.

He's carrying enough guilt. He won't accept any more.

Leaving the province is easy. The prison rolls on beyond. He walks through more districts that look like the ones he knows, then districts that do not. His plans return, at first unwillingly but then more eagerly, to thoughts of escape—escape on his own terms, powered only by himself, risking only himself. If he walks deep enough into the prison, he reasons, he will start walking outward again.

He does his best to walk in the direction of the setting sun, away from the gate that he entered through. This is not always possible, because the terrain is growing more rugged. He climbs slopes that are misty in the mornings, prisoners' tents pitched awkwardly up the sides of hills amidst wet undergrowth. When it rains the water rushing downhill is strong enough to flood a district of prisoners down the slope, washing away their tents and pots and pans, spoiling their food, knocking adults off their feet, and stealing children away. At the top of such hills perch the privileged districts largely immune to floods, usually with metal huts and a grand view. These are peopled by prisoners of higher races and approved castes, invariably followers of the Path Behind. On the slopes, he mostly encounters faiths and unfaiths that he doesn't know. Once he walks past somebody teaching a version of the story of the Walking. It sounds garbled, so he doesn't stop to listen.

Descending hills should be easier, but he is continually tempted to run down in great floating leaps. There are too many eyes on him for that. He imagines a room with a chair and spikes on the ceiling, cutting tools on a gleaming metal tray. And anyway, if the floating is gone, he would fall all the way downhill. He digs his heels in as he walks, and so trudging downhill is even harder than climbing up.

He groups those districts together in his mind, forming an image of that province based on terrain, but he does not come across a provincial secretariat in the hills. Beyond lies a valley of marshes.

Sentry boxes grow scarcer the further he goes, but still appear at logarithmically regular intervals. Perhaps that's how he'll know when he's crossed the centre and is approaching the outer fence again, when they begin to return in frequency. The hillside sentry boxes were damaged by floods, abandoned as the soldiers shifted to a hilltop encampment. Down in the valley of marshes, there are days of walking between sentry boxes. Roads have given way to muddy paths. Fresh soldiers arrive by bicycle every few days, though in the gloomy, mangrove-shrouded swamp it's hard to tell the passage of time. The slowly writhing overstory closes overhead and blocks out the sun; the world is grey and green, liquid. Fetter feels submerged, almost gliding, despite the ache in his calves and feet.

It's quiet enough that Fetter can hear bicycles coming from a distance, and deserted enough that he feels the need to hide, for the first time in his imprisonment. He opts out of hiding among the roots or in the water, from fear of crocodiles or snakes or devils; he climbs and tries to feel a lightness in his bones. It's safe to float here, he tells himself, beneath the ceiling of the overstory, with so many handholds and barriers against the sky, and with no eyes to see and snitch. But he can't quite make himself unlock from the earth—he twitches convulsively for a few seconds, then climbs the trees with his hands and feet, balancing with his toes on the knee roots. The trunks move slowly, as if restless; the lighter branches writhe faster. He sticks to the heavier ones, unsure of his own weightedness. The constant movement all around is disconcerting, but it makes it easier to hide from cyclists. After they've passed and he returns to the ground, he walks with his eyes down, following the rut the bicycle left in the wet mud.

There are many inhabited districts in the valley, he discovers, but they are small and widely spaced. Wherever the marshes part a little to allow some dry earth, or at least shallow mud, he finds clusters of huts or tents. Sometimes little wooden huts rest on low stilts over the water. The prisoners look much the same as all the others, except their prison life is slower and less intense. Food supplies are less frequent and everyone is a little hungrier. He is refused food and driven away several times, until he finds a district where a small group of people are trying to repair their huts over the water and are glad to feed him in exchange for another pair of hands. He stays there for a few days, working and resting.

They are not certain what their district's number is, they tell him, so they can't direct him to his own; some of them claim to have lived here before there was a marsh, or a prison. They cannot agree on which direction he might be likeliest to find an outer boundary fence.

He leaves after he looks down from a hut's doorway to see a devil's tail in the water. He's not even sure he sees it: it was submerged and might have been a trick of the light in the gloaming. But it made him freeze and shudder, because it was that same great and twisted crocodilian tail that he once saw in Acusdab as a child, the tail of the devil that came out of Nine Yellow Oxen in Luriat. Or another just like it, he tells himself; surely these repeated sightings indicate a type, not a unique devil.

But *is* there such a thing as a type of devil? Isn't that more race science? Isn't it just a simplifying habit of thought, no different from the pervasive Luriati nonsense of higher and lower types? Perhaps, he thinks, peering carefully into the murk, every devil is unique and that they sometimes look like each other only reflects that they are kin. What difference does it make, when the devil is in the water at his feet?

He makes his excuses and leaves, but someone must have noticed him react to an unseen thing in the water. Rumour begins to outpace him. At his next stop, he's asked for advice on a child's illness, whether he thinks it is the work of invisible powers. Startled by the use of the older phrase, and seeing no devils, he says *no*. He doesn't know how to explain that the child may have been touched by a white-armed antigod. It's not like its touch leaves a mark, so the absence of a devil in the moment doesn't indicate . . . he tries to explain all this but has to cut himself off because he's only confusing the family. He performs a basic blessing instead, one of his mother's early lessons in gramarye, which he's seen the devil-doctors of Acusdab do a thousand times.

That meaningless *no* and that tiny blessing create a new figure in the valley: Fetter the adura, Fetter the devil-doctor. The valley of marshes is a dangerous place, and its people are superstitious; they hunger for reassurance of any kind, and he finds a role, once again, thrust upon him. He considers refusing or refuting it, but he's just grateful to have something he can trade for food and shelter other than the work of his hands. So what if it's a lie? He admits freely to clients and petitioners how little he knows, but this only seems to make him more authentic in their eyes.

Sometimes it's hard to find the lie, when they question him. *Yes*, he answers, searching for the lie in his mouth. *Yes, I am from Acusdab. Yes, I was taught by the one who taught doctoring to the aduro there. Yes, I know the gramarye.* He almost says *Yes, I can see them, which is more than any adura ever did*, but manages to hold that truth back with his teeth. He coughs it up and spits it into the swamp, and even this affirms his legitimacy for his new fanbase, because aren't the aduro famous for their betel addiction, their constant spitting, their blood-red mouths? How is there so much truth in this lie?

His clients apologize for not being able to pay him in betel or tobacco or money. They can only feed and shelter him, try to guide him to where he's going, though most habitations in the valley don't know their own district numbers and not a single prisoner knows their prisoner number. Some fish, or eke crops from the ground where the terrain allows, but the valley depends heavily on supplies. This is the most rural and poverty-ravaged province that Fetter has seen in the prison country. Perhaps this is why they are so desperate they'd even believe in him.

He keeps moving through the valley of marshes, following the rutted paths, meandering by necessity but heading roughly west. Prison villages expect his coming, and always have a list of things ready for him to do. They ask for blessings of various subtypes, most of which he remembers the protocols for, and the rest of which he fakes. It's not like any of them can tell the difference. Even soldiers ask him for blessings, and he gives them. Everyone in the valley of marshes lives in terror of being struck by devils, devoured by wild beasts, or disappeared by the prison authorities. He performs blessings against all of these, though he cautions that the gramarye is not enough against that last threat. In truth it won't hold out against any of them, but he doesn't want to depress people any more than they already are.

At high noon in a village deep in the marshes, in what seems to Fetter to be the uttermost depths of this wild valley, in a village of three faded-grey tents that doesn't deserve the name—it has no sentry box and the bicycle ruts approaching it have almost faded away—set in a small area of cleared damp earth surrounded by writhing mangrove swamp on all sides, a familiar face finds him and asks for an exorcism.

Fetter blinks up at the man. They are about the same age, he remembers, but the other man now looks much older.

"Siculu?" he says, and the man nods.

"So *you're* Fetter the adura," Siculu says. "I thought you were a student. You were called Peroe."

Fetter hesitates, then shrugs. "I haven't seen you since that dinner at Tomarin's house."

Siculu looks at him steadily, as if trying to decide something. "Were you lying then?" he asks, at last. "Or now? I've heard so many stories about Fetter the adura. Are those the lies?"

"I was lying then," Fetter says. "I was pretending to be Peroe to—well, it doesn't matter. Will you report me?"

Siculu snorts. "Report you to what? I just want to know if you're a real adura. Can you do an exorcism or no?"

Fetter considers. The technical answer is no, because there is no such thing in the gramarye as an exorcism: this is a confusion with superficially similar rites of the Alabi church, whose rhetorical framework became well-entrenched during the Third Occupation. This is the exact mechanism through which the invisible laws and powers became *devils*. What the gramarye has is not a rite of exorcism, but a rite of hostage negotiation. But that's not the question he's being asked.

"Yes," Fetter says.

Siculu leads him to the last tent. It stands alone, set apart from the other two and the cluster of families around them.

Crouched inside is a tall young woman Fetter remembers, Siculu's fellow servant in Tomarin's house. He remembers noticing that they looked alike then: less so, now. Siculu looks like he's aged a decade, and the woman looks like she's aged a century. Her face is twisted and hollow and her hair is white, and she has a devil on her back. Fetter cries in alarm and takes several steps back before remembering that he's supposed to be the doctor.

"What is it, what is it," Siculu shouts, and Fetter controls himself with difficulty. The other villagers are hurriedly packing their belongings and bringing their tents down.

Fetter's seen hostage negotiation rites before, and the devil is usually present at those—he's seen them stalking and encircling, he's seen them hover and even touch possessively. But he's never seen them climb on and dig their nails in. The woman bleeds from her scalp and her neck where the devil grips her.

"She's not bleeding much," Siculu says, somewhere behind him. "But her wounds won't heal, and she's been frozen like this for two days. I didn't know what to do, until I heard the adura was coming this way."

Fetter sighs and squats in front of the woman. He looks her in the eye, then, with a shudder, turns his head to stare the devil down.

The devil looks almost human. He has never seen anything like it—small and naked, but so soaked in blood that it seems fully dressed, fully armored, every inch of skin so stained in red. The blood isn't dry: it's a film of liquid, running, flowing along the devil's surfaces in a red tide. Where the blood film passes, the skin glistens damply. It has four arms, all of which are clamped around the woman. So are its legs, digging into her sides. If she stood up, she'd carry it on her back like a sleepy child. It has four curved fangs curling out at each corner of its mouth, distending its lips outward and exposing the grin of its flat, human inner teeth and its pink gums. Every few seconds, it opens its mouth to lick at the residue of blood film as it washes across its face, forming a brief mask before it flows up into the devil's long straight hair, a red wig, and then down its back again.

It's digging its fingers, which have no claws but only ordinary human nails, into the woman's skin. Her bleeding under those nails is slight, but it doesn't clot; she bleeds and bleeds, and the devil's red shroud grows. The blood disappears from her skin, as if evaporating. Where it stains her camisa, the fabric reddens, then browns, then fades back to dirty white.

The devil would need five or six times this much blood to cover its entire body and still the blood tide, if that's what it wants. Fetter is sure that would kill her. Her eyes are empty: she doesn't seem to see him. The devil looks at him, the whites of its eyes startling in the red.

"What's her name?" Fetter asks, at last. His voice trembles, but not as much as he thought it would.

"Ucalas," Siculu says. "My sister. We're twins."

"Do you have a knife?" Fetter asks. He doesn't know a protocol for this. This is not like the usual hostage negotiation, where a devil's gaze has caught someone and the adura must force it to look away. This is not that. This is something uglier and more raw. Predation? Parasitism? Something unknowable? Whatever it is, he has to put a stop it, and he can't fake this. Nothing in the gramarye tells him what to do next.

"What are you going to do with a knife?" Siculu demands. "Don't hurt her. She's been cursed, or possessed. Can you drive the devil out?"

Fetter considers this. The devil looks at him, as if asking the same questions. He's filled with terror to be so close to one, to allow one to know that he sees it, but it's a little easier, he thinks shamefacedly, because it already has a victim. As long as it's gripping Ucalas, he's safe. He waits for his gut to churn through the probabilities, but no certainty rises in him. He tries to remember the skills he is now famous for.

"Do you have anything you can burn?" Fetter asks. "For smoke."

There is the indistinct sound of arguing behind him. Fetter doesn't dare take his eyes off the devil, but he risks a quarter-turn of his head. The other families are packed and leaving.

Siculu is shouting after them. It seems they're taking all the dry firewood and means of making fire.

Siculu returns to his side. "They were going to leave last night, but they were afraid of moving in the dark. Now that you've come, they're terrified of death magic."

Fetter finds it within him to roll his eyes. "This isn't *death magic*," he says. "Filling in fucking citizenship forms in post-Occupation Luriat is death magic. This is just . . . doctoring."

"I don't understand," Siculu says. He's holding one of his hands in the other, by the wrist, as if he were taking his own pulse, or perhaps as if he were pretending that he was a child again, safe with an adult holding his hand.

Fetter shakes his head, never taking his eyes off the devil. "Tell me about Ucalas," he offers. He's making this up as he goes along: her story isn't relevant to any rite, any script that he knows. But he needs to keep Siculu calm, otherwise he'll have two situations to deal with.

"She's my sister," Siculu says, again.

"How did both of you come to work for Tomarin?" Fetter asks. He takes Ucalas by the hand and tests her pulse. He's squatting in the entrance: he can't stand up because Ucalas fills the tent, but he can't sit because he would feel too vulnerable with the devil so close and staring. The arches of his feet ache.

"He was our patron," Siculu says. "Most of our family worked for his family."

"And why are you in prison?" It's the first time he's asked that question.

Siculu looks startled, as if he had forgotten. He doesn't answer.

"Did Tomarin fire you?" Fetter asks.

"No," Siculu says, immediately. "There was . . . did you say *prison*? No, we're . . . we were going home. We had to take the path through the valley of marshes because . . . because the trains don't run in the White Year. If Ucca was well, we'd have been home by now. Past the marshes and up into the mountains. That's where our family's from."

"This is a prison," Fetter insists, but he's troubled all over again. At first he thought Siculu was perhaps embarrassed, but now he thinks the man truly doesn't know. He's forgotten. And what force does Fetter know that can cause that kind of forgetting? An awful idea is growing in his belly. Perhaps Siculu and Ucalas are in prison because Tomarin's household was arrested for consorting with Peroe, and the reason they don't remember is because his father's temporal rewrapping undid Peroe's crime. It seems likely that Tomarin would have thrown Siculu and Ucalas to the jackals so he could evade arrest. With Peroe's crime undone, they could be in prison without a reason—unremembered, unremembering.

"Where's Tomarin now?" he asks, in the hope that this sideways approach will lead to illumination.

"On holiday," Siculu says. "It's a White Year. He's in the mountains."

"Near where your family are?" Fetter asks, unthinkingly, and this draws a chuckle from Siculu, and unexpectedly, from Ucalas.

It's throaty and sounds painful and dry, but it is unmistakably a laugh, not a cough or a moan. Siculu exclaims and tries to kneel next to his sister, but Fetter blocks him with an outstretched arm and waves him back. He doesn't want Siculu too close to the devil.

Ucalas's eyes focus slowly. Fetter is reminded of watching Janno wake up from his trance. Ucalas seems to be coming from a greater distance.

"It hurts," Ucalas says. At first Fetter thinks she's talking to him, but she's looking at Siculu. Only her eyes move; she can't turn her head because of the devil's grip, but she wouldn't know that. To her it must seem that she's lost control of parts of her own body.

"Siculu," Fetter says. "Please back away as far as you can. Go up the path, maybe. And Ucalas—please remain very still, and don't say anything."

Steps fade away. Ucalas meets his eyes, but remains silent. He's not sure if she's following his instructions. He doesn't know if she can understand or hear them.

Fetter rolls his neck to the side and bares his throat. He taps it with a finger, looking at the devil.

"I don't remember any rites for something like this," he says, to the devil. "I see you, though, and I know there's no rite for that."

The blood film washes over the devil's face, covering its eyes like a blink.

"I don't have a drum or rough smoke to calm you. I don't have a rooster to sacrifice to you. I don't know what you want," Fetter says. "Is it blood? All I can offer you is my own."

The devil says something. It sounds like a rustle. If there are words, they are indistinct.

"I could try to force you off her neck," Fetter says. "I admit this was my first thought. But you look strong. It would probably hurt her if I tried to pry you away."

The devil blinks, this time with its eyelids.

Fetter leans forward, putting his arms around Ucalas's shoulders, encompassing the devil. He doesn't quite touch either of them, but holds his arms close in a half-circle. Ucalas breathes raggedly on his chest. His face is so close to the devil's that it could dart forward and bite him with only the slightest tilt of its neck. Slowly, very slowly, looking it in the eye the whole time, he reaches for the devil's upper right hand, which is tightly gripping the crown of Ucalas's head, its fingers digging into her scalp just above the hairline. He touches it; the devil's skin is cool and wet. The blood film washes past, agitated, staining the tips of his fingers. He leans his head against Ucalas's, and slowly tugs the devil's fingers toward his own head. At first, it resists—it is far stronger than him—but at his insistent tugging the hand moves in a quick scuttling gesture. He feels the nails dig into his scalp.

Having persuaded it to move one limb, he finds the others are easier. One by one, he gently guides its arms from Ucalas to himself. One arm encircles his neck before the fingers dig in below his ear. The last two arms grip his torso, one over and one under the shoulders. The arms are longer than a human's and multi-jointed; they bend and bend all the way around him. The legs wrap around his waist. He lifts, and the devil is on him now, not Ucalas. He gently scuffles backward on his knees until he's out of the tent, and then he stands up as carefully as he can. He hears Ucalas murmur and slump, boneless, finally able to move and too weak to do so. The devil in his arms is indeed like a sleepy child. It clings tightly to him, puts its fangs against his neck, the distended lips wet against his skin, and does something with its human teeth like blowing a bubble. He feels weak, but he's not sure if it's blood loss or simply raw terror. He has never been so afraid in his life.

He walks out into the marsh with the devil in his arms. The mud squishes under Fetter's feet as he leaves the cleared area. Running footsteps behind him—good, the brother will see to the sister. If Fetter stops he begins to sink, so he keeps moving, ducking under squirming branches and around veils of hanging-creeper. The devil is heavy and solid, but cold. The blood film has stained Fetter's skin and clothes at every point of contact. He feels lighter with every step, as if drained of heavy blood. The mud beneath his feet is more and more liquid, but it bears his weight and the devil's too, as if they weighed only as much as a dry fallen leaf. The devil turns its head—Fetter flinches inwardly at the movement and feels his skin ripple, the hairs standing up—but it only looks at him as if it hadn't seen him before. And then it's gone, leaping from him like a monkey, climbing up and up with its long arms, swinging from root to trunk to branch, its unnatural grace seamlessly melding into the writhing of the uppermost overstory as it heads for the noonday sun.

In the morning, exhausted and weak, Fetter wakes to the sound of a bell, which at first he thinks is the call of some strange devil. He slept on the ground outside the tent and is sore, his clothes stiff with dried mud and perhaps blood underneath. He tries to go back to sleep, ignoring the sounds of activity in the village, until a rubber tyre nudges him in the ribs and he looks up to see a policeman straddling a bicycle.

"Summons for you. Good that you found your way to your assigned district," the policeman says, looking around. "This is pretty fucking desolate. I'm surprised there's anybody out here." He hands Fetter a letter with his name and a number on it, folded in such a way to be its own envelope.

"*This* is my district? But—" Fetter cuts himself off and opens the summons. It's incomprehensible jargon. He asks for an explanation, but the policeman waves him away.

"It's a long way, we'd better get started."

Is he being summoned to court? Is he being moved to yet another prison? He asks these questions, but the policeman shrugs.

"Not that I would tell you if I knew," the policeman says, as if confiding. "But I don't know."

Fetter says goodbye to Siculu and Ucalas. It's brief. Things are awkward between them: the twins are grateful and Fetter is guilty. The other families, who Siculu persuaded to come back the previous evening, keep their distance. They've pitched one tent but are still arguing about whether to pitch the second one.

When they leave, Fetter sits on the top tube of the bicycle frame with the policeman's arms around him, hunching at the neck. The policeman cycles slowly with his knees splayed out.

They pedal west for hours, the policeman huffing all the way. He hands Fetter off to another policeman at a sentry box, who has a bigger bicycle with a pillion seat. Sentry boxes start to appear more frequently as they travel. He had been equally distant from the prison's eastern and western boundaries. It takes days of travel, accompanied by various policemen and sometimes soldiers. Fetter is hazy for much of the journey. They travel by bicycle, motorcycle, and four-wheel drive vehicle, first on muddy swamp paths, through mountain passes, on narrow hilly roads, then on long roads of packed earth lined with metal huts and tents, and finally on lonely asphalt roads under an oppressively low sky. At last they reach buildings of brick and plaster.

Here, they finally come to rest, and he is ushered into a building, which, going by the number of people in uniform, appears to be a police station or headquarters of some sort. He is transferred into the custody of a tall, severe man in austere, almost threadbare robes. Words and papers are exchanged between this priest and the policeman who accompanied him on the last leg of his journey, but Fetter doesn't notice. He is staring at the tall priest's face. It's clean-shaven, hairless except for thick brows. The eyes are shadowed under those brows, and the mouth unsmiling. It's a face he was taught from his earliest days.

"I am Salyut," the Saint-General says, in a voice like burned honey. "Your father wants to see you."

# 28

The Saint-General does not, of course, drive or handle money with his sainted hands. He is accompanied by a lay attendant, a young and devout woman named Isla who Fetter later learns is a Luriati volunteer who gives up hours of every week to perform tasks for Gerau's group but has never spoken to Gerau herself. Isla does the driving, fetching, and carrying for the Saint.

Fetter sits in the passenger seat, because the Saint-General peremptorily took the back seat and started answering calls, texts, and emails as the vehicle drove away from the police station and the prison, through a different set of gates than the ones he entered through. Isla speaks to Fetter in a tone of awed respect. It's almost as bad as how she speaks to Salyut, when she dares speak to the Saint-General at all.

"I didn't even know the son of the Perfect and Kind lived in Luriat," Isla says, in a soft murmur so as to not interrupt Salyut's strident phone conversations, which are either in a language that Fetter doesn't know or one he lost during his incarcerations. "I would have made pilgrimage years ago."

"I'm not a priest," Fetter says. He isn't sure how to explain anything about his life—Fetter is at most a few years older than her, but he feels decades older. His back aches.

"Am I still a prisoner?" Fetter addresses this over his shoulder at Salyut. It's worrying to have the Saint-General sitting behind him. His aching back feels raw and skinned, completely exposed. He feels vulnerable, luckless, lost. The old man has no visible knife to plunge into him, but there are all kinds of knives.

Salyut covers his phone with his hand instead of muting it, frowning. "You were never a prisoner," he says. His speaking voice is deeper than his phone voice, rougher and sweeter. Fetter can imagine him giving sermons. "This was merely a brief quarantine and mandatory distancing."

"They gave me a number," Fetter tries to explain. "They took my DNA. I'm in the system."

"Systems are nothing to the systematic," Salyut says. Peering over his shoulder, Fetter sees that Salyut is still covering his phone with his hand and doesn't seem impatient to return to his previous conversation. "You have proper identification waiting for you with your father. You were released after routine questioning and the completion of your quarantine."

I was never questioned, Fetter wants to say, but at the same time he feels that he *was* questioned. There were the questions the policeman asked him when he was first . . . arrested? Detained? And if not that, he thinks, I have questioned myself. I have done nothing but question myself. He doesn't ask why his father has his identification. Obviously someone went to his apartment and found it. He wonders if his father went himself. What a jarring thought, the Perfect and Kind standing amidst the ruins of his life. More likely it was a volunteer lay attendant, someone like Isla.

After Fetter is silent for a few seconds, Salyut returns to his conversation on the phone. His voice seems higher, shriller. He *is* talking in hellspeak, Fetter thinks, after picking out a few words that he recognizes. But it's a dialect Fetter doesn't know. It sounds old, rolling and multisyllabic and liquid. He wonders if this is what Mother-of-Glory spoke when she was young, when Salyut was last on the island, when it was still an island.

They drive east, stopping at temples and barriers and checkpoints for Isla to get out and put money in tills and tollbooths and pockets. Fetter sees no devils.

Speaking softly, almost under her breath, Isla tells Fetter about herself. She's not from Luriat originally, either: her parents moved there when she was a child. She was born in Singing Fish, the city on the west coast of the peninsula that mirrors Luriat on the east coast. Singing Fish has seen Behinder pogrom after pogrom for decades, Isla remarks: both her parents lost family to violence, and so converted to the Path when Isla was born, to protect her. Isla says this without irony. To her, this was a fortunate and wise decision that led to the family's safety and prosperity. Look at Isla now, driving the Saint-General himself, not to mention the very son of the Perfect and Kind! This is proof of the Path's egalitarianism and meritocracy. The spiritual consequences of this blessing will distribute themselves to Isla's kin and loved ones, their honoured dead and their yet unborn, curling like smoke through the tree of this family to mark their place in history.

Fetter does not have it in him to deny Isla her blessing, so he doesn't question it a second time.

As Luriati urbanity gradually reifies around them, their stops at police and military security checkpoints grow shorter: they are waved past after a peek in the back seat. Eventually, and with a shock, Fetter recognizes Cooksferry. They drive past the road that leads to Pipra's mall. He wonders if she's in there, and Janno and Avli and the others. The vehicle does not pause. How long did it take to get here from the prison gates? An hour? Two? It seemed like a long time, but not nearly enough. His distance from the city grew in his head with every week he spent in prison country, until it seemed he must be a world away from any world that he might have called his own. And here they are, a short drive later, back in Luriat.

The city looks the same, except far less crowded than Fetter remembers. There is no traffic; there are no crowds; there are hardly any devils and almost as few people. Flags line the streets, hanging from lampposts and telephone poles and trees and traffic lights and balconies and open windows. Different flags in bright colours. The sun and the moon, or a great enweaponed snarling beast.

There are pillars of smoke in the distance like grey flags, black flags, white flags. How long has he been away?

He shrinks from the flags and shudders at the smoke. He has never been in Luriat as the son of the Perfect and Kind—at least, not outside the safety of group meetings. He has never seen the city maddened and savaging itself. This is not the city he wanted to return to upon becoming free.

And is he free? With the Saint-General at his back and the city flagged and burning, Luriat feels like just another district of that unending prison country.

The car keeps moving, and then they are in the Plantations— they drive past where the bright door Nine Yellow Oxen used to be, but it's gone, that fragment of wall finally demolished— and on Boiling Point, and turning into the Godsfaction Dedicatory Convention Centre. The park grounds of the GDCC are crowded with tents. There are thousands of people in every direction. The vehicle drives slowly, crowds spilling into the path. He sees no devils here, but he can't see much beyond massed human bodies.

Then the vehicle stops and Isla ushers him out and into the GDCC through a side door, a heavy mesh over a frame backed by a transparent sealed membrane to keep the air-conditioning from leaking out. Fetter allows himself to be herded without thinking, without recognizing that his body is out of the vehicle, out of the prison, now moving under an open sky, now under a heavy ceiling. Salyut brushes past him, and Fetter would have let him leave, standing confused in an empty maintenance corridor, if Isla didn't whisper and prod and instruct him to follow the Saint-General. Fetter moves, obedient in his daze, and doesn't register the attendant not following in turn. He never sees Isla again.

Salyut holds the barred elevator door open, radiating impatience without any overt sign. Fetter follows him in. He feels that he's in a dream of falling, a long, long fall from the point where he picked up the phone in the prison's provincial secretariat—or did it start earlier, at the pyre?—down into this moment, where Salyut knocks at a frosted glass door and opens it without waiting for a response, this moment when Fetter goes inside, the moment when his fall comes to a hard stop in front of his father, the Perfect and Kind.

"You tried to kill me," the Perfect and Kind says. His voice is even. He doesn't sound accusatory, merely factual. He tosses something small to Fetter, who catches it automatically with a powerful sense of déjà vu.

He looks at his hand. It's the tooth. Relic *a*. Just as dead as it was when Pipra tossed it at him, just like this. Still he feels caught in a sudden squall, cold water soaking and sluicing over him.

"I left this in my mother's pyre," Fetter says, at last. His voice feels dry, as if he hasn't spoken in days. He looks around the suite, which is luxuriously minimalist in polished concrete and exposed wood beams overhead. Large windows let in soft light through gauzy curtains.

His father is a man of average height and weight, like himself, dressed in thin saffron robes with one bare shoulder. He is clean-shaven, but unlike Salyut, he is not bald. His head is covered in short tight curls like Fetter's own, more grey than black. He seems entirely unaffected by Relic *a*, but it would have no power now.

"Did someone dig this out of the ash for you?" Fetter asks. He's closed his fist around the tooth, mirroring how he carried it south like a weapon. He opens his fingers with difficulty. "Or did you change the world so that it never left the city?"

The Perfect and Kind nods, not in answer, but as if acknowledging the confirmation of long-held suspicions. "So she told you such things. I wondered." He opens his hand, fingers dipped down, and holds it out.

Fetter recognizes the gesture from Behinder statues: the seal of compassion and acceptance. He tosses the tooth lightly back into his father's palm. The Perfect and Kind closes his fingers over the tooth, and when he opens his hand again, it's gone.

"Conjuring tricks," Fetter says. He tries to feel the contempt he's putting into his voice. "I've seen that one from street magicians trying to earn a few casi."

"What makes you think some of them aren't doing real magic?" the Perfect and Kind says. "Many puissant penitents and ascetics end up turning tricks on the street, one way or the other."

"Won't you break the world by changing it so much?" Fetter says. He wants to take control of this conversation, to discomfit his father in some way, or at least to provoke a reaction beyond equanimity.

"I have so changed the world only twice," the Perfect and Kind says. "Both times to survive your mother's curse. It is not an easy thing, even for me."

Fetter points at his father's hand, where the tooth so recently lay, and the Perfect and Kind laughs.

"This was not that," he says. "A brief opening into an empty realm. Changing this world is not the only power I have mastered, son."

"Don't."

"Fetter, then. It's a name—"

"That you gave me, I know. I've made it mine."

"Very good." The Perfect and Kind seems genuinely appreciative. "I have much more to give you, if you were to ask for it."

"What could you offer me?"

"I have been an absent father," the Perfect and Kind says. "Though self, identity, predication, time, fatherhood, and absence are all constructs whose meanings dissolve under scrutiny. There are two levels to every utterance. Do you understand? There is surface, and then there is depth."

"The Path Behind and the Path Above?" Fetter says.

"No," the Perfect and Kind says, smiling. There is something deeply frightening about the smile; Fetter finds himself looking away from it. "The path—there is only one path, despite your mother's unforgivable breaking of its nonduality. The path is part of the surface of things. It must act in the world, and so it must have robes and titles, events and funding, a social media strategy and political patrons."

"Prisons," Fetter says. "Pogroms. War."

"Yes," the Perfect and Kind says. "I'm sure your mother taught you the price of changing the world."

"It's all just magic for you, no?" Fetter says. He waves his hands. "Like this, and the world is different. Mountains where there were no mountains—why didn't you just undo my birth? Or make it so I died years ago?"

"Because you are my child, and I love you," the Perfect and Kind says. "This feeling belongs to the surface of things, but there is no world without its surfaces. I want you to exist. I want you to be happy. Killing me will not make you happy. It will only thrust you deeper into anguish."

"And you can't be killed anyway," Fetter says.

"Oh, I can be killed," the Perfect and Kind says. "In fact, I will be. But not by you."

"Oh? Who, then?"

"Nobody you know," the Perfect and Kind says, smiling as if at a joke. "You probably think I came to Luriat in triumph after your mother's death. Even my inner circle thinks this. But in fact, I came here to die." His face betrays no anguish or pain. It's as if the surface of that face is disconnected, unmoored from the words and thoughts in his depths. "But my death will not change the world."

Fetter lets this go, trying to match his father's disconnectedness. Is this, he asks himself, the only time we will speak? What if he sends me back to prison after this? Or simply casts me out and refuses to see me again? Should I ask my questions now? Should I try to kill him with my bare hands? But there is no strength in his hands and he can't think of any real questions, only an old feeling that he must have had so many questions for his father over the years of his life. One way or the other, it feels like they have all been answered along the way. He only has new questions from this very conversation itself. So he asks them. "You can see the future—you know what's going to happen? And what is an *empty realm*?"

"No," says the Perfect and Kind, and for a moment Fetter wonders if that's all, if all his questions will be answered with a *no*. But then his father continues. "There is no such thing as a seeable future; I know some things that are going to happen—only through experience, planning, and the judicious exercise of overwhelming power, both mundane and supramundane." The Perfect and Kind smiles again, his eyes half-lidded and still. "An empty realm is an overwritten past, a dead world of no further consequence, one of a vast array. They are themselves complicated territories with their own contested histories; your mother's devils come from empty realms. But these realms are causally unbound to this membrane—they have fallen outside of the past we acknowledge, our light cone that narrows as it stabs deep into history's heart—and so they are safe places to dispose of dangerous things."

"There is a world of devils?"

"Endless worlds, Fetter," his father says. "And there is no such thing as *devils*. They are the people of lost histories. We see them only in translation, the only way they can exist in this realm. They come because your city is a fraying lacework; every bright door is an open wound bleeding into the water. Once that was this whole island. I tried to contain the damage."

Questions were a mistake, Fetter thinks. They lead to more questions, and what's worse, to answers. He tries, uselessly, to gather the focus and killing intent that he had once folded so well into his body—as a child with a knife, or on a train with a bared tooth in his hand. But he feels weak, scattered. He shouldn't have run from Caduv's rescue attempt, if that was what it was. Perhaps then he would not be here now, facing his father and feeling . . . what is he feeling? It isn't the rage that he expected, or the fear. It's almost like disappointment.

The Perfect and Kind must have seen this realization in Fetter's face, his surface undetached from his depths. "You've spent your whole life building me up in your head," his father says. It sounds gentle, though it isn't. "Even one such as I cannot be all things to you. Go rest and gather yourself. We will speak again."

Fetter doesn't move. "I don't understand what you want with me," he says, at last. "Why are you here? What will you do?" He means, in large part, *What will you do with me?* But he cannot force those last two words off the tip of his tongue. "Will you tell me?"

"I have no secrets from you," the Perfect and Kind says. His face is still. "Your mother kept you and this land from me for as long as she lived. She broke my Path, which is unforgivable, but not undoable. I am here to heal it and set things right. I am here to undo the toxicity and corruption of the Path Behind, and to reconnect with my son. I cannot offer you the throne I was cast out of, but I have made my own. If you wish it, I will make you a prince of the Path as you should have always been. I will teach you power and wisdom: I am confident that you can achieve the fourth level of awakening. You could be like Salyut and Magellan; a saint sitting at my side."

Fetter is silent for what feels, to him, like an hour. He stares at his father's face, tries to count his heartbeats, wonders if his voice would be steady if he spoke. He waits until he is sure it will be. "You already have a Saint-General and a Saint-Errant," Fetter says, at last. "Aren't they a matched set? Order and disorder—don't they cover all eventualities between them?"

"I try to avoid dualities," the Perfect and Kind says, and smiles his terrifying smile. "I will give you a title and a rank befitting your ancestry and respectful of both lines of your heritage. You could be Luriat's Saint of Bright Doors. I would have you be guardian of this place. I will teach you how to seal bright doors, to give you power over those that come through. You will gain much knowledge from them. You could heal this city's fractured power structure by placing yourself at its apex. The Absent King and Absent Queen will bow their absent knees; both presidents already swear fealty to the sun and the moon, and if I were to appoint you my prince regent in the north—"

"No," Fetter says. It's through gritted teeth, though he tells himself it is easy.

"You would have the power to undo the wrongs you hate," the Perfect and Kind says. "You could close the prisons and open the borders. You could defrock the corrupt monks and end the pogroms. You could save lives and hearts and minds. You would soon eclipse the Saint-General and the Saint-Errant in both mundane and supramundane power. Eventually, you would surpass me. I could die at peace, knowing that the Path I've made would continue to save this world without me."

Fetter shakes his head—this vision, this *ridiculous* vision of himself as a Saint, this thing completely opposed to anything he has ever wanted for himself, which proves that his father doesn't know him and doesn't care to, that his father only wants to make him an instrument, and *yet*, the vision of empowerment and knowledge is still tempting. He imagines himself chosen at last, invested with power and agency beyond his wildest dreams; he imagines a great expansion of his rib cage, bringing the island within his chest, being its gaoler instead of it being his. He imagines a long-held tightness inverted. What could he do with the power, no matter how ill-gotten, how tainted, how compromised, to undo even some of the wrongs of the world? Wouldn't it be self-indulgence to turn down that chance? In his instinctive refusal, is he not placing his own choice, his assessment of what he can and cannot bear, above the suffering of others—suffering that he could alleviate, or even end?

The Perfect and Kind looks out of the window, up at the sky, not down at the crowded park below. "You have not, technically, been released. You are on supervised probation, by a special order of the Storm Court at my request," he says. "The formal boundaries of your probation are simple: you may not leave Luriati jurisdiction; you must report in person every day to either the North Luriat Police Station, or to myself or the Saint-General as my representative; and you may not associate with known criminals, including your seditionist friends who produced the banned play. Within those constraints, you may do as you wish, but violations of these terms may lead to serious charges from which even I cannot save you. Do you understand? Very good. You may go. Sign and date the register on the table—your identification is there, don't forget it this time."

Fetter swallows the words and the humiliation that knot in his throat. He signs the register, which is just a cheap blank notebook clearly acquired for this sole purpose, and picks up that small laminated piece of paper that would have made so much of a difference when he was accosted on the train—or would it have? He studies the card and its strings of haecceity, the photograph in which he is squinting and unrecognizable to himself. He remembers his headache from when that photograph was taken, but nothing else about that day.

He thought the Perfect and Kind would turn his back and look out the window while Fetter leaves, but—glancing back as he leaves the room—his father is standing there, staring at him, his face unreadably serene, his smile modest and unchanging. The Perfect and Kind holds his right hand lightly raised in the seal of the boon: the gift that is given, palm up and fingers downturned, as if handing out freedoms.

The Perfect and Kind is not looking at Fetter. He's looking at me. He can't *see* me—it's not possible—but he is looking, regardless.

Fetter pauses with his hand on the door, holding it open. The glass is cold. "Salyut told me I wasn't a prisoner," he says. "That I was never a prisoner, only quarantined. Which of you is lying?"

"I thought you said you made your name your own," his father says. "Is the chain ever free?"

# 29

There is nothing to suggest that anyone has been in Fetter's apartment, except his certain knowledge and the ID card heavy in his pocket.

First, he sleeps. It's late, and he is as exhausted as if he had broken out of prison by force, instead of being confusingly and unceremoniously released. Or transferred to a third prison, this time all of Luriat itself.

In the morning, he is starving. He thought that being home would feel like home, but it doesn't. It's just the apartment he lived in before; now it feels like he's only visiting. His books are covered in a thick layer of dust. He was expecting a rotten smell of food gone bad, but there is nothing more than a faint mustiness. Hadn't there been a bag of sliced fruit on the counter? Did he throw it out, or did an intruder clean up? There is nothing in the house that can be consumed, except a bottle of tea leaves and the little cloth bag of painkillers by his bed. He has not had a headache since the pyre, as if the tiny blood vessels in his face had expanded in the heat and then become fixed in this new configuration, a stronger, broader flow opening within him.

He showers and changes into his own clothes for the first time in a long time. When dressed, he sees he's mixed up what used to be his own wardrobe with Peroe's; he's wearing his own loose breeches, a bright mustard yellow, but one of Peroe's sober, fitted, sleeveless camisas in pale grey. He's grown used to

bare arms. He runs his fingers over them, the faint white traceries of old scars, the scabs of the new.

Outside, the streets are still much emptier than he's used to.
He finds a free kadé and eats breakfast. A policeman stops him
on the way out and demands to see his identity card. Fetter
produces it immediately, his heart pounding, but the policeman only glances at it and hands it back.

"Wear a mask," the policeman says, and hands him a wad-
ded-up disposable mask from a bulging pocket. "Anybody not
wearing a mask is supposed to be quarantined for two weeks.
I'll go easy on you, but don't let me see you out here bare-faced
again."

Fetter nods, though he does not understand this casual interaction at all. He looks at his own identity card in some confusion.
It looks the same at first, but . . . have the strings of haecceity
changed? He tries to remember them, but only fragments come
to mind, like the fragment that Koel once told him marked him
as almost-chosen. He can't find it now, but he might be misre-
membering or failing to see it. He shoves the card back in his
pocket and puts on the mask he was given—the policeman corrects him when he has it inside out—and tucks it over his nose
and mouth. The policeman is wearing a cloth mask himself, but
shoved down below his chin.

Inside the mask, Fetter's breath is faster and hotter than it
should be. The mask smells of someone else's body.

He walks toward the sea, drawn by its distant salt and rumble, but when he remembers he's walking toward the beach of
executions his feet come to a convulsive halt. He turns west
instead and walks toward the Pediment, but slows again, wondering if he's being observed. His father knew about the play,
but the play was meant to be known. Banned now, which is not
a surprise. The Perfect and Kind called Koel and Caduv seditionists, not terrorists. Fetter isn't sure what, if anything, the

police know. He is obviously not wanted under his own name and haecceity, otherwise that policeman would surely have . . . The thought trails off into confusion, as he is no longer sure what the police might do in any situation, or even if his haecceity is the same as before. Perhaps his father has had it tampered with. Is he being surveilled? No, it's probably Koel and Caduv who are being surveilled, if they haven't gone into hiding. No matter what the situation, he shouldn't violate the terms of his parole on his very first day.

What day *is* it, he wonders. What time is it? He feels untethered from time; he can't even remember the phase of tonight's moon. He looks up to check the position of the sun, and freezes when he sees a saffron flutter far above him, unmoving in the sky, alone in the blue where nothing should be so still.

But no, it isn't still: it's moving, slowly, heedless of the wind; it makes sharp turns that should not be possible for anything airborne; it reverses direction at a whim.

He stares for a few minutes, mouth a little open in shock, eyes squinting in the sun. It's a person, hovering—no, standing, as if the air were solid—hundreds of metres high, above the tallest buildings, moving in something almost like a grid pattern over the city, but with jagged angles and sudden reversals, sudden increases and decreases of speed.

"Don't let him notice you," mutters a voice, and when Fetter brings his eyes down to street level, blinded by the bright sky, he sees a woman carrying groceries in a plastic bag, already many paces away.

The other thing marring the sky are the pillars of smoke over the city. There are none nearby, but they seem to be rising in all directions. They remind him of his mother's pyre, though they are not so tremendous. Smaller fires, but burning all across the city. The thought fills him with dread.

Fetter goes back to his own building—back *home*, he tries,

but it's not there, and maybe it won't ever be again—and knocks at apartment doors, looking for familiar faces. The Sands is as volatile as ever. Many are gone and he doesn't know if they've moved or fallen sick or been taken. New faces are wary of him and mumble excuses through their masks. His reputation as a helpful elder statesman of the neighbourhood is gone as if it had never been. Perhaps in his absence, people have stopped telling newcomers to *ask Fetter*. Even the faces that he does recognize—at least, the unmasked parts that seem familiar— treat him with caution and a condescension that he recognizes and is belatedly shamed by, the superiority of the ones who have *been* here and who *know* to the newcomer who hasn't, and doesn't. He is not invited in, but that may be quarantine protocol. From the few willing to speak to him across the bars of a closed door, he learns how much the city has changed while he's been gone, over what seems to be a few months but feels like years.

It is the White Year, they tell him, where have you *been* that you don't know this? And he tries and fails to explain. He learns not to mention prison, and he is unable to speak of Acusdab, and what happened there.

He asks about the flags and the pillars of smoke and the saffron blur in the sky, though he doesn't need the last question answered so much as confirmed. He doesn't know Magellan at all, but he understood the message as clearly as anybody else in the city when he saw the Saint-Errant in the sky.

The message is this: *the saints are here now, and this place belongs to them.*

෴

Fetter takes his time. He has a base of operations, even if it doesn't feel like home. He reads his own books, for the pleasure of it and as a rebuke to the occupied sky. He asks questions of his neighbours and of people in the street, and, carefully, even of policemen.

This last is possible because something about his identity card *has* been tampered with. He is sure of it. The police now treat him with an unfamiliar measure of respect. The haecceity strings that mark his race and caste must have changed. He has no way of knowing whether it is a legitimately reissued card or a forgery at the hands of his father's supporters, but the police treat it as legitimate, so Fetter tries to stop worrying about the authenticity of his false new status. He reminds himself that his old status was equally false. Status is a rainbow on a proud soap bubble, inflated to its uttermost.

Bright doors go neglected across the city, familiar sights made unfamiliar by the lack of tending and study and worship. Sometimes he sees a basket of rotting fruit before one, little snail's trails of ash from long-gone joss sticks. He is careful not to go near any of the doors. The city is pockmarked with them, bright wounds bleeding into empty waters, attracting . . . he'd learned to call them *devils* so habitually that he stopped using his mother's phrase for them—the invisible laws and powers of the world. But his father named them people: the lost peoples of forgotten histories, translated through a bright and bloody membrane. How close am I, he wonders, to becoming one? Am I defeated enough? Am I lost enough? Is my world ready to shatter, to empty like a cracked cup?

He checks in at the North Luriat Police Station every day, as instructed. He has the option of meeting with his father or the Saint-General, but that feels like an insult he doesn't need to seek out. The police are bad enough, but his new haecceity smoothes down the experience. He wonders if his father expected Fetter to come talk to him. He claimed to be good at predicting what would happen next, so probably not. His father gave Fetter the escape route himself, after all. Perhaps that was another insult: perhaps he is supposed to feel cowardly for taking the easy way out. The thought amuses him. He has no fear of cowardice, and if his father doesn't understand that, then the limits to the Perfect and Kind's power and knowledge are not as unreachable as they first seemed.

It's almost a week before he runs into a pyre, on the way back from one such check-in, the root of one of those tall pillars of smoke. It is a funeral pyre of a sort, after all—except there is no grand firestorm, no towering flammable construction, no dancing mourners, no oil of sweet basil. There is only the stench of kerosene and burning meat, and a blackened body slumped in the street with a burning tyre around its neck, a slender column of flame. There are people watching all around, and it is impossible to tell which of them set the fire and which came upon it in horror. He moves toward the fire—it can't harm him, after all; his relationship to fire is very different now—wondering if there is any possibility that the person is still alive, though they are not moving and the fire seems to have been burning for a while, but before he can do more than reach forward toward the flame, he's grabbed and dragged away. He still can't tell if he's being stopped by murderers intent on their work continuing undisturbed or by people trying to save him from burning. They don't speak, or if they do, he doesn't hear them over the crackle and roar in his ears. When they let him go, outside the circle of observers, they walk back to their positions. They are not uniformed or armed. From behind they look like ordinary people, walking away, locking back into place.

The twinge in his gut strikes again one day, a rare occurrence after its long silence, as if his luck has been keeping a cautious distance. It drags him up several streets and around a corner to another fire and a familiar face in it, a cold shock that almost quenches hot terror and rage. It's Janno wearing the burning tyre necklace.

He has seen half a dozen such pyres in recent weeks, but it is infinitely worse to recognize a face. Fetter's hands spasm, uselessly, but Janno is already and very obviously dead. Fetter does not get any closer. He tries to remember Janno's face sleeping and then waking, the pupils wide and hazy, but Fetter's own eyes, despite his attempts to draw them away, are pulled back again and again as if by hooks, to char and caricature. He backs away, clawing at his throat, choking behind his plague mask on bile and vomit from his roiling gut. It feels as if he should be coughing up blood.

∽

The city's fires are diverse. Most of Luriat is staying home and the streets are a desert, but Fetter can't stop himself from venturing out into the city to track down the beacons of smoke.

Sometimes he finds burning vehicles, the flames so intense that he can't tell if anybody is inside them. Tuktuks, cars, once even a bus that flamed enough to blacken the walls and darken the windows of the building behind it. By the time Fetter comes upon it, is merely a smouldering husk licked by small red tongues. Sometimes the fires are bright doors burning: he can tell from the faint underscent beneath the smoke. The burning buildings may be homes or shops, the latter identifiable from the remnants of signs. He can tell, from the charred fragments of hellspeak, that the shops were not randomly selected but targeted by the assigned race and caste of their owners.

He thinks all this is the aftermath of a pogrom that must surely have run its course, until he chances on a crowd of running young men led by a monk of the Path Behind. It is only then he understands that the pogrom is alive, still surging and flowing through the city. The monk directs his army with a booming voice. Some wear masks, but most do not. The monk is bare-faced. There are policemen present: they hover indulgently in the margins, mutter to each other as if critiquing the pogrom's technique, cluck their tongues at every error and inefficiency, sometimes step forward to correct a stance or issue an instruction. Sometimes, too, they pick off stragglers, avuncular scavengers in the pogrom's wake.

Fetter feels utterly exposed, caught in broad daylight with no cover and no luck; he and the few others on the street all quickly back away, try to obscure themselves. Fetter turns off the main street and down a narrower residential lane, but there's even less cover here. The small houses have their windows and doors tightly shut, not breathing. He moves down the street as quickly as he can without running. He doesn't want to attract attention, he thinks, until he hears running footsteps behind him. He hesitates, then quickens his pace, then breaks into a run himself. Crashing sounds suggest doors at the top of the lane being broken down. Are they chasing him? The lane is short and narrow, and it leads to another street that has plenty of escape routes. Nearly at the end, he skids to a halt to look behind him and judge the level of danger, and later he will berate himself for this error. He will wonder if in looking back he changed time like his father, whether the men behind him were always there or whether they were only there because he looked. Perhaps in another world, an empty realm rapidly receding, he kept running, never hesitating or looking back, and escaped without further misadventure.

In this world, they grab him. He's swung around, pushed roughly against a wall. He feels his feet leave the ground and panics, tightening the deep clench in his belly, lowering his centre of gravity. To the three men who've caught up with him, it must look like he's grovelling, lowering himself to a squatting position. They don't seem to have noticed his overlong moment in the air. Perhaps they feel strong for tossing him about like a feather. They're asking him questions, but he can't hear or understand; his ears are full of a soft roar of fire or blood. They are unmasked. He watches their lips move. He struggles for the identity card in his pocket and lifts it up at them, brandishing his haecceity. One of the men looks at it and curls a lip.

"Fake," the man says, with absolute conviction. Fetter hears this word clearly, cutting through the static. The man is big, much bigger than Fetter, and his head is shaved as if he's a soldier or Behinder monk in civilian clothes. There are screams and crashes from the direction they'd come, and heat besides, but Fetter doesn't dare take his eyes off this man. He tries to remember his training in violence, but it seems to have abandoned him. He hasn't felt physically confident since prison—no, since he walked through his mother's pyre, as if it burned her training out of him, as if she took her gifts back when she left.

"Real," Fetter says, but he's immediately conscious this was a mistake, because the man narrows his eyes and the other two—who seemed more interested in whatever was happening up the lane—focus on him, flanking the big man and crowding Fetter.

"You're not Luriati," the big man says. "We can tell from the way you talk. Take off the mask."

Fetter takes off the mask. I'm not Luriati, he wants to agree, and so what? What is Luriat to me, that I should give a shit? But it is never truth that seems called for, only violence, and he has too much of the one in him now for any of the other. That well is dry and his bones feel brittle. He can barely make a fist.

It's not so bad, in the end. They beat him but they don't kill him. They don't necklace him with a tyre. He feels grateful, eventually, or at least he tells himself he does, to only lose one of his front teeth, to only break one of his ribs, to never quite breathe easy again—from then on, for the rest of his life, something in his chest is always raw, scraping, making him struggle with a deep breath or a long sentence. Despite the intimacy of this interaction, he does not catch the plague again.

He heals badly, slow and painful, in his own bed, out of a fear of hospitals. He won't consign himself to institutions that will make a number of him. He fears being found there, weak and vulnerable, to be dragged out and burned. He finishes his bag of painkillers, one by one.

He starves, feverish, until one of his neighbours—someone new to the city, she says, he doesn't know her—checks in on him. She says she walked in because the door was open and she wanted to see. He forgot to lock it or lost the key: he doesn't remember how he made it back. Only flashes of staggering and a forensic record of bruising. She brushes aside his bedroom curtain and finds him huddled in bed. He can't see her properly, only a blur, lost in harsh daylight striking tears from his swollen-shut eyes. She never gives him her name, or he doesn't remember it. The first thing he understands from her is *the door is open*, so he misunderstands and thinks of her as Bright Door, though he's too foggy to remember the reference.

She brings him food and water, putting it in his room while he's sleeping or dazed. This unexpected generosity is how he lives. He never gets a good look at her because she stops coming before he heals enough to bear the light. He remembers a smile that seems to stretch too wide across her face, but perhaps it is just that the smile is all he remembers. It gets bigger and broader every time he summons it in his memory, until her face is all teeth.

Strangers seem to come and speak to him in his fever: some humanoid, others devilish; some masked and defaced, others armed and heralded by faint drums. He doesn't feel safe. His bedroom echoes with questions whispered and shouted in languages that he doesn't recognize, a territory constantly invaded through a door that is permanently open. He tried to tell Bright Door to close it behind her, to lock up for him, but he couldn't speak.

Afterward, when his fevers subside and the swellings go down and he can't stop tonguing the empty space where his front tooth used to be, he limps door to door through the entire building but never finds Bright Door again, or anybody who will claim to know her, or, for that matter, him.

# 30

There comes a point where pillars of smoke mark the city's crematoria as much as sites of murder. The crematoria are overloaded with victims of the plague. There are queues, and protestors flanking the queues, the bereaved whose traditions demand burial in earth or sky, both forbidden during the White Year by special gazette from the Storm Court: they found a way to make mourning a fresh injury. Behind the deathly white is fire, all the shades of red and yellow you might see staring into naked flame—robes and arson and pyres and blood.

When Fetter limps back out into the city, he finds there are more fires than the ones he knows. He watches a Behinder monk immolate himself in the street, chanting a slogan. The monk burns stoically for a few seconds before he screams and runs. The crowd of the weeping faithful attempt to douse the flames, or perhaps to hold him down, but they only burn their hands. Around them, the slightly less faithful take up his chant, which becomes clear to Fetter slowly, as if through a fog.

"No speaking, only ashes! No ashes! Only speaking!"

Fetter tries to find out what the burning monk was protesting. He asks a man on the edge of the chanters when he takes a moment to breathe, who says it was a call for the new government to make it illegal for believers to leave the Path, to disavow belief or to convert to other faiths.

"To the Path Above?" Fetter asks.

"To the Path, above us all!" The man seems cheered by this novel salutation.

Fetter moves to the crowd's periphery to find an outer circle of onlookers less engaged with the material, but they are also less certain of what the protest is about. One suggests that as a monk of the Path, that man was overwhelmed by compassion for animals being slaughtered for meat. Another says the man burned to escape a summons from the Summer Court to be tried for fraud. Others begin to show interest in his questions and gather to come up with new explanations—Fetter extricates himself and moves away even as they present their theories to each other.

The city authorities still demand people stay at home and avoid creating new plague clusters. The TV, loudspeaker announcements from passing trucks, the occasional newspaper still being printed, even shouted instructions from teams of public health inspectors proceeding door to door, flanked by armed soldiers: everything tells Luriatis to stay indoors. Going outside is forbidden except for essential services and emergencies; essence and emergence are judged on a case-by-case basis by police holding court on the street. But it seems to Fetter that three-quarters of the city is on the street anyway. Some are engaged in the grand project of pogrom: it has not ended, though it seems to be tiring. He is much more careful now, staying apprised of its movements and making sure he's never anywhere near the main column. He's learned not to rely on fortunate spasms of his gut. He can, he thinks ruefully, approximate good sense by paying close attention to the world and learning from his mistakes.

There are networks of command and control to the pogrom. He recognizes them by observing from a distance, reading the reports in the independent press, watching videos on social media. Phone calls that are instantly obeyed, ringing sounds followed by apparently involuntary movements of the limbs, the subsumption of the hearer's will in the caller's design. On the street the wave of ringtones can be like tinnitus, a buzzing and a music coming all together, a summoning for a moveable and many-headed beast. But it is the opposite of mindless: there are too many minds at work, too much intention.

Fetter walks the city ever careful of escape routes and the present location and vector of trouble, ensuring that he is always moving away from it. At a distance from the city's trouble, he has more time to think about his own. Why hasn't he been arrested for violating the terms of his parole? It's been days—no, weeks?—since he attended his last mandatory daily check-in. There has not even been a summons delivered to his apartment.

Perhaps his father has been covering for him. Or perhaps, Fetter thinks while walking through the burning city, rubbing shoulders with the lost and the looters, listening to breaking glass and the ever-present crackle of fire, coughing up the gritty ashes in his throat, perhaps he is simply low priority. He should not take the absence of action against him as an indication that his punishment isn't all stacking up somewhere, a tide held back only by this dam of circumstance.

He doesn't risk going back to the North Luriat Police Station for a belated check-in, in case they interpret this as a provocation to arrest him at once.

He doesn't go near the GDCC, either; he avoids the whole Plantations district. He can't predict what his father would do, and Fetter is vulnerable again—is he more so than he was before, when his father so generously gave him the freedom of this burning city? How real are the terms of his parole? How real was his release in the first place? His prison is now the world entire. Whatever he does, he will always be in violation.

He goes to Koel's house, since his parole is already broken, but she's not there. Other people have taken it over and claim to have no idea who she is or where she might have gone. Caduv's apartment is the same. In increasing recklessness, he goes to Hej's apartment—he will explain his absence somehow, he thinks; he will forgive somehow, if Hej did snitch on him, or be forgiven somehow for his own betrayals, for the lies and omissions, for throwing his life away—but the door, a stolid cage with thick bars and a fine grey mesh, is firmly secured with a huge padlock. There is no answer to his hails. Most of the apartments in Hej's building are similarly locked up. He vaguely recalls Hej talking about spending much of the White Year in some exclusive getaway in the hill cities, a nice holiday away from the mess: Fetter took that for a joke about privilege, but perhaps it was simply privilege. *It's too depressing, I need a vacation. Come with me?* Is that what Hej said? He can't remember the exact words. *Let them kill each other.*

Fetter had said no; Hej had shrugged.

Fetter remembers the shrug clearly, though the words that surrounded it are lost. That shrug dislodged Fetter's heart; it slid and fell and spiderwebbed with cracks. He told himself then that it didn't matter, that a relationship meant you had to work through some differences. Now—well, it feels like it doesn't matter now, either. He shakes the bars and tells himself it doesn't matter and he spits for good measure, imagining his hands on Hej's throat and the spit in Hej's mouth. The thought would have made him hard once. He feels the ghost of something pass through his body, as if a devil had walked through him, and then it's gone.

Fetter approaches Cooksferry on foot, since the buses and light rail are no longer running. The streets are empty apart from the occasional speeding vehicle, fleeing or chasing, their metal surfaces shining so bright in the sun that they pierce through his eyes into his brain. He is now desperate to find anyone who might know him by face, even if under another name. He's unsure if he means to seek out Pipra or whether it would be enough to know she's alive, and whether she knows about him, and *what* she knows, now that he betrayed her, and his father undid it, and his history with her is hopelessly snarled—what has he done or not done now, what are they to each other, would she even know him? He thinks of the ghost of a white lotus, a note written and unwritten.

But none of this matters. The mall is a black, burned-out husk. He stands and stares at it for a long time. It seems like the work of an old fire, any embers long since extinguished by rain, much of the ash blown away by wind, most of the walls collapsed. He wonders if any of the bright doors have survived, but does not risk entry: the ruins look unsafe. It is not possible that they all died here, Pipra and Janno—no, Janno died later, in a different fire—and Avli and the others. No, not here. They would have had warning, they would have fled long before fire brought the building down. He cannot bear the thought of blackened bones in that rubble.

As he turns away to begin his long, weary trudge back across the city to the Sands, a car pulls up. For an absurd moment he fears that it's the Saint-General come to fetch him, before he bends to look through the window. The top of the car, the hood and the roof, has been painted in a reflective material: it is blinding, reflecting the sun. This is what many vehicles have done—they each feel like a stab through his eyeballs as they pass. A middle finger to the sky, chaff to dazzle and confuse the eye above. He hoods his eyes to peer, and sees Ulpe at the wheel. They are not wearing a mask, and their face looks older and grimmer than Fetter remembers.

He gets in and closes the door. He is trembling. He thinks it is exhaustion, or shock, or the weight of grief held in abeyance.

Several questions jam against each other in his throat, dislodging ash from his mouth. Or no, that is just the taste that he has not been allowed to forget since his mother's pyre. "The paint," he says. "Does it work?"

Ulpe shrugs. "We think so," they say. "We've distributed it to as many vehicles as possible to make life harder for Magellan."

"Doesn't he have supramundane powers?" Fetter says, sinking into his seat as Ulpe swings the car around and accelerates. The road is empty of traffic but pockmarked with ruin. They weave between burnt-out wrecks, things that could have been vehicles, perhaps, or people. Fetter looks at them in passing, trying to swallow. It hurts to breathe, but now it always does. He takes off his mask, too, and tries to smile, to soften what may have sounded like a criticism. "Who's *we*? Are the others all right?"

Ulpe glances at him. "Are *you* all right? You've lost a . . . I mean—"

"A tooth, I know," Fetter says. He laughs, then groans when his ribs grind. "Not the prettiest one any more."

Ulpe glances in his direction again and though Fetter keeps his eyes facing forward, he can sense their smile, perhaps of relief. "You were *never* the prettiest one," they say. "Caduv and Koel are all right. We're going to them now."

"You've been watching me?"

"Yes. No. We've been in hiding since the play was banned. Your apartment was surveilled, so we didn't dare get close," Ulpe says. "And we kept losing track of you in the city— between Magellan and the cops and the pogrom, it was too hard to approach you without being seen. Too risky. Sorry. But someone spotted you coming out this way, and Koel told me where you'd be."

Fetter nods. He stretches his legs with difficulty in the cramped vehicle; his feet and calves ache.

Ulpe drives them to a district called White Teak. Fetter is unfamiliar with it. Unlike most of Luriat, it is urban-grey with no greenery in sight. There are vast concrete amphitheatres that Ulpe says are the campuses of tech companies, marked off by giant signs that Fetter has difficulty parsing, acronyms and slogans like incantations. They remind him of the sponsorship signs in the prison.

Further into the district, staggered ranks of high-rise apartment buildings recede into the distance. They are taller and seemingly better-appointed than Fetter's own or anything in the Sands, but they are still grey stained black with age and rain, not glassy and gleaming like the luxury towers that dot the Plantations. Ulpe drives deeper into this maze.

Fetter peers up through the windows, looking for Magellan, but less and less of the sky is visible as they drive between the towering buildings. The narrow strip of blue above is cut by power lines and washing and flags and cables, slashed by ropes of mysterious purpose, parallel and in tension. He wonders aloud if some of them are bridges, providing passage between the upper floors of nearby buildings.

"It's part of the culture here," Ulpe says. "People on the high floors live up there as much as possible. They run their own rooftop markets and pass their properties down the generations and hold their own elections for representation in local government. They're having one next week, in fact; that's why there are so many posters."

Fetter knows land disputes well—he grew up listening to his mother adjudicate them for his contentious far-kin in Acusdab— but here it seems that the concept of property extends into the sky. Are these people not laying claim to a block of air, he thinks.

If the building came down, only the likes of Magellan could visit their property.

According to his father, Fetter too could master such powers. He tries to imagine that perspective. What would White Teak look like from above? Concrete roofs blistering in the sun; tangles of ropes and fluttering flags; an impenetrable hive of humanity. He fails to imagine what he doesn't know: What the world looks like to an adept of the supramundane who can walk on air. Are they in truth blinded by some shiny paint? Are they unable to see through a concrete wall? He hazily remembers his mother's elucidations of Behinder theory. Someone who has reached the higher levels of awakening should perceive the world as a great emptiness, the apparently solid exposed by the vast spaces between its atoms, the unreality of time and distance, the hollow at the heart of essence. The always-borning empty realms are but the husks shed by an empty world.

Magellan might be looking directly at him right now, seeing through ten thousand barriers as if they were a film of clear water. Fetter can't stop his face from twitching in a smile—a bitter one, a grimace, a baring of teeth. He looks out of the window instead.

Amidst election posters and banners full of smiling faces next to names and numbers, White Teak has no shortage of the other flags that Fetter has been seeing all around Luriat: the sun and the moon, the beast with its guns and blades.

Ulpe parks the car and hustles Fetter into the shelter of an apartment building and up a flight of stairs. The steps are polished concrete, too narrow. They both walk at a slight angle.

On the second floor, far below the tiers of the aired gentry, Koel and Caduv are hiding out, together with several other people—Fetter recognizes one from Koel's theatre crew, but not the others. Koel looks up at him almost without reaction, her face a mask of worry lines, and at first he thinks she's reverted to the angry, sniping Koel of their early acquaintance. But then she rises to embrace him, smiling. He returns both the press and the smile, muttering brief explanations and reassurances to her noises of concern, at his bereavement, his imprisonment, his assault, his injuries.

They sit on the floor, which is covered in mattresses in place of furniture. He counts the mattresses: this hideaway shelters more people than are now present in it. Someone offers him tea. He drinks it. Koel, Caduv, and Ulpe sit around him, and it's like the old days. The other people shift to another room, and he can't tell if they are giving them privacy or seeking their own.

Fetter talks about everything except Relic *a*. He does not attempt to explain his assassination attempt or his father's ability to undo events: it would only fill them with despair. It's when he says he met his father that Caduv speaks up.

"You were in the room with the Perfect and Kind, and you didn't kill him?" Caduv says. It's the first thing he's said. He's been sitting across from Fetter, his expression shuttered. "Isn't that the whole point of you?"

Koel waves a hand at Caduv. Her face is serious, her jaw set. Fetter thinks about the white teeth tattooed underneath her clavicles, now covered by her camisa. "Destinies are hard when they come upon us," she says. "To refuse, to accept, to bend or to break—whatever you choose to do with them, they're hard."

"What *destinies*," Caduv scoffs. "Our whole group was made of unchosen ones. That was what defined us. We have no destinies except the ones we make."

Unexpectedly, it's Ulpe who answers. "We've each chosen to chase the destinies we weren't given, though." They sound wry. It's a knowing tone that Fetter isn't used to hearing in their voice. "You tried to use a song to change the world, didn't you? Koel walked and told the truth. Fetter is trying to fight his father . . . It's just that none of it *worked*. And I . . ."

"Have you found him yet?" Koel asks, gently, her eyes shadowed. Fetter thinks it's concern for Ulpe, but there's a deeper worry, something raw.

"No," Ulpe says. "Not yet, though I go to every one. But I can feel it. He is coming. The White Year, it's—he will come."

"What . . ." Fetter trails off. "The fires? Is it . . . ?" He doesn't know how to ask this question.

Ulpe smiles. It is brittle, crumbling at the edges. They look like they haven't slept well in weeks. Their eyes are bloodshot and bagged, their lips dry and bleeding. "I won't let it happen. Don't worry."

This is met with silence: weighty from the others, ignorant from Fetter. He wants to ask what *it* is, who *he* is, but there is too much pain on everybody's face.

"I should go," Ulpe says, at last. The others are silent while they leave, so Fetter is too. Fetter will never see Ulpe again, though he has no way of knowing this was a final leavetaking.

After the door closes, Fetter turns to Koel and finally asks the question. "The Man in the Fire . . . ?"

"It's unfair," Koel says, heavily. It looks like she's not going to say anything more, but she looks at Fetter's face and ekes out a few more words. "It's unfair, but *we* can't deal with that right now. We're relying on Ulpe to . . . handle it."

"We should *help* them," Caduv says, and almost immediately Koel cuts in, as if this is an argument they've been having often.

"And we *will*," she says. "But the White Year is well underway, and we're *failing*. We have to survive the war we're in."

Caduv responds with something Fetter doesn't understand, about some action somewhere else in the city that's already happened or is about to happen. The conversation has shifted firmly away, as if they really don't want to talk about the Man in the Fire, and whatever Ulpe is doing about him—going from pyre to pyre, looking for . . . someone. A person in the flame? A devil, coming out of the fire? He tries to remember what his father said about empty realms. Could the fires across Luriat be openings, like the bright doors? He has not sensed anything supramundane about them. No strange scent, no otherworldly aura. Nothing like the bright doors at all. Only murder and arson, very much of this world.

Fetter shifts his attention back to the room, the conversation he's only half following. He waits till they fall silent.

"What happened?" Fetter asks, and he means, to every-thing, to the city, to their plans—he tries to indicate this with a gesture, a confused swirl of his hand that encompasses the world and the times, which Koel seems to understand.

"I didn't anticipate the extent to which the Perfect and Kind could centralize moral and temporal authority under himself once he arrived," Koel says, after thinking for a moment, as if he had asked *What was your mistake?* "And I didn't anticipate how much worse that would make the White Year. All our tac-tics relied on pitting the factions of Luriat against each other, but we had a far briefer window of productive chaos than I hoped for. We barely managed to pull off the prison break."

"We barely *survived* it," Caduv says.

Koel nods. She ticks off failed plans on her fingers, most of which Fetter doesn't recognize. "The soft power push is dead in the water. We never managed to get to phase two after the play was banned by the Summer Court. Now that even skep-tics like Coema are formally taking to the Path, there's a level of ideological lockstep that we've not had to deal with before."

"And street-level opposition is impossible with Magellan in the air," Caduv says. Perhaps because he was himself such a major component of the play, he seems uninterested in dissecting its failure. "Otherwise we might have been able to break the pogrom's organizational structure weeks ago."

"We keep losing people to Magellan," Koel says. She sounds very tired. "He has to be stopped."

"Surface to air missile," Caduv says, and laughs. It's an ugly laugh. "I'm not joking."

"We can't source *that* kind of weaponry," Koel says.

"Magellan takes people?" Fetter asks. "Where do they go?"

"Prison, we hope," Koel says. "We're trying to figure that out, but Salyut purged the prison administration and most of our contacts were swept up. Magellan picks out our people one by one—he only seems to need a direct line of sight to identify someone, and can reach them in moments. He comes down and disappears them. They're gone in a blink."

Fetter thinks about empty realms and how casually his father uses them as dumping grounds. *Prison, we hope.* Yes, he understands that. Prisons you can at least try to break people out of.

"I'm sorry," he says to Caduv, who immediately stands up as if he's been waiting for this. Koel leans back against the wall, looking resigned.

"Fuck you," Caduv says. "We nearly lost people just getting *ready* to break you out. And then you . . . you fucking checked out on your father's say-so, like it was a hotel. I'm glad we didn't waste ourselves on you."

"I'm still . . . It's a parole. I'm not really free," Fetter tries, but Caduv is too enraged to listen.

"You've made it clear that *you* don't need our help," Caduv says, his voice so full of bile that he has to stop to cough. "We're not fighting the Perfect and Kind for you. We're doing it for everybody *except* you. You're the only one who's safe, no matter what you do or don't do. He'll never hurt his precious and only son."

Caduv walks away, going into the other room and drawing the curtain behind him.

Fetter groans and shifts to a seat next to Koel, leaning on the wall. They sit in silence for a while. He's surprised to find himself smiling, baring his missing tooth. Koel looks at him sidelong.

"I don't know that look on your face," she says. "Is that a good sign?"

"You said you couldn't source a missile," Fetter says. "But it sounded to me like there were weapons you *could* source."

Koel raises an eyebrow. "You said you wouldn't kill again."

"I lied," Fetter says. The baldness of this sticks in his throat, but he coughs it away. "I want to help. I have . . . there are things I want to make up for." He doesn't specify which things, because he's not sure. He's not sorry that Koel and Caduv didn't get themselves killed trying to rescue him. It sounds like they managed to rescue others. That sounds like a win.

Maybe he's digging for victories in the middle of all this defeat.

"Magellan only comes down to ground level for moments," Koel says. "He's so fast. He only seems to need the briefest contact to disappear someone. I've seen it twice in person and several more times on video. There's that ugly flutter of robes in the sky, and then a smear across the world like blood, and he's on the ground. He takes his target by the upper arm, like a cop. His fingers dig in—I remember the way my friend's tattoos distorted when Magellan grabbed her—and then she was gone. His hand was still in the same grabbing posture, the fingers like a claw."

"Who was she?" Fetter asks.

"Nobody you know," Koel says. "It was at a protest, one of the few that seemed like it stood a chance of drawing more people in. She was a teacher. I mean, she was also literally a teacher of children—she taught gramarye and dialectics at the University College of South Luriat, in the Alabi Literature Department—but that was her role in the world. I admired her. I'm not going to see her again, am I?"

Fetter shakes his head. "I don't think so. I'm sorry." Maybe if she comes back through a bright door, he thinks, but you wouldn't see her then, or be able to recognize her even if you could.

"The other time I saw it happen was at a rally by one of the smaller revolutionary parties. Their spokesperson, who had been getting noticed online for being loud and critical— this was before they shut down the city's internet—anyway, it wasn't a well-attended rally, but I attended because I wanted to meet with them after. I was in the back, so I didn't get as good a look as I did with my friend, but it was the same. It happens very fast, and afterwards he just rises up into the sky again. He's gone before anybody can even shoot at him."

"Did anybody try?"

"Not that day," Koel says. "But it's been tried. He's either out of range, or moving too fast. One group I know, they had a sniper who swore he should have hit him. They say Magellan caught and disappeared the bullet. A few days later, he disappeared the sniper too."

Fetter thinks about this.

"There are a couple of other lies I should clear up," Fetter says, glancing at the closed curtain that Caduv vanished behind. "Lies of omission, but still."

Koel laughs. She's the only one of them still capable of laughter, Fetter thinks, and then to prove himself wrong, he laughs too.

"Tell me true things," Koel says, and he does.

# 31

He wears his own old clothes for what comes next: a big blousy camisa and wide breeches, only partly for concealment, but in some part also because he has that feeling again of things ending. This second life in Luriat, as a shackled ghost haunting the ruins of his first, is a mockery; he understands that now, the insult of it.

The site was carefully chosen by Koel—Caduv absented himself from planning. It's midway on a long, narrow, winding lane called Under the Canopy of Forgiveness, on the fringes of a district called Pale Black Moon right on the border of the Plantations. There are no witnesses, only small houses shuttered tight. This is one of two reasons that Koel picked it: so that Fetter would not be disturbed while he waits, looking up.

He feels strangely light in his bones, as if feverish. Perhaps this is what it feels like to unburden yourself.

The second reason is that just over the district boundary from Pale Black Moon to the Plantations, a border unmarked except in hearts and minds and property values, all the way down to the far end of Under the Canopy of Forgiveness, is the east wall of the GDCC. The Centre itself is further away, but the private park begins here. On the other side of that wall thousands of people camp: supporters of the Perfect and Kind, here to attend his every sermon and inch closer to spiritual improvement, if not awakening. Three times a day, sometimes more, Koel says, Magellan passes over Under the Canopy of

Forgiveness on his way to check in at the GDCC. There are other, less frequently used approaches on the west side, but they are deeper into the Plantations where Fetter is likely to be spotted. So he's here, in this little pocket of shuddering suburbia. He wonders if he's being observed through any windows, but he doesn't think so. Most of the houses around him are partly or entirely hidden by high walls. He walks a little further down Under the Canopy of Forgiveness and finds a canyon where there is nothing to see but wall. There is no foot traffic on this street, no sound except a distant bird he can't identify and the faint high susurrus of the crowd in the GDCC park.

When Magellan comes, he's already descending. Koel listed this as an additional advantage, though Fetter does not feel the need for it. He aligns himself along Magellan's flight path and runs down Under the Canopy of Forgiveness, giving himself momentum and direction before he unclenches the muscle in his gut that's been holding him down his whole life. When his feet leave the ground on his next bounding stride, they don't come down again.

Magellan doesn't fly, exactly. He doesn't hover. He doesn't float like Fetter does. His feet are flat and planted, as if he stands on a solid surface. Sometimes he even walks, though more often he simply moves, as if on an invisible conveyor in the sky, a ghost and tangled walkway. His head swivels constantly, looking at the city below him.

When Fetter launches himself, he, too, is not flying or floating: with his momentum and direction, he is a missile. The upward rush is exhilarating, the wind whipping his baggy clothes and forcing him to narrow his eyes, but his aim is true, and it only takes moments to near the descending saint. Fetter spares a glance down to see the park revealed, the tents and the cook-fires, plastic bottles glinting in the sun, the black-haired heads now turning to show indistinct brown faces—oh, they've seen him, they're pointing. Is there excitement in the buzz and burr of their distant collective voice, or is he imagining that?

His eyes flick up to Magellan, who is so close that Fetter can see the man's eyes widen. The Saint-Errant recognizes his master's son. Did any of them know he could do this? Fetter thinks not, from the expression on the older man's face.

It's not speed or precision that he's using to catch Magellan. It's not even surprise—it's curiosity.

Magellan says something and puts out a hand, as if to catch Fetter. The Saint-Errant doesn't look much like his counterpart—he is darker, more compact, and he wears his robes in a different style with both shoulders covered, as if it gets cold in the sky sometimes—but they have the same intensity, the same grim to their lip. Perhaps that's what it means to be a saint of the fourth level of awakening, Fetter thinks, reaching out his own hand to meet Magellan's.

He could have worn that saint's face. If he had chosen.

At close range, the tightness of Magellan's face is revealed to be wonderment.

Fetter grips Magellan by the hand and pulls, unbalancing them both—he needs to be below the other man for this to work—and the Saint-Errant gasps as he loses his standing posture. He has been yanked off his solid surface and is now, unexpectedly, floating in the air.

Fetter reaches inside his loose collar and triggers the infernal machine wrapped around his chest. It's been even harder to breathe for the past two hours, as if the tight vest with the packed explosives were a corset, so there is a moment of relief as it burns up and his chest expands, followed immediately by a sharp stabbing pain in his ribs—not the bomb, though, that's his injury—and soft cool fire licks his clothes off like a lover. The shockwave hits him late, as if it had to gather itself first; his field of vision is swallowed in flame until the fireball spits him out, the force of the explosion sending him hurtling down. He misjudged the angle a little: he is being hurled backward in the air, sending him over the park wall. He's turning, helpless to control his fall—he tucks his head down and his knees up, trying to protect himself, but this only makes him spin faster. And then there's a . . . he'd call it a crash, except his body has remembered that he weighs nothing; he's a feather, a shadow, so how could he crash? He lands, that's all, spins and tumbles and collides with soft warm flesh and plastic sheeting and heavy tarpaulin. Before he can bounce back up, he remembers to find that muscle in his gut and clench it tight again. He stumbles to his feet. He smells like smoke and he's surrounded by confused people and excited voices, but his vision is blurred and his thoughts staccato. He checks himself, even as others are checking him for injuries. He is naked but for charred rags, but doesn't seem seriously injured. Some cuts and bruises from his rough landing. He is unhurt from the explosion, as he thought he would be, though it's hard to breathe and he finds himself gasping.

He avoided looking at the open sky when he took his leap. He looked only at his target—a lifetime's habit of not falling into the sky, an old deep terror still rattling his bones from how close he risked it. He looks up and the explosion is still there in the sky, a massive black and red flower unnaturally slow in its unfoldings. It's obscene, hard to look away from now that he's looked at it. Everybody is looking at it. Even the people fussing over him keep turning to look at it. Someone gives him a long camisa to wear, and he pulls it on. It comes down to his knees; he felt no shame at his nakedness, but being clothed is a relief because it helps him blend in. They're asking him questions—oh, his ears are ringing. He doesn't answer, and they don't seem to mind. Dimly, he understands that they have already rationalized him away. He's not hurt, so he obviously

wasn't thrown too far, so they say: he must have been standing
in the park nearer the explosion and was flung away by the
shockwave. Even these people, at least a few of whom must
have seen him spat out of the fireball and watched him fall to
earth with their own eyes, have already persuaded themselves
that they saw no such thing.

His survival isn't like the miracle of the flying Saint-Errant,
which has a place in the Path's lore of the fourth level of awakening. Fetter is not legible, and so is not read.

He watches the fireball gently unfurl for a while, in community, in case a furious Saint-Errant comes flying out. But
Magellan does not emerge.

The Third Unforgivable. The sancticide of a votary who has
reached the fourth level of awakening. Or does he have to kill
them both to qualify? He turns to look at the Convention Centre in the distance, gleaming and white. Why did the Luriati
paint it white, if white is their colour of death? Did ingrained
Abjesili or Alabi taste override Luriati aesthetics? Or is it a
prophecy, a warning? Salyut is probably in there somewhere.
And his father. He could get to either of them, if he so chose.
Perhaps he's ready, now, to take back destinies that were stolen
from him.

He was supposed to find his way back to Koel, if he survived.
Did he survive? He contemplates the possibility of not having
survived, a little giddily. He's walked away from Koel's revolution before, and he could again. He just did something important for them, something they could not have done without
him—he's plucked the errant saint out of their sky. He laughs,
and this, finally, gets him the confused and angry looks that
he expected from the people around him who have finally understood that Magellan is dead, and are beginning to wail and
weep. But he's not the only one laughing. Perhaps the absurdity
of this heightened moment has led some closer to awakening,

if not the awakening they came for. He sees a laughing woman some yards in front of him be shoved by a weeper.

Fetter wonders if Koel expected him to survive. He asked for this, he reminds himself. He put himself in her hands and said *I am a coin, spend me.* That great black and red flower unraveling in the sky is what she bought.

He makes the decision with his head, not his heart or gut. He walks out of the GDCC park while the riot is still breaking out. For once, *riot* is not a euphemism. He does not look back to see the laughers and weepers go to war.

Fetter goes to an address he memorized a long time ago but never visited: the Acusdabi embassy.

Luriat doesn't have a diplomatic quarter as such. The major foreign embassies rent out space in the Plantations or in the upmarket end of the Port district. They set up court in grand manses, many of which date back to Abjesili slavers and Alabi governors-general. There is a long, discreet avenue called Tuft Street to the west of the Plantations where smaller embassies congregate. It takes him less than an hour to walk there from the gates of the GDCC, and another hour to walk its length, looking at the nameplates and signboards. The Acusdabi embassy, when he finds it, is a building smaller and less imposing than most. It isn't an embassy proper; the nameplate calls it a legation. There is no security at the door, unlike most of the other embassies on Tuft Street—guards eyed him suspiciously and spoke into their walkie-talkies as he walked past peering at their signs. Fetter being half-dressed, ash-faced, and barefoot probably has something to do with that.

The only grand thing about the Acusdabi embassy, and the strangest, is the door. The door is huge, wider and taller than usual, and made of thick, heavy wood, entirely without deco-ration. There is no window cut into it, no openings, which is a sight so unusual in Luriat that Fetter stares at it for a minute before finally realizing what's wrong with it. It's not a bright door, though, because it is wide open, flat against the wall and wedged into place with a heavy metal cylinder the size of his foot—faint traces of rust around it suggest that the door has been wedged open like this, in all weather, for a long time. The entranceway itself is slightly recessed under an overhang and curtained in heavy brocade.

Fetter rings the bell, then knocks on the wood of the door-jamb. He is about to knock again when the curtain is moved aside. The woman inside is dressed casually in a sleeveless t-shirt and faded sarong, and carries a bowl of colourful food—Fetter can't smell anything except ash. The woman is much older than him; her skin is weathered as if she'd spent a lot of time outdoors, her hair is a messy grey cloud, and there are faded tattoos on her upper arms. She looks startled.

"*Fetter?*" she says, and in that moment he knows he made a mistake, though he can't tell whether the mistake was coming here now or not coming here before.

He stands there, not knowing what to say, while she eats a spoonful, staring at him.

"Well, you'd better get inside," the Envoy Extraordinary says, gesturing with the spoon. "Do you want some fruit salad?"

The Envoy is insistently, aggressively hospitable. He showers and is given a change of clothes, probably her own—another t-shirt and sarong. He discovers fresh injuries in the shower. All his injuries are from the landing or the shockwave, because he wheedled with fate for a generous interpretation of his immunity to fire. An explosion is fire, isn't it? Mostly fire, like a person is mostly water. He isn't burned, but the new bruises are tender and some of the cuts are more serious than he thought, including one on his side which is wide enough that the Envoy insists on stitching him up. He looks away from the needle. He hopes any new internal injuries are not too severe. The old ones are painful enough.

She gives him fruit salad. He eats it, though everything is either astringent or slimy, unpleasant either way. His whole body aches and the cuts sting, but he doesn't feel tired.

"I thought you might be Salyut again," the Envoy says, confidingly. "Or one of his Behinder goons. I've been meaning to get that door fixed Luriati-style so I can slam it."

"Why is Salyut . . . no," Fetter decides, trying to force his thoughts back into some semblance of order. "How do you know who I am?"

"Oh, I see her in your face," the Envoy says.

"You knew my mother?" Fetter says. He tries to see her as something other than an untidy little old woman.

"We're old friends," the Envoy says.

"She's . . . you know she's dead?"

"Of course," the Envoy says. "I poured out the water at her funeral."

"You weren't at the pyre," Fetter says. "What funeral?"

"You went to the pyre," the Envoy says. She seems surprised. "None of the rest of us dared approach the house. The bloody doctors, you know. The great-grandniblings had a traditional funeral in the village, though I think I'm the only one left who remembers what the traditions are, which is why they invited me in the first place. That's good that you went. The doctors wouldn't stop *you*. Did she speak to you?"

"Yes," Fetter says, helplessly. This conversation is reminding him of talking to his mother. "I don't understand—the doctors—are you family? I'm sorry, I don't—"

The Envoy waves a hand. "It's all right. No, we're not kin, as they measure it now. But I was your mother's oldest friend. I was there when she met your father."

Fetter's blood runs cold, and he suddenly sees it on her, the twenty-five centuries. She wears them better than his mother did. "Oh," he says. "You were her lover."

The Envoy laughs. She sounds impressed, though not with him. "She told you, then! That's real growth for the repressed old harridan."

"She told me you died!"

"Ah," the Envoy says. She eats a meditative spoonful of fruit. "Yes, that sounds more like her."

"Was it all lies?"

"I don't know what *it all* is," the Envoy points out. "Summarize."

So he talks, and the Envoy listens, continuing to eat. There is something dreadful about the regularity of that movement, the spoon held loosely in her hand, moving from bowl to mouth and back, her shiny brown skin spiderwebbed in wrinkles.

"Self-serving," the Envoy says, at last. "Self-aggrandizing. Infuriating, in other words, as always. But yes, true enough."

"But you're not dead," Fetter says, clinging to a nugget of provable untruth.

"We've been dead to each other many times over," the Envoy says. "When she cheated on me with dickweasel, for instance"—it takes Fetter a moment to understand she is referring to the Perfect and Kind—"or after you were born. I was your other mother, for those few years, until she forced me away. We . . . disagreed strongly on her parenting strategy. She banned me from Acusdab when you were three."

"How did you become Envoy after being exiled?"

"It was her idea," the Envoy says. She doesn't quite roll her eyes, but there's something about the way she tilts her head back that suggests it. "I'd been in Luriat for years—I was living in the Pediment by then. She got in touch and did not, in fact, apologize even a little. She said you'd left home and offered to fund an embassy if I would go register myself with the Summer Court, and well, I like having a title and a nice house and a budget that's just about enough to buy the imported fruit. But we both knew she was asking me to look out for you when you got here."

"Did you?" Fetter regrets the question as soon as he asks it. It feels rude.

"Didn't I?" The Envoy looks at her empty bowl and back at Fetter, her eyes entirely calm. She licks her spoon. "What are you to me now, that I should give a shit? I figured you were grown, your bloody mother's son, quite capable of taking care of yourself. *And* I figured if you ever needed help, you'd end up at my door asking for it."

"I . . . wasn't expecting *you*," Fetter admits. "But I thought perhaps the Envoy could give me asylum—I'm sorry, do you have a name? My mother said you didn't, that none of you had names back then, but you must have one now?"

The Envoy laughs. "She remembers that time more clearly than me. No, we had endearments and epithets, not names in the modern sense. I've never had one. I am the Envoy Extraordinary and Minister Plenipotentiary for the Autonomous Territory of Acusdab. People here use honorifics or call me Envoy. *You* can call me Extraordinary."

Fetter smiles at this woman who was nearly a mother, entirely a stranger.

"Oh, all right," she says. "We are almost family, and I haven't been extra in centuries. You can call me Ordinary."

# 32

Fetter lives in the embassy for a few days before he hears a knocking—less a knocking, he thinks as it continues, more a banging, a closed fist hammering, perhaps on the wood of that permanently open door. Ordinary told him that door, the whole building in fact, was designed and built to his mother's exacting specifications. "I calibrated it myself," Ordinary says, which seems to invite congratulations, though he has no idea what she means.

The legation has no staff, security, or employees. Ordinary lives there alone, funded by whatever mechanism Mother-of-Glory put in place. His mother's machinations survive her.

He has spent most of his wakeful hours in this house healing from his injuries, talking to his almost-mother and reading through her library, which seems to include a copy of every book ever written about or even mentioning Acusdab. Some are familiar—he riffled through her copy of *Exorcism Rituals in the Luriati Hinterlands* with affection—and others he has never even heard of. He is reading when the hammering descends, so he only registers it distantly. He hears raised voices, first outside the house, and then inside; at this point, he closes the book and goes to see.

The intruders are still in the vestibule, and he hesitates before showing himself. But then he hears a familiar voice.

"We know he's here. Come out, Fetter; I can see you." Salyut's voice, from behind a wall, is rougher than it was. Perhaps he's been weeping over the loss of his brother saint. His is not the only voice. There is indistinct muttering and imprecations from a chorus, and a little further away, perhaps from outside, the murmur of a crowd.

Fetter turns the corner and shows himself. Salyut nods, not in greeting but in private acknowledgement to himself. His eyes are wide but there is a distance in them, a sense of shuttering that Fetter understands they did not have before. It is as if bars have swung shut behind the dilated pupils. The eyes are reddened. Perhaps Salyut has wept after all.

The Saint-General is flanked by four monks, three to his right in the familiar robes of the Path Behind, and one to his left in subtly different robes, who Fetter guesses is Path Above. He can't tell what the differences are, exactly; something in the fold and tuck, the polarity of the pleats, the exact colour that is slightly out of the standard Behinder range of colours familiar in Luriati territories—it all adds up to say *foreign*.

He thinks he recognizes one of the Behinder monks, too: Ripening Wisdom, wasn't it? He's seen him on TV often. A firestarter monk, one of the Path's street-level crisis engineers. Ripening is stalking the room, periodically going to the open door to shout slogans at the crowd outside. The heavy brocade curtain has been torn down and tossed aside, where it lies puddled like something dead. Fetter can only see a few faces through the door, but the crowd outside is shoulder to shoulder and packed at least twenty deep. That's more than enough to burn down all of Tuft Street, should they set their mind to it. Most of them are not robed monks but lay supporters of the Paths Above and Behind, the people of the pogrom, who constitute and replenish its serpentine body. Perhaps some of the people he last saw rioting in the park are among them: the weepers. He still has hope for the laughers. Many of them, even the monks, are wearing masks in grudging concession to the plague year.

Ripening Wisdom has his pulled down around his chin. Salyut is not wearing one at all.

"Are saints immune to infection, then?" Fetter asks, but he pitched his voice too low and it got lost in the noise. Perhaps fortunately. His voice is rough and unsteady, and it is too soon to betray weakness.

Ordinary stands in the middle of the room, between him and the monks. She glances back at him with, he thinks, resignation. She is dressed much as she was when he arrived at her door: she never has any official business and this is how she always dresses, in patterned sarongs and sleeveless t-shirts with obscure band names and logos. At least this time her hair is braided and she's not eating. It's about as formal as she gets.

"This is a fucking embassy," she says to Salyut, in a clear but low voice. "Don't embarrass yourself."

"He wants the boy," Salyut says, and his voice is just as low. It's as if the two of them are having a conversation under cover of Ripening Wisdom's stalking and sloganeering, the gradual movement of the other flanking monks deeper into the building, and the rumble outside rising to a roar.

"He must be used to not getting what he wants," Ordinary says.

Salyut looks confused, an expression that sits poorly on his face. He, too, stalks closer. "He's getting *everything* he wants. The Ugly is gone. Luriat has bent both knees. The boy will join the Path as rightful heir—" He stops speaking because Ordinary is chuckling.

No, Fetter thinks, not a chuckle. A cackle, perhaps. It sounds venomous, not amused. He drifts forward a step, then another, light on his feet, coming up behind Ordinary. He will not, he decides, allow this old woman to be harmed. He tries to summon up his old facility for violence. No strength answers, only a cold thread of weakness that winds its way up his legs and down his arms. He has no knife. The gap between the protection he wants to offer and his capability for violence yawns wide, a chasm that seems impassable. *No*, he tells himself. It doesn't *matter* if I'm injured or tired or weak. She doesn't die today.

He hums the song of sharpening, for what may be the last time, and tries to limber up as surreptitiously as he can.

The other monks have surrounded them. Ripening Wisdom is circling, spitting imprecations that Fetter hears as animal noise, wordless growls. Salyut's eyes flick from Ordinary to Fetter and back. Perhaps he recognizes the song in Fetter's mouth—there's a sharpness to those glances.

"*The Ugly*," Ordinary says. "I had forgotten that you all called her that." She makes a gesture with her left hand—palm forward, thumb and index finger touching; it looks almost like the Path's seal of teaching, Fetter thinks, but it can't be. He's behind her, so he can't see her face.

"What are you—" Salyut looks haunted, or perhaps hunted. "Everyone get back."

The other monks turn to look at him, puzzled.

There is a metallic clang and a long, drawn-out screech. Fetter and the monks look around in alarm, but the noise came from outside. Neither Salyut nor Ordinary moves.

The heavy door of the embassy slams shut. No visible hand or mechanism acts on it, but it closes so violently that the thud rings in Fetter's ears. The noise of the crowd outside only increases, as if they all began to shout when the door cut them off.

The other monks back away from Ordinary, retreating behind the Saint-General. Ripening Wisdom starts to say something to Salyut, but is cut off with a curt gesture. Salyut's eyes are on Ordinary. There is alarm in his eyes. Fetter has never seen a saint look afraid before. Not even Magellan showed fear before he died.

"You are wrong," Ordinary says. "On all counts. The boy is nobody's heir—she is not gone while that which she set in motion remains in motion—and Luriat's rulers may have bent at the neck and the knee, but so what? Rulers love to submit, and the Path has always paid too much attention to thrones and not enough to people."

Her voice has gone low and guttural. Fetter finds himself glad he can't see her face. The face this voice comes out of—

"The people follow the throne," Salyut says. "As they always have."

"This is the lie princes tell themselves," Ordinary says. "Power is in people."

"You think this uprising will win?" Salyut demands. "It's led by foreigners and cultists. They have no real support among the people."

This is Fetter's first indication in days that Koel and Caduv are still out there, and his heart lightens.

Ordinary snorts.

"They will be beaten," Salyut insists. "We are consolidating the militaries and courts. We already control the media. When we hold free and fair elections, we are guaranteed a two-thirds majority. The people will give *us* their mandate. Those rebels are nothing—a small band of seditionists attempting to graduate to terrorism. We'll hunt them down."

"You make the same mistake again and again," Ordinary says. "The sin of metonymy. I say *people* and you hear *the people*. I say *power* and you think of thrones and parliaments."

Salyut makes an impatient noise, but his eyes are darting from side to side. The other monks are attempting to open the door behind him.

"And you speak for the real people, do you?" Salyut sneers. "The authentic people who exist beyond the reach of mere democracy? The real people who can't possibly want what you don't want?"

"You're still doing it," Ordinary says, and then sighs. "I don't speak for anybody. Not even the Autonomous Territory of Acusdab, really, not since she died. It is not possible to speak for the unspeakable. I am pointing out something that the Path is unable to hear."

"Well, then," Salyut says. "Even by your own terms, you're wasting your time and mine."

"First true thing out of your mouth," Ordinary says, and Fetter smells bitterness on a wind from nowhere. A shiver goes through his entire body. It's only then he understands she's been stalling.

He breathes out hard, as if trying to expel that scent. "*Oh,*" he says, looking over Ordinary's head at Luriat's newest bright door. She said she'd calibrated it to his mother's specifications—he has a moment to consider the frustration load on a door whose translation must have been held in abeyance for years. Then things happen very fast.

What is it that comes out of the Embassy's bright door? Fetter never describes it clearly when he tells this story later, leaving his hearers to imagine a legendary monster. Monstrousness seems demanded by the mayhem. Some horrific and misshapen creature, twisted and ferocious, with invisible tentacles and claws and mandibles. Rumour will draw on old hinterlander stories to speak of devils, imaginatively extravagant because nobody knows what devils look like. The news will report it as malign foreign influences. Neither will make reference to bright doors at all.

What comes out of the new bright door is a young dark-skinned woman, broad-shouldered and wide-hipped, naked but for strings of pearls at neck and arms and waist, her hair a glossy black cloud, a short knife in her hand already in motion. She cuts Ripening Wisdom's throat like an overripe fruit before she enfolds the others in her dance, a single curving thread of momentum unarrested, feet stepping, hips swiveling, blade looping in tight arcs and never coming to a stop. Red flowers blossom; petal splatter. Salyut never turns around, but his red eyes roll back in his head when she inveigles the knife into the back of his neck with surpassing gentleness. When he falls, the knife must have gone down with him, because her hand is bare. But when Fetter looks at the body, there is no protruding hilt. It's as if the little knife crawled up all the way into the Saint-General's brain and nestled there, wrapping those folds around itself to sleep.

The young woman ignores Fetter: she does not appear to recognize him. She comes to Ordinary and takes her hands in both of her own.

Fetter doesn't recognize her either, though he knows who she is. It's just that he feels no recognition in him, no echo of his own life in hers. This is her long before she was the Mother-of-Glory; this is her unnamed and young, shard of a lost past, queen of an empty realm.

"Will you go?" he asks, uselessly. He's speaking to Ordinary, not to his mother. But she is already following the young woman toward the bright door with urgent steps. Ordinary does not look back. The two of them go through the bright door together hand in hand, as if it were air, as if it were no barrier at all. And when Fetter runs too late to the door and puts his hands on it, it is closed to him, smooth and impassable, the bitter wind fierce and howling in his heart.

⌒

He escapes the embassy through a window in the back. He doesn't go back toward the Tuft Street entrance. He can hear crashing noises from that direction; they seem to be breaking down the blank wall where the door used to be, trying to get in. When they succeed, that new bright door will be destroyed, and with it gone, that empty realm will be inaccessible forever.

No, not empty, is it? Not any more.

❧

The Perfect and Kind comes for him. There is no reprieve, no rest. Fetter is barely halfway down a side street, trying to put distance between himself and the Embassy, when the Perfect and Kind is walking beside him.

"Did you kill both my saints?" the Perfect and Kind asks, conversationally. "I did tell you that you would surpass them both in time. There was no need to be jealous."

Fetter turns to snap at him, to perhaps lunge at him, but he is gone again.

❧

Fetter thinks it might have been a hallucination brought on by stress until he turns a corner a few minutes later and finds the Perfect and Kind waiting for him, falling in stride as Fetter keeps walking. His father is not alone this time. There is another monk in robes, tall and gangly but struggling to keep up.

"I thought Vido should meet you," the Perfect and Kind says. "For the permanent record, as it were."

"She *specifically* wanted me to kill *you*," Fetter tells Vido, who looks discomfited.

The Perfect and Kind smiles. "I don't think Vido will forget you, even if he were capable of forgetting."

"Why is he not a saint?" Fetter says. "I've never understood that. If he remembers every word you've ever said, every teaching, every bit of lore, shouldn't *he* have reached the fourth level of awakening long ago?"

The Perfect and Kind shrugs. "It's not for lack of effort. Vido has been working diligently toward this goal for years. But recall is not understanding, much less mastery."

He does not elaborate on this insult. Fetter glances back at Vido's face and can't tell if the other man even knows he's been insulted. Perhaps this is the sea they swim in, these two.

They are now walking somewhere with intention, not merely fleeing Tuft Street. He'd hardly noticed the transition when the Perfect and Kind began to lead him, choosing turns and directions.

"I've always liked what became of the island in my absence," the Perfect and Kind remarks. "History is surprising. You shape a small stream's path with your hands as it comes down a mountain: on the plains, it becomes a great flood that even you couldn't stop. In the south, my Path is one of many reformist lifeways to come out of those visionary centuries: popular and powerful, but far from universal or absolute. The Path Above adapted to the competition by becoming syncretic and flexible, but in the process it diluted itself. It has become fragmented and diffuse. You understand?"

Fetter nods, exhausted. He isn't sure where in the city they are. It doesn't look like the Plantations or Pale Black Moon or any other neighbouring district that he's familiar with. It's too green. The houses are old-fashioned, their estates too sprawling, not walled off but fenced chest-high in tilting wooden posts and barbed wire.

"The Path Above was unable to compete with the gods of the south," the Perfect and Kind says. "It was not able to dethrone them. I did persuade much of the world of the merits of my system, but only, at best, as an alternative to both older and younger powers. The Path Above found a comfortable last place among the world's great organizing systems." He shrugs. "It decayed further under the repression of the Occupations— another consequence I did not see coming. I can redirect the river of time, but it pays me back with floods, with driftwood and wreckage and dangerous undercurrents. I hoped to build a systematic engine for the salvation of billions, but at this point, the Path Above is essentially a massive umbrella coalition of imitation poperies, strange cults, and personal development seminars, dispersed across a wide territory. I see it clearly."

The road is empty. It seems emptier than even lockdown would account for. The Perfect and Kind walks down the middle of the road as if entirely confident of not meeting anyone, so Fetter does too.

"This is what I admired about the Path Behind," the Perfect and Kind says. "Here in the north, you were still an island at heart. Things evolve faster here. Things that were small become big; things that were big become small. Rather than diffusing, the Path Behind adapted to the Occupations by becoming concentrated. By distilling and refining Occupier ideologies and world-systems and incorporating them. Alabi race science, for example—arguably, I invented that as a systematizing approach. Perhaps they were inspired. Consider the Five Unforgivables." The Perfect and Kind looks back over his shoulder at Fetter, and then at me. "They are based on the moral stratification of people into lesser and greater categories. The mother is less than the father; the saint is less than the chosen. The Path is greater than the pathless. Kin is greater than the stranger. It is a simple, circular logic, and one that hews close to the natural prejudices of the human animal: we care more for the ones we love than we do for those we hate, and as for those we don't know, their lives and deaths mean nothing to us. Alabi race science, like the Path, is a grouping and typing theory that recognizes this. The near are better than the far. The like are better than the unlike. We must know how we are fettered if we are to become free."

Fetter reaches into his pocket and takes out his identity card. "Did you change this for me?" He holds it up, running his finger under the string of haecceity that he thinks is different than it used to be.

The Perfect and Kind reaches out and takes the identity card, and puts it in an empty realm.

They come to an open field that could not exist in the city. No, not a field; a great clearing in jungle. What jungle is this? Has the Perfect and Kind taken him into an empty realm as well? There is dark foliage all around, a smudged circle at a distance. Or no, they are still in Luriat: those are buildings in the distance, a dirty low skyline in evening's gloom. Perhaps this is a park or a nature reserve. The only sources of light are the setting sun and the risen moon, and the pyres arranged in a diamond formation at the centre of the clearing. The bile has been high in Fetter's throat for hours. It threatens to spill into his mouth.

There are four pyres, each one a bound body, kneeling. Each body has burned to a featureless cinder. They are uniform, indistinguishable.

The Perfect and Kind leads Fetter into the centre of the diamond. Vido stands outside it, pointing at each in turn. When he speaks, his voice is not the reedy ingratiating quaver that Fetter expected, but a deep voice in a confident tone.

"Koel," Vido says, pointing from fire to fire to fire. "Hejmen. Caduv. Pipra."

"No ashes," the Perfect and Kind says. "Only speaking."

Fetter grits his teeth and refuses. "No," he says. "This is a lie."

The Perfect and Kind shrugs. His eyes are on me, not Fetter. He turns slowly to track my ever-freer passage in the thickening night. I circle at a distance outside the pyres, unwilling to be caught in their overlapping light. Afraid to get closer. Since we came back to the city, I've tried to keep my distance from Fetter—his father saw me, and I thought to hide from those eyes. But I now realize this is a trap he's laid for me.

"The Perfect and Kind never lies," Vido says.

Fetter's gaze darts from pyre to pyre. The bodies are degraded beyond recognition. He walks to the one Vido had named Caduv. He puts his hand on the cheek and feels it flake away into ashes. The fire is cool in the humid evening.

"I see you," the Perfect and Kind whispers. "At last, there you are." His voice is so quiet I don't think Fetter or Vido hears it. He is staring directly at me, unseeable as I am in the night. The light of his eyes is like a solid beam: it pierces me through, pins me in place.

Fetter's hand remains held out even when the face he touched is gone. I feel it when his heart breaks. There is no sign of it on his face or in the world, but to me the crack is loud as the thunderbolt that broke open the glaciers at the beginning of history, when time became time for the first time, bright as the lightning that slew the dragon and freed the waters. It marks a world ending, and a birth both bloody and cold.

"I told you about the empty realms," the Perfect and Kind says, eyes unmoving. He slides backward toward Fetter, whose hand still cups air; the cinder before him now ends at the neck. "There is one realm emptier than most, a formless realm of pure light where no shadow may be cast." The Perfect and Kind puts his hand on Fetter's shoulder, and the two of them are gone.

There is not even a clap of air rushing in to fill a sudden emptiness. It is simply as if they were never there.

The headless body falls over, still burning.

Vido squats where he stood, looking bored but prepared to wait. I suppose he has done this many times.

I approach behind him and I wrap my shadow hands around his neck, but they are useless and without weight. It is always like this. I observe the world, but I can only handle it with the lightest touch.

So instead I take his spine in my hand. It takes but a moment to invite myself in through layers of skin and muscle. I dip my thumb into the cervical spine and slowly up into the brainstem. Vido does not notice.

Most people don't react when I do this. They are insensible to the entanglement. A few, like Fetter, feel sensations of wrongness. They become queasy and nauseated; they think it is illness, or some sort of reaction from within their bodies. I've used this reaction to good effect many times, to nudge Fetter or sometimes others in one direction or another. It would be impossible on Vido, though. He is shielded from my influence by his utter insensitivity.

It doesn't stop me from tapping into his heart, lapping at the sea of his memories with my black tongue.

# 33

I was not named. I was garrotted at birth, nailed to the earth, and torn away. But I did not die, as Fetter always thought. A shadow cannot be killed, because a shadow isn't alive: a shadow is only cast. I will be cast as long as he lives—no, as long as his material body still exists, somewhere in the world, in *any* world. I was untimely ripped from him, so I go where I please, not tied to his heel like an unthinking shadow. Yet I am bound tight to him after all.

I was not named, but I named myself over the years, in love and irony and helplessness. Our mother taught me without knowing that I was, our father saw me without knowing what I am; I cannot speak or sing but I can dance: call me the Unfettered.

Even now, with Fetter gone from this realm, I can feel his feelings. He is too far away for me to hear his thoughts; for the first time in our lives, they are reduced to a whisper in a language I don't speak, an itching persistence without meaning or clarity. He is afraid where he is, and sick at heart. If he were in this world he would be weeping, or perhaps screaming. But I can feel the light on him. I flinch from it, the endless light of a realm without shadows. I thought I could follow him anywhere, but I could not follow him there. In my peculiar state of being cast and yet not cast, I can only exist within other shadows. So obscured, I move freely. I don't need much in the way of a host: I have hidden in the darkness of Fetter's inner ear, under his foot, the darkness between his clothes and his skin, the nooks of his body's inner cavities. Away from him I have hidden under a leaf, behind a mosquito, inside the tumbling of a lock, in the shadow between this page and the next.

But in that realm of pure light where the Perfect and Kind has taken Fetter, no such shadows exist. There the light comes from everything. It is a hell I'm barred from.

I learn this because Vido knows all about it in theory, though he has never seen it and is incapable of reaching it. Only saints and devils can cross realms: this too is his knowledge, marinated in millennia of resentment. He knows about me, or at least knows that I exist, or that *something* exists. The Perfect and Kind has not explained, but Vido has grown expert at picking up crumbs and fragments and assembling altogether wrong hypotheses. Vido thinks I am a devil plaguing the son of the Perfect and Kind, responsible for all his ills. Since the Perfect and Kind is perfect, his son must also be perfect. Therefore, every wrong thing the son does can only be the fault of malign outside influences. First the vile mother and now this monster of darkness; he is relieved to understand that it is a singular devil who may be exorcised, which is what he believes his teacher is doing at this very moment. He knows that I cannot exist in the realm where the light is not cast by any source but is the pure light of being itself: in this alone he is correct.

Much of his legendary knowledge is like this. In the darkness of his mind, I compare what Vido knows against what I have learned from a lifetime of observation. I find stray truths buried in a fog of false connections, tendrils of misconception, poison droplets of envy.

Vido has never seen a devil. He knows of them in theory. He knows more about them, in theory, than anybody else who only knows of them in theory. He was there when the Perfect and Kind—then called the Revelator—tamed the devils and learned power from them.

He was there when that power made mountains.

Vido did in fact suggest a boat that day, I discover, as our mother once surmised. The Revelator laughed at him before bending space and time instead, but there is no resentment in that memory. There is nothing but uncritical adoration for the Revelator, mixed with lust and guilt and self-abuse. All of Vido's resentment is aimed inward, as shame for his own failure to reach higher levels of awakening, or outward at the enemies of the Path. He has not been in Luriat long, but he has already absorbed the current Almanac's full matrix of race and caste; he identifies naturally and completely with its apex, which to him is simply the Path itself, and despises its designated inferiors. Most of all, he loathes the pathless, the unbelievers.

So many memories to sift through, but not, I think, because of his famed completeness of recall. His memory is vast, but not more so than others' of his age. The difference is simply that he has the same access to his own memories as I would have to anyone's, should I insert myself into their inner dark and learn the language of their mind. His memories are a little brighter, perhaps, for being accessed more often. His is the easiest mind I have ever had to learn.

I try to rifle through his memories faster, in search of the more recent memories I'm looking for. I need very recent memories, of the past hours. But I am frustrated, searching fruitlessly until the fallen burning body—the one Vido had called Caduv's—gives a loud pop, startling him. It summons a thread of associative recall that I swiftly follow and tug upon: the organized capture teams, the catching and binding, the oiling and burning, the begging and the screaming, and in the end, the snap and crackling, almost muffled.

༄

The Perfect and Kind comes back with Fetter in hand, gripping him by the upper arm like a cop. When he lets go, Fetter
stumbles to a knee before he rises again. His eyes are glassy
and blank, and I wonder if his mind has broken under the
Perfect and Kind's influence, or perhaps from the realm of
pure light, or from grief. But then I understand that Fetter
seems blank to me because my access to his interiority has not
returned. I can now hear his thoughts only dimly and unintel-
ligibly, as if he were muttering in the pit of his throat.

I hide in the shadow of Vido's corpus callosum. The Perfect
and Kind looks around for me, but he has long been tired of
Vido, his perfect sycophant: he does not look closely at him. I
knew to expect this, because Vido knows this himself. He has
not felt the close regard of the Perfect and Kind in decades.
He does not resent this. He finds pleasure in being the ever-
faithful follower of the great man, a deep erotic thrill in being
taken for granted, even when they fuck.

"I believe that worked," the Perfect and Kind says. "The
creature has retreated, and even if it returns, I believe its grip
on you is severed. It will never again be able to prey on you."

I am not sure if this is what the Perfect and Kind really says.
With my connection to Fetter's senses so attenuated, I am relying on Vido's senses, which feel fevered and claustrophobic in
comparison. I am relying on his mind to translate. These are
the words as Vido hears them.

The Perfect and Kind leads Vido and Fetter away from the
bodies. The fires have gone down somewhat, though they are
still smouldering.

I want so badly to tell Fetter that Vido was lying when he
named the bodies.

Those names were selected to cause him as much pain as

possible. It wasn't that Vido didn't *try* to capture the four of them for this exercise; every step of his plans, every twist and rill and convolution, is laid out for me in his memory.

I learn that Koel and Caduv were impossible to find, never mind capture. I rejoice in their freedom, even if that joy is tempered with bitterness at how we left things—no, I'm taking Fetter's part. It's my oldest habit, to confuse him with myself. A shadow's duty, perhaps, but I am not him, I remind myself as I have reminded myself since we were children. I am the Unfettered. Someday, I will earn that name in truth.

What of the others? Vido knows where Hejmen is, but he is protected by his family pedigree. Of course he is. Vido attempted to demand Hejmen's arrest, but his control over the military is still tenuous. No, that's not quite right. It's Vido who believes that this tenuousness will fade in time as he strengthens control. I study his memory: the mulish face of the officer who laughs off the possibility that Hejmen, a respectable young man of a good family, a high race, and an approved caste, with a job in the Summer Court no less, is in any way connected to an enemy of the state. The wrinkling brow, the raised eyebrows, at the suggestion that the enemy in question is himself the . . . son? Of the Perfect and Kind? Surely there is some mistake? Vido sweating and backpedaling, that is not what he meant to say, he only wanted to confirm the location—and so Hejmen's location has been doubly and triply confirmed, away on holiday in the hills in an enclave of wealthy Luriati families patiently waiting out the White Year. But the enclave is secure, and the military protect it. Vido could not conjure the support to breach it.

The Perfect and Kind leads Vido and Fetter back toward his base of operations, the Godsfaction Dedicatory Convention Centre. It's a long walk. He doesn't summon a vehicle or take to the air like Magellan. He just walks. Fetter follows like a dead body walking. Vido trudges. His memories are full of trudging.

I dig deeper. Pipra is pathless and should have been the most vulnerable of the four. A memory of frustration surfaces, though there is no face associated with it, only a sheet of paper and a series of phone calls. It seems that after Janno's death in a street pyre, Coema asked Gerau—perhaps at one of those dinners mediated by Tomarin, I think, an image that is not contained in Vido's memories but which I can supply myself, insincere titters and petty sniping around that table in the garden—to extend her protection to pathless Ministry employees. Pipra, probably without ever knowing, was protected from Vido by the flimsy, impassable barrier of a polite letter from Gerau, a favoured patron of the Perfect and Kind. To overrule her, Vido would have had to go to the Perfect and Kind himself and beg for his favour, and I can already see that he doesn't like to do this. He lives in terror that the answer will some day be *no*. To be refused by the Perfect and Kind in favour of someone like Gerau would be a humiliation too great to bear. Vido didn't risk it.

I learn the true identities of the bodies in the pyre as I see their faces in Vido's memories. I don't know any of them by face. One I know by name. The body that fell—the one that Fetter thought was Caduv—was Peroe, whose name Fetter borrowed for a time.

The real Peroe doesn't look much like Fetter to me. If I were human, I think I would turn away from the intensity of naked terror on his face, and on the faces of the other three. They are strangers to me, but perhaps not to Fetter. Vido was attempting to assemble a second group of known acquaintances, having been foiled in his first choices. All of them are people that Fetter has interacted with in the Sands, according to Vido, though I have no particular memory of them. One is a former fellow resident of the same building. The other two are people Fetter helped with their citizenship registration years ago. I call back the memories of their faces: Vido did not spend much time in their presence, leaving the beatings and bindings to others, so I have little to work with. I don't recognize them from these brief and disinterested memories. Perhaps Fetter would. Perhaps they interacted at times when I was not present, or was occupied doing something else. Fetter talks to far too many people, and I'm not always hanging about. I don't always pay attention.

Arriving at the GDCC, the Perfect and Kind vanishes into his private suite, leaving Vido to get Fetter settled in. All such menial, temporal matters have always devolved to Vido. Vido puts Fetter in a room on the floor below the Perfect and Kind, and calls Gerau to get a doctor in to see him.

I look for how Vido found Peroe in the first place. It seems that Gerau named Peroe in her letter, unthinkingly, when she defended Pipra from her association with this man. Coema, eager to prove himself the loyal opposition and not a traitor to the Path, willingly used his Ministry resources to locate Peroe for Vido. There were no more saints to deploy, but Peroe was recently recovered from the plague and weak in every sense of the word. In the White Year, there is no need for the fig leaf of justifiable provocation if the target is one that can be targeted. Peroe was from a middle-class family, despite being of a high race and an approved caste. Vido dispatched a capture team headed by one of the local Behinder demagogues eager to make a place for himself in the coming world, the rapidly descending Path Unitary.

I see him, too: the monk's name is Shining Jewel of Truth, a thin man with no lips. Vido dislikes him, but Vido dislikes almost everyone. Shining Jewel was given a military detachment as escort and support, and a quarantine enforcement unit from

the Ministry of Health, signed off by Coema himself. Soldiers
in protective gear dragged Peroe out of his house and accused
him of being an unquarantined plague carrier under the harsh
lights of TV cameras. They were surrounded by angry protestors demanding his immediate sequestration. Shining Jewel of
Truth made an impassioned speech to his crowd and cameras
about collective responsibility, and how these consequences
demonstrated that the actions of the state are neither racist nor
casteist. See, he said, the high are punished as surely as the low.

That, from Vido's perspective, was a wrap.

Vido was not there when the fires were set. He prides himself
on not micromanaging and has a mild distaste for the smell.

Time passes. I keep an eye on the watches of the day out of
habit—night used to mean freedom for me—but I have never
kept track of days of the week or months of the year.

Fetter's interiority remains distant. His mind is a cave in another mountain: I can see the flickering light of the fire within,
but there is a chasm between us. For all that I was torn from
him at birth, we have never been so completely separated before.
It's as if the light of that other realm still suffuses him from the
inside.

But very gradually, and little by little over many days, I regain a faint trace of his former legibility. My access to his mind
is more mediated now, through his face and his eyes, his body
language, his increasingly rare public utterances, rather than
immersion in the rushing river of his thoughts and emotions.
But I can feel his despair as if it were weather.

I am forced to notice his body, and its injuries. He walks
like an old man. He breathes with difficulty. He wheezes when
the humidity increases, coughs when it decreases. His tread is

heavy. I wonder if the light took his lightness from him, or if he is weighed down by his losses. His hair and beard are greying prematurely. He shaves both off when he joins the Path Unitary. I gather from Vido's schedule that it's been a month.

The robes do not suit Fetter. He lacks the discipline to stay clean-shaven, and the greying stubble makes him look twenty years older. He is careless with the drape, the upper robe baring both clavicles to hang lightly off his right shoulder. He looks shelled, vulnerable flesh exposed.

I do not dare leave the recesses of Vido's brain even for a moment. It is the only way I can remain near Fetter and unseen by the Perfect and Kind. If he sees me again, so close by, he will pluck me out and fling me into the realm of pure light. It will be the end of me.

If a shadow could have nightmares, I think that would be mine. Unsleeping as I am, it recurs to me again and again, forcing me to huddle deeper into my hiding place.

Another month goes by. I learn calendars from Vido. He is deeply conscious of the passage of time, in a way that Fetter never was. He tracks not only the progress of the Path Unitary and its capture of Luriat, but also what he believes to be the deterioration of his own failing body.

Prolonged exposure to me has finally begun to affect Vido. He hides his nausea from everyone. He does not tell the Perfect and Kind that his head hurts all the time, that he vomits some mornings, that there is a fever burgeoning in his bones, blood in his stool. He thinks he has the plague but he doesn't want to go into quarantine, though there are luxury facilities for VIPs like himself, because he's afraid that Fetter will use the opportunity to cozy up to his father. He's afraid Fetter will take his place as constant companion, as trusted right hand. It terrifies him—a cold slush at the ankles, a dragging sensation. It frightens him more than the plague.

◈

After he's worn the robe for almost three months, Fetter comes to Vido and asks about the names he'd given those pyres, that night.

"You want me to say them again?" Vido asks. It irritates me when he speaks. It is as if I am crouched in a shallow pool, and his speech ripples it, makes the water unquiet, makes it harder for me to stay under the waterline.

Fetter shakes his head. "I want to know the real names."

It's strange not to know what he's going to say before he says it. He doesn't look any better and his voice hasn't gotten stronger. It's only in the words, and perhaps the eyes, that I recognize him.

They are alone, in the room in the GDCC that has become Vido's office, a kind of secretarial chamber.

"Those were the real names," Vido says, after a very long pause. He is looking down at the letters on his desk instead of up at Fetter.

"No," Fetter says. His voice sounds gentle, but I have known it all my life and I can hear the rage in it: not a storm but a tide. Perhaps he has learned how to carry it better. Or perhaps this is what he always sounded like from the outside. "Koel and Caduv are well. I met with them a week ago. I've confirmed that Hejmen is alive. Gerau assures me that Pipra is fine and busy back at work at a new site. With a new team. Did you think I would just take your word for it?"

"You can't *meet* with terrorists," Vido says, startled into meeting Fetter's eyes. He is torn between the necessity of demanding—what would the generals call it?—*actionable intelligence* on the movements of these thorns in his flesh, and the deep need to protect the reputation of the son of the Perfect and

Kind, who might one day be the Saint of Bright Doors. "There'll be no end of trouble."

"Oh, there will be trouble," Fetter agrees.

"What are you—" Vido looks around the room in frustration. This room is where Luriat is run from, these days. The Perfect and Kind insists he is not a ruler. He has no interest in governance and considers it beneath him. The Luriati state, its fractures violently welded together with the hot metal of the Path Unitary, is at one level too cowed and at another too enmeshed in its internal rivalries to direct itself. So the various factions petition the Perfect and Kind, and power pools at Vido's feet, though it is not the kind of power he wants. He, too, tries to be rid of these responsibilities as quickly as possible, with the result that Luriat's governance is even more fragmented and haphazard than it was before. To retain control under these circumstances, it is necessary that the White Year never end, so this is also the room from which Vido directs the pogroms and manages the camps. All other furniture has been replaced with cabinets and spare tables to hold the paperwork. Everywhere Vido looks there are demands on him; decisions he cannot make but must, lives he doesn't want to take but, well.

He wonders if he should have Fetter killed, in a fit of wildness that I punish at once by tweaking his trigeminal nerve. Over the months, I have learned much greater precision than ever before. I've never spent so long within the body of a single person. I believed my shadow hands to be too light to affect the world, but there are places where a light touch is enough, once I've learned the subtleties of a particular body. Vido must make a grimace of pain, because even Fetter raises an eyebrow.

"What do you want from me?" Vido asks, at last. He massages his face. He thinks he is overworked. He feels sorry for himself.

"The names," Fetter says.

So Vido tells him the names, Peroe last.

"Your friends being alive doesn't set you free," Vido says. He puts his hands on the table and stands, though he feels small and petty, not intimidating. He hopes he looks intimidating. "You should think of them as hostages."

Fetter looks up at him and curls a lip. "You little shit," he says. "I should have listened to my mother." He grinds his teeth loudly enough to be heard across the table. "I knew that night that you might be lying. I knew it might not be them—I knew it probably *wasn't* them, at least, not most of them. It made no difference. What *mattered* was that you killed four people to make a gesture. It doesn't matter *who* they were. You killed them to make me put this fucking costume on."

Vido tries to say that he has never killed anybody and was in fact not even present when the fires were lit, but Fetter hawks up a ball of such venomous phlegm that when he spits it onto the papers on Vido's desk, it burns through them, sinking instantly. The browned edges of the burn curl down, like an impact crater.

Vido waits till Fetter leaves before he looks under the table to make sure it hasn't burned all the way through.

# 34

Vido waits for a night when he's feeling less sick. I observed his intentions form slowly like clouds over many days, so I collude: I huddle into the smallest fold of his cortex, behind his eyes, and allow him to feel as healthy and vital as he needs to be. I help him visit the Perfect and Kind in his room, a demon lover.

The two have become estranged as they aged, but they have a long history together. Vido is tired of feeling insecure in his position. This is a way to remind the Perfect and Kind that he's not just a functionary, not just a memory on legs. He knows the Perfect and Kind's body by heart, every touch that ever drew a response. He remembers as he re-enacts, whispering echoes of old whispers, touching echoes of old touches. Vido remembers, and in doing so parades before me, every morning sermon preaching loathing for the body that followed every nighttime fuck. The bag of flesh with its thirty-one impure parts—the involuntary body—the disgusting body—the unreliable body—the messy, ugly, fucking body.

The loathly, lonely body.

The Perfect and Kind puts his head back and closes his all-seeing eyes at the moment of climax, and I take that opportunity to pour out of Vido's brain into his mouth, a silky fall of shadow that enfolds the cock, that penetrates the cock, that hides underneath the foreskin in the shadow of the glans, then in the endless night of the ducts and vessels within. It slips softening out of Vido's mouth; I have transferred myself.

I could never hide unseen in the brain of the Perfect and Kind, which he prizes and holds up to the light of self-observation, but in his despised and forgotten gonads there is shadow enough.

When the Perfect and Kind sends Vido away, I almost miss him.

♋

I have never hidden, before this.

It is my nature to go unseen. I am an unfettered shadow who can only exist inside other shadows: of course I went unseen. But I was never *hiding*.

I have never stayed so still, before this.

It is my nature to flow. This is what separated me from other shadows, who remain bound to imitate their origins. I was freed at birth, and I have spent nearly all my life in ceaseless motion. I move from shadow to shadow. No sight or sound or smell or texture betrays me. Even devils don't see me. I am a devil to devils—as they are invisible to mortals of the local realm, so I am invisible to them. The Perfect and Kind is the only devil that sees me.

Before the Perfect and Kind, nobody ever looked directly at me. It is unsettling to be seen. No: it is terrifying.

I don't kill him for what he did to Fetter, or to Mother-of-Glory, or to decapitate the Path Unitary, or because of all the blood and death for which he is responsible. Maybe there's a little of all of those things, out of sympathy for how Fetter would have thought, but not really. Those are the reasons why Fetter would have killed him, but I am not Fetter and he doesn't know I exist. He will never praise me or love me or call me home.

In the end, I kill the Perfect and Kind because he looked at me and *saw* me, and in seeing me he trapped me, and I can't bear it.

I kill him because it's the only way I can be free. The only way I can move again like I've always moved, never stopping. The need to leave is a deep old ache in me, now compounded by the horror and frustration of being trapped, unmoving. It is like being buried. I want to finally, finally-finally, live up to my name. Did our mother free me from Fetter only so that I would orbit him forever?

Have I not done enough?

I wonder if Vido feels euphoric at being miraculously healed of the plague since I left him—since that night. He probably thinks he was cured by the touch of the Perfect and Kind.

I wonder what Fetter is doing, and what kind of trouble he's creating. What little I can sense of him feels more alive. Somewhere, he's coming back to himself, like he always does.

Our mother lost sight of me the moment I fell from her garrotte and slipped into the shield of other shadows. The first shadow I hid in was hers. She never found me again. I often wondered if she ever thought of me. I hope she did, but I fear she did not. Fetter was her project; I was simply something to be removed from him, to sharpen him into a perfect weapon. He was not, but what did she know about making weapons? She was no smith. She was a finder of precious things in dark places. If she never found me, that meant I was not precious.

I should have left then.

As the shadow of a boy, I stayed close to Fetter and our mother, because I didn't know any better. I didn't understand what I was, until the day Fetter found the nail in a box. Then I remembered. As he learned, I learned.

When our mother sent him out on his own to find and kill his father, I told myself I had my own mission—I conjured a vision of how she called me separately and told me what she wanted from me. How I was to follow him and protect him, that I was to keep him alive and to help him get the job done. She would never simply *say* that she was proud of me, but she might say something stuffy and pompous about changing the world; I would run after him in the bright morning, slipping from shadow to shadow under each blade of grass on the side of the road.

She didn't, but I went anyway.

I kept him alive through the violence of his teens. I stayed close to him, then. When he came to the city, I followed, and watched him make friends and build a life, and I was glad, because he didn't need me so badly any more. I began to spend more time away from him, to explore the city and the hinterlands on my own. I saw what Luriat was like long before Fetter did. The camps and the pogroms and the rolling, shifting wars in the hinterlands. I cannot turn a page, but I read over many shoulders; I attended talks and lectures; I watched the news in houses across the city, across many cities. I followed other lives, each only briefly. I went up into the hills and north to the coast to bask in the rippling shadows of waves on the water and swim in the shallows of the great world-ocean that stretches unbroken to the pole. I thought about going further still—over that ocean to the east or west, south past the mountains. There is an entire *world* out there, which Fetter never quite seemed to understand, and it doesn't much care about the Paths Above or Behind, it doesn't care at all about Luriat, and it especially doesn't care if everyone here lives or dies. I am not sure if I do either, except for Fetter: even then, sometimes only because I fear that when he dies and they burn him, I will disintegrate into the shadows of a billion particles of ash, and so pass from this world. I hate him for courting death, when *my* life still remains unlived.

I don't hate him. Never mind.

I came back. I was like a comet, my orbit growing looser over time, ranging further and further, but always coming back. Every time I came back, I would learn what he'd been doing, who he'd been talking to, what he was trying to accomplish, and I would help if I could, nudging him toward a house where he could safely steal what he needs, or to the papers that would uncover the experiment with his father's relic, or in a thousand smaller ways.

He thinks of me as his gut feeling, an oracular nausea, his luck. I suppose he is not wrong, but he has no sense of how hard I work: to surveil so many people, to spend hours reading over shoulders and eavesdropping on conversations, to scout ahead of him and find what he needs. Every time I led him to the right place at the right time, I first quietly eliminated all the places and times that were wrong. Luck is only someone else's labour.

I roil restlessly in the nethers and bowels of the Perfect and Kind as he goes about his days, which I can measure only in the circadian rhythms of his body. I don't dare access his sensorium and potentially draw his attention, so I have little idea what he's doing or who he's talking to. But he too seems withdrawn. Fetter seems to be avoiding him, and after that night, the Perfect and Kind seems to be avoiding Vido, and perhaps everyone.

He walks, instead. Having long since distanced himself from the exercise of worldly power, which he left so carelessly in Vido's hands: he walks.

I don't know for a fact where he walks. Perhaps he is only

walking in circles in his own room. Perhaps he is walking the corridors of the convention centre, or down in the park among his most enthusiastic supporters, or even in the streets of the burning city. But he does not seem to stop moving often enough to suggest passage through crowds of adoring fans. He doesn't stop every few steps to give blessings and answer questions and kiss babies. He just walks, without interruption. Perhaps the Perfect and Kind has decided to spy on his fandom. Perhaps he too has wrapped himself in shadow.

It's a famous story, isn't it? The king goes out in disguise to find the truth of his kingdom and how his subjects really live. The Perfect and Kind must know it, and he thinks himself a king.

But I am swimming in his state of mind—I may not have access to his thoughts, but I experience the chemicals they produce—and his endocrinal flow does not match the heightened state of curiosity and discovery that I would imagine if he were playing out this role. If anything the waters have calmed, like a deep lake in a mountain valley where no wind blows and no leaves fall. The surface is utterly still, a perfect mirror for the sky, undisturbed by wave or ripple.

Deep in the dark beneath, there are cold currents and swimmers in shadow. His stomach rumbles and churns like anybody else's. That is as high as I dare climb, staying in the shadows within and between his intestinal foldings, the darkness underneath his stomach acids. When his guts contract and cramp, I know he's finally sick—of me, though he doesn't know that.

His own teachings of disgust for the body betray him. The betraying body, the decaying body. I sink deeper into his tissues, into the shadows within the cells. I smother mitochondria in the dark.

I can tell when he stops his ceaseless walking and lies down, never to get up again. I can hear the rumblings of his voice as he gives his last advice, his final sermon. He's propped up a final time, under bright lights, I think—I cringe away from their heat—for what is probably a broadcast, or maybe a taping.

Fetter never comes to his father's deathbed. I still have a sense for his place in the world, at least a direction and an approximate distance. Fetter is in the city the whole time, sometimes in the building, sometimes on the same *floor*. He never comes. This wonderful pettiness—I am proud of him. I hope the Perfect and Kind remembers that Fetter walked through devils and fire to be there when his mother died.

The Perfect and Kind dies like anybody might die: sick and old, a body failing, a death rattle and a light going out. It's not special.

I give it a while longer, just to be safe.

Then I rise up his oesophagus, a lump of night. I slip out of his slightly parted lips. It's dark out. I had imagined him in his room at the convention centre, but I was wrong; we are outside. He is lying in state on an elaborate pyre encircled by a grand pavilion of white sheets and flags, dotted with coconut-leaf constructions. I wonder if Fetter made any of those.

The scene is only lit by the moon and the dancing flames of a thousand small lamps dotting the perimeter of the pavilion. There is plenty of shadow for me. The pyre has not been lit yet. Perhaps they are waiting for the son? No, I see Vido lighting it, wailing.

There are many monks outside the pavilion, some weeping, some stoic. Beyond them, a vast and sorrowful crowd. Nobody's laughing. We are still in the park: I recognize the lights of the convention centre beyond.

Fetter is not in the crowd. The shadows change and ripple, and so I know that a great fire is rising behind me: the funeral pyre of the Perfect and Kind. It means nothing to me, so I leave without looking back.

If I think about direction the way Fetter thinks, I know I'm moving north into the city. Given how close he feels, Fetter might be in the Pediment, or in the Sands beyond it. But these frames of reference don't come naturally to me: not the districts and streets of the city, nor the cardinal directions of the compass. To me, there have only ever been two directions to choose from: toward Fetter, or away from him. I choose my first direction.

Other fires are blossoming in the city as I move through it. Shadows dance tonight. I am dimly aware of noise and screaming. The Perfect and Kind's death has triggered change, or maybe it's been like this all along. The White Year that will not end as long as the banner of the sun and the moon still flies, even if that banner catches flame.

I find Fetter behind a barricade blocking the street that leads to the Pediment. The barricade includes metal police barriers, though there are no police here; vehicles, both parked and overturned; planks and pallets of heavy wood; blocks of concrete; bricks; paving slabs; what look like slabs of masonry torn from their rightful places; bags of sand and soil; bamboo lashed together with rough rope in towering, misaligned constructions. This diverse and composite barricade is stacked and layered and constructed well above head height, and completely blocks the street for vehicles and mortals, though devils are swarming, slipping past the barricade without touching it. There are ten thousand tiny shadowed openings sufficient for me to pass through without slowing down.

The other side is full of people. The ones I'm looking for are part of the crowd but not its leaders. Caduv is speaking, his voice resonant even at a distance, but he's only one of several speechmakers scattered across the crowd, addressing different groups.

There are many devils about. I see white-armed antigods

stalking. Almost nobody here is masked or distancing, so a fresh outbreak of plague is on its way. Koel and Fetter are in a corner right under the barricade, speaking quietly. Even as I loop back to them, Fetter steps aside to let a devil pass through the barricade, something long and cruel like a thornbush folded in upon itself. It has a human face and eyes that weep clean thick tracks down its hollow cheeks in a red so dark and thick that it seems purple in the dim. It nods to him, and he nods back.

"You're jumpy tonight," Koel says, not understanding his movements.

Fetter is back in his own clothes, though his hair and beard are stubble. I come up behind him and touch my heels to his in a way I haven't done since we were children. I pretend I'm his shadow, hidden in the greater shadow of the barricade, itself submerged in night.

"He's dead," Fetter says, after a while. He looks like he's listening. I don't know what it is that he's heard. Perhaps there is a change in the tenor of distant shouting, a shift in the pitch of terror abroad in the night. Perhaps he can sense his father's absence at a distance, the way I can sense his own presence. Heel to heel, I can feel his sorrows and joys like a nest of serpents, writhing: how it hurts in his chest when he breathes the cold air too deep; how there is no peace in his heart.

I wonder if he can feel me in his gut. Has he noticed the absence of his intestinal serendipities in recent months? I cannot reach his thoughts to find out. I don't know if he expected peace, or if he knew it would be like this. Perhaps he has been making his own luck for a change.

"So much for destiny," Koel says, offering a wry little laugh that invites Fetter to join in. But he doesn't.

"The only way to change the world," Fetter says, as if disagreeing with the part he doesn't speak out loud.

"You're not going to give me some individualist shit about personal growth?" Koel says. "Change yourself to change the world? Something you learned while meditating upon the mysteries of your own ass."

Fetter rolls his eyes. "Fuck you," he says. It's not quite as light-hearted as it sounds. "I'm here, aren't I?"

"You are," Koel says. She's peering through the barricade, though there's still nothing but night to see on the other side. Her fingers are loose, lightly curled, not at all clenched. She seems younger, eyes more anxious, shoulders more relaxed, infinitely more dangerous.

"Every lost past is a world," Fetter says. "I learned that from my . . . from the Perfect and Kind himself. I think it might be the only thing I learned from him that matters. Behind every bright door is a world full of lost hearts. It matters."

"I prefer to worry about living hearts," Koel says.

"It's the same thing," Fetter says. "*He* didn't see it that way, but it's true. They're our mistakes, I suppose . . . it's not surprising they're so hungry to haunt us—the histories we forgot, the crimes we buried. Devils know I've buried mine. I try not to think about it, you know? Blood on my hands."

"You'll have more before this is over," Koel says.

"No," Fetter says, but Koel just shakes her head.

They are silent for a while, as if this is an argument they've been having, whose ghosts are echoing in this quiet.

"No," Fetter says, again, as if refuting not only her assertion but the entire argument. "I need you to understand me, here. I know this isn't your politics, and I swear to every devil I know I'm not turning my back on that, because I'm fucking here, aren't I? I'm here, this time. But I need *you* to understand what I mean when I say I *am* the world."

Koel laughs, shortly. "And you've changed it?"

"And I've changed it," Fetter says. He raises one hand in the seal of the boon, turning around to take in the crowd—and the devils scattered in it—and me. He's smiling; it looks mocking to me, though I'm not sure who he would mock. Perhaps it's me. I've been away from him longer than I ever have before. Perhaps in my absence he sensed at last that I've always been here in his shadow. It's good to see him unknowable. It's good to see him alive.

I leave them with the world in their hands, and I walk in the only other direction I know.

# ACKNOWLEDGMENTS

I've been lucky to have a lot of love and support as a person and writer. I'm grateful to my family, Tilak, Padmini, and Ruchira, Thanusha, Ovini, and Okindu; to my beloved friends Nicola, Tania, Rudy, Nali, Aisha, the crew of *Strange Horizons* and the shape-shifting denizens of the Quinta del Mordaz; to my comrades-in-writing Nassos, Tess, and Rasha; to so many writers, readers, editors, critics, and friends who've helped me find life and art in these troubled decades. I can't imagine my life without all of you in it. I wish all of you had lived to see this.

A huge thanks to Indra Das, Samit Basu, Premee Mohamed, Sam J. Miller, Max Gladstone, Sequoia Nagamatsu, and all the readers, writers, editors, and booksellers who've had such kind words to say about this book, both in public and private, in its journey toward publication. Your generosity and encouragement mean so much to me.

It is not possible to thank every writer whose work I've found moving, influential, and inspiring, because there have been so very many over the decades. A few I've already named, and it is a privilege to be their contemporary. But I will name two more writers as ambassadors for the many yet unnamed: Sofia Samatar and Kuzhali Manickavel. Without them, and without the hundreds that they represent, this book would not exist.

My agent, Michael Curry, and my editor, Carl Engle-Laird, have both been amazing, wise, and patient with my many, many questions; a huge thank-you to both of you! Many thanks also to Debbie Friedman for being a wonderful copyeditor; to Norma Hoffman for catching so many errors at the last minute; to Ashley Hudson and Faceout Studio for an excellent cover; and to all the lovely people at DMLA and Tordotcom Publishing, including but not limited to Patricia Gostyla, Matt Rusin, Irene Gallo, Christine Foltzer, Michael Dudding, Samantha Friedlander, Ashley Spruill, Jeff LaSala, and Steven Bucsok, for walking me gently through the transformation of a manuscript to a book, for navigating the vagaries of doing this all across international borders and time zones, and for all the work you put into making this book happen. I am grateful and thankful for you all.

Nandini: I love you for many reasons, but ascendant among them is that you stormed into my life—with your passion for all knowledge and willingness to discuss theories of the fantastic for years on end—at exactly the right moment. You bring me joy, now and always. Also, I basically wrote this book to impress you, so all of this is your fault and I hope you're happy.